上海师范大学卓越教师培养专业建设项目成果

U0949849

西方文论思辨教程

卢敏　主编

Western Literary Theories:

A Bilingual Course to Develop Critical Thinking

WUHAN UNIVERSITY PRESS
武汉大学出版社

图书在版编目(CIP)数据

西方文论思辨教程/卢敏主编.—武汉：武汉大学出版社,2018.7(2021.10重印)

ISBN 978-7-307-20247-4

Ⅰ.西… Ⅱ.卢… Ⅲ.文艺理论—西方国家—高等学校—教材 Ⅳ.I0

中国版本图书馆CIP数据核字(2018)第107234号

责任编辑:谢群英　　责任校对:李孟潇　　版式设计:汪冰滢

出版发行：**武汉大学出版社**　(430072　武昌　珞珈山)

(电子邮箱：cbs22@whu.edu.cn　网址：www.wdp.com.cn)

印刷:武汉邮科印务有限公司

开本:787×1092　1/16　印张:18.5　字数:447千字　插页:1

版次:2018年7月第1版　2021年10月第2次印刷

ISBN 978-7-307-20247-4　定价:46.00元

版权所有,不得翻印;凡购我社的图书,如有质量问题,请与当地图书销售部门联系调换。

前　言

《西方文论思辨教程》(英汉双语)是为普通高等院校英语语言文学专业硕士研究生、本科生开设西方文论课程，以及越来越多的大学开设的跨文化通识课程而特别编写的。教材编写采用英汉双语形式，让学生沉浸在双语语言文化思想语境中，通过思辨性阅读来提高学生的思辨能力。

全书共分14章，选择了从柏拉图的《理想国》到爱德华·萨义德的《虚构、记忆与地方》共14位西方经典文论家的经典著作为学习内容。每章由导读、节选文、思考题三部分构成。导读包括作者和作品简介，为学生提供该作家作品在西方文论史上的坐标，节选文配有难点注释，思考题将进一步提高学生的深度阅读、深度思考、深度写作的能力。

本教材编写有以下特点。第一，教材编写紧密贴合我国大学教学学时学制安排，根据16周32课时的课堂教学时间，精心编选14章的教学内容，留出2周4课时为教学调整、巩固、答疑解惑等。选文篇幅在9000字左右，特别适合课堂讲解与讨论，并且在此篇幅内特别选择了3篇文论全文，以范文形式使学生充分感知西方文论的写作风貌和精髓。第二，教材采用英汉双语编写，旨在提高学生的英汉双语认知、感受和思辨能力，突破国内现有同类教材或英语或汉语的单语编写形式，帮助学生掌握精准的双语文论术语，形成较为理想的等值思维转换，进而促进中西思维的思辨性对话。第三，所选14位文论家的作品较清晰地勾勒了西方文论的发展脉络，较好地体现了各时期文论家之间的继承和创新，呼应和对话。

本教材编写对以下几点予以说明。第一，多数文论原文是用希腊文、德文、法文写作的，英文译本也有不同的译者和版本，因此本教材选文的英译版都特别注明了译者和出版社信息。第二，本教材所选的文论不仅有中文译本，而且还有不同的译者和译本，有些是从希腊文、德文、法文原文翻译的，有些是从英译本翻译的，所以有些译本的语言是比较晦涩难懂的。在参考多种汉、英译本的基础上，本教材编者提供了自己的中文翻译，所参考译文都列入参考文献。第三，选文注释主要从帮助读者理解的角度而选择注释条目，原文作者的某些冗长的佐证性注释因为与论文正文联系并不紧密而并未完全照搬。

本教材使用时的几点建议。第一，教学语言可以根据教师和学生的语言程度采用英语或汉语或英汉双语形式，以减少语言障碍，实现透彻理解为主。第二，思考题不仅可用于课堂讨论，而且可用于课后写作，适当增加课后写作将进一步提高学生的思维表达和思辨能力。第三，本教材具有引导学生走上西方文论探索之路的指导作用，每个节选文只展示了一位文论家的思想冰山的一角，深度的探索和研究需要全文阅读和全部相关著作的阅读。

前　言

2017年上海师范大学入选教育部卓越中学教师培养计划实施高校，并且成为上海市唯一一所全学段卓越教师培养计划实施院校。本书稿得到上海师范大学卓越教师培养专业建设项目资助。在此特别感谢上海师范大学校领导和外国语学院院领导的大力支持和鞭策鼓励。感谢上海师范大学广大师生与我一起走过西方文论经典阅读和研究的岁月。这样阅读和研究还将随着一批批新学者一直走下去。

编者

2018年1月

Contents
目　录

Chapter 1

第1章

1. Introduction to Plato

1. 柏拉图简介

Plato (427 B.C.?-347 B.C.) was a great philosopher in Classical Greece and the founder of the Academy in Athens, the first institution of higher learning in the Western world. Along with his teacher, Socrates, and his most famous student, Aristotle, Plato laid the very foundations of Western philosophy and science.

He was born into a well-to-do aristocratic family in Athens, and was the fourth child. His father was Aristo and mother was Perictione. Plato was a bright though modest boy who excelled in his grammar, music, and gymnastics. He started to learn philosophy from Socrates at the age of 20. In 399 B.C., Socrates was brought to trial on the charges of corrupting the youth, introducing new gods into the city, atheism, and engaging in unusual religious practices and was put to death. Then, Plato left Athens and traveled to Italy, Sicily, Egypt and Cyrene in a quest for knowledge. In 388 B.C., he visited Sicily and became a tutor of the King of Dionysios. In 387 B.C., he returned to Athens and founded the Academy. He never

柏拉图(公元前427年?—公元前347年)是古希腊伟大的哲学家,在雅典创办了西方世界第一所高等学校——阿卡德米学院。柏拉图及其老师苏格拉底以及最著名的学生亚里士多德共同奠定了西方哲学和科学的基础。

柏拉图出身于一个富裕的雅典贵族家庭,排行老四。他的父亲是阿里斯通,母亲是珀克里提俄涅。柏拉图自幼聪慧而谦虚,在语法、音乐、体育各方面表现优秀。20岁时,他开始师从于苏格拉底学习哲学。公元前399年,苏格拉底于被指控犯了毒害青年、在城市传播新神、宣扬无神论、从事异端宗教活动等罪而受到审判,被处以死刑。自此,柏拉图离开雅典,出游意大利、西西里岛、埃及、昔兰尼以寻求知识,丰富自身的学说。公元前388年,他出游西西里岛,成为国王狄奥尼西奥斯的老师。公元前387年,他返回雅典,并创办了阿卡德米学院。他

married and lived up to eighty.

Plato lectured extensively at the Academy, and wrote on many philosophical issues. The most important writings of Plato are his *Dialogues*. Except *Apology of Socrates* and some letters, Plato expressed his philosophical thoughts mainly in the form known as dialogue, and his words were laconic and beautiful, and his argumentation was rigorous and meticulous. Plato's influential works are *Crito*, *Phaedo*, *Philebus*, *The Ion*, *Statesman*, *Sophist*, *Meno*, *Symposium*, *Euthyphro*, *Menexenus*, *Protagoras*, *Gorgias*, *Phaedrus*, *Parmenides*, *Theaetetus*, *The Laws*, *The Republic*, and many others. Among them, *The Ion*, *Phaedrus*, *The Republic* mainly explain Plato's theory of art, which are the required readings for people who study Plato.

Plato theory of inspiration is clearly expressed in *The Ion*. According to Plato, inspiration is the creative resource of art. The creative action of a poet depends on the god's power and is irrational, for the poet is divinely inspired and possessed. This inspiration refers to not only the mental state of the poet but also the mental state of the appreciator. The poet writes a good poem driven by the inspiration from the god, and passes it to the rhapsode who chants the poem, like Ion, then by such rhapsode the audiences are inspired and lost in an ecstatic state. To Plato, the artistic creation and appreciation depend not on the techniques of writing and chanting poems, but on the artists and appreciators who are in an ecstatic state.

Plato's theory of imitation is expressed in *The Republic* and imitation is the core concept of his aesthetics. He believes that the idea world is created by God, and it is the changeless truth,

终生未娶,寿命长达 80 岁。

柏拉图在阿卡德米学院讲学,留下大量哲学著作。柏拉图最重要的作品是他的《对话》。除了《苏格拉底的申辩》以及一些书信体之外,他的哲学思想主要采用“对话”的形式来表现,辞藻简洁优美,论证严谨细致。柏拉图的代表作有《克力同篇》、《斐多篇》、《菲力帕斯篇》、《伊安篇》、《政治家篇》、《智士篇》、《美诺篇》、《会饮篇》、《游叙费伦篇》、《美涅克塞努篇》、《普罗泰戈拉》、《高尔吉亚篇》、《斐德若篇》、《巴曼尼得斯篇》、《泰阿泰德篇》、《法律篇》、《理想国》等。其中,《伊安篇》、《斐德若篇》、《理想国》三部著作集中阐述了柏拉图的文艺理论思想,是文艺界研究柏拉图的必读之作。

在《伊安篇》中,柏拉图提出灵感说。他认为,灵感是文艺创作的源泉。文艺创作活动是诗人凭借诗神附着的神力,在失去理智,陷入迷狂的一种精神状态下进行的非理性活动。这种灵感不仅指诗人的精神状态,而且也包括欣赏者的精神状态。诗人在诗神赋予的灵感的驱动下写出了好诗,将神的理念传给了像伊安这样的诵诗人,又通过诵诗人使听众获得灵感,陷入迷狂的状态。柏拉图认为艺术的创作和欣赏不是依靠写诗和诵诗的技巧,而是靠艺术家和欣赏者陷入一种迷狂、忘乎所以的精神状态。

在《理想国》中,柏拉图提出模仿说,模仿是其美学思想中的核心概念。他认为理念世界是神创造的,是永恒不变的真理,现实世界只是理念

while the real world is just the imitation of the idea world as well as its "appearances". Take the "bed" for example from Chapter Ten, Plato proposes three kinds of "bed": one in nature, made by God, is the idea and essence of the bed, and this bed is the real one; and the second is made by the carpenter according to the idea, which is very similar to the real one; then the third made by the painter is imitated from the bed made by the carpenter. So art is imitation of idea and art is the imitation's imitation.

世界的模仿品,是理念世界的"阴影"。卷十中以"床"为例,他提出三种"床":第一种是由神创造的天然的床,是床的理念和本质,这种床才是"床的真实体";第二种是木匠根据"理念"制作出来的个体床,这种床是近乎"床的真实体"的物体;第三种是画家笔下的床,这种床是画家模仿木匠制作的床而画出来的。总之,文艺的本源是理念,文艺是模仿的模仿。

The social function of art is Plato's another important opinion of art. He thinks that art should help govern the city as well as educate the people, and also help to set up a just republic. Firstly, he points out that art has great influence on people's psychology and character. He criticizes that Homer's works destroy one's reason, cater to the inferior, and make people give free rein to sorrow and pity, so Homer should be banished from the Republic. Secondly, he emphasizes the educational function of art and believes that art should help cultivate the ideal people. He advocates that suitable educational works should be chosen for children and favorable educational atmosphere should be created for children's moral education.

文艺社会功用说是柏拉图的又一重要的文艺理论观点。他认为文艺要对城邦的建设和人民的教育发挥作用,要有助于建立正义的理想国。首先,他指出文艺对人的心理和性格有着重大影响力。他批判了荷马的作品摧残理性,逢迎人性中低劣的部分,使人容易感伤和哀怜,应将其驱逐出理想国。其次,他强调文艺的道德教化功能,文艺要有利于培养理想的人。他提倡要为儿童选择恰当的教育作品,形成良好的教育氛围,对儿童进行道德方面的培养和教育。

2. Selections from *The Republic*

2.《理想国》选文

Republic X①

*Socrates—Glaucon*②

理想国

苏格拉底 —— 格劳孔

Socrates: Of the many excellences which I

苏:在我所构想的具有诸多优点

① Selected from *The Dialogues of Plato*, translated by Benjamin Jowett, Oxford: The Clarendon Press, 1892.

② 苏格拉底是主讲者,格劳孔是回应者。原英译本中没有对话者的名字,只有"I said"、"he said",为了便于阅读,本书添加了对话者名而省略了"I said"、"he said"。国内多个中译本中也都添加了对话者名。

perceive in the order of our State, there is none which upon reflection pleases me better than the rule about poetry.

Glaucon: To what do you refer?

Socrates: To the rejection of imitative poetry, which certainly ought not to be received; as I see far more clearly now that the parts of the soul have been distinguished.

Glaucon: What do you mean?

Socrates: Speaking in confidence, for I should not like to have my words repeated to the tragedians and the rest of the imitative tribe—but I do not mind saying to you, that all poetical imitations are ruinous to the understanding of the hearers, and that the knowledge of their true nature is the only antidote to them.

Glaucon: Explain the purport of your remark.

Socrates: Well, I will tell you, although I have always from my earliest youth had an awe and love of Homer①, which even now makes the words falter on my lips, for he is the great captain and teacher of the whole of that charming tragic company; but a man is not to be reverenced more than the truth, and therefore I will speak out.

Glaucon: Very good.

Socrates: Listen to me then, or rather, answer me.

Glaucon: Put your question.

Socrates: Can you tell me what imitation is? For I really do not know.

Glaucon: A likely thing, then, that I should know.

Socrates: Why not? For the duller eye may often see a thing sooner than the keener.

Glaucon: Very true, but in your presence, even if I had any faint notion, I could

的国家里,我认为我对诗歌的做法是最为满意的。

格:什么样的做法?

苏:它拒绝诗歌模仿,那些模仿之作绝对不能接受。须知,既然我们已经辨别出了心灵的不同组成部分,那么拒绝模仿的理由就更清楚了。

格:你的意思是?

苏:我们私下里说说,因为我不想让那些悲剧诗人或是别的模仿者听到我说的话。但是我愿意说给你听:这种艺术对于所有没有预先受到警告不知道它的危害性的那些听众的心灵,是有腐蚀性的。

格:请解释你的观点。

苏:我不得不直说了。虽然我从小就对荷马怀有敬爱之心,现在也依然如此。因为他是所有这些伟大的悲剧诗人的祖师爷呢。但是,我不能把对一个人的尊敬看得高于真理。因此,我必须说出我的心里话。

格:很好。

苏:那么请听我说,或者回答我的问题吧。

格:你问吧。

苏:你能告诉我什么是模仿吗?因为我自己也确实不太清楚。

格:那我就更不懂了。

苏:那倒不一定。视力差的人可能会比视力好的人更快看见某物。

格:这倒也是。不过在你面前,即使我看见什么,也没有勇气说出来。

① 荷马(Homer),古希腊诗人,著有《伊利亚特》(*Iliad*)和《奥德赛》(*Odyssey*)。这两部史诗被认为是希腊最伟大的文学作品,大约完成于公元前 800 年—前 700 年之间。在古代希腊,它们被奉为圣典。

not muster courage to utter it. Will you enquire yourself?

Socrates: Well then, shall we begin the enquiry in our usual manner: Whenever a number of individuals have a common name, we assume them to have also a corresponding idea① or form. Do you understand me?

Glaucon: I do.

Socrates: Let us take any common instance; there are beds and tables in the world—plenty of them, are there not?

Glaucon: Yes.

Socrates: But there are only two ideas or forms of them—one the idea of a bed, the other of a table.

Glaucon: True.

Socrates: And the maker of either of them makes a bed or he makes a table for our use, in accordance with the idea—that is our way of speaking in this and similar instances—but no artificer② makes the ideas themselves: how could he?

Glaucon: Impossible.

Socrates: And there is another artist—I should like to know what you would say of him.

Glaucon: Who is he?

Socrates: One who is the maker of all the works of all other workmen.

Glaucon: What an extraordinary man!

Socrates: Wait a little, and there will be more reason for your saying so. For this is he who is able to make not only vessels of every kind, but plants and animals, himself and all other things—the earth and heaven, and the things which are in heaven or under the earth; he makes the gods also.

还是你自己看吧。

苏：那我们下面还是按照我们惯常的程序开始讨论问题吧。在凡是我们能用同一名称称呼多数事物的场合，我们总是假定它们也是有一个相对应的理念或是形式。你明白吗？

格：我明白。

苏：那让我们现在就举出一些平常的东西吧，例如世界上有许多床和桌子，对吧？

格：是的。

苏：但是它们都可以归纳为两个理念或是形式——一个是床的理念，一个是桌子的理念。

格：是的。

苏：那么根据这个理念工匠制造出了床和桌子供我们使用。我们所熟悉的其他东西也是这么来的。至于理念或形式本身则不是任何匠人能制造出来的，这是肯定的，是吗？

格：是的，工匠不可能。

苏：还有另一种工匠，你该怎么称呼他呢？

格：什么样的工匠？

苏：一种能制造出所有其他工匠所制造的东西的工匠。

格：多么不寻常的人啊！

苏：请稍等一下，他的伟大之处不止这些。因为他不仅制造了各种各样的工具，而且还创造了植物、动物、他自己以及所有的一切——天和地以及天地间的万物；他还创造了诸神。

① 理念是柏拉图哲学中的基本观念，即概念或普遍的道理。
② 柏拉图认为，艺术本质上是技艺，是制作的技巧，工匠就是制造者。

Glaucon: He must be a wizard and no mistake.

Socrates: Oh! You are incredulous, are you? Do you mean that there is no such maker or creator, or that in one sense there might be a maker of all these things but in another not? Do you see that there is a way in which you could make them all yourself?

Glaucon: What way?

Socrates: An easy way enough; or rather, there are many ways in which the feat might be quickly and easily accomplished, none quicker than that of turning a mirror round and round—you would soon enough make the sun and the heavens, and the earth and yourself, and other animals and plants, and all the other things of which we were just now speaking, in the mirror.

Glaucon: Yes; but they would be appearances only.

Socrates: Very good, you are coming to the point now. And the painter too is, as I conceive, just such another—a creator of appearances, is he not?

Glaucon: Of course.

Socrates: But then I suppose you will say that what he creates is untrue. And yet there is a sense in which the painter also creates a bed?

Glaucon: Yes, but not a real bed.

Socrates: And what of the maker of the bed? Were you not saying that he too makes, not the idea which, according to our view, is the essence of the bed, but only a particular bed?

Glaucon: Yes, I did.

Socrates: Then if he does not make that which exists he cannot make true existence, but only some semblance of existence; and if any one were

格：那他肯定是一位奇才！没错。

苏：哦，难道你不相信吗？你是说世界上根本就没有这样的一位匠人吗？或者你认为在一种意义上存在着这样的一位匠人，而在另一种意义上这种人是不存在的？你不知道其实你自己也能在某种意义上制造出所有这些东西？

格：在哪种意义上？

苏：这很简单，或者说有很多方法可以制造出所有这些东西。较快的办法就是你拿着一面镜子转圈——你就会很快地制造出太阳、天堂、大地和你自己，以及别的动物和植物。你还能在镜子中制造出所有我们刚刚讲过的其他东西。

格：是的。但是这些东西只是影像而已。

苏：很好。你现在慢慢理解我的意思了。我认为画家也属于诸如此类制造影像的匠人。难道不是吗？

格：当然是的。

苏：那么我猜想你肯定会说画家制造的不是真的。尽管如此在某种意义上画家也是制造了一张床，对吧？

格：是的，但不是真的床。

苏：那么制造出床的木匠呢？根据我们的观点，你是不是说木匠制造出的床也不是本质上的床，而只是一张具体的床而已？

格：是的，我是这么说的。

苏：那么如果他不能制造出实际存在的东西，他就不能制造出真实的存在，而只是制造出一些像真实的

to say that the work of the maker of the bed, or of any other workman, has real existence, he could hardly be supposed to be speaking the truth.

Glaucon: At any rate, philosophers would say that he was not speaking the truth.

Socrates: No wonder, then, that his work too is an indistinct expression of truth.

Glaucon: No wonder.

Socrates: Suppose now that by the light of the examples just offered we enquire who this imitator is?

Glaucon: If you please.

Socrates: Well then, here are three beds: one existing in nature, which is made by God, as I think that we may say—for no one else can be the maker?

Glaucon: No.

Socrates: There is another which is the work of the carpenter?

Glaucon: Yes.

Socrates: And the work of the painter is a third?

Glaucon: Yes.

Socrates: Beds, then, are of three kinds, and there are three artists who superintend them: God, the maker of the bed, and the painter?

Glaucon: Yes, there are three of them.

Socrates: God, whether from choice or from necessity, made one bed in nature and one only; two or more such ideal beds neither ever have been nor ever will be made by God.

Glaucon: Why is that?

Socrates: Because even if He had made but two, a third would still appear behind them which both of them would have for their idea, and that would be the ideal bed and not the two others.

Glaucon: Very true.

Socrates: God knew this, and He desired to

东西。如果有人说造床的木匠或其他任何手艺人造出的东西是真实存在的,那么他不可能说出真知。

格:无论如何,哲学家们会说他没有说真知。

苏:难怪。那么,木匠的工作也是一种对真实事物的模糊表达了。

格:可不嘛。

苏:那么根据我们刚刚所提供的例子,我们来看看真正的模仿者到底是谁呢?

格:好的。

苏:那么下面我们假设有三种床:一种是自然的床,我认为我们大概说是上帝制造的。因为不可能是别的人制造的。

格:对的。

苏:另一种是木匠制造出的床。

格:是的。

苏:第三种床是画家画的床,是吧?

格:是的。

苏:那么床有三种,分别是由上帝、木匠和画家三位艺术家制造的,对吧?

格:是的,是这三种人。

苏:上帝无论是出于选择还是需要只能制造出一张床;上帝从未制造出两张以上的床,以后也不会。

格:为什么?

苏:因为即使上帝制造了两张床,这两个床后面就会有一个公共的理念,这才是床的真实体,而原来那两个就不是了。

格:那倒是真的。

苏:上帝正因为知道这一点,并

be the real maker of a real bed, not a particular maker of a particular bed, and therefore He created a bed which is essentially and by nature one only.

且希望自己成为那个真正的床的制造者,而不是只会制造出某种特定的床的木匠。因此,上帝就只制造出了一张本质的床。

Glaucon: So we believe.

Socrates: Shall we, then, speak of Him as the natural author or maker of the bed?

Glaucon: Yes, in as much as by the natural process of creation He is the author of this and of all other things.

Socrates: And what shall we say of the carpenter—is not he also the maker of the bed?

Glaucon: Yes.

Socrates: But would you call the painter a creator and maker?

Glaucon: Certainly not.

Socrates: Yet if he is not the maker, what is he in relation to the bed?

Glaucon: I think, that we may fairly designate him as the imitator of that which the others make.

格:看来是的。

苏:那么我们能否把上帝叫做床的自然作者或制造者呢?

格:可以。既然上帝是自然之床和其他一切事物的自然过程的制造者。

苏:那么我们该如何称呼木匠呢——他不是也制造出了床吗?

格:是的,木匠也是床的制造者。

苏:那么你会把画家也称作创造者和制造者吗?

格:当然不会。

苏:如果他不是床的制造者,那么他与床有什么关系呢?

格:我认为我们应该称他为那两人所造的东西的模仿者比较合适。

Socrates: Good, then you call him who is third in the descent from nature an imitator?

Glaucon: Certainly.

Socrates: And the tragic poet is an imitator, and therefore, like all other imitators, he is thrice removed from the king① and from the truth?

Glaucon: That appears to be so.

Socrates: Then about the imitator we are agreed. And what about the painter? —I would like to know whether he may be thought to imitate that which originally exists in nature, or only the creations of artists?

Glaucon: The latter.

Socrates: As they are or as they appear? You have still to determine this.

Glaucon: What do you mean?

苏:很好。因此你把与自然隔着两层的作品制造者称作模仿者?

格:是的。

苏:那么悲剧诗人就是模仿者,因此,如其他的模仿者一样,他也与王者和真实隔着两层。

格:看来是这样的。

苏:那么关于模仿者我们的意见已经达成一致了。关于画家呢?我想知道画家究竟是模仿制作了原来就已经存在的东西呢,还是他只是对工匠作品的模仿?

格:后者。

苏:因此这是事物的真实还是影像?你必须明确这点。

格:我不明白你的意思。

① King:比喻性用语。“王者”即“最高”、“真理”的意思。

Socrates: I mean, that you may look at a bed from different points of view, obliquely or directly or from any other point of view, and the bed will appear different, but there is no difference in reality. And the same of all things.

Glaucon: Yes, the difference is only apparent.

Socrates: Now let me ask you another question: Which is the art of painting designed to be—an imitation of things as they are, or as they appear—of appearance or of reality?

Glaucon: Of appearance.

Socrates: Then the imitator, is a long way off the truth, and can do all things because he lightly touches on a small part of them, and that part an image. For example: a painter will paint a cobbler, carpenter, or any other artist, though he knows nothing of their arts; and, if he is a good artist, he may deceive children or simple persons, when he shows them his picture of a carpenter from a distance, and they will fancy that they are looking at a real carpenter.

Glaucon: Certainly.

Socrates: And whenever any one informs us that he has found a man who knows all the arts, and all things else that anybody knows, and every single thing with a higher degree of accuracy than any other man—whoever tells us this, I think that we can only imagine him to be a simple creature who is likely to have been deceived by some wizard or actor whom he met, and whom he thought all-knowing, because he himself was unable to analyse the nature of knowledge and ignorance and imitation.

Glaucon: Most true.

Socrates: And so, when we hear persons saying that the tragedians, and Homer, who is at their head, know all the arts and all things human, virtue as well as vice, and divine things too, for that the good poet cannot compose well unless he

苏：我的意思是你可以从不同的角度看这张床，从侧面或是正面或从其他角度看，床可能都会不同，但实际上这张床并没有什么不同。其他的事物也是如此。

格：是的，只是表象不同，实质都是一样的。

苏：现在我再问你一个问题：画家在作画时，是在模仿事物本身还是在模仿事物的表象呢？是对事物表象的模仿还是对事物本质的模仿？

格：是对事物表象的模仿。

苏：那么我认为模仿术和真实的距离是很远的。这也是画家能够模仿制造出其他事物的原因吧，他只是把握了事物的一小部分，而且是表象的一小部分。例如，画家会画出鞋匠、木匠或其他工匠，尽管他对这些工匠的技术一无所知；但如果他是个优秀的画家，他把他的画陈列得离观众有一定的距离，他还是能够骗过小孩和一些笨人，使他们信以为真。

格：当然了。

苏：那么无论何时如果有人告知我们说他发现了一位精通一切技艺，懂得一切其他人都知道的事情，并且比其他人都懂得更加精确的全才时，我们只能说这个人是一位头脑简单，很容易被他遇到的他认为是全才的一些巫师或是表演家所欺骗了。他之所以被骗是因为他自己无法辨析知识、无知和模仿的本质区别。

格：是的。

苏：那么，当我们听到人们说起悲剧诗人，说起荷马，他们的领袖时，会说他知道一切技艺和一切与人类有关的事，善恶皆知，还有神的事情，

knows his subject, and that he who has not this knowledge can never be a poet, we ought to consider whether here also there may not be a similar illusion. Perhaps they may have come across imitators and been deceived by them; they may not have remembered when they saw their works that these were but imitations thrice removed from the truth, and could easily be made without any knowledge of the truth, because they are appearances only and not realities? Or, after all, they may be in the right, and poets do really know the things about which they seem to the many to speak so well?

因为好诗人只有知道他所写的东西，才能写好诗，没有这种知识的人永远也无法成为诗人，这时我们应该考虑这些人是否也碰到了那些巫师或是表演家了，受了他们的欺骗了。他们看到的作品只是从真实中所模仿出来的作品而已。因此，即使不知道真实的事物也能很容易地制造出这些东西。因为这些模仿之作只是事物的表象，而非真实。或许这些人说的也是对的吧，优秀的诗人对他们所描述的事物还是有一定了解的。

Glaucon: The question, should by all means be considered.

格：这个问题我们应该全面考虑一下。

Socrates: Now do you suppose that if a person were able to make the original as well as the image, he would seriously devote himself to the image-making branch? Would he allow imitation to be the ruling principle of his life, as if he had nothing higher in him?

苏：那么现在如果一个人既能制造被模仿的东西又能制造影像，你认为他会认真地致力于他的影像制造工作吗？他允许模仿成为他生活的统治原则，就好像他内心没有更高的追求一样？

Glaucon: I should say not.

格：我不这样认为。

Socrates: The real artist, who knew what he was imitating, would be interested in realities and not in imitations; and would desire to leave as memorials of himself works many and fair; and, instead of being the author of encomiums, he would prefer to be the theme of them.

苏：真正知道他在模仿的工匠将会对真实更感兴趣，而不愿模仿。他会渴望制造出许多出色的真品留下来作为自己的纪念。他会宁愿成为一名被羡慕的人，而不只是去羡慕别人。

Glaucon: Yes, that would be to him a source of much greater honour and profit.

格：是的。那对他而言将会是更大的荣誉和利益。

Socrates: Then, we must put a question to Homer; not about medicine, or any of the arts to which his poems only incidentally refer: we are not going to ask him, or any other poet, whether he has cured patients like Asclepius①, or left behind him a school of medicine such as the Asclepiads were, or whether he only talks about medicine and

苏：那么我们来问荷马一个问题。这个问题不是关于医术的或是其他方面的，荷马对这些问题只是顺便提了一下。我们也不会问荷马或是其他任何诗人他们是否像阿斯克勒比俄斯（医学上的神或英雄）那样

① 阿斯克勒比俄斯（Asclepius）是医术之始祖。

other arts at second hand; but we have a right to know respecting military tactics, politics, education, which are the chiefest and noblest subjects of his poems, and we may fairly ask him about them. "Friend Homer," then we say to him, "if you are only in the second remove from truth in what you say of virtue, and not in the third—not an image maker or imitator—and if you are able to discern what pursuits make men better or worse in private or public life, tell us what State was ever better governed by your help? The good order of Lacedaemon① is due to Lycurgus②, and many other cities great and small have been similarly benefited by others; but who says that you have been a good legislator to them and have done them any good? Italy and Sicily boast of Charondas③, and there is Solon④ who is renowned among us; but what city has anything to say about you?" Is there any city which he might name?

治好了病患,或是在他身后教育了一批像阿斯克勒比俄斯那样医术高明的学生,或是他们只是间接地提起了医术和其他工艺。但是我们有权提问荷马关于军事战术、政治和教育方面的问题,因为这些都是荷马诗歌里面重要的谈论主题。而且我们也可以这样公道地请教荷马下面的问题:"亲爱的荷马,假定你虽然是我们定义为模仿者的那种影像的制造者,但是离美德方面的真实并不隔开两层,而只是相隔一层,并且能够知道怎样的教育和训练能够使人们在公私生活中变好或变坏,那么请问有哪一个城邦曾在你的帮助下而治理好了的?古代斯巴达的良好秩序归功于斯巴达的立法者莱克尔加斯,而且其他一些大小不等的城市也因为有别的立法者。但有谁曾说过你曾经是个很好的立法者,并对这些城邦有过帮助?意大利和西西里人曾归功于卡雍达斯,而我们则归功于梭伦。但是有谁曾归功于你?"荷马能说出自己曾对哪个城邦的治理有过帮助吗?

Glaucon: I think not, said Glaucon; not even the Homerids themselves pretend that he was a legislator.

格:我想没有,连荷马的崇拜者们也不曾有人说荷马是一位优秀的立法者。

Socrates: Well, but is there any war on record which was carried on successfully by him, or aided by his counsels, when he was alive?

苏:那么历史记录上有哪次战争是荷马有生之年指挥打胜的,或是在他的参谋下打胜的?

Glaucon: There is not.

格:没有。

---

① Lacedaemon 是斯巴达(Sparte)控制下的一个城邦,斯巴达是与雅典(Athens)争夺希腊统治权的主要对手,以其秩序和纪律闻名。

② 莱克尔加斯(Lycurgus),斯巴达的立法者。

③ 卡雍达斯(Charondas,约公元前 600 年),西西里(Sicily)的立法者。

④ 梭伦(Solon,约公元前 629 年—前 559 年),雅典的立法者、诗人和改革家。

Socrates: Or is there any invention of his, applicable to the arts or to human life, such as Thales① the Milesian or Anacharsis② the Scythian, and other ingenious men have conceived, which is attributed to him?

Glaucon: There is absolutely nothing of the kind.

Socrates: But, if Homer never did any public service, was he privately a guide or teacher of any? Had he in his lifetime friends who loved to associate with him, and who handed down to posterity and Homeric way of life, such as was established by Pythagoras③ who was so greatly beloved for his wisdom, and whose followers are to this day quite celebrated for the order which was named after him?

Glaucon: Nothing of the kind is recorded of him. For surely, Socrates, Creophylus④, the companion of Homer, that child of flesh, whose name always makes us laugh, might be more justly ridiculed for his stupidity, if, as is said, Homer was greatly neglected by him and others in his own day when he was alive?

Socrates: Yes, that is the tradition. But can you imagine, Glaucon, that if Homer had really been able to educate and improve mankind—if he had possessed knowledge and not been a mere imitator—can you imagine, that he would not have had many followers, and been honoured and loved by them? Protagoras⑤ of Abdera, and Prodicus⑥

苏：或者你听到过有关荷马在技艺或是人们生活方面的发明吧？有像米利部的泰勒斯和斯基泰人阿那卡尔西那样的发明？或者其他聪明的人构想出的与荷马有关的发明？

格：绝对一项也没听说过。

苏：如果荷马从未担任过什么公职，那么他有没有私下里担任过导师或是老师的工作呢？在他的有生之年有朋友爱与他交往，并且把他的生活方式流传给了子孙后代的吗？就像毕达哥拉斯那样？毕达哥拉斯曾因他的智慧深受大家的喜爱，并且他的追随者至今依然称赞以毕达哥拉斯命名的定律。

格：荷马这方面没有任何的记录。当然了，苏格拉底，荷马的学生克瑞俄菲洛斯作为荷马教育的一个标本，比起他的愚蠢来，他的名字更让人可笑。据说荷马在世时这个学生以及他同时代的其他人就轻视荷马。

苏：是的，是有这个传说。但是，格劳孔你想象一下，如果荷马真的能够教育和提高人类的品德，如果他真拥有知识而不只是一位模仿者，那么，你想象一下，他肯定会有许多的追随者尊敬他、爱戴他，对吧？阿布德拉的普罗泰戈拉和开奥斯的普

① 泰勒斯(Thales,公元前636年—前546年)是一位自然哲学家,他认为水是基本元素,它构成了世界上的一切。

② 阿那卡尔西(Anacharsis),公元前6世纪的哲学家,据说是锚和陶轮的发明者。

③ 毕达哥拉斯(Pythagoras,公元前582年—前507年),哲学家和数学家,以发明"毕达哥拉斯定理"(Pythagorean Theorem)而著名。他的门徒形成了一个秘密团体,其中的成员必须受其教育。

④ 克瑞俄菲洛斯(Creophylus)是与荷马同时代的史诗作家。

⑤ 普罗泰戈拉(Protagoras,公元前480年—前410年),希腊哲学家,著名智者,以他的格言"人是一切东西的尺度"(Man is the measure of all things.)而闻名。柏拉图把他作为某个苏格拉底的对话对象。

⑥ 普洛蒂卡斯(Prodicus),公元前5世纪时的一位诡辩家。

of Ceos, and a host of others, have only to whisper to their contemporaries: "You will never be able to manage either your own house or your own State until you appoint us to be your ministers of education"—and this ingenious device of theirs has such an effect in making men love them that their companions all but carry them about on their shoulders. And is it conceivable that the contemporaries of Homer, or again of Hesiod①, would have allowed either of them to go about as rhapsodists②, if they had really been able to make mankind virtuous? Would they not have been as unwilling to part with them as with gold, and have compelled them to stay at home with them? Or, if the master would not stay, then the disciples would have followed him about everywhere, until they had got education enough?

Glaucon: Yes, Socrates, that, I think, is quite true.

Socrates: Then must we not infer that all these poetical individuals, beginning with Homer, are only imitators; they copy images of virtue and the like, but the truth they never reach? The poet is like a painter who, as we have already observed, will make a likeness of a cobbler though he understands nothing of cobbling; and his picture is good enough for those who know no more than he does, and judge only by colours and figures.

Glaucon: Quite so.

Socrates: In like manner the poet with his words and phrases may be said to lay on the colours of the several arts, himself understanding their nature only enough to imitate them; and other

洛蒂卡斯以及其他的智者仅仅只是给他们的同代人悄悄地传道说:"你只有让我们这些人成为你们的教育传道者,你们才可以管理好你们自己的家务或是国家事务"——并且这些智者的策略对人们有着非常大的影响。人们非常爱戴他们以至于差点把这些智者顶在自己的肩膀上走路了。同样的,如果荷马真能帮助同时代人得到美德,人们还能让他或是赫西俄德流离颠沛,以卖唱为生吗?人们会依依不舍,把他看得跟黄金一样重要,而把他强留在自己家里的。或是如果荷马坚持要走的话,那么这些信徒则会跟随他走到天涯海角,直到他们得到了荷马的教育为止。

格:是的,苏格拉底。我认为你说的确实如此。

苏:那么我们是不是可以推断出自荷马以来所有的诗人都只是模仿者。他们模仿美德之类的影像,但却从不知道真实?诗人就像我们之前讨论过的画家一样,会画出像鞋匠那样的人来,而诗人自己对鞋匠的技艺却一无所知。他所画的画足以让那些跟他一样对鞋匠的技艺不懂的人,仅仅从颜色和形象来判断他的画的好与坏。

格:确实如此。

苏:同样的,诗人通过他的词语来描绘各种技艺,而诗人自己对这些技艺却不甚理解。其他与诗人一样无知的人则仅仅从诗人的语言来判断诗的好坏。假设他用韵律、音步和

① 赫西俄德(Hesiod),古希腊与荷马齐名的伟大诗人,他对神的起源的描述为希腊神学奠定了基础,通常认为他晚于荷马。

② 即吟游诗人,是诗的背诵者,特别是背诵荷马和赫西俄德的诗。当时,希腊实质上只有口头文学,但到柏拉图写作的时期,这种情况开始变化。

people, who are as ignorant as he is, and judge only from his words, imagine that if he speaks of cobbling, or of military tactics, or of anything else, in metre and harmony and rhythm, he speaks very well—such is the sweet influence which melody and rhythm by nature have. And I think that you must have observed again and again what a poor appearance the tales of poets make when stripped of the colours which music puts upon them, and recited in simple prose.

Glaucon: Yes.

Socrates: They are like faces which were never really beautiful, but only blooming; and now the bloom of youth has passed away from them?

Glaucon: Exactly.

Socrates: Here is another point: The imitator or maker of the image knows nothing of true existence; he knows appearances only. Am I not right?

Glaucon: Yes.

Socrates: Then let us have a clear understanding, and not be satisfied with half an explanation.

Glaucon: Proceed.

Socrates: Of the painter we say that he will paint reins, and he will paint a bit?

Glaucon: Yes.

Socrates: And the worker in leather and brass will make them?

Glaucon: Certainly.

Socrates: But does the painter know the right form of the bit and reins? Nay, hardly even the workers in brass and leather who make them; only the horseman who knows how to use them—he knows their right form.

Glaucon: Most true.

Socrates: And may we not say the same of all things?

Glaucon: What?

Socrates: That there are three arts which are

曲调谈论鞋匠或军事策略或其他任何事情,听众由于和荷马一样对这些事情不甚了解,而仅仅通过诗歌的语言认识事物,就会认为荷马的诗歌描绘得很好,这是旋律和节奏本身具有的魅力。我想你一定也观察到了如果去掉了音乐带给诗歌的华丽包装,而只是像散文那样诵读的话,那诗人的形象该是多么的可怜啊!

格:是的,我已经注意到了。

苏:它们就像那些并非天生丽质,而只是因为年轻而显得漂亮的面孔,现在青春已逝,容华尽失。

格:确实如此。

苏:还有一点:影像的制造者或是模仿者对真实一无所知;他们只知道表象。是这样吗?

格:是的。

苏:那么让我们把这个问题理解清楚了,不要一知半解。

格:那请继续说吧。

苏:我们说画家可以画马缰和嚼子吧?

格:是的。

苏:然而却是皮匠和铜匠制造出这些东西的吧?

格:当然了。

苏:但是画家知道缰绳和嚼子应该是什么样子的吗?当然不知道。就连制造出这些东西的皮匠和铜匠恐怕也不知道吧。只有使用它们的骑马者才知道吧?

格:完全正确。

苏:那我们能不能说其他事物也是如此呢?

格:你指什么?

苏:我是说所有事物都与这三

concerned with all things: one which uses, another which makes, a third which imitates them?

Glaucon: Yes.

Socrates: And the excellence or beauty or truth of every structure, animate or inanimate, and of every action of man, is relative to the use for which nature or the artist has intended them.

Glaucon: True.

Socrates: Then the user of them must have the greatest experience of them, and he must indicate to the maker the good or bad qualities which develop themselves in use; for example, the flute-player will tell the flute-maker which of his flutes is satisfactory to the performer; we will tell him how he ought to make them, and the other will attend to his instructions?

Glaucon: Of course.

Socrates: The one knows and therefore speaks with authority about the goodness and badness of flutes, while the other, confiding in him, will do what he is told by him?

Glaucon: True.

Socrates: The instrument is the same, but about the excellence or badness of it the maker will only attain to a correct belief; and this he will gain from him who knows, by talking to him and being compelled to hear what he has to say, whereas the user will have knowledge?

Glaucon: True.

Socrates: But will the imitator have either? Will he know from use whether or not his drawing is correct or beautiful? Or will he have right opinion from being compelled to associate with another who knows and gives him instructions about what he should draw?

Glaucon: Neither.

Socrates: Then he will no more have true opinion than he will have knowledge about the goodness or badness of his imitations?

种技术有关:使用者的技术,制造者的技术和模仿者的技术,对吧?

格:是的。

苏:那么优秀的、漂亮的或是真实的体系,无论是否有生命,人类的每一个举动都与这些使用者相关呢!

格:是的。

苏:那么使用者一定是最有经验的,他把使用过程中发现的该事物的好与坏都会告知制造者。例如,吹奏长笛的人告知制造长笛的人,他会把长笛在演奏中表现出来的性能如何告知制造者应该如何制造,而制造者则按照他的指示去制造长笛。

格:当然了。

苏:了解长笛的人把长笛的好坏告知长笛的制造者,这些制造者信任他,并按照他所说的去制造长笛。

格:是的。

苏:虽然这种长笛乐器是相同的,但是关于长笛的好坏,制造者只能从了解长笛的使用者那里通过交谈得知,并且不得不听从使用者所说的,而只有长笛的使用者对它有真实的知识。

格:是的。

苏:那么模仿者对自己所描绘的事物有真实的知识吗?他能通过使用了解到他所画的事物是否正确或漂亮吗?或是他能从与另一个有真知的人交往中听从他的关于正确描绘事物的要求之后而形成自己正确的意见吗?

格:不能。

苏:那么模仿者关于自己模仿的优劣质量既无真实知识也无正确意见了。

Glaucon: I suppose not.

Socrates: The imitative artist will be in a brilliant state of intelligence about his own creations?

Glaucon: Nay, very much the reverse.

Socrates: And still he will go on imitating without knowing what makes a thing good or bad, and may be expected therefore to imitate only that which appears to be good to the ignorant multitude?

Glaucon: Just so.

Socrates: Thus far then we are pretty well agreed that the imitator has no knowledge worth mentioning of what he imitates. Imitation is only a kind of play or sport, and the tragic poets, whether they write in iambic① or in Heroic verse②, are imitators in the highest degree?

Glaucon: Very true.

Socrates: And now tell me, I conjure you, has not imitation been shown by us to be concerned with that which is thrice removed from the truth?

Glaucon: Certainly.

Socrates: And what is the faculty in man to which imitation is addressed?

Glaucon: What do you mean?

Socrates: I will explain: The body which is large when seen near, appears small when seen at a distance?

Glaucon: True.

Socrates: And the same object appears straight when looked at out of the water, and crooked when in the water; and the concave becomes convex, owing to the illusion about colours to which the sight is liable. Thus every sort of confusion is revealed within us; and this is that weakness of the human mind on which the art of conjuring and of

格：我想是那样的。

苏：那么诗人作为一种模仿者关于他所创作的东西的智慧是最美的了？

格：不是，恰恰相反。

苏：那么他虽然不知道自己创作的东西是否优劣，他依然继续模仿。也许对于那些一无所知的大众来说还是显得很美的。

格：仅此而已。

苏：那么我们已经取得了一致意见：模仿者对他所模仿的东西没有真实的知识。模仿只是一种游戏。这些悲剧诗人无论他们是以抑扬格还是以英雄体诗写作，他们充其量都只是模仿者。

格：确实如此。

苏：那么现在告诉我，我们是不是还没有展示模仿是否与隔真理两层的第三级事物相关的呢？

格：是的。

苏：那么模仿是人的哪一部分功能呢？

格：你指什么？

苏：我是说：当我们近看一个东西的时候，它看上去很大；当我们远看的时候，它看上去很小。

格：确实如此。

苏：同一事物在水之外看是笔直的，而从水里看却是弯曲的；凹面变成了凸面。这些现象都是由于视觉所依赖的颜色假象所造成的。因此我们的心灵里有各种各样诸如此类的困惑。这也是人类的弱点，而这些工匠通过光、影子以及其他奇特的

① iambic：抑扬格，短长格，主要用于戏剧对话中。

② heroic verse：英雄体诗，在古希腊文学中，多用于史诗写作，如著名史诗《伊利亚特》和《奥德赛》。希腊语诗歌的结构与英语诗歌不完全相同，它以音节的长度而不是重音为基础。

deceiving by light and shadow and other ingenious devices imposes, having an effect upon us like magic.

Glaucon: True.

Socrates: And the arts of measuring and numbering and weighing come to the rescue of the human understanding—there is the beauty of them—and the apparent greater or less, or more or heavier, no longer have the mastery over us, but give way before calculation and measure and weight?

Glaucon: Most true.

Socrates: And this, surely, must be the work of the calculating and rational principle in the soul.

Glaucon: To be sure.

Socrates: And when this principle measures and certifies that some things are equal, or that some are greater or less than others, there occurs an apparent contradiction?

Glaucon: True.

Socrates: But were we not saying that such a contradiction is the same faculty cannot have contrary opinions at the same time about the same thing?

Glaucon: Very true.

Socrates: Then that part of the soul which has an opinion contrary to measure is not the same with that which has an opinion in accordance with measure?

Glaucon: True.

Socrates: And the better part of the soul is likely to be that which trusts to measure and calculation?

Glaucon: Certainly.

Socrates: And that which is opposed to them is one of the inferior principles of the soul?

Glaucon: No doubt.

Socrates: This was the conclusion at which I was seeking to arrive when I said that painting or

设计则正是利用人类的这些弱点,像变魔术一样欺骗了人类。

格:确实如此。

苏:测量、数字和称重是用来帮助人类理解事物,这是它们的美丽之处。这些表象的多或少、大或小、轻或重已经不能满足我们对事物精确掌握的需求了,替而代之的是数过的数、量过的大小和称过的重量等更准确的数字。

格:确实如此。

苏:这些测量活动正是心灵理性部分的工作。

格:确实如此。

苏:但是,当这种测量确认了某些事物是相等的,或是一些事物比其他事物大些或小些时,却常常看上去是矛盾的。

格:是的。

苏:但是我们不是说过:我们的同一感官对同一事物同时不能有两种相反的看法吗?

格:是的,我们是这样说的。

苏:那么心灵的那个与测量有相反意见的部分,和那个与测量一致的部分不可能是同一个部分。

格:当然不是同一个部分。

苏:那么心灵更好的那部分很可能是信任后测量和计算的。

格:一定是的。

苏:而反对测量和计算的那部分心灵则是低贱的。

格:是的。

苏:这就是我起初谈论绘画以及一般的模仿时想取得一致的结论。

drawing, and imitation in general, when doing their own proper work, are far removed from truth, and the companions and friends and associates of a principle within us which is equally removed from reason, and that they have no true or healthy aim.

Glaucon: Exactly.

Socrates: The imitative art is an inferior who marries an inferior, and has inferior offspring.

Glaucon: Very true.

Socrates: And is this confined to the sight only, or does it extend to the hearing also, relating in fact to what we term poetry①?

Glaucon: Probably the same would be true of poetry.

Socrates: Do not rely, on a probability derived from the analogy of painting; but let us examine further and see whether the faculty with which poetical imitation is concerned is good or bad.

Glaucon: By all means.

Socrates: We may state the question thus:—Imitation imitates the actions of men, whether voluntary or involuntary, on which, as they imagine, a good or bad result has ensued, and they rejoice or sorrow accordingly. Is there anything more?

Glaucon: No, there is nothing else.

Socrates: But in all this variety of circumstances is the man at unity with himself —or rather, as in the instance of sight there was confusion and opposition in his opinions about the same things, so here also is there not strife and inconsistency in his life? Though I need hardly raise the question again, for I remember that all this has been already admitted; and the soul has

他们在进行工作时是在创作远离真实的作品,并且我们内心的伴侣、朋友及其交往的那部分都是远离理性的,它们是不以健康或是真理为目的的。

格:确实如此。

苏:模仿术是低贱的父母所生的低贱的孩子。

格:确实如此。

苏:这个道理仅限于眼睛看的事物呢,还是也适用于耳朵听到的事物以及我们所定义为诗歌的事物呢?

格:可能也适用于诗歌吧。

苏:我们不要只根据绘画而得出的大概来下结论吧,我们还是进一步地考察一下从事模仿诗歌所打动的那个心灵的部分是好的还是坏的吧。

格:当然可以。

苏:我们可以这么说吧:模仿术是自愿或不自愿地模仿人的行为,如他们想象的那样一个好的或坏的结果已经产生了,他们也因此而开心或是悲伤。还有别的什么吗?

格:没有了。

苏:但是在所有这些感受里,人的心灵是统一的呢,或者还是像眼睛看到的那样,对同一事物会有困惑或是相反的看法。那么在他的生活中也有冲突和不一致吧?尽管我根本不需要再提出这个问题,因为我记得我们已经确认过这些问题了。我们也已经承认了我们的心灵在任何时

① poetry:古代诗歌的两种主要形式,史诗和悲剧,都是吟唱的,所以听众都是用耳朵的。

been acknowledged by us to be full of these and ten thousand similar oppositions occurring at the same moment?

Glaucon: And we were right.

Socrates: Yes, thus far we were right; but there was an omission which must now be supplied.

Glaucon: What was the omission?

Socrates: Were we not saying that a good man, who has the misfortune to lose his son or anything else which is most dear to him, will bear the loss with more equanimity than another?

Glaucon: Yes.

Socrates: But will he have no sorrow, or shall we say that although he cannot help sorrowing, he will moderate his sorrow?

Glaucon: The latter, is the truer statement.

Socrates: Tell me: will he be more likely to struggle and hold out against his sorrow when he is seen by his equals, or when he is alone?

Glaucon: It will make a great difference whether he is seen or not.

Socrates: When he is by himself he will not mind saying or doing many things which he would be ashamed of any one hearing or seeing him do?

Glaucon: True.

Socrates: There is a principle of law and reason in him which bids him resist, as well as a feeling of his misfortune which is forcing him to indulge his sorrow?

Glaucon: True.

Socrates: But when a man is drawn in two opposite directions, to and from the same object, this, as we affirm, necessarily implies two distinct principles in him?

Glaucon: Certainly.

候都是充满了这样的冲突。

格：我们是对的。

苏：对是对的，不过还是漏掉了一点，我们现在必须补上。

格：漏了什么？

苏：我们是不是说过一个伟大的人，当他遇到了失去儿子或是其他他特别心爱的事物时，他会比别人更能泰然处之？

格：是的。

苏：那么他是因为不觉得痛苦呢，还是因为他虽然非常痛苦，却依然克制了这种痛苦的感觉呢？

格：应该是后一种吧。

苏：那么请告诉我他是当着别人的面更能克制自己的悲痛呢还是独处的时候？

格：是否在公众场合还是独处的时候能控制情绪还是有很大区别的。

苏：当他独处时他是不会在意说什么、做什么的，但是在公众场合他还是会很在意别人听到或是看到他做的事情。

格：是的。

苏：他的理智要求他克制自己的悲痛，正如他的情感迫使他深陷悲痛之中一样。

格：是的。

苏：那么一个人对同一事物有两种相反的看法的话，我们认为他心里必定存在着两种不同的原则。

格：一定是的。

3. Questions for Discussion

(1) How do you understand "the bed made by god"?

(2) Why is Plato opposed to imitative art?

(3) Why should Homer be banished from the Republic?

3. 讨论题

(1)你如何理解"上帝造的床"?

(2)为什么柏拉图反对模仿艺术?

(3)为什么要将荷马驱逐出理想国?

Chapter 2

1. Introduction to Aristotle

Aristotle (384 B.C.-322 B.C.) was an ancient Greek philosopher and scientist. He wrote on diverse subjects, including physics, metaphysics, poetry (including theater), logic, rhetoric, politics, government, ethics, biology, and zoology. One of Aristotle's most important contributions was defining and classifying the various branches of knowledge and laid the foundation of most of the sciences of today.

Aristotle was born of a well-to-do family at Stagirus. His father was a court physician to King Amyntas of Macedonia. Under the influence of his father, Aristotle was interested in science. At the age of 17, he went to Plato's Academy and began his 20 year's study. At the death of Plato in 347 B.C., Aristotle left Athens and went to Assos, and then Mytilene. In 342 B.C., at the invitation of King Philip of Macedonia he became the tutor of his 13-year-old son Alexander. Three years later, he left the court and went back to his hometown. In

第2章

1. 亚里士多德简介

亚里士多德(公元前384年—前322年),是古希腊哲学家、科学家。他的研究涉猎广泛,包括物理、形而上学、诗歌(包括戏剧)、逻辑学、修辞学、政治学、政府管理、伦理学、生物学和动物学。亚里士多德最重要的贡献之一是对各种知识进行定义和分类,为多数现代科学奠定了基础。

亚里士多德出生在斯塔基拉一个富裕的家庭。他的父亲是马其顿国王阿敏塔斯的宫廷御医。受父亲的影响,亚里士多德对自然科学颇有兴趣。17岁时前往阿卡德米学院开始了长达20年的学习。公元前347年,柏拉图逝世,亚里士多德离开雅典,先去阿苏斯城,后到米提利尼城游学考察。公元前342年,他应马其顿王腓力之召担任13岁的亚历山大王子的老师,三年后离开宫廷返回故乡。公元前335年,亚里士多德回到

335 B.C., Aristotle returned to Athens and founded a school called the Lyceum. In 323 B.C., the pro-Macedonian government in Athens was overthrown. To escape prosecution he fled to Chalcis and died of illness the next year.

雅典,建立了自己的吕克昂学院。公元前323年,雅典亲马其顿政府被推翻。为躲避迫害,他避难于卡尔基斯城,次年病逝。

Aristotle learned philosophy from Plato, but he was different from his teacher in many ways. He once said "Plato is dear to me, but dearer still is truth." Aristotle considered the world was composed of forms and materials and harmonious things. He laid down the standard professional approach to scientific research. The arguments he used were of two types: dialectical, that is, based on logical deduction; and empirical, based on practical considerations. Aristotle's school, his philosophy, and his followers were called "peripatetic", taken from the Greek word meaning walking around, because Aristotle taught while walking with his students at the Lyceum.

亚里士多德在哲学上师从柏拉图,但是他与柏拉图在很多方面持不同观点。他曾说"吾爱吾师,吾更爱真理"。亚里士多德认为世界乃是由各种本身的形式与质料和谐一致的事物所组成的。他为科学研究奠定了标准而专业的方法。他所使用的论证方法主要有两类:基于逻辑推断的辩证法;基于践行性考量的实证法。在吕克昂学院,亚里士多德常和学生边讲课边漫步,故其学院、哲学和弟子被称为"peripatetic",希腊语,意为"逍遥派"或"漫步派"。

Aristotle's famous aesthetic works are *Rhetoric* and *Poetics*. In *Rhetoric*, Aristotle defines rhetoric as the ability to see what is possibly persuasive in every given case. Aristotle discusses three rhetorical settings and divides oratory/speech into three categories: deliberative / political oratory, epideictic/ceremonial oratory, forensic oratory. Aristotle proposes three modes of persuasion: ethos, pathos and logos.

亚里士多德著名的美学作品有《修辞学》和《诗学》。《修辞学》中,亚里士多德将修辞定义为在每一给定的事例中发现可行的说服方式的能力。亚里士多德根据场合将演讲分为三类:政治演讲、仪式演讲和法学演讲。亚里士多德提出三种说服方式:人格诉诸、情感诉诸和逻辑诉诸。

There are twenty-six chapters in *Poetics*, Aristotle expresses his views on arts in *Poetics*, that the essence of epic, tragedy or music and other artistic forms is imitation, while these artistic forms differ from one another in three respects: the medium, the objects, the manner or mode of imitation. Aristotle provides both a history of the development of poetry and drama, and a critical framework for evaluating tragedy.

《诗学》现存26章。亚里士多德在《诗学》中表达了对于艺术的观点,认为史诗、悲剧或音乐等艺术形式的本质皆是模仿,而这些艺术形式之间的区别表现在模仿中采用不同的媒介、对象和方式。亚里士多德梳理了诗歌和戏剧的发展史,并为评价悲剧提供了批评框架。

Poetics can be divided into the three parts. The first part (Chapter one to five) analyzes the importance of imitation, the origin of poetry, the development of tragedy and comedy. Imitation is man's inborn instinct which can give people pleasure. And there are different objects of imitation and narrative perspective among different poets or dramatists. Epic or tragedy imitates men of a higher type.

The second part (Chapter six to twenty-two) describes the constitution, types and functions of tragedy in detail, and explains six essential elements of tragedy: plot, character, thought, diction, spectacle and song respectively. Tragedy imitates acts that produce either pity or fear. Aristotle's tragic heroes are flawed individuals who commit, without evil intent, great wrongs or injuries that ultimately lead to their misfortune, often followed by tragic realization of the true nature of events that led to this destiny. Aristotle created the literary term catharsis. "Catharsis" in Greek can mean purification. Aristotle believes that the appreciation of tragedy can arouse people's feelings of fear and pity and purify the emotions and/or mind of the audience.

The third part (Chapter twenty-three to twenty-six) compares epic with tragedy. They differ in diction, language, length and logic. Aristotle believes that the tragedy should follow the three unities and the length should not be too long.

The *Poetics* is the first systematic essay in literary theory, full of insight, and showing a high degree of flexibility in the application of its general rules. This framework has had a strong influence up to the present day.

《诗学》可划分为三大部分。第一部分(第1—5章)分析了模仿的重要性、诗的起源、悲剧和喜剧的发展。模仿是人与生俱来的本能,给人以愉悦感。并且不同的诗人或戏剧家模仿的对象、叙述的角度也不同,而史诗或悲剧更多模仿的是高尚的人或行为。

第二部分(第6—22章)详细地描述了悲剧的构成、类型和功用,对悲剧的六要素:情节、性格、思想、言语、戏景、唱段分别做了详细阐释。悲剧所模仿的应该是能激起人们怜悯或恐惧的行为,而亚里士多德的悲剧的主人公并非一个完美的人物,并往往由于自身的缺陷以及一些过失导致了灾祸,事后则对导致悲剧命运的事件本质幡然醒悟。亚里士多德创造了净化这一文学术语。希腊语中的"catharsis"有净化之意。亚里士多德认为,欣赏悲剧可以激起人们心中的恐惧和怜悯之情,进而可以净化人的情感和思想。

第三部分(第23—26章)将史诗和悲剧进行了比较。两者在言语、语言、篇幅以及逻辑的运用上皆不相同。亚里士多德认为悲剧应遵循三一原则,篇幅不宜过长。

亚里士多德的《诗学》是文学理论中首篇成体系的文论,充满真知灼见,其普遍原则在运用中具有高度的灵活性,其批评框架至今仍具有极强的影响力。

2. Selections from *Poetics*

2.《诗学》选文

Poetics①

Aristotle

诗学

亚里士多德

I

I propose to treat of Poetry in itself and of its various kinds, noting the essential quality of each, to inquire into the structure of the plot as requisite to a good poem; into the number and nature of the parts of which a poem is composed; and similarly into whatever else falls within the same inquiry. Following, then, the order of nature, let us begin with the principles which come first.

Epic Poetry and Tragedy, Comedy also and Dithyrambic② Poetry, and the music of the flute and of the lyre in most of their forms, are all in their general conception modes of imitation. They differ, however, from one another in three respects,—the medium, the objects, the manner or mode of imitation, being in each case distinct.

For as there are persons who, by conscious art or mere habit, imitate and represent various objects through the medium of color and form, or again by the voice; so in the arts above mentioned, taken as a whole, the imitation is produced by rhythm, language, or "harmony",③ either singly or combined.

Thus in the music of the flute and of the lyre, "harmony" and rhythm alone are employed; also in

第*1*章

我认为对于诗歌本身和诗的类型,需要注意每种类型的本质,把探讨情节结构作为一首好诗必不可少的部分,讨论诗的组成数量和性质的部分以及探讨其他同一范畴类似的问题。让我们循着自然的顺序,先从原则的问题谈起。

史诗、悲剧、喜剧还有酒神颂歌,绝大部分长笛和竖琴演奏的音乐,总体来讲都是模仿的形式。它们的差别有三点,即在模仿中采用不同的媒介、不同的对象以及不同的方式。

因为有人借技艺或仅仅习惯,通过色彩、形态或声音的媒介模仿和展现不同的事物。所以上文提及的艺术,作为一个整体来讲,模仿是通过节奏、话语和音调来产生的——或用其中的一种,或混合采用。

因此长笛乐、竖琴乐仅用音调和

---

① Selected from *Aristotle's theory of poetry and fine art, with a critical text and translation of the Poetics*, by S. H. Butcher, New York: The Macmillan Company, 1902.

② dithyrambic: 狂热的;热情洋溢的;酒神颂歌的。

③ harmony: 音乐中的和声,此处译为"音调"。

other arts, such as that of the shepherd's pipe, which are essentially similar to these. In dancing, rhythm alone is used without "harmony"; for even dancing imitates character, emotion, and action, by rhythmical movement.

节奏即可,还有其他一些音乐,比如牧笛乐,与这些都是相似的。而舞蹈的模仿只用节奏,不需要音调,因为舞蹈是通过运动的节奏来模仿人的性格、情感和行动的?

There is another art which imitates by means of language alone, and that either in prose or verse—which verse, again, may either combine different meters or consist of but one kind—but this has hitherto been without a name. For there is no common term we could apply to the mimes of Sophron① and Xenarchus② and the Socratic dialogues on the one hand; and, on the other, to poetic imitations in iambic, elegiac, or any similar meter. People do, indeed, add the word "maker" or "poet" to the name of the meter, and speak of elegiac poets, or epic (that is, hexameter) poets, as if it were not the imitation that makes the poet, but the verse that entitles them all indiscriminately to the name. Even when a treatise on medicine or natural science is brought out in verse, the name of poet is by custom given to the author; and yet Homer and Empedocles③ have nothing in common but the meter, so that it would be right to call the one poet, the other physicist rather than poet. On the same principle, even if a writer in his poetic imitation were to combine all meters, as Chaeremon④ did in his *Centaur*, which is a medley composed of meters of all kinds, we should bring him too under the general term poet.

另有一种艺术只通过语言来模仿,所用的是散文或者诗歌(或混用的诗或单用一种风格),但这种艺术至今没有名称。一方面,我们没有一个共同的术语来称呼索弗荣和塞那耳科斯的哑剧及苏格拉底对话。另一方面,抑扬格、对句格或类似的格律也没有统一的称谓。人们的确会将"诗人"一词附在格律名称后面,称作者为句格诗人,或史诗(六音步)诗人,好像不是因为模仿才称其为诗人,而是因为他们都使用了相应的格律文。即使作者用格律文撰写医学专著或自然科学,人们也会习惯性地称之为诗人。然而,除了格律之外,荷马和恩培多克勒没有什么相似之处。因此,称前者为诗人是合适的,后者与其称他为诗人,不如称他为自然哲学家。同样,如果一个作者在诗中模仿时混合采用所有格律,就像开瑞蒙在他的叙事诗《马人》中混用了所有的诗格一样——我们仍应把他看作诗人。

So much then for these distinctions.

关于上述区别,就谈这些。

There are, again, some arts which employ all

还有一些艺术应用了上述提到

① 索弗荣(Sophron,约公元前 470 年—公元前 400 年),哑剧作家。
② 塞那耳科斯(Xenarchus,公元前 5 世纪末),索弗荣之子,哑剧作家。
③ 恩培多克勒(Empedocles,公元前 493 或 495 年—公元前 432 或 435 年),古希腊哲学家。
④ 开瑞蒙(Chaeremon)公元前 4 世纪雅典戏剧家。《马人》(*Centaur*)是开瑞蒙的作品。

the means above mentioned,—namely, rhythm, tune, and meter. Such are Dithyrambic and Nomic① poetry, and also Tragedy and Comedy; but between them originally the difference is, that in the first two cases these means are all employed in combination, in the latter, now one means is employed, now another.

Such, then, are the differences of the arts with respect to the medium of imitation.

II

Since the objects of imitation are men in action, and these men must be either of a higher or a lower type (for moral character mainly answers to these divisions, goodness and badness being the distinguishing marks of moral differences), it follows that we must represent men either as better than in real life, or as worse, or as they are. It is the same in painting. Polygnotus② depicted men as nobler than they are, Pauson as less noble, Dionysius drew them true to life.③

Now it is evident that each of the modes of imitation above mentioned will exhibit these differences, and become a distinct kind in imitating objects that are thus distinct. Such diversities may be found even in dancing, flute-playing, and lyre-playing. So again in language, whether prose or verse unaccompanied by music. Homer, for example, makes men better than they are;

的所有媒介,即节奏、音调和格律,比如酒神颂歌和诺摩斯诗歌以及悲剧和喜剧。它们之间的差别在于前两者同时使用这些媒介,而后两者则把它们用于不同的部分。

以上所述是关于艺术通过媒介进行模仿之间的区别。

第 2 章

既然模仿的对象是行动中的人,而这些人必然是高雅抑或粗俗之人中的一种(因为道德品性基本说明了这些区分,善与恶就是道德差异的标志),所以我们描绘的人要么比人物本身更好,要么更差,也可能是人物本身。正如画家作画一样:波利格诺托斯画里的人物比人物本身更加高贵,保森的人物却比人物本身低俗,而狄奥尼修斯描绘的人物更接近人物本身。

上文所提及的每种模仿方式显然也展现了这些区别,也会因为模仿对象的差别而有所不同。这些区别甚至可能在舞蹈、长笛乐和竖琴乐里出现,也可以出现在语言里,不管是散文或是无音乐伴奏的格律文里。比如,荷马将人物塑造得比人物本身

① nomic:诺摩斯的。名词是 nomos(复数 nomoi 希腊文/nomes 英文),意为"调子"、"曲调"。作为一种类型,诺摩斯有自己的音乐程式和格律形式(nomos 亦作"条律"和"标准"解)。诺摩斯的内容以对神的赞颂和祈求为主,日神阿波罗(Apollōn 希腊文/Apollo 英文)是出现率较高的主人公。

② 波利格诺托斯(Polygnotus),公元前 5 世纪画家。

③ 亚里士多德以三位画家作为例子说明作诗和作画都可以采用同样的艺术手法,即"美化"、"丑化"、"写实"。

Cleophon① as they are; Hegemon the Thasian②, the inventor of parodies, and Nicochares③, the author of the *Deiliad*, worse than they are. The same thing holds good of Dithyrambs and Nomes; here too one may portray different types, as Timotheus④ and Philoxenus⑤ differed in representing their Cyclopes⑥. The same distinction marks off Tragedy from Comedy; for Comedy aims at representing men as worse, Tragedy as better than in actual life.

更好,克里奥丰描述的人物则是人物本身,滑稽诗发明者萨索斯人赫革蒙和《得利亚特》的作者尼科卡瑞斯描绘的人物都比人物本身差。这些差别同样会出现在酒神颂歌和诺摩斯诗歌中。每个人都会描绘出不同类型的人物,正如提谟修斯和非罗森诺以不同方式描写他们的独目巨人一样。这些区别也将悲剧和喜剧区别开来:喜剧旨在将人物塑造得比其本身差,悲剧则将人物塑造得比其本身好。

III

There is still a third difference—the manner in which each of these objects may be imitated. For the medium being the same, and the objects the same, the poet may imitate by narration—in which case he can either take another personality as Homer does, or speak in his own person, unchanged—or he may present all his characters as living and moving before us.

These, then, as we said at the beginning, are the three differences which distinguish artistic imitation,—the medium, the objects, and the manner. So that from one point of view, Sophocles⑦ is an imitator of the same kind as Homer—for both imitate higher types of character; from another point of view, of the same kind as Aristophanes⑧—for both imitate persons acting and

第 *3* 章

这些艺术的第三点差别是模仿上述各种对象时采取了不同的方式。由于媒介一样,对象一样,诗人既可凭叙述——或进入角色,此乃荷马的做法,或以本人的口吻讲述,不改变身份——也可通过扮演,表现行动和活动中的每一个人物。

正如我们在开篇时所说的,艺术模仿的区别体现在三个方面——媒介、对象和方式。所以,从某个角度来讲,索福克勒斯是与荷马同类的模仿艺术家,因为他们都会模仿一些较高贵的人物角色;从另一个角度来看,又与阿里斯托芬相似,他们都会模仿行动中的人物。因此,有人说"戏剧"

① 克里奥丰(Cleophon),公元前4世纪古希腊悲剧诗人。
② Thasian:萨索斯岛(Thasos)的。
③ 尼科卡瑞斯(Nicochares),公元前3世纪古希腊戏剧家。《得利亚特》(*Deiliad*)是尼科卡瑞斯的作品。
④ 提谟修斯(Timotheus,公元前450年—公元前360年),古希腊音乐家、诗人。
⑤ 非罗森诺(Philoxenus,约公元前435年—公元前380年),古希腊酒神颂诗人。
⑥ Cyclopes:意思是"圆目",是希腊神话中的只有一个眼睛的怪物,一般称为独眼巨人,或圆目巨人。
⑦ 索福克勒斯(Sophocles,公元前496年—公元前406年),古希腊三大悲剧诗人之一。
⑧ 阿里斯托芬(Aristophanes,约公元前446年—公元前385年),古希腊喜剧诗人。

doing. Hence, some say, the name of "drama" is given to such poems, as representing action. For the same reason the Dorians① claim the invention both of Tragedy and Comedy. The claim to Comedy is put forward by the Megarians②,— not only by those of Greece proper, who allege that it originated under their democracy, but also by the Megarians of Sicily, for the poet Epicharmus③, who is much earlier than Chionides④ and Magnes⑤, belonged to that country. Tragedy too is claimed by certain Dorians of the Peloponnese⑥. In each case they appeal to the evidence of language. The outlying villages, they say, are by them called κωμαι, by the Athenians δημοι: and they assume that comedians were so named not from κωμαζειγ, "to revel," but because they wandered from village to village (κατα κωμα), being excluded contemptuously from the city. They add also that the Dorian word for "doing" is δραγ, and the Athenian, πραττειν.

This may suffice as to the number and nature of the various modes of imitation.

IV

Poetry in general seems to have sprung from two causes, each of them lying deep in our nature. First, the instinct of imitation is implanted in man from childhood, one difference between him and other animals being that he is the most imitative of living creatures, and through imitation learns his earliest lessons; and no less universal is the

是指那些展现人物行动的诗歌。同样的,多里安人声称他们发明了悲剧和喜剧。喜剧的起源说是由麦加拉学派提出来的,不仅仅是希腊人宣称喜剧来源于他们的民主时代,西西里的麦加拉人也认为喜剧是他们首创的,因为他们国家的诗人埃庇卡尔摩斯要比基奥尼得斯和马格内斯的年代早得多。伯罗奔尼撒的某些多里安人也声称他们首创悲剧,他们举了不同例子为证:他们称乡村为κωμαι,而雅典人称之为δημοι:他们认为喜剧演员的称谓不是来源于κωμαζειγ,而是因为这些人因受人鄙视而被逐出城外,在各个乡村之间游荡。他们还说多里安人称"做"为δραγ,而雅典人称之为πραττειν。

对于不同的模仿方式的数量及其特征就讲这么多。

第4章

总体来说,诗歌的产生有两个原因,都与人的天性息息相关。首先,从孩提时代起人便有了模仿的本能。人与其他动物的一个不同点就是,人最善于模仿活的生物,通过模仿获得最初的知识。其次,通过模仿产生愉悦感是具有普世性的。我们可以通

① Dorian:多利安人,古希腊主要部落之一。
② Megarians:麦加拉学派,古希腊小苏格拉底学派之一。
③ 埃庇卡尔摩斯(Epicharmus,公元前540年—公元前450年),西西里人,喜剧作家。
④ 基奥尼得斯(Chionides,公元前5世纪),古希腊喜剧诗人。
⑤ 马格内斯(Magnes,公元前5世纪),古希腊喜剧诗人。
⑥ Peloponnese:伯罗奔尼撒半岛,位于希腊南部,古称摩里亚半岛。

pleasure felt in things imitated. We have evidence of this in the facts of experience. Objects which in themselves we view with pain, we delight to contemplate when reproduced with minute fidelity: such as the forms of the most ignoble animals and of dead bodies. The cause of this again is, that to learn gives the liveliest pleasure, not only to philosophers but to men in general; whose capacity, however, of learning is more limited. Thus the reason why men enjoy seeing a likeness is, that in contemplating it they find themselves learning or inferring, and saying perhaps, "Ah, that is he." For if you happen not to have seen the original, the pleasure will be due not to the imitation as such, but to the execution, the coloring, or some such other cause.

过一些经验常识来证明。一些在生活中我们讨厌看到的实物,比如最令人鄙夷的某些动物形体和尸体,当它被极其逼真的艺术再现时,我们却会禁不住地感到兴奋。这是因为求知不仅于哲学家,而且对普通人来说都是一件非常快乐的事,尽管后者的学习能力稍差一些。因此,人们乐于看到相似物,是因为通过思考他们可以从中获得学习或对其进行推论,当看到某个人物时会说,"啊,这是他"。倘若你从未见过作品的原型,便不会从模仿的作品中得到快感,而是会从作品的技术处理、颜色或诸如此类的原因得到愉悦。

Imitation, then, is one instinct of our nature. Next, there is the instinct for "harmony" and rhythm, meters being manifestly sections of rhythm. Persons, therefore, starting with this natural gift developed by degrees their special aptitudes, till their rude improvisations gave birth to Poetry.

模仿是人的天性之一,其次还有我们天生的音调感和节奏感,格律文显然是节奏的部分。因此,在初期人们利用这种自然天赋逐步地发挥特殊才能,直到粗浅的即兴创作孕育了诗歌的诞生。

Poetry now diverged in two directions, according to the individual character of the writers. The graver spirits imitated noble actions, and the actions of good men. The more trivial sort imitated the actions of meaner persons, at first composing satires, as the former did hymns to the gods and the praises of famous men. A poem of the satirical kind cannot indeed be put down to any author earlier than Homer; though many such writers probably there were.

依作者性格的不同诗歌发展成两大类。较严肃者模仿高尚的以及好人的行动,而较平庸的人则模仿低劣小人的行径,其起始于创作谩骂式的讽刺诗,而前者却起始于创作颂神歌和赞美诗。我们找不到一首在荷马之前所作的此类讽刺诗,虽然在那之前可能存在过许多讽刺诗作者。

But from Homer onward, instances can be cited—his own *Margites*, for example, and other similar compositions. The appropriate meter was also here introduced; hence the measure is still called the iambic or lampooning measure, being

但从荷马及其以后的作者的作品里,我们却可以找出一些例子,例如荷马的《马耳吉忒斯》以及其他类似的作品。由此适合此类诗歌的格律便应运而生了,由于人们在互相嘲

that in which people lampooned one another. Thus the older poets were distinguished as writers of heroic or of lampooning verse.

讽时喜用这种格律，所以它至今仍被称作抑扬格或讽刺格。因此，早期的诗人被分为英雄诗诗人或是讽刺诗人。

As, in the serious style, Homer is pre-eminent among poets, for he alone combined dramatic form with excellence of imitation so he too first laid down the main lines of comedy, by dramatizing the ludicrous instead of writing personal satire. His *Margites* bears the same relation to comedy that the *Iliad* and *Odyssey* do to tragedy. But when Tragedy and Comedy came to light, the two classes of poets still followed their natural bent: the lampooners became writers of Comedy, and the Epic poets were succeeded by Tragedians, since the drama was a larger and higher form of art.

荷马不仅是严肃作品的最杰出的大师，唯有他将喜剧形式和卓越的模仿结合起来，而且他还是第一位为喜剧勾勒出轮廓的人，他将荒唐可笑的事戏剧化而不是进行谩骂式的讽刺。他的《马耳吉忒斯》同喜剧的关系，就如他的《伊利亚特》和《奥德赛》同悲剧的关系一样。当悲剧和喜剧出现以后，这两类诗人遵循着他们的天性：讽刺诗人成了喜剧作者，史诗诗人则演变成悲剧作者，因为戏剧是一种形式上更广泛和更高尚的艺术。

Whether Tragedy has as yet perfected its proper types or not; and whether it is to be judged in itself, or in relation also to the audience,—this raises another question. Be that as it may, Tragedy—as also Comedy—was at first mere improvisation. The one originated with the authors of the Dithyramb, the other with those of the phallic songs, which are still in use in many of our cities. Tragedy advanced by slow degrees; each new element that showed itself was in turn developed. Having passed through many changes, it found its natural form, and there it stopped.

悲剧是否已经完善了它的种类，它是否依据自身或是观众来判断——这又是另一论题。不管怎样，悲剧——喜剧亦然——是从即兴表演发展而来的。前者起源于酒神颂歌的作者，后者则来自生殖崇拜活动的颂歌中，此种活动至今仍在许多城市沿用。悲剧缓慢地发展起来，每一个展现出来的新成分都被加以改进。经过多次演变，它建立起自然的形式以后便停止了发展。

Aeschylus① first introduced a second actor; he diminished the importance of the Chorus, and assigned the leading part to the dialogue. Sophocles raised the number of actors to three, and added scene-painting. Moreover, it was not till late that the short plot was discarded for one of greater

埃斯库罗斯最早将演员扩至两名，并缩减了合唱的重要地位，从而使话语成为主导部分。索福克勒斯又将演员增至三名，并增加了画景的使用。此外，直到较迟的阶段人们才

① 埃斯库罗斯(Aeschylus，约公元前 525 年—公元前 456 年)，古希腊三大悲剧诗人之一。

compass, and the grotesque diction of the earlier satyric① form for the stately manner of Tragedy. The iambic measure then replaced the trochaic tetrameter②, which was originally employed when the poetry was of the satyric order, and had greater with dancing. Once dialogue had come in, Nature herself discovered the appropriate measure. For the iambic is, of all measures, the most colloquial we see it in the fact that conversational speech runs into iambic lines more frequently than into any other kind of verse; rarely into hexameters, and only when we drop the colloquial intonation. The additions to the number of "episodes" or acts, and the other accessories of which tradition tells, must be taken as already described; for to discuss them in detail would, doubtless, be a large undertaking.

摒弃短促的情节，扩大了悲剧的篇幅，早期萨图罗斯剧式的形式中怪诞的言语被演变为悲剧作为一种庄严的艺术。抑扬格的使用取代了扬抑格四音步，早期使用扬抑格四音步因为当时诗歌采用萨图罗斯剧的规则并与舞蹈有着较大的关系。话语的产生使自然本身发现了合适的格律。在所有格律中，抑扬格是我们所见的最口语化的格律。事实上，我们的交谈对话比其他任何诗歌更容易发展为抑扬格的格式。六音步几乎不被使用，只有当我们不使用口语化的语调时才偶尔用到。至于情节或场次的增加以及传统上其他部分的描述，就权当已经谈过了，因为再去详细地讨论这些，无疑是一件工程浩大的事情。

V

Comedy is, as we have said, an imitation of characters of a lower type,—not, however, in the full sense of the word bad, the ludicrous being merely a subdivision of the ugly. It consists in some defect or ugliness which is not painful or destructive. To take an obvious example, the comic mask is ugly and distorted, but does not imply pain.

The successive changes through which Tragedy passed, and the authors of these changes, are well-known, whereas Comedy has had no history, because it was not at first treated seriously. It was

第5章

如前所述，喜剧模仿较粗俗的人物，然而，这些人也不是完全意义上的穷凶极恶，其滑稽的成分仅仅是丑恶的一部分。滑稽的事物存在一些不完美或其貌不扬的地方，但不会让人觉得难受或痛苦。举一个尽人皆知的例子，滑稽的面具既丑陋又扭曲，但却不会给人造成痛苦。

我们都知道悲剧经过了连续性的改革，也经过了做出这些改革的知名者。然而喜剧却没有历史，因为在

① satyric：萨图罗斯剧（satyras）式的。萨图罗斯剧又称"羊人剧"，由演员装扮成山羊模样的酒神崇拜者来演出的剧目。

② trochaic tetrameter：扬抑格四音步，四步格。

late before the Archon① granted a comic chorus to a poet; the performers were till then voluntary. Comedy had already taken definite shape when comic poets, distinctively so called, are heard of. Who furnished it with masks, or prologues, or increased the number of actors—these and other similar details remain unknown. As for the plot, it came originally from Sicily; but of Athenian writers Crates② was the first who abandoning the "iambic" or lampooning form, generalized his themes and plots.

一开始它就没有被认真对待。执政官同意指派歌队给诗人已是相当迟的时候了,而在那之前歌队的表演者都是自愿参加的。当喜剧诗人成为有区别度的称呼,被人们听说时,喜剧已经形成了一定的模式。是谁引入了面具,或开场白,或增加了演员的数目,这些及其他类似的细节仍是未知的。至于情节,虽源于西西里,但雅典诗人克拉忒斯最先摒弃抑扬格或讽刺诗格,使主题和情节得以推广。

Epic poetry agrees with Tragedy in so far as it is an imitation in verse of characters of a higher type. They differ in that Epic poetry admits but one kind of meter and is narrative in form. They differ, again, in their length: for Tragedy endeavors, as far as possible, to confine itself to a single revolution of the sun, or but slightly to exceed this limit, whereas the Epic action has no limits of time. This, then, is a second point of difference; though at first the same freedom was admitted in Tragedy as in Epic poetry.

史诗与悲剧的相似之处在于它模仿较高尚的人物。不同之处在于史诗只有一种格律,采用的是叙述的形式。其次,它们的长度不一样,悲剧的作者尽可能地控制在"太阳的一周",或稍微地超过限制,而史诗是没有时间限制的。这是第二点不同之处,尽管在早期时同史诗一样,悲剧的创作在时间上也是自由的。

Of their constituent parts some are common to both, some peculiar to Tragedy: whoever, therefore knows what is good or bad Tragedy, knows also about Epic poetry. All the elements of an Epic poem are found in Tragedy, but the elements of a Tragedy are not all found in the Epic poem.

至于成分,有的为二者所共有,有的则为悲剧所独有。因此,能判断悲剧优劣之分的人也能辨别史诗的好坏。史诗中的所有成分都可以在悲剧中找到,而悲剧中的成分却不一定都能在史诗中找到。

VI

第 *6* 章

Of the poetry which imitates in hexameter verse, and of Comedy, we will speak hereafter. Let us now discuss Tragedy, resuming its formal definition, as resulting from what has been already

用六音步模仿的诗歌和喜剧我们以后再谈。现在我们来继续谈论悲剧,根据上文所述来给它的形式下个定义。

① Archon:古希腊统治者或者执政官。
② 克拉忒斯(Crates),古希腊喜剧诗人。

said. Tragedy, then, is an imitation of an action that is serious, complete, and of a certain magnitude; in language embellished with each kind of artistic ornament, the several kinds being found in separate parts of the play; in the form of action, not of narrative; through pity and fear effecting the proper purgation of these emotions.① By "language embellished", I mean language into which rhythm, "harmony" and song enter. By "the several kinds in separate parts", I mean, that some parts are rendered through the medium of verse alone, others again with the aid of song.

Now as tragic imitation implies persons acting, it necessarily follows in the first place, that Spectacular equipment will be a part of Tragedy. Next, Song and Diction, for these are the media of imitation. By "Diction" I mean the mere metrical arrangement of the words; as for "Song", it is a term whose sense everyone understands. Again, Tragedy is the imitation of an action; and an action implies personal agents, who necessarily possess certain distinctive qualities both of character and thought; for it is by these that we qualify actions themselves, and these—thought and character—are the two natural causes from which actions spring, and on actions again all success or failure depends. Hence, the Plot is the imitation of the action—for by Plot I here mean the arrangement of the incidents. By Character I mean that in virtue of which we ascribe certain qualities to the agents.

Thought is required wherever a statement is proved, or, it may be, a general truth enunciated. Every Tragedy, therefore, must have six parts, which parts determine its quality—namely, Plot,

悲剧是对严肃的、完整的、有一定长度的行动的模仿,通过被艺术美化的语言,以不同的形式分别用于戏剧不同部分。它的模仿方式是借助人的行动而不是叙述方式,通过引发怜悯和恐惧从而达到净化感情的目的。所谓"美化的语言",指包含节奏、音调和唱段的语言;所谓"以不同的形式分别用于不同的部分",指戏剧的某些部分仅采用格律文,而其他的一部分则会使用唱段。

既然悲剧的模仿包含人物行动,首先有必要说明的是,戏景的装备就是悲剧的一部分。其次,唱段和言语是模仿的媒介。所谓"言语",是指语言韵律的排列;至于唱段,这是一个人人皆能理解的观念吧。既然悲剧是对行动的模仿,这种模仿是通过行动中的人物进行的,这些人物身上必然携带着反映其性格和思想的不同特点。通过性格和思想我们才能估量行动本身,而且这两者是行动产生的两个自然因素,而人的成与败取决于自己的行动。因此,戏剧的情节是对行动的模仿 ——所谓"情节",指事件的安排。所谓"性格",是指通过性格我们将这些特点归结于某个人。

我们都知道任何论述都需要思想,这也是一个普遍存在的真理。因此,悲剧必须包括以下六个决定其性质的部分:情节、性格、言语、思想、

① 亚里士多德的净化说:亚里士多德认为观众可以通过欣赏悲剧产生怜悯或恐惧之情,进而净化感情。

Character, Diction, Thought, Spectacle, Song. Two of the parts constitute the medium of imitation, one the manner, and three the objects of imitation. And these complete the fist. These elements have been employed, we may say, by the poets to a man; in fact, every play contains Spectacular elements as well as Character, Plot, Diction, Song and Thought.

But most important of all is the structure of the incidents. For Tragedy is an imitation, not of men, but of an action and of life, and life consists in action, and its end is a mode of action, not a quality. Now character determines men's qualities, but it is by their actions that they are happy or the reverse. Dramatic action, therefore, is not with a view to the representation of character: character comes in as subsidiary to the actions. Hence the incidents and the plot are the end of a tragedy; and the end is the chief thing of all.

Again, without action there cannot be a tragedy; there may be without character. The tragedies of most of our modern poets fail in the rendering of character; and of poets in general this is often true. It is the same in painting; and here lies the difference between Zeuxis① and Polygnotus. Polygnotus delineates character well; the style of Zeuxis is devoid of ethical quality. Again, if you string together a set of speeches expressive of character, and well finished in point of diction and thought, you will not produce the essential tragic effect nearly so well as with a play which, however deficient in these respects, yet has a plot and artistically constructed incidents. Besides which, the most powerful elements of emotional

戏景和唱段。其中有两个部分构成模仿的媒介,一个指模仿的方式,另外三个是模仿的对象。这些部分形成了悲剧艺术的整体。我们可以这样说,一些诗人将这些成分应用到一个人物身上,每个戏剧都包括戏景、性格、情节、言语、唱段和思想。

所有部分中最重要的便是事件的结构。因为悲剧是对行动和生活的模仿,不是对人物的模仿。而生活包括了行动,它的目的是某种行动而不是品质。虽然性格决定人的品质,但他们的幸福与否却取决于自己的行动。因此,戏剧中的行动不是为了展现人物的性格才行动,而是有了行动之后才凸显出人物的性格。由此可见,事件和情节是悲剧的目的,而目的是一切事物中最重要的。

此外,没有行动就没有悲剧,没有性格悲剧却依然可以存在。大多数现代诗人的悲剧在于性格的渲染失败。一般来说,许多诗人的作品都有这样的问题。同样,在绘画中我们可以通过性格区分宙克西斯和波利格诺托斯的作品。波利格诺托斯将性格刻画得很好,而宙克西斯的作品缺乏道德品质。再则,如果你只将一系列能表现性格、言语和思想处理完善的话语连接起来,是不会产生如悲剧一样的功效。然而,悲剧即使在这些方面有所缺陷,但只要有情节和艺术性构造的事件就可以达到成效。

① 宙克西斯(Zeuxis,公元前5世纪),古希腊画家。

interest in Tragedy—Peripeteia① or Reversal of the Situation, and Recognition scenes—are parts of the plot. A further proof is, that novices in the art attain to finish of diction and precision of portraiture before they can construct the plot. It is the same with almost all the early poets.

除此之外,悲剧在情感上最有力的成分是突转和发现,属于情节的部分。还有一点可资证明的是,刚接触艺术的人在他们学会构造情节之前会完善言语的使用和描绘的精准度。大多数早期诗人也是如此。

The Plot, then, is the first principle, and, as it were, the soul of a tragedy. Character holds the second place. A similar fact is seen in painting. The most beautiful colors, laid on confusedly, will not give as much pleasure as the chalk outline of a portrait. Thus Tragedy is the imitation of an action, and of the agents mainly with a view to the action.

因此,情节是悲剧的第一原则,也就是说,是悲剧的灵魂;其次是性格。同样的原则见之于绘画:一幅黑白素描画比各种被混在一起的最美的颜色更能给人带来愉悦感。因此,悲剧是对行动的模仿,而模仿行动中的人物主要是为了模仿行动。

Third in order is Thought,—that is, the faculty of saying what is possible and pertinent in given circumstances. In the case of oratory, this is the function of the political art and of the art of rhetoric: and so indeed the older poets make their characters speak the language of civic life; the poets of our time, the language of the rhetoricians. Character is that which reveals moral purpose, showing what kind of things a man chooses or avoids. Speeches, therefore, which do not make this manifest, or in which the speaker does not choose or avoid anything whatever, are not expressive of character. Thought, on the other hand, is found where something is proved to be or not to be, or a general maxim is enunciated.

排在第三位的是思想,是指在特定的情况下能阐述可能和相关事物的能力。在演说中,这是政治和修辞艺术的功能:过去的诗人让他们的人物讲公民生活化的语言,而到我们这个年代则要像修辞学家那样子地去讲话。性格可以揭露道德目的,展现人类对事物的取舍。因此,没有明显表现出取舍的话语,或这段话中说话者没有进行任何抉择,就不能表现性格。此外,思想体现在论证事物真伪或解释普遍道理的言论中。

Fourth among the elements enumerated comes Diction; by which I mean, as has been already said, the expression of the meaning in words; and its essence is the same both in verse and prose.

上述所列举的成分中,第四位是言语。所谓"言语",正如我说过的,就是话语意思的表达,它的本质在诗和散文中都一样。

Of the remaining elements Song holds the chief place among the embellishments.

剩下的部分中唱段占据主要"装饰"的地位。

① peripeteia:情节的突然转变。reversal:反转;突转和发现(或认出、意识到)。

The Spectacle has, indeed, an emotional attraction of its own, but, of all the parts, it is the least artistic, and connected least with the art of poetry. For the power of Tragedy, we may be sure, is felt even apart from representation and actors. Besides, the production of spectacular effects depends more on the art of the stage machinist than on that of the poet.

戏景就其自身而言是情感的吸引力,但在整体当中是最不艺术化的一部分,与诗艺的关联最少。因为我们确信,即使没有布景和演员也能感受到悲剧的力量。此外,戏景效果的产生更依赖舞台机械人员的艺术而不是诗人的艺术。

VII

第 7 章

These principles being established, let us now discuss the proper structure of the Plot, since this is the first and most important thing in Tragedy.

建立好这些原则之后,我们来谈论合适的情节建构,因为这是悲剧的第一原则,也是最重要的部分。

Now, according to our definition Tragedy is an imitation of an action that is complete, and whole, and of a certain magnitude; for there may be a whole that is wanting in magnitude. A whole is that which has a beginning, a middle, and an end. A beginning is that which does not itself follow anything by causal necessity, but after which something naturally is or comes to be. An end, on the contrary, is that which itself naturally follows some other thing, either by necessity, or as a rule, but has nothing following it. A middle is that which follows something as some other thing follows it. A well constructed plot, therefore, must neither begin nor end at haphazard, but conform to these principles.

根据我们的定义,悲剧是对完整的、有一定长度的行动的模仿,因为有些行动可能是完整的但长度却不够。完整的定义是要有起始、中段和结尾。起始指事物本身不刻意地跟随他者,但接受自然存在或后来者的部分。与之相反,结尾指出于必要性或作为一个规定,其本身自然地跟随着其他某个事物,但不再有可跟随的事物。中段指随着其他事物对它的跟从而自然地跟从某些其他的事物。因此,一个建构良好的情节,一定不可以随意地开始或者结束,而要符合这些原则。

Again, a beautiful object, whether it be a living organism or any whole composed of parts, must not only have an orderly arrangement of parts, but must also be of a certain magnitude; for beauty depends on magnitude and order. Hence a very small animal organism cannot be beautiful; for the view of it is confused, the object being seen in an almost imperceptible moment of time. Nor, again, can one of vast size be beautiful; for as the eye

此外,无论是一个有生命的有机体还是由部分组成的整体,一个漂亮的对象不仅要对其部分要有井然有序的安排,还要有一定的长度,因为美依赖长度和顺序。因此,一个非常小的动物机体不可能是美的,因为在几乎难以察觉的时间里它给人的视觉感受是模糊混乱的。同样的,体积太大也不美,因为人眼不能一眼看到

cannot take it all in at once, the unity and sense of the whole is lost for the spectator; as for instance if there were one a thousand miles long. As, therefore, in the case of animate bodies and organisms a certain magnitude is necessary, and a magnitude which may be easily embraced in one view; so in the plot, a certain length is necessary, and a length which can be easily embraced by the memory.

整个事物,观看者便失去了对事物的整体感——好像观看一千公里那么长远的动物似的。因此,生命体和有机体必须要有一定的长度,这种长度是指可以很容易地一览而尽。所以在情节中也需要一定的让人快速地可以记得住的长度。

The limit of length in relation to dramatic competition and sensuous presentment is no part of artistic theory. For had it been the rule for a hundred tragedies to compete together, the performance would have been regulated by the water-clock①,—as indeed we are told was formerly done. But the limit as fixed by the nature of the drama itself is this:—the greater the length, the more beautiful will the piece be by reason of its size, provided that the whole be perspicuous. And to define the matter roughly, we may say that the proper magnitude is comprised within such limits, that the sequence of events, according to the law of probability or necessity, will admit of a change from bad fortune to good, or from good fortune to bad.

戏剧完整性和美感的呈现在长度的限制上不属于艺术理论的部分。因为它已成为大多数悲剧互相竞争的规则,它们的表现也随着时间而调整,就像人们传说的那样。但是,从戏剧本身的性质调整其限制来看,如果作品整体描述清晰,其篇幅越长,作品越美。简单来说,合适的长度应该遵守这些限制,根据可能性或必然性的定律,事件发生的顺序将会包括由逆境到顺境或顺境到逆境的变化。

XI

第 *11* 章

Reversal of the Situation is a change by which the action veers round to its opposite, subject always to our rule of probability or necessity. Thus in the *Oedipus*②, the messenger comes to cheer Oedipus and free him from his alarms about his mother, but by revealing who he is, he produces

突转是指行动的发展转向其反方向的变化,这种转变通常符合可能性或必然性的原则。例如在《俄狄浦斯》一剧里,信使到来本想让俄狄浦斯高兴并将他从娶母为妻的预言中

① water-lock:以流水计时的装置。

② 《俄狄浦斯》(*Oedipus*),古希腊悲剧,主人公俄狄浦斯(Oedipus)在不知情的情况下杀死了自己的父亲,并娶了自己的母亲。

the opposite effect. Again in the *Lynceus*,① Lynceus is being led away to his death, and Danaus goes with him, meaning to slay him; but the outcome of the preceding incidents is that Danaus is killed and Lynceus saved.

Recognition, as the name indicates, is a change from ignorance to knowledge, producing love or hate between the persons destined by the poet for good or bad fortune. The best form of recognition is coincident with a Reversal of the Situation, as in the *Oedipus*. There are indeed other forms. Even inanimate things of the most trivial kind may in a sense be objects of recognition. Again, we may recognize or discover whether a person has done a thing or not. But the recognition which is most intimately connected with the plot and action is, as we have said, the recognition of persons. This recognition, combined with Reversal, will produce either pity or fear; and actions producing these effects are those which, by our definition, Tragedy represents. Moreover, it is upon such situations that the issues of good or bad fortune will depend.

Recognition, then, being between persons, it may happen that one person only is recognized by the other—when the latter is already known—or it may be necessary that the recognition should be on both sides. Thus Iphigenia is revealed to Orestes by the sending of the letter; but another act of recognition is required to make Orestes known to Iphigenia.②

解放出来,但是随着身世的揭露,却造成了相反的结果。又如在《伦丘斯》里,伦丘斯被带去处死,达那俄斯跟去行刑,但以此为铺垫的结果是达那俄斯被杀了,伦丘斯反而得救。

发现,顾名思义,是指从不知到知的变化,由诗人指定的在顺境或逆境中人物之间产生的爱与恨。发现的最好形式是与突转同时发生,如《俄狄浦斯》中的发现一样。当然,还有一些其他的形式。从某种意义上来说,即使是最普通的无生命的事物也是发现的对象。此外,我们可以发现一个人是否做过某事。但是,我们说过,与情节和行动密切相关的发现是对人物的发现。这种发现与突转联系在一起就能引发人的怜悯或恐惧,而根据我们的定义,能产生这些效果的是悲剧所展现出来的行动。此外,人物的顺境或逆境也是依赖此类事件的。

那么,置于两者中的发现,一种情况下仅有一方的身份被另一方发现(另一方的身份是已知的),还有一种可能是双方互相发现。例如,俄瑞斯忒斯通过伊菲革涅娅托人送信而认出了她,而伊菲革涅娅却需要再次的发现才能认出俄瑞斯忒斯。

---

① 《伦丘斯》(*Lynceus*),古希腊悲剧。伦丘斯是埃及国王埃古普托斯(Aegyptus)之子。埃古普托斯强迫达那俄斯(Danaus)的 50 个女儿嫁给自己的 50 个儿子。达那俄斯命令女儿们在新婚之夜杀死自己的丈夫,但是其中一个女儿许珀耳涅斯特拉(Hypermnestra)没有听从父亲的命令对丈夫伦丘斯下手。伦丘斯后来杀死达那俄斯夺取了王位。

② 伊菲革涅娅(Iphigenia)是阿伽门农(Agamemnon)的长女。特洛伊战争前夕,阿伽门农杀死了本该献给阿耳忒弥斯(Artemis)的牡鹿而得罪了这位女神,为了摆脱阿耳忒弥斯所制造的无风天气,不得已决定献祭其亲生女儿伊菲革涅亚。祭献时,伊菲革涅亚被风带走,是阿耳忒弥斯救了她并让她在陶里斯(Tauris)担任祭司。

Two parts, then, of the Plot—Reversal of the Situation and Recognition—turn upon surprises. A third part is the Scene of Suffering. The Scene of Suffering is a destructive or painful action, such as death on the stage, bodily agony, wounds, and the like.

突转和发现是情节的两部分，取决于意外的发现。第三个成分是苦难。苦难是指毁坏性或痛苦的行动，例如舞台上的死亡，身体的痛苦、伤痛以及类似的情况。

XII

The parts of Tragedy which must be treated as elements of the whole have been already mentioned. We now come to the quantitative parts—the separate parts into which Tragedy is divided—namely, Prologue, Episode, Exode, Choric song; this last being divided into Parode and Stasimon①. These are common to all plays: peculiar to some are the songs of actors from the stage and the Commos.②

The Prologue is that entire part of a tragedy which precedes the Parode of the Chorus. The Episode is that entire part of a tragedy which is between complete choric songs. The Exode is that entire part of a tragedy which has no choric song after it. Of the Choric part the Parode is the first undivided utterance of the Chorus: the Stasimon is a Choric ode without anapaests or trochaic tetrameters; the Commos is a joint lamentation of Chorus and actors. The parts of Tragedy which must be treated as elements of the whole have been already mentioned. The quantitative parts—the separate parts into which it is divided—are here enumerated.

第 *12* 章

悲剧被看作整体的一部分在上文已做过说明。现在我们进入量的部分，即悲剧被分成单独的部分：开场白、场、退场、合唱歌曲，合唱最终被分为帕罗道斯和斯塔西蒙。这两者在所有戏剧中都是共有的，少数特殊的如演员在戏台上唱的段子以及孔摩斯只有在某些剧里才有。

开场白指在悲剧中先于合唱中的帕罗道斯的整个部分，场是指在悲剧中处于两次完整的合唱之间的整个部分，退场是指在悲剧中所有合唱之后的整个部分。在合唱部分，帕罗道斯是歌队第一次完整的表述；斯塔西蒙是没有短抑扬格或长短格诗行的合唱颂歌；孔摩斯是歌队和演员轮唱的挽歌。悲剧被看作整体的一部分在上文已做过说明。现在我们从量的部分列举了悲剧的部分，即悲剧被分成单独的部分。

XIII

As the sequel to what has already been said, we must proceed to consider what the poet should aim at, and what he should avoid, in constructing

第 *13* 章

综上所述，我们接着讨论在建构情节时诗人的意图，应避免什么，以及通过哪种方式才能产生悲剧特殊

① Stasimon：通常指戏剧表演中，当合唱队登上舞台，保持站立后再演唱的歌曲。

② Commos：孔摩斯，通常指挽歌。

his plots; and by what means the specific effect of Tragedy will be produced.

的效果。

A perfect tragedy should, as we have seen, be arranged not on the simple but on the complex plan. It should, moreover, imitate actions which excite pity and fear, this being the distinctive mark of tragic imitation. It follows plainly, in the first place, that the change of fortune presented must not be the spectacle of a virtuous man brought from prosperity to adversity: for this moves neither pity nor fear; it merely shocks us. Nor, again, that of a bad man passing from adversity to prosperity: for nothing can be more alien to the spirit of Tragedy; it possesses no single tragic quality; it neither satisfies the moral sense nor calls forth pity or fear. Nor, again, should the downfall of the utter villain be exhibited. A plot of this kind would, doubtless, satisfy the moral sense, but it would inspire neither pity nor fear; for pity is aroused by unmerited misfortune, fear by the misfortune of a man like ourselves.

如我们所见,一个完美的悲剧安排应该是复杂的而不是简单的。此外,它应该模仿引发怜悯和恐惧的行动,这是悲剧模仿的特点。那么很明显,首先,悲剧不应出现道德高尚的人由顺境转入逆境的场景,因为这既不能引发怜悯,亦不能引发恐惧,倒是会使人反感。其次,也不可以出现一个低劣的人由逆境转为顺境的场景,因为这与悲剧精神背道而驰,它不可能拥有独立的悲剧品质,它满足不了人们的道德感,也不可能引发怜悯或恐惧。再者,不应展现极恶之人转为落魄的场景。这种安排无疑满足了道德感,但却不会引发怜悯或恐惧,因为怜悯是由不该遭受的不幸引起的,恐惧的产生是因为遭受不幸的人是和我们一样的人。

Such an event, therefore, will be neither pitiful nor terrible. There remains, then, the character between these two extremes,—that of a man who is not eminently good and just, yet whose misfortune is brought about not by vice or depravity, but by some error or frailty. He must be one who is highly renowned and prosperous,—a personage like Oedipus, Thyestes①, or other illustrious men of such families.

因此,这类事件既不令人怜悯也不令人恐惧。还有介于这两种极端之间的人物,这类人不是十分的完美和公正,然而他们的不幸不是由恶行或邪恶所导致,而是因为犯了某些错误或本身具有的弱点。这类人名声显赫且家族兴旺,如俄狄浦斯、堤厄斯忒斯和其他类似有如此家族背景的人。

A well constructed plot should, therefore, be single in its issue, rather than double as some maintain. The change of fortune should be not from bad to good, but, reversely, from good to bad. It should come about as the result not of vice, but of some great error or frailty, in a character either such as we have described, or better rather than

因此,一个构思精良的情节应该是单线的,而不是某些人主张的双线。悲剧所反映的人物命运的变化不应从逆境到顺境,相反,应该是由顺境到逆境。人之所以会遭受逆境不是因为其本身邪恶,而是因为他犯了某种严重的错误,人物的性格应该

① 堤厄斯忒斯(Thyestes),古希腊神话中悲剧人物,曾误食自己子女的血肉。

worse. The practice of the stage bears out our view. At first the poets recounted any legend that came in their way. Now, the best tragedies are founded on the story of a few houses,—on the fortunes of Alcmaeon①, Oedipus, Orestes, Meleager②, Thyestes, Telephus③, and those others who have done or suffered something terrible.

如我们上文所述的那样,或较之好一点或差一点。实践证明我们的想法是正确的。起初,诗人们记录了碰到的任何传说故事,而现在最好的悲剧取材于少数几个家族的故事,如阿尔克迈翁、俄狄浦斯、俄瑞斯忒斯、墨勒阿革耳、堤厄斯忒斯、忒勒福斯的家族命运,还有其他做过或遭受过可怕之事的人。

A tragedy, then, to be perfect according to the rules of art should be of this construction. Hence they are in error who censure Euripides④ just because he follows this principle in his plays, many of which end unhappily.

根据这些艺术规则我们得出:一个追求完美的悲剧应该是这样的结构。因此,那些仅仅因为欧里庇得斯在他的戏剧里按照这一原则编写,且很多的戏剧以不幸结尾而批评他的人是错误的。

It is, as we have said, the right ending. The best proof is that on the stage and in dramatic competition, such plays, if well worked out, are the most tragic in effect; and Euripides, faulty though he may be in the general management of his subject, yet is felt to be the most tragic of the poets.

我们在前文说过,这恰恰是合适的结尾。最好的证明是在戏场和戏剧比赛中,如果这类戏剧经过精心编写,一定会产生最好的悲剧效果。因此,即使欧里庇得斯在整体的编排上不太完美,他仍被我们作为最好的悲剧诗人。

In the second rank comes the kind of tragedy which some place first. Like the *Odyssey*, it has a double thread of plot, and also an opposite catastrophe for the good and for the bad. It is accounted the best because of the weakness of the spectators; for the poet is guided in what he writes by the wishes of his audience. The pleasure, however, thence derived is not the true tragic pleasure. It is proper rather to Comedy, where those who, in the piece, are the deadliest

第二等的结构——一些人将它排在第一等——比如《奥德赛》,它的情节有两条线索,结局是好人和坏人分别受到了赏惩。由于观众自身软弱才会把这类结构当成是最好的,而诗人写作时会投观众之喜好。然而,如此得到的愉悦感不是真正的悲剧快感,却更像是喜剧式的。喜剧中的

① 阿尔克迈翁(Alcmaeon),古希腊神话中的悲剧人物,希腊传说中先知安菲阿剌俄斯(Amphiaraus)的儿子,曾带领兄弟摧毁了底比斯后杀死了自己的母亲厄里芙勒(Eriphyle),最后死于菲盖厄(Phegeus)之手。

② 墨勒阿革耳(Meleager),希腊神话中的英雄,狩猎卡吕冬野猪(Calydonian Boar)的发起者。

③ 忒勒福斯(Telephus),希腊神话中的人物,赫拉克勒斯(Heracles)之子。

④ 欧里庇得斯(Euripides,公元前480年—公元前406年),古希腊三大悲剧诗人之一。

enemies—like Orestes① and Aegisthus②—quit the stage as friends at the close, and no one slays or is slain.

人物是势不两立的仇敌,如俄瑞斯忒斯和埃吉索斯,到剧终时成了朋友,一起退场,谁也没有杀害谁。

XIV

Fear and pity may be aroused by spectacular means; but they may also result from the inner structure of the piece, which is the better way, and indicates a superior poet. For the plot ought to be so constructed that, even without the aid of the eye, he who hears the tale told will thrill with horror and melt to pity at what takes place. This is the impression we should receive from hearing the story of the Oedipus. But to produce this effect by the mere spectacle is a less artistic method, and dependent on extraneous aids.

Those who employ spectacular means to create a sense not of the terrible but only of the monstrous, are strangers to the purpose of Tragedy; for we must not demand of Tragedy any and every kind of pleasure, but only that which is proper to it. And since the pleasure which the poet should afford is that which comes from pity and fear through imitation, it is evident that this quality must be impressed upon the incidents.

Let us then determine what are the circumstances which strike us as terrible or pitiful.

Actions capable of this effect must happen between persons who are either friends or enemies or indifferent to one another. If an enemy kills an enemy, there is nothing to excite pity either in the act or the intention,—except so far as the suffering in itself is pitiful. So again with indifferent persons. But when the tragic incident occurs between those who are near or dear to one another—if, for

第 *14* 章

恐惧和怜悯可能由戏景引起,也可出自作品的内部构造,后者是更好的方式,这样做才称得上是有造诣的诗人。因为只有这样去设计结构,才能在不看演出的情况下,仅仅听故事的叙述,仍会因恐惧而激动,产生怜悯之情。这便是我们在听他人叙述俄狄浦斯的故事时应该产生的感受。但是仅仅通过戏景产生的效果是不太艺术化的方式,且需要一些外部的帮助。

利用戏景方式只能制造出一些丑陋怪诞而不是可怕的事物,这些诗人只能是悲剧的门外汉。我们不应要求悲剧应该具有任何一种愉悦感,它拥有的应该是由它引发的适合它的愉悦感。既然诗人通过模仿产生怜悯和恐惧继而使人从中得到愉悦感,那么很明显,诗人应该让人们从事件中牢记此品质。

下面我们讨论什么样的情况会使人恐惧和怜悯。

产生此种效果的行动通常发生在亲友之间、仇敌之间或非亲非仇者之间。若是仇敌之间相互残杀,除非人物受尽折磨苦难,不然无论是什么行动或意图,都不会引起怜悯。非亲非仇者之间也是如此。但当悲剧事件发生在彼此亲近的人之间,例如,

① 俄瑞斯忒斯(Orestes),希腊神话中的人物,古希腊远征特洛伊的统帅阿伽门农的儿子。

② 埃吉索斯(Aegisthus),希腊神话中克吕泰涅斯特拉(Clytemnestra)的情人。他同克吕泰涅斯特拉一起谋杀了她的丈夫阿伽门农。8 年后,阿伽门农的儿子俄瑞斯忒斯替父报仇,杀死了埃吉索斯。

example, a brother kills, or intends to kill, a brother, a son his father, a mother her son, a son his mother, or any other deed of the kind is done—these are the situations to be looked for by the poet. He may not indeed destroy the framework of the received legends—the fact, for instance, that Clytemnestra was slain by Orestes and Eriphyle① by Alcmaeon—but he ought to show invention of his own, and skillfully handle the traditional material. Let us explain more clearly what is meant by skillful handling.

The action may be done consciously and with knowledge of the persons, in the manner of the older poets. It is thus too that Euripides makes Medea② slay her children. Or, again, the deed of horror may be done, but done in ignorance, and the tie of kinship or friendship be discovered afterwards. The Oedipus of Sophocles is an example. Here, indeed, the incident is outside the drama proper; but cases occur where it falls within the action of the play: one may cite the Alcmaeon of Astydamas③, or Telegonous④ in the *Wounded Odysseus*. Again, there is a third case—to be about to act with knowledge of the persons and then not to act. The fourth case is when someone is about to do an irreparable deed through ignorance, and makes the discovery before it is done. These are the only possible ways. For the deed must either be done or not done,—and that wittingly or unwittingly.

兄弟杀死或意图杀掉自己的兄弟，同样的，儿子对父亲、母亲对儿子、儿子对母亲以及其他诸如此类的行为，这些都是诗人应该寻找的事例。诗人不可以完全毁坏故事原本的框架——比如，俄瑞斯忒斯杀死克吕泰涅斯特拉或阿尔克迈翁杀死厄里芙勒这样的事实——但应该有自己的创新，巧妙的处理此类传统素材。下面我们进一步解释什么是“巧妙的处理”。

像早期诗人那样，行动可以是人物在意识地了解情况下去完成——正如欧里庇得斯笔下的美狄亚杀掉自己孩子那样。此外，人物会做出可怕的行为，但是在无知情况下，才发现互相间有亲属或朋友关系——索福克勒斯笔下的俄狄浦斯便是这样的例子。诚然，此事不在悲剧之内，但悲剧也会发生类似事件：如阿斯图达马斯笔下的阿尔克迈翁或《俄底修斯负伤》一剧里忒勒戈诺斯的行为。此外，第三种情况是人物已知与对方的关系后准备开始行动，但又没有行动。第四种情况是在无知的情况下将要做一些无可挽回的行动，但在动手之前发现彼此的关系而停止。这些就是可能的方式。因为行动必然是完成或未完成，人物也必然是了解情况或不了解情况。

---

① 厄里芙勒（Eriphyle），古希腊神话中的英雄安菲阿剌俄斯（Amphiaraus）的妻子，阿尔克迈翁（Alcmaeon）的母亲。

② 美狄亚（Medea），古希腊神话中科奇斯岛（Colchis）会施法术的公主，爱上了来到岛上寻找金羊毛的伊阿宋（Jason），帮他取得金羊毛，并夺取了王位。后来伊阿宋移情别恋，美狄亚毒死了自己的两个幼子和伊阿宋的新欢逃离 。

③ 阿斯图达马斯（Astudamas），公元前4世纪悲剧作家。他的《阿尔克迈翁》将传说中的蓄意杀母改为出于无知（不知情）。

④ 忒勒戈诺斯（Telegonous），俄底修斯（Odysseus）和基耳凯（Circe）之子。受母命外出寻父，却最终误杀其父。《俄底修斯负伤》乃索福克勒斯所作，现已失传。

But of all these ways, to be about to act knowing the persons, and then not to act, is the worst. It is shocking without being tragic, for no disaster follows. It is, therefore, never, or very rarely, found in poetry. One instance, however, is in the *Antigone*①, where Haemon threatens to kill Creon. The next and better way is that the deed should be perpetrated. Still better, that it should be perpetrated in ignorance, and the discovery made afterwards. There is then nothing to shock us, while the discovery produces a startling effect. The last case is the best, as when in the *Cresphontes* Merope is about to slay her son, but, recognizing who he is, spares his life. So in the *Iphigenia*, the sister recognizes the brother just in time. Again in the *Helle*, the son recognizes the mother when on the point of giving her up. This, then, is why a few families only, as has been already observed, furnish the subjects of tragedy. It was not art, but happy chance, that led the poets in search of subjects to impress the tragic quality upon their plots. They are compelled, therefore, to have recourse to those houses whose history contains moving incidents like these.

但在所有方式中,人物在知情的情况下准备行动,没有行动是最糟糕的。其结局让人吃惊,但无悲剧效果,因为没有不幸发生。因此,几乎没有或是很少有诗歌用这样的方式。不过《安提戈涅》中有个例子是海蒙威胁要杀掉克瑞恩。较之稍好点的方式是最终付出了行动。更好的方式是,行动要在不知情的情况下完成,事后才发现互相之间的关系。如此处理不会使人反感,而人物身份的发现还会产生令人吃惊的效果。最后一种情况是最好的,比如在《克瑞斯丰忒斯》里,梅罗珮打算处死儿子,但在杀他之前认出并赦免了他;同样的,在《伊菲革涅娅》里,姐姐及时地认出了弟弟;在《赫蕾》里,儿子在交出母亲的前一刻认出了她。这就是为什么只有少数的家族会被留意到,成为悲剧的素材。这不是艺术而是令人愉快的机遇带领诗人在情节中搜索产生悲剧效果的题材。因此,他们不得不去追索那些经历过此类惊人事件的家族。

Enough has now been said concerning the structure of the incidents, and the right kind of plot.

关于事件结构以及合适的情节类型,以上所述足矣。

XV

In respect of Character there are four things to be aimed at. First, and most important, it must be good. Now any speech or action that manifests

第15章

关于性格的刻画,诗人应该做到以下四点。第一,也是最重要的一

① 《安提戈涅》(*Antigone*),希腊悲剧作家索福克勒斯创作的悲剧。安提戈涅是俄狄浦斯的女儿,她不顾国王克瑞翁(Creon)的禁令,将自己的兄长——反叛城邦的波吕尼刻斯(Polynices)安葬,后被关在一座石洞里,自杀而死,而一意孤行的国王也遭遇妻离子散的命运。海蒙(Haemon)是克瑞恩之子,安提戈涅的未婚夫。安提戈涅被塑造成维护神权/自然法,而不向世俗权势低头的伟大女英雄形象,激发了后世的许多思想家如黑格尔、克尔凯郭尔、德里达等的哲思。

moral purpose of any kind will be expressive of character: the character will be good if the purpose is good. This rule is relative to each class. Even a woman may be good, and also a slave; though the woman may be said to be an inferior being, and the slave quite worthless. The second thing to aim at is propriety. There is a type of manly valor; but valor in a woman, or unscrupulous cleverness is inappropriate. Thirdly, character must be true to life: for this is a distinct thing from goodness and propriety, as here described. The fourth point is consistency: for though the subject of the imitation, who suggested the type, be inconsistent, still he must be consistently inconsistent. As an example of motiveless degradation of character, we have Menelaus① in the *Orestes*; of character indecorous and inappropriate, the lament of Odysseus in the *Scylla*, and the speech of Melanippe; of inconsistency, the *Iphigenia at Aulis*②,—for Iphigenia the suppliant in no way resembles her later self.

点,性格应该好。任何显现道德意图的言语或行动都可以表现出人物的性格:若意图是好的,那么性格也是好的。各阶层皆如此。好人可能是一个妇人也可能是个奴隶,尽管这个妇人可能较为低劣,而奴隶则更是卑微。第二,性格应该适宜。人物性格有硬汉类型的,但将勇猛或不择手段的机敏用在女性身上是不合适的。第三,性格应该贴近生活,这与上文提及的好性格与合适的性格有所不同。第四,性格应该一致。尽管被模仿的人物本身性格不一致,而诗人又想表现这种性格,他仍应做到寓一致于不一致之中。人物性格无意义的堕落,以《俄瑞斯忒斯》中墨奈劳斯为例;欠妥的和不合适的性格,以《斯库拉》中俄底修斯的恸哭以及梅拉尼珮的言语表现的性格为例;不一致的性格,以《伊菲革涅娅在奥里斯》中伊菲革涅娅的性格为例:求生的伊菲革涅娅与后来的她完全不一致。

As in the structure of the plot, so too in the portraiture of character, the poet should always aim either at the necessary or the probable. Thus a person of a given character should speak or act in a given way, by the rule either of necessity or of probability; just as this event should follow that by necessary or probable sequence. It is therefore evident that the unraveling of the plot, no less than the complication, must arise out of the plot itself, it must not be brought about by the *Deus ex Machina*③—as in the *Medea*, or in the return of the Greeks in the *Iliad*.

同情节的结构一样,人物性格的刻画也是如此,诗人应始终追寻必然或可能的原则。因此,一个给定的人物应该以给定的方式说话和行动,即通过必然或可能的原则,只有这样才能使事件的承继符合必然或可能的原则。因此,情节的解(包括其混乱纠纷的解)显然是产生于情节本身,而不应产生于"机械降神"——如在《美狄亚》和《伊利亚特》中希腊人准备返航那一节中。

---

① 墨奈劳斯(Menelaus),俄瑞斯忒斯的叔叔,没有帮助危难中的侄儿俄瑞斯忒斯,有失英雄和长辈的风度。

② 《伊菲革涅娅在奥里斯》(*Iphigenia at Aulis*)是欧里庇得斯的作品。当伊菲革涅娅得知其父阿伽门农要祭献她时,她惊恐中表现出求生的愿望。其后,为了希腊的利益,她又毅然表示愿意牺牲自己。

③ Deus ex Machina:机械降神,指通过舞台机械装置,降下一位神。神的突然出现起着调解冲突的作用。

The Deus ex Machina should be employed only for events external to the drama,—for antecedent or subsequent events, which lie beyond the range of human knowledge, and which require to be reported or foretold; for to the gods we ascribe the power of seeing all things. Within the action there must be nothing irrational. If the irrational cannot be excluded, it should be outside the scope of the tragedy. Such is the irrational element the *Oedipus* of Sophocles.

Again, since Tragedy is an imitation of persons who are above the common level, the example of good portrait painters should be followed. They, while reproducing the distinctive form of the original, make a likeness which is true to life and yet more beautiful. So too the poet, in representing men who are irascible or indolent, or have other defects of character, should preserve the type and yet ennoble it. In this way Achilles① is portrayed by Agathon② and Homer.

These then are rules the poet should observe. Nor should he neglect those appeals to the senses, which, though not among the essentials, are the concomitants of poetry; for here too there is much room for error. But of this enough has been said in our published treatises.

"机械降神"应该只应用在剧外的事——或是先前的超出凡人认知范围的事抑或是以后的须经告示或预言的事,因为我们认为神有洞察一切的能力。在行动中不应有不合理的内容。若不合理的内容难以排除,应将它放在悲剧范围之外。比如在《俄狄浦斯》中,索福克勒斯就是这样处理不合理内容的。

再则,既然悲剧是对比人物本身好的人的模仿,诗人就应该向杰出的肖像画家学习。他们在再现原型特有形式的同时,使得模仿作品贴近生活,且更加的美。这与诗人一样,在重现性情暴躁、懒散之人或其他性格有缺陷之人时,也应保留人物原型,将人物塑造得好一点。如荷马和阿伽颂描绘的阿喀琉斯就是用了这样的方式。

这些便是诗人应该注意的原则。还有诗人不可以忽视那些吸引人感官的事物,尽管不是必要的,但却是诗歌中共存的特点,因为在这方面很容易出错。这部分在我们已经出版的著述中已作过足够的说明。

3. Questions for Discussion

(1) What are the six elements of the tragedy?

(2) What are the Reversal of the Situation and the Recognition?

(3) Analyze a tragedy that you have ever read with the theory in *Poetics*.

3. 讨论题

(1)什么是悲剧六要素?

(2)什么是"突转"和"发现"?

(3)根据《诗学》中的理论分析你所阅读过的悲剧。

---

① 阿喀琉斯(Achilles),古希腊神话中的英雄,出生后便被母亲浸泡在冥河中,所以他是战无不胜刀枪不入的。只有脚踝是弱点,最终他被箭射中脚踝而死。

② 阿伽颂(Agathon,公元前5世纪),古希腊悲剧诗人。他是首位通过想象人物构成虚拟主题的作家。此外,他还擅长于音乐。柏拉图与阿里斯多芬均对其有所叙述。

Chapter 3

1.Introduction to Immanuel Kant

Immanuel Kant (1724-1804) is the founder of the German classical philosophy and aesthetics. He synthesized early modern rationalism and empiricism, set the terms for much of 19th and 20th century philosophy, and continues to exercise a significant influence today in metaphysics, epistemology, ethics, political philosophy, aesthetics, and other fields.

Kant was born into an artisan family of modest means in Konigsberg on April 22, 1724. In 1740, he entered Konigsberg University. In 1746 financial difficulties forced him to withdraw from the University. After nine years supporting himself as a tutor to the children of several wealthy families in outlying districts, he returned to the University, finishing his degree and entering academic life, teaching as an unsalaried lecturer for many years. As an unsalaried lecturer at the University, Kant was paid directly by the students who attended his lectures, so he needed to teach an enormous amount and to attract many students in order to earn a living. He often published works during these years. His theses contain different subjects

第3章

1. 康德简介

伊曼努尔·康德(1724—1804)是德国古典哲学和美学的奠基人。他综合了早期现代理性主义和经验主义,确立了19世纪和20世纪哲学中的众多术语,至今仍对形而上学、认识论、伦理学、政治哲学、美学及其他领域产生重要影响。

1724年4月22日,康德出生在柯尼斯堡的一个手工业者家庭。1740年,康德进入柯尼斯堡大学。1746年由于家境贫寒,他被迫中断学业,在科尼斯堡附近的小城镇为几个富裕家庭的孩子做家庭教师以养活自己。9年后,康德重返柯尼斯堡大学,完成学业并进入学术圈,在以后的许多年一直担任柯尼斯堡大学的编外无俸讲师。作为无俸讲师,康德的收入由听其讲座的学生直接支付,为了生存,他需要大量授课,并吸引大量学生。任职期间,康德经常发表著作。他的论题包罗万象,从自然科学、美学、神学甚至到巫术应有尽有。

from natural science, aesthetics, theology, and even to witchcraft. In 1770, Kant was given a University chair in Logic and Metaphysics at Konigsberg University. Since then, Kant had focused on his critical philosophy without publishing a paper for ten years. In 1786, Kant became the rector of Konigsberg University and quit the job title in 1797. Kant was elected as the academician of Berlin Science Academy. On February12, 1804, he passed away in Konigsberg.

1770年,康德被任命为柯尼斯堡大学逻辑学与形而上学教授。当上教授以后,康德沉寂十年没有发表一篇文章,而是潜心研究他的批判哲学。1786 年,康德升任柯尼斯堡大学校长,1797 年辞去校长职务。康德在柯尼斯堡大学任教期间当选为柏林科学院院士。1804 年 2 月 12 日,康德在柯尼斯堡去世。

Kant's works can be divided into two stages. Before 1770, his works concentrate on natural science. One of his early works is *Universal Natural History and Theory of the Heavens* (1755), in which he developed the nebular hypothesis about the formation of the solar system. Since 1781, he had published a series of original works concerning vast fields, mainly including *The Critique of Pure Reason* (1781), *The Critique of Practical Reason* (1788), *The Critique of Judgement* (1790). The publications of the three critiques mark the completeness of Kant's philosophical system, concerning epistemology, ethics, and aesthetics respectively.

康德的著作可分为两个阶段。1770 年前,他的著作主要研究自然科学,主要成果有《自然通史和天体论》(1755),其中他提出了太阳系起源的星云假说。从 1781 年起,康德出版了一系列涉及领域广阔、有独创性的伟大著作,主要包括:《纯粹理性批判》(1781)、《实践理性批判》(1788)、《判断力批判》(1790)等。“三大批判”的问世标志着康德哲学体系的完成,分别涉及认识论、伦理学以及美学。

Kant introduces transcendental idealism in *The Critique of Pure Reason*. In both the groundwork of *The Critique of Practical Reason* and *The Metaphysics of Morals* (1797), Kant gives a more detailed argument for the conclusion that morality and freedom reciprocally imply one another.

康德在《纯粹理性批判》中引入了先验唯理念论。在《实践理性批判》和《道德形而上学》(1797)两部奠基之作中,康德通过细致论证就道德和自由的关系议题做出结论:道德和自由密不可分,互为前提。

The first part of *The Critique of Judgement* is "Critique of Aesthetic Judgement". This part is composed of "Analytic of Aesthetic Judgement" and "Dialectic of Aesthetic Judgement". "Analytic of Aesthetic Judgement" is composed of "Analytic of the Beautiful" and "Analytic of the Sublime". In "Analytic of the Beautiful" Kant analyzes aesthetic judgement from four moments: moment of quality, moment of quantity, moment of the relation and moment of modality. Kant draws conclusions that

《判断力批判》上卷论及美学,即“审美判断力的批判”。上卷又分“审美判断力的分析”和“审美判断力的辨证论”。“审美判断力的分析”由“美的分析”和“崇高的分析”两部分构成。在“美的分析”中,康德从质的契机、量的契机、关系的契机和方式的契机四个契机对审美判断进行分析,得出结论:从质的契机看,审美判断具有无利害的特点;从

from the first moment, aesthetic judgments are disinterested; from the second moment, aesthetic judgments behave universally; from the third moment, the beautiful has to be understood as finality, but without any definite end; from the fourth moment, the beautiful is apart from a concept, while it is cognized as object of a necessary delight.

量的契机看,审美判断是普遍有效的;从关系契机看,美没有明确的目的,却有合目的性;从方式契机上看,审美判断不涉及概念,但美的对象产生快感是必然的。

Kant divides the sublime into the "mathematically" and the "dynamically". The sublime feeling is a kind of "rapid alternation" between the fear of the overwhelming and the peculiar pleasure of seeing that overwhelming overwhelmed.

康德将崇高分为两种:数学的和力学的。崇高感来自于恐惧和愉悦之间的"迅速转换",是克服恐惧后的愉悦。

2. Selections from *The Critique of Judgement*

First Section. Analytic of Aesthetic Judgement①

First Book. Analytic of the Beautiful

First Moment. Of the Judgement of Taste: Moment of Quality

Immanuel Kant

§ 1. The judgement of taste is aesthetic.

If we wish to discern whether anything is beautiful or not, we do not refer the representation of it to the Object by means of understanding with a view to cognition, but by means of the imagination (acting perhaps in conjunction with understanding) we refer the representation to the Subject and its feeling of pleasure or displeasure. The judgement of taste, therefore, is not a cognitive judgement, and so not logical, but is aesthetic—which means that it is one whose determining ground cannot be other

2.《判断力批判》选文

第一部分 审美判断力的分析

第一卷 美的分析

第一契机 鉴赏判断:质的契机

伊曼努尔·康德

§ 1. 鉴赏判断是审美的

如果我们想辨别某物是否美丽,我们并不通过认知理解从其表象联系到客体,而是通过想象力(也许表演和理解相结合)从其表象到主体来体会,愉快和不愉快的情感。因此,鉴赏判断不是认知判断,不是逻辑判断,而是审美判断,这意味着鉴赏判断的决定因素是主观的。一切表象的联系、甚至感觉联系都可以是主观的(在这种情况下,联系就是指经验

① Selected from Kant's *Critique of Aesthetic Judgement*, translated by James Creed Meredit, Oxford: The Clarendon Press, 1911.

than subjective. Every reference of representations is capable of being objective, even that of sensations (in which case it signifies the real in an empirical representation). The one exception to this is the feeling of pleasure or displeasure. This denotes nothing in the object, but is a feeling which the subject has of itself and of the manner in which it is affected by the representation.

To apprehend a regular and appropriate building with one's cognitive faculties, be the mode of representation clear or confused, is quite a different thing from being conscious of this representation with an accompanying sensation of delight. Here the representation is referred wholly to the Subject, and what is more to its feeling of life—under the name of the feeling of pleasure or displeasure—and this forms the basis of a quite separate faculty of discriminating and estimating, that contributes nothing to knowledge. All it does is to compare the given representation in the Subject with the entire faculty of representations of which the mind is conscious in the feeling of its state. Given representations in a judgement may be empirical, and so aesthetic; but the judgement which is pronounced by their means is logical, provided it refers them to the Object. Conversely, be the given representations even rational, but referred in a judgement solely to the Subject (to its feeling), they are always to that extent aesthetic.

§ 2. The delight which determines the judgement of taste is independent of all interest①.

The delight which we connect with the representation of the real existence of an object is called interest. Such a delight, therefore, always involves a reference to the faculty of desire, either as its determining ground, or else as necessarily implicated with its determining ground. Now, where

主义表象中的实在之物)。唯一例外的就是愉快或不愉快的情感。它没有表示客体的任何东西,而是主体因表象的影响产生的自我及其方式的感觉。

用认知能力来理解一座规则合适的大厦,不论其表象方式是清晰的还是含混的,绝不同于凭借愉悦的感觉来意识这个表象。这种表象在愉快或不愉快的名义下完全与主体相联系,甚至是主体的生命,这形成了一个具有分辨和评估的完全独立能力的基础,这对知识没有丝毫贡献。它所能做的就是比较主体的给予表象和感觉状态中思想意识到的全部表象力。在一个判断中的给予表象可能是经验的,也是审美的;但是通过它们的方式断言出来的表象却是逻辑的,如果只将它们同主体相联系。相反,如果给予表象是理性的,但在一个判断中只将它与主体(它的情感)相联系,那么就此而言它们在任何时候都是感性的审美。

§ 2. 决定鉴赏判断的愉快是不带任何利害的

与一个物体真实存在的表象相联系的愉快称之为利害。所以,这样的一个愉快总是涉及与欲求能力相关的联系,要么作为它的决定因素,要么与这种决定因素必然 相 连 。现

① interest: 利害。

the question is whether something is beautiful, we do not want to know, whether we, or any one else, are, or even could be, concerned in the real existence of the thing, but rather what estimate we form of it on mere contemplation (intuition or reflection). If any one asks me whether I consider that the palace I see before me is beautiful, I may, perhaps, reply that I do not care for things of that sort that are merely made to be gaped at. Or I may reply in the same strain as that Iroquois sachem① who said that nothing in Paris pleased him better than the eating-houses. I may even go a step further and inveigh with the vigour of a *Rousseau* against the vanity of the great who spend the sweat of the people on such superfluous things. Or, in fine, I may quite easily persuade myself that if I found myself on an uninhabited island, without hope of ever again coming among men, and could conjure such a palace into existence by a mere wish, I should still not trouble to do so, so long as I had a hut there that was comfortable enough for me. All this may be admitted and approved; only it is not the point now at issue. All one wants to know is whether the mere representation of the object is to my liking, no matter how indifferent I may be to the real existence of the object of this representation. It is quite plain that in order to say that the object is beautiful, and to show that I have taste, everything turns on the meaning which I can give to this representation, and not on any factor which makes me dependent on the real existence of the object. Every one must allow that a judgement on the beautiful which is tinged with the slightest interest, is very partial and not a pure judgement of taste. One must not be in the least prepossessed in favour of the real existence of the thing, but must preserve complete indifference in this respect, in order to play the part of judge in matters of taste.

在,既然问题是某物是否美丽,我们不想知道我们自身、或任何其他人是否,或曾经是否与该物的真实存在相连,但是我们想知道在单纯的沉思中(直觉或反思)我们会怎样评判它。如果有人问我眼前看到的宫殿是否美丽,也许我会回答我并不喜欢那种被建造出来仅仅用于观看的物体。或者我会像北印第安人酋长一样回答,那位酋长说在巴黎没有比小吃店更让他高兴的事了。或许我可以更进一步,用卢梭的气势谩骂那些大人物的虚荣心,他们把人们的血汗浪费在一些不必要的事情上。最后,我很容易说服我自己如果我处在一个荒无人烟的小岛,没有重返人类世界的希望,即使我凭借自己的愿望就能变出一座宫殿,我也绝不会为此麻烦,只要我有一个足够让我舒服的小茅屋。这一切都会被承认,赞同,但是这并不是争论的焦点。人们只想知道单是物体的表象是否博得我的喜爱,无论我对这个物体表象的真实存在多么不在意。很清晰地看出为了说明这个物体的美丽,显示我的品位,一切都取决于我怎样评价这个表象,而不是我在某个方面依靠物体的真实存在。每个人都必须承认对于美的事物的判断,若是夹杂着丝毫的利害关系,都是不公正的,也不是纯粹的鉴赏判断。每个人对于事物的真实存在也不能有丝毫的倾向性,必须在这个方面保持绝对的漠视,以便在鉴赏中让判断起作用。

① sachem:(北美印第安人的)部落酋长。

This proposition, which is of the utmost importance, cannot be better explained than by contrasting the pure disinterested① delight which appears in the judgement of taste with that allied to an interest—especially if we can also assure ourselves that there are no other kinds of interest beyond those presently to be mentioned.

§ 5. Comparison of the three specifically different kinds of delight.

Both the Agreeable② and the Good③ involve a reference to the faculty of desire, and are thus attended, the former with a delight pathologically conditioned (by stimuli), the latter with a pure practical delight. Such delight is determined not merely by the representation of the object, but also by the represented bond of connection between the subject and the real existence of the object. It is not merely the object, but also its real existence, that pleases. On the other hand, the judgement of taste is simply contemplative, i. e., it is a judgement which is indifferent as to the existence of an object, and only decides how its character stands with the feeling of pleasure and displeasure. But not even is this contemplation itself directed to concepts; for the judgement of taste is not a cognitive judgement (neither a theoretical one nor a practical), and hence, also, is not grounded on concepts, nor yet intentionally directed to them.

The agreeable, the beautiful, and the good thus denote three different relations of representations to the feeling of pleasure and displeasure, as a feeling in respect of which we distinguish different objects or modes of representation④.

这个至关重要的命题再也不能被更好地解释,除非我们将出现在鉴赏判断中的纯粹无利害的愉快和利害相联系的愉快进行对比,尤其是如果我们能够确定除了即将要提到的利害之外,再也没有其他的利害了。

§ 5. 三种不同特性的愉悦之比较

快适和善都涉及了欲求能力的联系,前者伴随着受制于病理上(通过刺激)的愉快,后者伴随着纯粹实践性的愉快。这种愉快不仅由物体表象所决定,而且由主体和客体的真实存在的表象联系所决定。不仅仅是客体,它的真实存在也是让人愉快的。另一方面,鉴赏判断也是沉思的,它对于客体的存在是漠不关心的,只是决定它的性格如何和愉快、不愉快的情感一致。但是这种沉思本身也不是针对概念的;鉴赏判断不是认知判断(既不是理论上的认知判断也不是实践性上的认知判断),也不是建立在概念之上的,试图指向它们的判断。

快适、美、善意味着对愉快和不愉快的情感三种不同的表象联系,我们通过表象联系区分不同的客体和表象方式。然而预示着我们满意的一致表达也是不同的。快适就是指

① 对于一个愉悦的对象所作的判断可以完全是无利害的,但却是非常有兴趣的,就是说,它并非建立在任何利害之上,但它却产生某种兴趣;一切纯粹的道德判断就是这类判断。

② the agreeable: 快适。

③ the good: 善。

④ mode of representation: 表象方式。

Also, the corresponding expressions which indicate our satisfaction in them are different. The agreeable is what GRATIFIES① a man; the beautiful what simply PLEASES② him; the good what is ESTEEMED (approved)③, i.e., that on which he sets an objective worth. Agreeableness is a significant factor even with irrational animals; beauty has purport and significance only for human beings, i.e., for beings at once animal and rational (but not merely for them as rational—intelligent beings—but only for them as at once animal and rational); whereas the good is good for every rational being in general—a proposition which can only receive its complete justification and explanation in the sequel. Of all these three kinds of delight, that of taste in the beautiful may be said to be the one and only disinterested and free delight; for, with it, no interest, whether of sense or reason, extorts approval. And so we may say that delight, in the three cases mentioned, is related to inclination, to favour, or to respect. For FAVOUR is the only free liking. An object of inclination, and one which a law of reason imposes upon our desire, leaves us no freedom to turn anything into an object of pleasure. All interest presupposes a want, or calls one forth; and, being a ground determining approval, deprives the judgement on the object of its freedom.

So far as the interest of inclination in the case of the agreeable goes, every one says: hunger is the best sauce; and people with a healthy appetite relish everything, so long as it is something they can eat. Such delight, consequently, gives no indication of taste having anything to say to the choice. Only when men have got all they want can we tell who among the crowd has taste or not.

使人快乐的东西,美是指让他喜欢的东西,善是指被赞同的东西,在此他设定了客观价值。对于非理性的动物而言,快适也是一个重要的因素;美只对人类有意义,即是动物性的也是理性的存在物(不仅是理性、智慧的存在物,也是动物性的、理性的存在物);一般而言,善适用于每一个理性存在物——这个命题只有在后面才能有完整的辨别和解释。在这三种愉快当中,对美的鉴赏愉快可以说是独一无二的、无私利的自由的愉快。因为没有任何利害,无论是感性还是理性的利害来强迫它赞同。我们也可以认为上述提到的三种愉快与爱好、喜爱、尊敬相联系。喜爱是一种自由的喜欢。一个爱好的客体,一个理性规则强加于我们欲望的客体,没有赋予我们任何自由来将一些事物转化成愉快的客体。所有的利害都预示着一个需要,或者号召着一个需要;而作为赞许的一个决定因素剥夺了自由客体的判断。

就快适上的爱好的利害而言,每个人都说,饥饿是最好的调味品;这是拥有健康胃口的人期待着一切,只要是能吃的东西。因此这样的愉快对于鉴赏没有任何指示,更谈不上选择了。只有当人类得到他们想要的一切,我们才能辨别人群中谁有品

① 使快乐。
② 使喜欢。
③ 被尊敬的,被赞成的。

Similarly there may be correct habits (conduct) without virtue, politeness without good-will, propriety without honour, etc. For where the moral law dictates, there is, objectively, no room left for free choice as to what one has to do; and to show taste in the way one carries out these dictates, or in estimating the way others do so, is a totally different matter from displaying the moral frame of one's mind. For the latter involves a command and produces a need of something, whereas moral taste only plays with the objects of delight without devoting itself sincerely to any.

位,而谁没有品位。相似的是,也有无美德的正确习惯(行为),无善意的礼貌,无荣誉的得体等等。凡是受道德律影响的地方,客观而言,关于该做什么事的自由选择的空间是没有的;为了在实施这些指示时表现鉴赏,或在评估别人的行为时的鉴赏是完全不同于表现自己的道德境界的。因为后者包含一个命令并产生某物的需要,然而道德鉴赏只是和愉快的客体做游戏,而并不致力于任何一个对象。

Definition of the Beautiful Derived from the First Moment

来源于第一契机的美的定义

Taste is the faculty of estimating an object or a mode of representation by means of a delight or aversion apart from any interest. The object of such a delight is called beautiful.

鉴赏是通过不带任何利害的愉快或不悦而对一个对象或一个表象方式所作的评判能力。一个这样的愉悦对象就叫做美。

Second Moment. Of the Judgement of Taste: Moment of Quantity.

第二契机　鉴赏判断:量的契机

§ 6. The beautiful is that which, apart from concepts, is represented as the Object of a universal delight.

This definition of the beautiful is deducible from the foregoing definition of it as an object of delight apart from any interest. For where any one is conscious that his delight in an object is with him independent of interest, it is inevitable that he should look on the object as one containing a ground of delight for all men. For, since the delight is not based on any inclination of the subject (or on any other deliberate interest), but the subject feels himself completely free in respect of the liking which he accords to the object, he can find as reason for his delight no personal conditions to

§ 6. 美是不依赖概念而作为一个普遍愉快的对象被表现出来的

这个关于美的定义是从前面的定义引申而来的,即美是无任何利害关系的愉快的对象。因为人意识到,那愉快的对象与他无利害关系,他必然会认为,那对象具有让每个人都愉快的理由。因为它既不是基于主体的任何偏爱,(也不是基于任何其他一种经过考虑的利害),而是主体感受到他自己与令他感到愉快的对象之间完全是自由的,于是他就不能找到私人的,只和他的主体有关的条件作为这愉快的根据,因此他必须认为

which his own subjective self might alone be party. Hence he must regard it as resting on what he may also presuppose in every other person; and therefore he must believe that he has reason for demanding a similar delight from every one. Accordingly he will speak of the beautiful as if beauty were a quality of the object and the judgement logical (forming a cognition of the object by concepts of it); although it is only aesthetic, and contains merely a reference of the representation of the object to the subject; because it still bears this resemblance to the logical judgement, that it may be presupposed to be valid for all men. But this universality cannot spring from concepts. For from concepts there is no transition to the feeling of pleasure or displeasure (save in the case of pure practical laws, which, however, carry an interest with them; and such an interest does not attach to the pure judgement of taste). The result is that the judgement of taste, with its attendant consciousness of detachment from all interest, must involve a claim to validity for all men, and must do so apart from universality attached to objects, i.e., there must be coupled with it a claim to subjective universality.

这种愉快是根据他所设想的人人共有的东西。因此他必须相信他有理由设想每个人都同时感到此愉快。他将会这样谈到美,好像美是对象的一种性质,而他的判断是逻辑的(凭借概念以构成的对于对象的知识);虽然这种判断只是审美的,并且仅包含着对象对于主体的一种关系;然而因为它究竟还是与逻辑的判断相似,人们能够设定它适用于每个人。但是从概念上也不能产生这种普遍性来。因为概念是不能过渡到快感及不快感的(除非在纯粹的实践规律里面,而它自身却伴着一种利害关系,这又是和纯粹的鉴赏判断无关)。所以鉴赏的判断,既然意识到在它内部并没有任何的利害关系,它就必须只要求对于每个人都能适用,而并不要求客体具有普遍性,这就是说,它只是和主观普遍性的要求连接着的。

Definition of the Beautiful drawn from the Second Moment

The beautiful is that which, apart from a concept, pleases universally.

从第二个契机总结出对美的定义

美是不凭借概念而普遍令人感到愉快的。

Third Moment. Of Judgements of Taste: Moment of the relation of the Ends brought under Review in such Judgements

§ 11. The sole foundation of the judgement of taste is the form of finality① of an object (or mode

第三契机　鉴赏判断:按照它里面观察到的目的的关系

§ 11. 鉴赏判断的唯一根据是一个客体(或其表象方式)的合目的

① finality:合目的性。

of representing it).

Whenever an end① is regarded as a source of delight, it always imports an interest as determining ground of the judgement on the object of pleasure. Hence the judgement of taste cannot rest on any subjective end as its ground. But neither can any representation of an objective end, i. e., of the possibility of the object itself on principles of final connection, determine the judgement of taste, and, consequently, neither can any concept of the good. For the judgement of taste is an aesthetic and not a cognitive judgement, and so does not deal with any concept of the nature or of the internal or external possibility, by this or that cause, of the object, but simply with the relative bearing of the representative powers so far as determined by a representation.

Now this relation, present when an object is characterized as beautiful, is coupled with the feeling of pleasure. This pleasure is by the judgement of taste pronounced valid for every one; hence an agreeableness attending the representation is just as incapable of containing the determining ground of the judgement as the representation of the perfection of the object or the concept of the good. We are thus left with the subjective finality in the representation of an object, exclusive of any end (objective or subjective)—consequently the bare form of finality in the representation whereby an object is given to us, so far as we are conscious of it as that which is alone capable of constituting the delight which, apart from any concept, we estimate as universally communicable, and so of forming the determining ground of the judgement of taste.

§ 17. Ideal of beauty

There can be no objective rule of taste by which what is beautiful may be defined by means of

性形式

无论何时,目的都被视作愉快的来源,它总是迁入某个利害作为评价愉快客体的决定因素。因此鉴赏判断不能让任何主观目的作为它的决定因素。但是一个客观目的的表象,也就是主体本身按照目的关联原则的可能性的表象也不能决定判断鉴赏,因此善的概念也不能。判断鉴赏是审美判断,不是认知判断,它无需因这个那个因素去处理客体的任何自然概念、外在、内在可能性,它仅仅只需处理被表象决定的表象力之间的相对关系。

客体被认为是美的时候呈现的这种联系和愉快是紧密结合的,这种愉快通过判断鉴赏被宣称对每个人都是有效的;因此伴随着表象的一致同客体的完美表象、或善的概念一样,不能囊括判断的决定因素。因此一个客体表象的主观目的性落在了我们这儿,排除一切目的(主观的或客观的)——因此表象目的的单纯形式通过客体被给予我们,只要我们意识到它能构建成没有概念,我们所评判的能普遍传达的愉快以及构成鉴赏判断的决定因素。

§ 17. 美的理想

任何通过概念来规定什么是美的客观鉴赏规则都是不可能有的。

① end:目的。

concepts. For every judgement from that source is aesthetic, i. e., its determining ground is the feeling of the subject, and not any concept of an object. It is only throwing away labour to look for a principle of taste that affords a universal criterion of the beautiful by definite concepts; because what is sought is a thing impossible and inherently contradictory. But in the universal communicability of the sensation (of delight or aversion)—a communicability, too, that exists apart from any concept—in the accord, so far as possible, of all ages and nations as to this feeling in the representation of certain objects, we have the empirical criterion, weak indeed and scarce sufficient to raise a presumption, of the derivation of a taste, thus confirmed by examples, from grounds deep seated and shared alike by all men, underlying their agreement in estimating the forms under which objects are given to them.

因为一切出自这一来源的判断都是审美的,它的决定因素是主体的情感,不是客体的概念。寻找通过确切概念来提供美的普遍标准的鉴赏原则是浪费精力的;因为寻求的是不可能的,并且内在自相矛盾的东西。但是在感觉(愉快或不悦)的普遍传达中,就所有年龄段、民族对于特定客体的表象情感而言,这种无概念的传达性是一致的,我们有鉴赏来源的经验主义性标准,这种标准很微不足道,不足以引起假想。这些鉴赏由处在深层、为所有人类分享的实例证明,以评判给予它们物体形式的一致性为基准。

For this reason some products of taste are looked on as exemplary—not meaning thereby that by imitating others taste may be acquired. For taste must be an original faculty; whereas one who imitates a model, while showing skill commensurate with his success, only displays taste as himself a critic of this model. Hence it follows that the highest model, the archetype of taste, is a mere idea, which each person must beget in his own consciousness, and according to which he must form his estimate of everything that is an object of taste, or that is an example of critical taste, and even of universal taste itself. Properly speaking, an idea signifies a concept of reason, and an ideal the representation of an individual existence as adequate to an idea. Hence this archetype of taste—which rests, indeed, upon reason's indeterminate idea of a maximum, but is not, however, capable of being represented by means of

因此我们把一些鉴赏作品看做典型化的:这并不是说通过模仿别人可以获得鉴赏。因为鉴赏必须是原创力;一个模仿典范的人,尽管成功地显示了其技能,但只有将自己作为这种典范的批评家时,他才显示出鉴赏。由此看出最高的典范,鉴赏的原型,仅仅是一个人在意识中产生的理念,他必须据此构成一切事物的评估,物体的鉴赏、批评鉴赏的一个实例、甚至是鉴赏本身。严格说来,理念意味着一个理性概念,而理想则意味着一个单一存在物,作为符合某个理念的存在物的表象。这种最大化程度上依赖理性的不确定理念的鉴赏原型不能通过概念表现出来,只能通过个人的描绘表现出来——这更能被称之为美的理想化。尽管我们

concepts, but only in an individual presentation①—may more appropriately be called the ideal of the beautiful. While not having this ideal in our possession, we still strive to beget it within us. But it is bound to be merely an ideal of the imagination, seeing that it rests, not upon concepts, but upon the presentation—the faculty of presentation being the imagination. Now, how do we arrive at such an ideal of beauty? Is it a priori or empirically? Further, what species of the beautiful admits of an ideal?

First of all, we do well to observe that the beauty for which an ideal has to be sought cannot be a beauty that is free and at large, but must be one fixed by a concept of objective finality. Hence it cannot belong to the object of an altogether pure judgement of taste, but must attach to one that is partly intellectual. In other words, where an ideal is to have place among the grounds upon which any estimate is formed, then beneath grounds of that kind there must lie some idea of reason according to determinate concepts, by which the end underlying the internal possibility of the object is determined a priori. An ideal of beautiful flowers, of a beautiful suite of furniture, or of a beautiful view, is unthinkable. But, it may also be impossible to represent an ideal of a beauty dependent on definite ends, e.g., a beautiful residence, a beautiful tree, a beautiful garden, etc., presumably because their ends are not sufficiently defined and fixed by their concept, with the result that their finality is nearly as free as with beauty that is quite at large. Only what has in itself the end of its real existence—only man that is able himself to determine his ends by reason, or, where he has to derive them from external perception, can still compare them with essential and universal ends, and then further pronounce aesthetically upon their accord with such

不能拥有理想,我们仍需努力在心中创造它。但是它一定仅仅是想象的理想,鉴于它不是建立在概念之上的,而是描绘之上的——描绘即是想象。那么我们怎样才能达到美的理想呢?它是先天性的还是经验性的?更或者,什么种类的美能成为一种理想?

首先,我们必须观察到的是能够从中寻求理想的美一定不能是自由自在、不受束缚的美,却一定是主观合乎目的性概念的固定的美。因此它不属于一个纯粹鉴赏判断的客体,而是部分智慧化的鉴赏判断的客体。换句话说,理想放置于决定哪种评估形成的因素之中,在这种因素之下按照决定性概念必须存在理性概念,客体的内在可能性由优先权决定。漂亮的花朵、漂亮的家具、美丽的风景,它们的理想是不可想象的。但依附于某个特定的目的,如美丽的住宅、美丽的树、美丽的花园等等去展现美的理想也似乎不太可能,也许这些目的不能通过他们的概念来充分定义和固定,因而他们的目的就像自由自在的美一样,无拘无束。只有自身具有真实存在的目的性的东西——只有人类能够通过理性决定自己的目的,或者他从外部知觉中得到这些目的,并且将这些目的同本质的普遍的目的比较,相一致时,进一步审美地声称在世间的所有客体中,他是唯一一个能成为美的理想,正如人性、智慧是完美的理想。

① presentation:描绘。

ends, only he, among all objects in the world, admits, therefore, of an ideal of beauty, just as humanity in his person, as intelligence, alone admits of the ideal of perfection.

Two factors are here involved. First, there is the aesthetic normal idea①, which is an individual intuition (of the imagination). This represents the norm by which we judge of a man as a member of a particular animal species. Secondly, there is the rational idea②. This deals with the ends of humanity so far as capable of sensuous representation, and converts them into a principle for estimating his outward form, through which these ends are revealed in their phenomenal effect. The normal idea must draw from experience the constituents which it requires for the form of an animal of a particular kind. But the greatest finality in the construction of this form—that which would serve as a universal norm for forming an estimate of each individual of the species in question—the image that, as it were, forms an intentional basis underlying the technic of nature, to which no separate individual, but only the race as a whole, is adequate, has its seat merely in the idea of the judging Subject. Yet it is, with all its proportions, an aesthetic idea, and, as such, capable of being fully presented in *concreto* in a model image. Now, how is this effected? In order to render the process to some extent intelligible (for who can wrest nature's whole secret from her?), let us attempt a psychological explanation.

It is of note that the imagination, in a manner quite incomprehensible to us, is able on occasion, even after a long lapse of time, not alone to recall the signs for concepts, but also to reproduce the image and shape of an object out of a countless number of others of a different, or even of the very

这里涉及两个因素。第一,审美的规格概念,这是个体直觉(或想象)。它代表着一种规范,通过这种规范,我们将人类评判为一个特殊动物种类的一员。第二,是理性概念,它通过感觉表象处理人性的目的,将它们转化成评估外在形式的一种原则,借此这些目的暴露于不同的现象效应中。规格概念必须从经验中获取成分,它需要一个特殊种类的动物形式。但这种形式的建造是最合乎目的——作为形成带有质疑的个体种类的评估的一个普遍的标准——意象,正如原本那样,仿佛试图为大自然的技艺奠定基础。没有独立的个体,只有种族整体在主体评判中才有一席之地。它的各个比例都是一个美学的理念,能够在典范意象中完全地呈现出来。这是怎样产生效果的呢? 为了在可理解的程度上实施这个过程(谁能够强迫大自然说出自己的秘密呢?),让我们尝试做一个心理学的解释吧。

重要的是想象力以一种我们很难理解的方式,不仅能够偶尔,甚至很长一段时间后召唤概念符号,而且能够从不同种类、甚至同一种类的数不清的客体中产生一个客体的意象

① normal idea: 规格概念,标准概念。
② rational idea: 理性概念。

same, kind. And, further, if the mind is engaged upon comparisons, we may well suppose that it can in actual fact, though the process is unconscious, superimpose as it were one image upon another, and from the coincidence of a number of the same kind arrive at a mean contour which serves as a common standard for all. Say, for instance, a person has seen a thousand full-grown men. Now if he wishes to judge normal size determined upon a comparative estimate, then imagination (to my mind) allows a great number of these images (perhaps the whole thousand) to fall one upon the other, and, if I may be allowed to extend to the case the analogy of optical presentation, in the space where they come most together, and within the contour where the place is illuminated by the greatest concentration of colour, one gets a perception of the average size, which alike in height and breadth is equally removed from the extreme limits of the greatest and smallest statures; and this is the stature of a beautiful man. (The same result could be obtained in a mechanical way, by taking the measures of all the thousand, and adding together their heights, and their breadths [and thicknesses], and dividing the sum in each case by a thousand.) But the power of imagination does all this by means of a dynamical effect upon the organ of internal sense, arising from the frequent apprehension of such forms. If, again, for our average man we seek on similar lines for the average head, and for this the average nose, and so on, then we get the figure that underlies the normal idea of a beautiful man in the country where the comparison is instituted. For this reason a Negro must necessarily (under these empirical conditions) have a different normal idea of the beauty of forms from what a white man has, and the Chinaman one different from the European. And the process would be just the same with the model of a beautiful horse or dog (of a particular breed). This

和形状。更进一步说,如果我们思想着重于比较时,我们也许会推断出它实际上可以将一个意象叠加于另一个意象之上,从多数同类中的一致性得到一个大致轮廓,这可以当做一切形象的共同标准,尽管这个过程是无意识的。比如说,某人看见一千个成年人。现在他要依赖可以比较的评估去判断标准尺寸,想象力会让大量的形象(也许是那上千的成年人)一个接一个落在脑海里,并且如果允许我用光学的表现方式来延伸这些事件的类比时,它们会在一个有限的轮廓内聚集到一起,聚集到颜色集中照亮的地方,这个人可以得到平均尺寸的概念,不论是从身高还是宽度,它距离最大值和最小值都是等距离的,这就是一个美男子的形象。(我们也能从机械的方式中得出这一点,通过测量上千个人,然后将他们的身高、宽度、体重相加,最后把总和除以一千。)但是想象力通过对内在感觉器官的动态影响完成了这一切,这源于对此类形式的频繁理解。如果我们以类似的方式为我们这个平均的男子寻求平均的头、鼻子等等,那么在这个美男子标准的概念之下我们将得到一个形体,这个标准只能应用于比较而来的国家。因此,(在这些经验条件之下),黑人肯定有一个不同于白人的美学规格概念,中国人则有不同于欧洲人的美学概念,这种情况也适用于一匹美丽的马和狗(属于某一种类的)。这个标准概念并不来自于经验的各种比例,即规定准则,而是通过这一概念形成第一评估的准则成为可能。它是所有的单一个体直觉的中介,这些个体有各式各样的变化形式——整个物种的浮游意象,大自然将这意象定格为同类物种的

normal idea is not derived from proportions taken from experience as definite rules: rather is it according to this idea that rules forming estimates first become possible. It is an intermediate between all singular intuitions of individuals, with their manifold variations—a floating image for the whole genus, which nature has set as an archetype underlying those of her products that belong to the same species, but which in no single case she seems to have completely attained. But the normal idea is far from giving the complete archetype of beauty in the genus. It only gives the form that constitutes the indispensable condition of all beauty, and, consequently, only correctness in the presentation of the genus. It is, as the famous "Doryphorus①" of Polycletus② was called, the rule (and Myron③'s "Cow" might be similarly employed for its kind). It cannot, for that very reason, contain anything specifically characteristic; for otherwise it would not be the normal idea for the genus. Further, it is not by beauty that its presentation pleases, but merely because it does not contradict any of the conditions under which alone a thing belonging to this genus can be beautiful. The presentation is merely academically correct.

产品原型,但是似乎没有在一种情况下能够完全得到它。但是标准概念远远不能给予这种美的完整原型。它仅仅给出了构成美的必要条件的形式,仅仅是种类表象的正确性。它正如波利克里托斯的著名雕像《荷矛者》一样,被声称为一种准则(米隆的母牛也类似于此)。正因为如此,标准概念不能包含特别有个性特质的事物;否则它就不属于这个种类的标准概念。甚至它不再通过表象的美让人愉快,而是它不和任何条件相冲突,在此条件下属于此类的事物是美丽的。这种表象仅仅理论上是正确的。

But the ideal of the beautiful is still something different from its normal idea. For reasons already stated it is only to be sought in the human figure. Here the ideal consists in the expression of the moral, apart from which the object would not please at once universally and positively (not merely negatively in a presentation academically correct). The visible expression of moral ideas that

但是美的理想不同于标准概念。原因已经说明了:它只能在人的形象中可以找到。在这里,理想在于表露道德,除此,客体不会普遍地、积极地让人愉快,(不仅仅消极于理论上正确的表露)。统治人的内在思想的道德理念的明显表达只能从经验中提取,但是它们与我们所有理性的结

① Doryphorus:《荷矛者》,古希腊雕塑家波利克里托斯的作品,雕像的人体比例表现得十分完美,成为后人追求理想化人体比例的标准。

② 波利克里托斯(Polycletus,约公元前5世纪),古希腊著名雕塑家,以比例精确著称。

③ 米隆(Myron,公元前5世纪中叶),古希腊著名雕塑家,善于运用写实手法塑造人物在剧烈运动时的动态,并善于刻画人物个性,代表作《掷铁饼者》(Discobolus)。

govern men inwardly can, of course, only be drawn from experience; but their combination with all that our reason connects with the morally good in the idea of the highest finality—benevolence, purity, strength, or equanimity, etc.—may be made, as it were, visible in bodily manifestation (as effect of what is internal), and this embodiment involves a union of pure ideas of reason and great imaginative power, in one who would even form an estimate of it, not to speak of being the author of its presentation. The correctness of such an ideal of beauty is evidenced by its not permitting any sensuous charm to mingle with the delight in its object, in which it still allows us to take a great interest. This fact in turn shows that an estimate formed according to such a standard can never be purely aesthetic, and that one formed according to an ideal of beauty cannot be a simple judgement of taste.

合与最高目的性理念中的道德之善——仁慈、纯洁、力量、沉着等等相关,它们在身体表象中(内在效果)变得明显可见:想判定它,甚至谁想表现在人身上必须拥有理性纯洁思想和伟大想象力的结合。美的理想化的正确性表现在:它不允许任何感官的魅力混进客体的愉快中,但却可以对此抱有极大的兴趣。事实反过来说明通过这样一个标准概念形成的评估不可能是纯粹审美的,通过美的理想化形成的评估也不可能仅仅是一个鉴赏判断。

Definition of the Beautiful Derived from this Third Moment

Beauty is the form of finality in an object, so far as perceived in it apart from the representation of an end.

从第三个契机总结出来的美的定义

美是一个对象的合目的性的形式,在它不是具有一个目的的表象而在对象身上被知觉时。

Fourth Moment Of the Judgement of Taste: Moment of the Modality of the Delight in the Object

§ 20. The condition of the necessity advanced by a judgement of taste is the idea of a common sense.

Were judgements of taste (like cognitive judgements) in possession of a definite objective principle, then one who in his judgement followed such a principle would claim unconditioned necessity for it. Again, were they devoid of any

第四契机　鉴赏判断:按照对象愉悦的方式来看

§ 20. 鉴赏判断所要求的必然性条件是共通感的观念

假使鉴赏判断(像认知判断那样)具有一个一定的客观原理,那么谁要是依据这原理下了判断,他将会宣称他的判断具有无条件的必然性。假使鉴赏判断没有任何原理,像单纯

principle, as are those of the mere taste of sense, then no thought of any necessity on their part would enter one's head. Therefore they must have a subjective principle, and one which determines what pleases or displeases, by means of feeling only and not through concepts, but yet with universal validity. Such a principle, however, could only be regarded as a common sense. This differs essentially from common understanding, which is also sometimes called common sense (sensus communis): for the judgement of the latter is not one by feeling, but always one by concepts, though usually only in the shape of obscurely represented principles.

The judgement of taste, therefore, depends on our presupposing the existence of a common sense. (But this is not to be taken to mean some external sense, but the effect arising from the free play of our powers of cognition.) Only under the presupposition, I repeat, of such a common sense, are we able to lay down a judgement of taste.

感官的趣味判断,那么人们就完全不会想到它们的必然性。所以鉴赏判断必须具有一个主观性的原理,这个原理通过情感而不是通过概念,但仍然普遍有效地规约着何物令人愉快,何物令人不愉快。一个这样的原理却只能被视为一共通感,这种共通感是与人们有时也称作共通感(sensus communis)的一般理解在本质上又是有区别的:后者是不按照情感,而是按照概念判断,固然通常只按照不明了地表示的原理判断着。

因此,鉴赏判断依赖于我们假定的共通感的存在(不是理解为外在的感觉,而是从我们认识诸能力的自由活动中来的结果),只在一个这样的共通感的前提下,我说,才能做出鉴赏判断。

Definition of the Beautiful drawn from the Fourth Moment

The beautiful is that which, apart from a concept, is cognized as object of a necessary delight.

从第四个契机总结出美的定义

美是不依赖概念而被当作一种必然的愉快的对象。

3. Questions for Discussion

(1) How do you understand that aesthetic judgments are disinterested?

(2) What are the differences between the agreeable, the beautiful and the good?

(3) What's the difference between an idea and an ideal of beauty?

3. 讨论题

(1)你是如何理解审美判断的无利害性?

(2)快适、美以及善之间的区别是什么?

(3)理念和美的理想之间的区别是什么?

Chapter 4

1. Introduction to Hegel

Georg Wilhelm Friedrich Hegel (1770-1831) was a major figure in German idealism and classical aesthetics. At the end of the 18th century till the beginning of the 19th century, since Immanuel Kant, Hegel had proceeded the development of German classical aesthetics and literary theories to reach the climax of Western modern aesthetics and literary theories. Following Kant in philosophy, Hegel established a colossal system to comprehend the history of philosophy and the world surrounding us.

Hegel was born in Stuttgart in the Duchy of Württemberg in Germany. His father was secretary to the revenue office. Hegel's mother was the daughter of a lawyer at the High Court of Justice at the Württemberg court and was devoted to religious faith. Hegel studied in Tübinger Stift from 1788 to 1793, and developed sincere friendship with Hölderlin and Schelling. Hegel had been a tutor for several years after graduation. As a teacher at the University of Jena from 1801 to 1807, he accomplished the first edition of *Phenomenology of Spirit* (1807) and it was published officially. From

第4章

1. 黑格尔简介

乔治·威廉·弗里德里希·黑格尔(1770—1831)是德国唯心论哲学及古典美学的主要人物。18世纪末至19世纪初,黑格尔在康德之后,推动德国古典美学和文学理论继续发展,使之达到西方现代美学和文学理论的顶峰。哲学上,在追随康德哲学的基础上,黑格尔建立了一个庞大的体系来理解哲学的历史和我们身处的世界。

黑格尔出生于德国符腾堡公国首府斯图加特城。父亲是税务官,母亲是符腾堡法庭高级法院律师的女儿,一位虔诚的宗教徒。1788—1793年,他在图宾根神学院求学,与荷尔德林、谢林成为同窗挚友。毕业后,黑格尔做了几年家庭教师。1801—1807年,在耶拿大学任教期间,黑格尔完成了《精神现象学》(1807)第一版并正式出版。1808—1815年,黑格尔在纽伦堡任大学预科校长及哲学教师。1816年,他获得海德堡大学哲

1808 to 1815 Hegel was the headmaster and philosophy teacher at a gymnasium in Nuremberg. In 1816 he was appointed to a chair in philosophy at the University of Heidelberg. In 1818, he was the chair of philosophy at the University of Berlin, and in 1829, he was appointed the rector of the University.

学教授职位。1818年,他任柏林大学哲学教授,并于1829年任柏林大学校长。

Hegel's major publications include *Science of Logic* (1812, 1813, 1816), *Encyclopedia of the Philosophical Sciences* (1817), *Lectures on the Philosophy of Religion* (1832), *Lectures on the History of Philosophy* (1833), *Lectures on Aesthetics* (1835), and *Lectures on the Philosophy of History* (1837).

黑格尔的主要作品有《逻辑学》(1812, 1813, 1816)、《哲学全书》(1817)《宗教哲学讲演录》(1832)、《哲学史讲演录》(1833)、《美学讲演录》(1835)、《历史哲学讲演录》(1837)。

Hegel's aesthetics and literary theories are mainly expressed in *Lectures on Aesthetics* (1835), compiled by his student and colleague H. G. Hotho (1802-1873) at the University of Berlin. There are two well-known English translated versions, *The Philosophy of Fine Art* (1920) by F. P. B. Osmaston and *Aesthetics: Lectures on Fine Art* (1975) by T. M. Knox. Hegel's philosophy of art is a wide ranging account of beauty in art, the historical development of art, and the individual arts of architecture, sculpture, painting, music and poetry. It contains distinctive and influential analyses of Egyptian art, Greek sculpture, and ancient and modern tragedy, and is regarded by many as one of the greatest aesthetic theories to have been produced since Aristotle's *Poetics*.

黑格尔的美学思想和文艺理论主要见于《美学讲演录》(1835),由其柏林大学的学生和同事霍托(1802—1873)编撰出版。该书有两个有名的英译本:奥斯马斯顿版译名为《艺术哲学》(1920),诺克斯版译名为《美学:美学讲演录》(1975)。黑格尔的艺术哲学对艺术美进行了广泛的论述,梳理了艺术发展史,阐述了建筑、雕塑、绘画、音乐和诗歌五大艺术体系。它对埃及艺术、希腊雕塑、古典和现代悲剧的分析独特而影响深远,被认为是继亚里士多德《诗学》之后最伟大的艺术理论之一。

Hegel's theory of tragedy, like that of Aristotle, is an integral part of his whole philosophy. It is so basic a part of his system that it is found scattered throughout his works rather than contained in a single volume. Hegel thinks that the essence of tragedy is the diremption of the ethical substance and the reconciliation.

黑格尔的悲剧理论,与亚里士多德的一样,是他整个哲学体系不可分割的一部分。作为他哲学体系的基本部分,其悲剧理论遍布在他所有的著作中,而不只在一卷书中。黑格尔认为悲剧的实质是伦理实体的分裂与重新和解。

Hegel's theory of tragedy consists of three elements: a collision, a division of the ethical substance and the resolution of the collision. In

黑格尔的悲剧理论有三个构成要素:冲突、伦理实体的分裂、冲突

"Collision", Hegel points out three kinds of collision and illustrates them with vivid and detailed examples.

的和解。在"冲突"部分,黑格尔提出三种冲突并以生动翔实的例子阐释了这些冲突。

2. Selections from *Aesthetics: Lectures on Fine Art*

2.《美学》选文

Chapter Ⅲ The Beauty of Art or the Ideal①
(c) Collision

Georg Wilhelm Friedrich Hegel

第三章 艺术美,或理想(c) 冲突

乔治·威廉·弗里德里希·黑格尔

All the situations hitherto considered, are, as has already been touched upon, neither actions themselves nor, in general, stimuli to action proper. Their determinate character remains more or less a purely occasional state of affairs or an action insignificant in itself in which a substantial content is so expressed that its determinate character is now revealed as a harmless play which cannot be taken seriously. The seriousness and importance of the situation in its special character can only begin when its definiteness comes into prominence as an essential difference and, by being in opposition to something else, is the basis of a collision.

以上所说的一切情境,像我们已经约略指出的,本身既不是动作,一般也不是激发真正动作的原因。这些情境的定性仍然或多或少地只是纯粹机缘式的情况或是一种本身无意义的行为,其中一种有实体性的内容借此方式来表现:定性像是一种无害的游戏,用不着有真正的严肃性。只有在定性现出本质上的差异面,而且与另一面相对立,因而导致冲突的时候,情境才开始现出严肃性和重要性。

In this respect the collision has its basis in a transgression, which cannot remain as such but must be superseded; it is an alteration of the state of affairs which was otherwise harmonious and is itself to be altered. Nevertheless the collision is still not an action; on the contrary, it contains only the beginnings of an action and its presuppositions, and therefore, by being merely a stimulus to action, it retains the character of situation. Nevertheless, the opposition, in which the collision is disclosed, may be the result of an earlier action.

就这一点看来,冲突要有一种破坏作为它的基础,这种破坏不能持续,而必须被替代。它是对先前存在的和谐情况的一种改变,而这改变本身也在改变之中。尽管如此,冲突还不是动作,它只是包含着一种动作的开端和前提,因此,仅仅作为动作的刺激物,它保留情境的特性。尽管冲突所揭开的矛盾可能是前一个动作的结果。拿古希腊悲剧三部曲为例,

① Selected from Hegel's *Aesthetics: Lectures on Fine Art*, Vol. 1, translated by. T. M. Knox, Oxford: Clarendon Press, 1975.

For example, the trilogies of Greek tragedy are continuations, in the sense that out of the end of the first drama a collision arises for the second, which demands its resolution in the third.

从前一部剧本的结尾引出第二部的冲突,而这个冲突又要在第三部里得以解决。

Now since collision as such requires a solution which follows on the battle of opposites, a situation pregnant with collision is above all the subject-matter of dramatic art, the privilege of which is to represent beauty in its most complete and profound development; while sculpture, for example, is in no position to give complete configuration to an action which reveals the great spiritual powers in their conflict and reconciliation; and even painting, despite its wider scope, can never bring before our eyes more than one feature of the action.①

因为冲突一般都需要解决,作为两对立面斗争的结果,所以充满冲突的情境特别适宜于用作戏剧艺术的对象,戏剧艺术可以把美的最完满最深刻的发展表现出来。相反,雕塑却不能充分表现出可以显现伟大心灵力量的分裂与和解的那种动作;就连绘画,尽管它的范围是广阔的,也永远只能把动作的某一瞬间呈现出来。

But these serious situations bring with them a difficulty of their own already present in their nature. They rest on transgressions and give rise to circumstances which cannot subsist but necessitate a transforming remedy. But the beauty of the Ideal lies precisely in the Ideal's undisturbed unity, tranquility, and perfection in itself. Collision disturbs this harmony, and sets the Ideal, inherently a unity, in dissonance and opposition. Therefore, by the representation of such transgression, the Ideal is itself transgressed, and the task of art can lie here only, on the one hand, in preventing free beauty from perishing in this difference, and, on the other hand, in just presenting this disunion and its conflict, whereby out of it, through resolution of the conflict, harmony appears as a result, and in this way alone becomes conspicuous in its complete essentiality. But on the question of to what limit dissonance may be driven, no general specifications can be laid

这些具有悲剧意味的情境引发了处理它们固有概念时特有的困难。由于它们产生于世界情境的破坏之中,它们提供的考虑情形也是不能持续存在的,因此弥补性质的事物应用于转化它们。但是理想的美恰恰在于它自身未经打扰的统一性、静穆和自身完满。冲突破坏了这种和谐,使得理想的统一性成为不和、敌对状态。通过表现此种破坏,理想本身也遭受了破坏。艺术的功能一方面使得自由之美在这种差异中免于完全被破坏,一方面使得统一性与冲突的破坏产生的和谐作为此种冲突解决的结果而恢复。以这种方式,美的完美本质才能体现出来。然而,我们不可能基于一种普遍的原则,得出此种冲突受制于实行的具体限制,从而几种艺术方式可以在这方面保留它们独立的特性。例如,我们的内心思想

① 莱辛(Gotthold Ephraim Lessing,1729-1781)在《拉奥孔》(*Laocoon*: *An Essay on the Limits of Painting and Poetry*,1767)里的观点:造型艺术不像诗那样能叙述动作的过程,只能在动作时间里抓住某一时刻来表现。

down, because in this matter each particular art follows its own special character. Our inner ideas, for example, can endure far more dissonance than immediate intuition can. Poetry therefore has the right to proceed, in describing the inner feelings, almost to the extreme torment of despair, and, in describing the external world, to downright ugliness. But in the visual arts, in painting, and still more in sculpture, the external shape stands there fixed and permanent without being superseded and without vanishing again fleetingly, like musical notes. Here it would be a blunder to cling to the ugly when the ugly cannot be resolved. Therefore to the visual arts not everything can be allowed which can perfectly well be permitted to dramatic poetry, since it lets an ugly thing appear just for a moment and then vanish again.

比瞬间的直觉经得起更强烈的分裂。诗在描述内在感受时,甚至可以达到极端的绝望,而且它对外部对象的描述可以达到绝对的丑。造型艺术却是相反的,在绘画,甚至在雕塑中,外部形式保持着不可改变的固定性,也不会被消除,抑或像音符般被忽略而后再次出现。在此种情况下,彻底地表现丑将会成为严重的缺陷,而这也是不可能改变的。因此在戏剧诗中表现片刻的出现而后再次消失是十分可行的,但在造型艺术中则不然。

In examining the kinds of collision in more detail we can cite at this stage once again only the most general considerations. In this connection we must treat three main aspects:

在这里我们将对冲突最主要的类型展开最概括的讨论。我们将重点关注相互协调的三个基本方面:

(i) collisions which arise from purely physical or natural circumstances in so far as these are something negative, evil, and therefore disturbing;

(ii) spiritual collisions which rest on natural bases, which, although inherently positive, still bear in themselves for the spirit the possibility of differences and oppositions;

(iii) disunions which have their ground in spiritual differences and which alone are entitled to appear as the truly interesting oppositions, because they proceed from man's own act.

第一,由物理的或自然的情况所产生的冲突,这些情况本身是消极的、邪恶的,因而是有危害性的;

第二,由本身虽是积极的自然条件带来的心灵冲突,但是对于心灵,却带有差异对立的可能性。

第三,由心灵性的差异而产生的分裂,这才是真正重要的矛盾,因为它起源人所特有的行动。

(α) As for conflicts of the first kind, they can count only as mere occasions for action, because here it is only external nature with its illnesses and other evils and infirmities which produces circumstances disturbing the original harmony of life and with differences as a consequence. In and by themselves such collisions are void of interest and are given a place in art only on account of the

(α)关于第一种冲突,它们只能作为单纯的原因而发生作用,因为这里所涉及的只是外在的自然,以及自然所带来的疾病、罪孽和灾害,这些东西破坏了原来的生活和谐,结果造成差异对立。单就它们本身,这种冲突是没有意义的,之所以采用艺术的

disunions which may develop out of a natural misfortune as its consequence. So, for example, in the *Alcestis*① of Euripides, which provided the material too for Gluck's② *Alceste*, the foundation is the illness of Admetus. The illness as such is no material for genuine art, and it becomes so, even in Euripides, only owing to the individuals for whom this misfortune leads to a further collision. The oracle proclaims: Admetus must die unless a substitute is devoted to the underworld. Alcestis submits to this sacrifice and resolves to die in order to avert death from her husband, the father of her children, the King. In the *Philoctetes* of Sophocles too, it is a physical evil which is the basis of the collision. In their voyage to Troy the Greeks put the patient ashore on Lemnos because of his wounded foot, the result of a snake-bite at Chrysa. Here the physical misfortune is likewise only the most external point of connection and occasion for a further collision. For, according to the oracle, Troy is to fall only when the arrows of Hercules are in the hands of the besiegers. Philoctetes refuses to give them up because he has had to endure the wrong of being marooned for nine years full of agony. Now this refusal, like the wrong of being marooned in which it originated, could have been brought about in all sorts of other ways, and the real interest lies not in the illness and its physical distress but in the conflict which arises as a result of Philoctetes' decision not to give up the arrows.

The position is similar with the plague in the Greek camp before Troy, which, apart from being already represented as a consequence of earlier transgressions, is also represented as punishment. In general, after all, it pertains to epic poetry rather than dramatic to present disturbances and

题材,是因为自然灾害可以发展出心灵性的分裂,作为它的结果。例如,欧里庇得斯的悲剧《阿尔刻提斯》就以阿德墨托斯的病为前提,格鲁克的同名歌剧即取材于此剧。疾病本身并不足以为真正艺术的对象,欧里庇得斯采用它,只是因为它导致患者的进一步冲突。预言告诉阿德墨托斯,如果他找不到一个替身替他到阴间,他就必死。阿尔刻提斯自愿牺牲,决定替死,来挽救她的丈夫、她儿女的父亲和一国之君。索福克勒斯的悲剧《斐罗克特》的冲突也是以身体上的灾祸为基础。希腊人在远征特洛伊途中把斐罗克特放在勒姆诺斯岛上,因为他的脚在克里莎斯被一条毒蛇咬伤了。这里身体上的灾祸也只是进一步冲突的最远的原因和出发点。因为按照预言,只有赫拉克勒斯的箭落在攻城军的手里,特洛伊城才能打下,而斐罗克特却拒绝把这支箭交给他们,因为他们把他丢在勒姆诺斯岛上,让他遭受了整整九年的痛苦,很不公道。这个拒绝以及引起它的不公待遇可能产生各种不同的结果,因此真正的兴趣不在他的足疾和连带的痛苦,而在他拒绝交出箭时所引起的矛盾。

希腊军营的瘟疫也是如此,这在剧本里本来被看作从前一种罪过的结果,即看作一种惩罚。一般说来,追究风暴、沉船、旱灾之类自然灾祸的原因较适合于史诗而不适合于戏

① 传说阿尔刻提斯(Alcestis)是阿德墨托斯(Admetus)的妻子,丈夫生病必死,她到阴间做丈夫的替死鬼,后来被救回人间。欧里庇得斯(Euripides)借此传说创作。

② 格鲁克(Christoph Willibald Gluck,1714-1787),德国著名作曲家,创作多取材于希腊悲剧。

hindrances by means of a natural misfortune, a storm, a shipwreck, a drought, etc. But, on the whole, art does not represent such an evil as a pure accident, but as a hindrance and misfortune, the necessity of which assumes precisely this shape instead of another.

(β) But in so far as the external power of nature as such is not the essential thing in the interests and oppositions of the spiritual sphere, so, secondly, when it appears linked with spiritual matters, it emerges only as the ground on which collision proper leads to breach and disunion. In this class are all conflicts grounded in natural birth. Here in general we can distinguish three cases in more detail:

(αα) First, a right linked to nature, as, for example, kinship, right of inheritance, etc., which precisely because it is tied up with nature, immediately permits of a number of natural specifications while the right, the thing at issue, is unique. In this matter the most important example is the right of succession to the throne. If this right is to be the occasion for the sort of collisions in question here, then it must not be explicitly regulated and established yet, because otherwise the conflict at once becomes one of a totally different sort. I mean that if the succession is not yet established by positive laws and their valid organization, then it cannot be regarded as absolutely wrong if it is all one whether the elder or the younger brother or some other relative of the royal house is to rule. Now since ruling is something qualitative, and not quantitative like money and goods which, owing to their nature, can be divided with perfect justice, it follows that dissension and strife are present at once in the case of such unregulated succession. So, for example, when Oedipus leaves the throne without a ruler, his sons, the Theban pair, confront one another with the same rights and claims; the brothers adjust the

剧。总之,艺术对于灾祸,并不是把它只作为一种偶然事件来表现,而是把它作为一种阻碍和不幸事件来表现,这种阻碍和不幸事件按其必然性只能取这种形象而不能取另一种形象。

(β)其次,外在的自然力量,单就它是外在的自然力量来说,在心灵的旨趣和矛盾中不是本质的东西,所以在它和心灵的关系紧密结合时,它只是一种基础(或背景),使真正冲突导致破坏和分裂。凡是以自然的家庭出身为基础的冲突都属于这一类。这类约略可分为三种:

(αα)第一,与自然密切联系的权利,例如亲属关系、继承权之类,正因为这种权利是与自然性(或出身情况)相联系的,它就可以有杂多的自然定性,但是权利这个主要的东西,却只是单一的。这方面最主要的例子是王位继承权。作为这一类冲突的原因,这种继承权不应该是明白规定的,否则冲突就会属于另一类型。如果这种继承权还没有由法律明文和它所代表的社会秩序加以规定,哥哥、弟弟,或是皇室的其他亲属就都可以继承统治权,谁继承都不能被看作违法。因为统治权关乎质不关乎量,不像金钱和货物那样可以很公平地分摊,所以总不免引起争执和纠纷。例如俄狄浦斯死了,没有指定继承人,他的两个儿子就都有同样的继承权,他们约定逐年轮流居王位,其中艾提阿克理斯破坏了约定,于是波吕尼刻斯就带兵打忒拜,来维护他的权利。弟兄间的仇恨在各时代都是艺术中的一个突出的冲突,从《旧约》里该隐杀死他的兄弟亚伯就已开始

matter by arranging to rule in alternate years, but Eteocles broke the agreement and Polynices returned to Thebes to fight for his right. The enmity of brothers as such is a collision which crops up in every period of art: it begins with Cain① who slew Abel. Also in the *Shahnameh*, the earliest Persian hero-book, the starting-point for all sorts of battles is a dissension about succession to the throne. Feridu divided the earth between his three brothers. Salm received Rum and Khavar; Thur's share was Turan and Jin; and Iraj was to rule over the land of Iran. But each makes claims over the territory of the other and the resulting dissensions and wars are without end. In the Christian Middle Ages too the stories of dissensions in families and dynasties are without number. But such discords appear in themselves as accidental; for it is not absolutely necessary for brothers to be at enmity. Special circumstances and loftier causes must be added, as for example the hateful birth of the sons of Oedipus②, or as too in *The Braut von Messina*③ an attempt is made to ascribe the quarrel of the brothers to a loftier fate. In Shakespeare's *Macbeth*④ the basis is a similar collision. Duncan is King, Macbeth is his next eldest relative and is therefore strictly heir to the throne even in preference to Duncan's sons. And so the first inducement to Macbeth's crime is the wrong done to him by the King in naming his own son as his successor. This justification of Macbeth, drawn from Chronicles, is altogether omitted by Shakespeare, because his only aim was to bring out the dreadfulness of Macbeth's passion, in order to

了。在波斯最早的英雄故事《夏拿墨》里,王位的争夺也是许多斗争的出发点。斐里杜把土地分给三弟兄,色尔姆分得腊姆和查维尔,屠尔分得都兰和德金,伊越基则统治伊朗。但是三人都要争夺弟兄间的土地,于是就酿成无穷的纠纷和战争。在基督教的中世纪,家族和王朝的纷争故事也是说不完的。但是这种纠纷本是偶然的,弟兄互相敌视的事情本身并无绝对必然性,所以这种纠纷还必须有别的情况和更基本的原因,例如俄狄浦斯的两个儿子的诞生本身就很不祥,或是像在《麦西纳的新娘》里,席勒设法把两弟兄的争执归咎于较高的命运。莎士比亚的《麦克白》也以同样的冲突为基础。邓肯是国王,麦克白是他的最近而且最年长的亲属,所以在王位继承上他比邓肯的儿子还有优先权。但是邓肯却指定他的儿子继承王位,这件不公正的事是造成麦克白罪行的最初原因。麦克白的这一点可辩护的理由在编年史里是载明了的,但是莎士比亚却把它完全抛开,因为他的目的是要展示麦克白欲望的可怕,来讨好英王詹姆士,把麦克白写成一个罪犯,才符合英王的利益。因此,按照莎士比亚的处理方式,我们找不到理由来说明麦克白不杀邓肯的儿子们而让他们逃走,贵族们也没有想到这件事。但是《麦克白》这个剧本的全部冲突已经超过了我们现在所

① 该隐杀死亚伯,受神刑罚。《创世记》第四章。

② 俄狄浦斯在不知不觉中娶了自己的母亲,生下了这俩兄弟。

③ 《麦西纳的新娘》(*The Bride of Messina*),席勒的作品,模仿希腊悲剧而写成。麦西纳王后在临产前,有人预言生下来的孩子将会致两个哥哥于死命,因此生下女儿后,王后将女儿藏匿起来。女儿长大后,两个哥哥不知道她的出身,争着要娶她,结果两个都送了命。

④ 麦克白谋杀国王篡位,后国王邓肯的两个儿子出兵报仇,麦克白发疯自尽。

make a bow to King James who must have been interested in seeing Macbeth represented as a criminal! Thus, according to Shakespeare's treatment of the subject, there is no reason why Macbeth did not murder Duncan's sons too, but let them escape, and why none of the nobles thought of them. But the whole collision on which *Macbeth* turns is already beyond the situation-stage which was our subject here.

谈的这个阶段的情境范围了。

(ββ) Now, secondly, the converse within this sphere consists in this, that differences of birth, which in themselves involve a wrong, are given by custom or law the power of an unsurmountable barrier, so that they appear as a wrong that has become natural, as it were, and they therefore give rise to collisions. Slavery, serfdom, castes, the position of Jews in many states, and, in a certain sense, even the opposition between the birth of nobles and commoners, are to be reckoned in this group. Here the conflict lies in the fact that, while the man has rights, relationships, wishes, aims, and requirements which belong to him by the nature of man, these are stemmed by one or other of the above-mentioned differences of birth as a natural force obstructing them or endangering them. On this sort of collision the following is to be said.

(ββ)这类冲突的第二种情境与上述我们谈论过的恰恰相反,其中作为一种本身就有失公平,由于习俗和法律的影响,出身的差异变成了不可克服的界限,好像已经成为一种习以为常的不平之事,而成为冲突的原因。奴隶地位、农奴地位、等级上的差别、犹太人在许多国家中的处境,贵族和市民的相反出身都可以归为这一种。这类冲突在于这一事实方面,即从人的本性看,人应具有权利、关系、欲望、目的和要求,而由于上述的出身差别中的某一种关系,它们受到了一种自然力量的阻碍和危害。关于此种类型的冲突,我们将做出以下评价。

Differences between classes, between rulers and ruled, etc., are of course essential and rational, for they have their basis in the necessary articulation of the whole life of the state, and they are validated everywhere by the specific kind of occupation, turn of mind, disposition, and the whole of spiritual development. But it is another thing if these differences in respect of individuals are to be so determined by birth that the individual is from the beginning to be relegated, not by his own doing, but by the accident of nature, to some class or caste irrevocably.

阶级的差别,统治者与被统治者的差别等等当然是重要的而且是合理的,这些差别根源在于国家全部生活所必有的分工组织,它们在职业、方向、思想方式和整个精神文化各方面都可以体现。但是如果将每个人的差别都用出身地位来决定,而他们不是由于自己,而是由于自然中的某种偶然,被抛到某一阶级或等级,且无法改变,这就不能应用上述的看法,说是合理的了。

In that event these differences prove to be

因为在这种情况下,这些差别本

purely natural and yet they are invested with a supreme determining might. How this fixity and power originated does not matter at present. For the nation may originally have been one, and the natural difference between free men and serfs, for example, may only have developed later, or the difference of castes, classes, privileges, etc., may have arisen from differences of nation and race, as has been maintained in relation to the caste system in India. For us here this is of no consequence; the chief point lies only in the fact that such relationships of life, regulating the whole being of man, are supposed to derive their origin from nature and birth. Of course, in the nature of the case, difference of class is to be regarded as justified, but at the same time the individual should not be deprived of his right to align himself of his own free will with this or that class. Aptitude, talent, skill and education alone have to lead to a decision in this matter and to decide it. But if the right of choice is annulled from the very beginning by birth, and if therefore a man is made dependent on nature and its fortuitousness, then within this lack of freedom a conflict may arise between (a) the position assigned to a man by his birth and (b) his different measure of spiritual education and its just demands. This is a melancholy and unfortunate collision, for it rests entirely on a wrong which true free art has not to respect. In our contemporary situation, class differences, a small group excepted, are not tied to birth. The sole exception is the ruling dynasty and the peerage, for higher reasons grounded in the essential nature of the state itself. This apart, birth makes no essential difference in relation to the class which an individual can or wishes to enter. But on this account after all we at once link with the demand for this perfect freedom the further demand that the individual shall, in education, knowledge, skill, and disposition make himself equal to the class to

来只是从自然产生来的,却具有最大的力量去决定个人命运。这种阶级差别的固定性和威力是怎样来的,不在我们现在讨论的范围之内。一国人民可能本来是整体的,到后来才形成自由人与奴隶之类出身差别;等级、阶级、特权者之类差别也可能缘于民族与种族的差别,例如,印度的等级就有人以为是这样来的。这对于我们是无关宏旨的。要点在于这类支配个人整个生命的生活关系(社会关系)是由自然产生的地位来决定的。按照事物的概念来看,阶级的差别当然是有理由可辩护的,但是个人凭借自由意志去决定自己属于这个或那个阶级的权利却不应该被剥夺。只有资禀、才能、适应能力和教育才有资格在这方面做出决定。如果一个人从出生起就被剥夺这种选择的权利,他因此就被迫服从自然和它的偶然性,在这种不自由的情况之下,就可能造成(a)由出身而定的个人地位,(b)他的精神文化及其连带的合理要求间的冲突。这是一种悲惨的、不幸的冲突,因为它来自一种不公平,这种不公平不是真正自由的艺术所应敬重的。按照我们现代的情况,除了少数人以外,阶级差别与出身地位是无关的。只有处于统治地位的王室和贵族才是例外,这是基于国家本质较高层面的理由。对于其余的人来说,出身与阶级差别没有本质的关系,每个人可以按他的能力和意愿进入某一个阶级。因此我们把这种完全自由的要求与更高要求结合,即个人的教养、知识、能力和思想能符合他所选择的阶级。如果一个人的精神能力和活动满足某一阶级的要求,但他的出身地位却成

which he aspires. But if birth places an unsurmountable obstacle to the claims which a man, without this restriction, could satisfy by his own spiritual force and activity, then this counts for us not only as a misfortune but essentially as a wrong which he suffers. A purely natural and in itself unjust wall, over which his spirit, talent, feeling, inner and outer education have lifted him, separates him from what he was capable of attaining, and something natural, consolidated by caprice alone into this legal provision, presumes to set insuperable barriers to the inherently justified freedom of the spirit.

为一种不可逾越的障碍,这对我们来说,不只是一种不幸,而在本质上是一种他所遭受的冤屈。一堵纯属自然但本身不合理的墙把他挡住了,他的精神、才能、情感和内外的修养本使他可以越过这堵墙,可是他却被阻隔无法获得他本来有能力获得的东西,这种自然情况是由人的任意武断加以合法固定的,为本身合理的心灵自由设下了不可逾越的障碍。

Now in the more detailed appreciation of such a collision, the essential points are these:

进一步估计这种冲突,我们可以看到以下三个主要的方面:

First, the individual with his spiritual qualities must already have actually overstepped the natural barrier and its power which his wishes and aims are meant to surmount, or otherwise his demand is over again just a folly. If, for example, a lackey with only a lackey's education and skill falls in love with a princess or a lady of high degree, or she with him, such a love affair is only absurd and ridiculous, even if the representation of this passion comprises all the depth and full interest of the glowing heart. For in this instance it is not the difference of birth which really separates the parties, but the whole range of higher interests, broader education, aims in life, and modes of feeling which cuts a lackey off from a woman highly placed in class, means, and social position. If love is the one point of union, and does not also draw into itself the remaining scope of what a man has to experience in accordance with his spiritual education and the circumstances of his class, it remains empty and abstract, and touches only the sensuous side of life. To be full and entire, it would have to be connected with the entirety of the rest of the mind, with the full nobility of disposition and interests.

第一,个人必须以他的精神素质超越这种自然界限,使自然界限的力量屈服于他的愿望和目的,否则他的要求便是愚蠢的。比如,如果一个仆人只是拥有仆人的知识和才能,却爱上了贵族社会的公主或小姐,或者相反地,公主或小姐爱上了他,那么这种爱情便是荒谬且低级趣味的,即使这种激情在艺术表现中是深沉而热烈的。在这种情况下,出生地位的差别并没有构成障碍,而真正能将一位在地位、财产及社会条件上高高在上的小姐与仆人之间分隔开的是更高的兴致、更广泛的教育、生活目的以及情感方式。如果爱情是双方结合的唯一纽带,而不考虑其所在阶级的精神教养和社会关系所应有的生活方式,那么它就是空洞的和抽象的,只关乎感官而已。爱情要达到完满,就必须达到完全自觉的生命的真正和谐,并分享和欣赏全然高贵的情感。

The second case, in this context, consists in this, that dependence on birth is imposed as a legally obstructive shackle on the inherently free spirit and its justified aims. This collision too has something unaesthetic in itself which contradicts the Concept of the Ideal, however popular it may be and however readily art may have a notion to make use of it. If, that is to say, differences of birth are made into a definite wrong by positive laws and their validity, as, for example, birth as a pariah, a Jew, etc., it is in a way a perfectly correct view if a man in the freedom of his inner being, rebelling against such an obstacle, regards these laws as dissoluble and knows himself free from them. To fight them seems therefore to be absolutely justified. Now in so far as, owing to the power of existing circumstances, such barriers become unsurmountable and are consolidated into an invincible necessity, this can only afford a situation of misfortune and one inherently false. For the reasonable man must bow to necessity, when he has not the means to subdue its force, i.e. he must not react against it but must bear the inevitable calmly and patiently; the interest and need demolished by such a barrier he must sacrifice, and so what is insuperable he must endure with the still courage of passivity and tolerance. Where battle is of no avail, a reasonable man is quit of it so that he can at least withdraw into the formal independence of subjective freedom. In that event the might of wrong has no might at all over him, while he at once experiences his utter dependence if he opposes it. Yet neither this abstraction of a purely formal independence nor this futile snatching at victory is really beautiful.

第二种情形是出身地位的依存性成了一种法定的起妨碍作用的枷锁,套在本身自由的心灵以及它的正当的目标上。这种冲突并不适应于艺术审美,而且与理想的概念也是相悖的,尽管人们乐于采用也便于采用这种冲突。如果出身地位的差别通过正规的法律及其效力变成一种固定的冤屈,例如,生为贱民或者犹太人,那么,从这一方面来看,显而易见他完全可以有权利凭借自己内在生命的所有能量来抵抗此种阻碍,并且消除它,从而在隔离的过程中认识自我。抵抗此种障碍看似完全合理,但是出于目前的状况,克服此种障碍已然成为不可能,并且转化为不可克服的必然状态,这种状态只能被当作一种不幸,具有固有的错误性。而且理性的人无法征服此种对立的必然性,他会不可避免地被迫屈服于此:即不再抵抗这种不可避免的障碍,而只能静默地任其凌驾之上。他必须放弃兴趣和需求的意识,用被动忍受的静默勇气来接受这种障碍。在斗争产生不了作用的时候,合理的方法就是放弃斗争,这样至少可以恢复主体形式的独立自主性。如此一来,那种错误对他而言就起不了作用;反之,如果他硬要抵抗,就必然感受到他所受的限制。然而,无论是抽象形式的独立,还是无结果的斗争,都不能真正算得上美。

A third case, directly connected with the second, is equally remote from the genuine Ideal. It consists in this, that individuals whose birth has given them a really valid privilege owing to religious regulations, positive laws, or social

第三种冲突的类型,与第二种是密切相关的,也是一样远离于真正的理想。在这种情形下,个人从出身地位、宗教条文、国家法律和社会习惯

circumstances, uphold their privilege and wish to insist on it. For in that event independence is there, according to the reality of external and positive law, but, as the subsistence of what is inherently unjust and irrational, it is a false and purely formal independence, and the Concept of the Ideal has vanished. Of course one could suppose that the Ideal is preserved, on the ground that even subjective life goes hand in hand with the universal and the legal, and remains in consistent unity therewith; yet, in this case, on the one hand the universal does not have its force and might in this individual, as the Ideal of the heroic requires, but only in the public authority of the positive laws and their administration; on the other hand, what the individual claims is just a wrong and he therefore lacks that substantiality which, as we have seen, likewise is implicit in the Concept of the Ideal. The concern of the ideal individual must be inherently true and justified. What is relevant here is, for example, the legal dominion over slaves and serfs, the right to rob foreigners of their freedom, or to sacrifice them to the gods, and so on.

得到某种特权,他就要求享受这种特权。按照实在的和外在现实情况来说,独立是存在的,但是它本身是非正义的、不合理的,所以是一种虚伪的、纯粹形式的独立,艺术理想的概念也就此消失了。毫无疑问,我们很可能劝说自己,理想会得以保持,因为我们作为主体按照普遍法律行事,并与其处于统一之中。但是我们也可以看出普遍法律对特定的人起不了根本的作用,就像我们发现英雄理想所需要的那样,在于国家权力,即实际法律和执行上面;其次,当事人所要求享受的是一种非正义的事,这就失去了我们所提到的艺术理想所应具备的实体性质。艺术的理想主体本身必须本质上是正确并且合理的。对于奴隶和农奴法定的统治权,剥夺外国人的自由或是用他们的牺牲来献神的权利等都属于这种情况。

It is true that such a right can be pursued by individuals innocently, in the belief that they are defending their valid right, as in India, for example, the higher castes take advantage of their privileges, or as Thoas ordered the sacrifice of Orestes, or as in Russia the masters rule their serfs; indeed those in authority may wish to assert rights of this kind as right and legal because of their own interest in them. But in that case their right is only the unrighteous right of barbarism, and they themselves look, in our eyes at least, like barbarians who resolve on and carry out what is absolute injustice. The legality on which the subject relies is to be respected and justified for his time and its spirit and level of civilization, but for us it has through and through been merely laid down

要求这种权利的人当然自以为是维护正当的权利,例如,在印度属于较高级别的人要利用特权,托阿斯命令把俄瑞斯忒斯杀死献神,以及俄国地主鞭挞他们的农奴之类;事实上,那些高高在上的人们都认为这些符合他们自身利益的事就是合法的权利。但他们的权利只是野蛮人一种不正义的权利,因而他们自己规定并实行这种不正义的事,至少在我们看来,也就显得多少有些像野蛮人了。这些人所依据的法律以他们的时代精神以及教养标准来看,都是应当受到尊重和维护的,但是对于我们而言,它彻头彻尾只是一种规定罢了,并无道理和力量。如若当事人仅

without validity or power. Now if the legally privileged individual just uses his right for his own private ends, from a particular passion and selfish intentions, we have before us not just barbarism but a bad character into the bargain.

从个人情欲和自私动机出发,利用其特权去达到个人目的,那么他就不仅是个野蛮人,而且品格也堪称恶劣。

Through such conflicts attempts have often been made to arouse pity, and even fear as well, according to the law of Aristotle who lays it down that fear and pity are the aim of tragedy; but we entertain neither fear nor awe in the presence of the power of such rights accruing from barbarism and the misfortune of the times, and the pity that we might feel changes at once into repugnance and indignation.

根据亚里士多德把恐惧和同情作为悲剧对象的原则,诗人常常通过展现这种冲突来激发我们的同情,甚至是恐惧。但当我们遭遇只存在于野蛮人和未开化时代不幸情况的特权时,我们体会到的既不是恐惧,也不是尊敬,我们可能感到的同情会立即转化成愤怒和敌意。

The only true issue of such a conflict can therefore consist solely in the fact that these false rights are not finally asserted, as for example when neither Iphigenia nor Orestes is sacrificed in Aulis① and among the Tauri.

这种冲突在艺术上唯一真正的终结便是,我们会发现这种不合法的权利并未实现,就如伊菲革涅娅没有在奥里斯牺牲,俄瑞斯忒斯也并未在陶里斯牺牲。

(γγ) Now, finally, a last element in collisions which derive their basis from natural conditions is subjective passion when it rests on natural foundations of character and temperament. The best example of this is Othello's jealousy. Ambition, avarice (and love too indeed to some extent) are examples of the same sort. But these passions lead to collisions of substance only in so far as they induce individuals who are gripped and dominated by the exclusive power of such a feeling to turn against what is genuinely moral and absolutely justified in human life, and who consequently fall into a conflict of a profounder kind.

(γγ)依据于纯粹自然情境的第三种也是最后一种类型的冲突是由性情和品质的自然特性而引发的个人情感。其中最显著的例子是奥塞罗的妒忌。野心、贪婪(某种程度来说,爱情也是)都属于这一类型。但是这些情感只有在下列情况下,才能引发真正的冲突,从而使得完全受这种情感支配的人违反了真正的道德,以及人类存在中本质合理的进程,从而导致一种更严重的冲突。

This leads us to consider a third chief kind of dissension, namely that which has its proper ground in spiritual forces and their variance, in so far as this opposition is called up by the deed of the

这就使我们开始探究冲突原始分类的第三种主要形式,这类冲突主要依据精神力量的冲突,因为此种对

① 出自古希腊悲剧作家埃斯库罗斯(Aeschylus)的《阿伽门农》(*Agamemnon*)。伊菲革涅娅、俄瑞斯忒斯注释参见第2章相关注释。

man himself.

(γ) It has already been noticed above in relation to purely natural collisions that they form only the connecting point for further oppositions. The same is more or less true of conflicts in the second category also considered just now. In works of art of more profound interest, none of these stops at the antagonism hitherto indicated; they introduce such disturbances and oppositions only as the occasion out of which the absolute spiritual powers of life are presented in their difference from one another and their struggle with one another. But the spiritual realm can only be activated by spirit, and so spiritual differences must also win their actuality by man's act in order to be able to come on the scene in their proper shape.

立是人类活动的结果。

(γ)在上述讨论纯粹自然的冲突时,我们提到它们只是构成进一步冲突的起点。这一点多多少少也同样适用于刚讨论过的第二类冲突。在具有更深刻意义的艺术作品中,这些冲突都无法保持我们上述的对立形式。这些干扰和冲突元素只是证实了这种恰当的时刻,精神生活真正本质的力量在差异中是互相对立,互相斗争的。精神领域只有通过精神才能激活。因此,精神方面的差异也必须从人的行动中得到实现,才能显现于它们所特有的形象。

Thus now we have, on the one hand, a difficulty, an obstacle, a transgression brought about by an actual human deed; on the other hand, a transgression of absolutely justified interests and powers. Only both of these characteristics taken together are the basis of the depth of this final kind of collision.

因此,一方面我们须有一种由人的某种现实行动所引起的困难、障碍和破坏;另一方面须有本身合理的旨趣和力量所受到的伤害。只有把这两方面定性结合在一起,才会有这最后一种冲突的根源。

The chief cases which can occur in this sphere may be distinguished as follows:

在这一范围可能出现的主要例子可以分为以下几类:

(αα) While we are now only just beginning to leave the province of those conflicts which have their foundation in nature, the first case of this new sort still stands in connection with the earlier ones. But if human action is to be the ground of the collision, then the natural result produced by man, otherwise than by man as spirit, consists in the fact that unknowingly and unintentionally he has done something which later proves in his own eyes to have been a transgression of ethical powers essentially to be respected. The consciousness of his deed, which he acquires later, then drives him on, through this previously unconscious transgression, into dissension and contradiction with himself, once he imputes the transgression to

(αα)当我们开始离开依据于自然的那一类冲突的范围时,我们将要讨论的这类新的冲突与前面所讲的冲突仍是相连的。但是这种冲突依据于人类行动的自然性,而不是其精神,就是说,人不自觉地、无意地做了某一件事,后来他才认识到那件事在本质上破坏了某种应受尊重的道德力量。后来他对自己的行动有了认识,承认他原先没有认识到的那种破坏行为还是出于他自己,这样,他就被迫进入分裂和矛盾。这类冲突的根源在于行动开展时的意识和目的与随后对行动本质的认识之间的矛

himself as caused by him. The antagonism between his consciousness and intention in his act and the later consciousness of what the act really was constitutes here the basis of the conflict. Oedipus and Ajax can count here as examples for us. Oedipus's act, so far as his will and knowledge went, consisted in the fact that he had slain a stranger in a quarrel; but it was what was unknown that was the actual and essential deed, namely the murder of his own father. Ajax, conversely, in a fit of frenzy slaughters the cattle of the Greeks, believing them to be the Greek princes. Then when, with awakened consciousness, he considers what has happened, he is gripped by shame at his deed, and this produces collision. What, in a way like this, a man has unintentionally transgressed must yet be something which essentially and in accordance with his reason he has to honour and regard as sacrosanct. If, on the other hand, this reverence and veneration is a mere opinion and false superstition, then for us at least such a collision can no longer have any deeper interest.

盾。俄狄浦斯和阿雅斯可以作为我们的例子。俄狄浦斯的行动,如果仅就他的目的和知识而言,也仅仅是他在一次争斗中杀害了一个完全陌生的人。但是他的这个行动本身却是在不知不觉中杀了自己的父亲,这是确凿无疑的。阿雅斯在一阵狂怒中,杀死希腊军队的牛,并坚信它们是希腊的将领们。他在恢复意识后,意识到自己的所作所为,为之羞愧难当,于是陷入了自身的冲突之中。然而,我们必须意识到,在冲突之中被人类无意破坏的必须是他在理性判断时所骄傲并敬重的。如果这种敬重只是出于一种无根据的见解和错误的迷信,那么至少对我们来说,这种冲突根本引发不了真正深刻的兴趣。

(ββ) But now since, in the kind of conflict we are concerned with at present, a spiritual transgression of spiritual powers is to come about through a man's deed, then, secondly, the collision more appropriate to this sphere consists in a transgression which is known and which issues from this knowledge and the intention involved. The starting-point may here too once again be passion, violence, folly, etc. The Trojan war, for example, has its beginning in the abduction of Helen; next, Agamemnon proceeds to sacrifice Iphigenia and thereby commits a transgression against her mother because he kills the dearest fruits of her womb; Clytemnestra therefore slays her husband; Orestes, because she has murdered his father, the King, takes revenge by the death of his mother. Similarly, in *Hamlet* the father is treacherously sent to his grave, and Hamlet's mother defames the shades of

(ββ)然而,因为我们现在所讨论的冲突来源于人类行为的精神力量的精神性破坏之中,那么更适用于这种冲突应来自于有意识的,并且是由这类意识和目的引发的破坏之中。这里的出发点还可以再次集中于激情、暴力、愚蠢及其他类似的特性之中。例如特洛伊战争缘起海伦被抢夺。阿伽门农牺牲了伊菲革涅娅,因而伤害了其母亲的感情,因为伊菲革涅娅是她这辈子的最爱。克吕泰涅斯特拉因此谋杀了她的丈夫。俄瑞斯忒斯为了给他的国王父亲复仇而杀害了他的母亲。同样类似的还有《哈姆雷特》,其中父亲被暗算而死,他母亲却很快嫁给了谋杀者,从而侮辱了死者的魂灵。

the dead by an almost immediate marriage with the murderer.

Even in the case of these collisions the chief point is still that what is fought against is something absolutely ethical, sacrosanct, and genuine which the man has roused against himself by his act. Were this not so, then for us, in so far as we have a consciousness of the genuinely ethical and sacrosanct, such a conflict would be without value and substance, as, for instance, in the familiar episode in the *Mahabharata*①, Nala and Damayanti. King Nala had married Damayanti, the prince's daughter, who had had the privilege of choosing of her own accord amongst her suitors. The other claimants hover as genii in the air. Nala alone stands on the earth, and Damayanti had the good taste to select him. Now on this account the genii are angered and they keep a watch on King Nala. But for many years afterwards they could bring nothing against him, because he was not guilty of any offence. But at last they win power over him because he commits a great crime by making water and treading on the ground thus urine-infected. According to Indian ideas this is a serious offence which cannot escape punishment. Hereafter the genii have him in their power; one instills into him the desire for play; the other provokes his brother to be his opponent; and Nala must at last, losing his throne, wander unarmed with Damayanti into misery. At length he has to endure even separation from her, until in the end, after numerous adventures, he is raised once more to his former good fortune. The real conflict, on which the whole thing turns, is only for the ancient Indians an essential transgression of something sacrosanct. In our eyes it is nothing but an

在这些事例的冲突中,要点在于当事人所力争追求的对象本身是道德的、神圣的、真实的。如果不是如此,我们就觉得这种冲突没有什么价值,没有什么真实性,因为我们对真正的道德和神圣有所认识,人们所熟悉的《摩诃婆罗多》中那罗和达摩衍蒂的插话就是个反例。国王那罗和达摩衍蒂公主结了婚。这位公主本来有权在求婚者之中作出自由选择。其他的求婚者都是在空中飘荡的神怪,只有那罗站在地上,她很有见地,就选择了他。神怪们因此怀恨在心,瞄准机会想谋害那罗。过了许多年,他们都找不出他的岔子,因为他没有做什么坏事。但是他们终于得到制伏他的权力,因为他犯了一宗大罪过,在小便之后,用脚践踏了尿湿了的土地。按照印度人的观念,这是一种不能免于刑罚的重罪。从此以后,神怪们就把他掌握在自己的权力之下,一神怪引发他嬉戏的欲念,另一神怪怂恿他的弟兄去反对他,终于逼得那罗丧失王位,和达摩衍蒂过起流离困苦的生活。最后他又被迫和她分离,经历了许多奇遇之后,才恢复到原来幸福的状态。这整篇故事所环绕的真正冲突,对于古代印度人来说,是一种对于神圣事物的真正的亵渎,但是对于我们的意识来说,却是一种荒诞不经的事。

① *Mahabharata*:《摩诃婆罗多》是著名印度史诗,与《罗摩衍那》(*Ramayana*)并列为印度的两大史诗。《那罗传》(Nala and Damayanti)是《摩诃婆罗多》第 3 篇《森林篇》中一个著名的插话。黑格尔对此插话的分析出于西方美学观,未必符合东方美学观。

absurdity.

(γγ) But, thirdly, the transgression need not be direct, i.e., it is not necessary for the deed as such, taken by itself, to be productive of collision; it only becomes such owing to the known relations and circumstances within which it is done and which work against it and contradict it. Romeo and Juliet, for example, love one another; in love as such no transgression is inherent; but they know that their families live in hatred and enmity with one another, that the parents will never consent to their marriage, and they get into a collision owing to this presupposed ground of antagonism.

In relation to the specific situation, as contrasted with the general state of the world, these most general remarks may suffice. If one wished to consider, and go through, all its aspects, shades, and nuances, and assess every possible kind of situation, then this chapter alone would provide an occasion for discussions of endless prolixity. For the invention of different situations has an inexhaustible wealth of possibilities, and then the essential question always is of their applicability to a specific art, depending on its genus and species. To fairy-tales, for example, much is allowed which would be forbidden to another mode of treatment and representation. But in general the invention of the situation is after all an important point which commonly presents great difficulty to artists. In particular we hear today the frequent complaint about the difficulty of finding the right material from which the situations and circumstances are to be drawn. In this connection, at first sight it may seem to suit the dignity of a poet better to be original and to invent situations by himself. Yet this sort of originality is not an essential matter. For the situation does not in itself constitute what is spiritual, or the artistic form proper; it affects only the external material in which and on which a character and temperament is to be unfolded and

(γγ)第三,破坏并不一定是直接的,这就是说,一种行动单就它本身来看,并不一定就是一个引起冲突的行动,但是由于它发生的那些跟它对立矛盾的而且是已知的关系和情境,它就变成一种引起冲突的行动。例如,罗密欧与朱丽叶相爱,这爱情本身并没有破坏什么;但是他们认识到双方家庭是互相仇恨的,双方父母都不会允许他们结婚,由于这种原已假定存在的分裂,他们就陷入冲突了。

关于一般世界情况和具体情境的差别,以上所说的一些最概括的话就够了。如果要把这种研究推广到这个问题的各个方面,各种变化和细微差别,并且对于每一种可能的情境都加以讨论,那么,单是这一章就会牵涉无限的枝节问题上去。因为可能发现的不同情境是无穷的,而在每一事例中问题都在于怎样使某一具体情境应用于某一具体艺术的体裁和表现方式。例如,童话所能表现的是其他艺术种类处理和表现方式所不允许的。一般说来,发现情境是一项重点工作,对于艺术家往往也是一件难事。特别在现代,人们常听到一种抱怨,说找适当的题材来组成背景和情境有多么困难。第一眼看来,诗人如果有独创性,能自己去创造情境,他就会显得更有价值。但是这种独创性并不是艺术的主要方面,因为情境本身还不是灵性的东西,还不能组成真正的艺术形象,它只涉及一个人物性格和心境所揭露和表现的外在材料。只有把这种外在的起点刻画成动作和性格,才能表现出真正的艺术本领。所以如果诗人自己创造

represented. Only by elaborating this external starting-point into actions and characters is genuine artistic activity evinced. Therefore we cannot thank the poet at all for having manufactured this inherently unpoetic aspect by himself; he must remain entitled to create always anew from what is already there, from history, saga, myths, chronicles, indeed even from materials and situations previously elaborated artistically; as, in painting, the external element in the situation is drawn from legends of the saints and often enough repeated in a similar way. In the case of such representation the strictly artistic production lies far deeper than in inventing specific situations.

出这本身非诗的一方面,我们用不着为此感谢他;应该允许他取材于现成的历史、传说、神话、编年纪事乃至于早已被艺术家运用过的旧材料和情境,并且他应该经常能推陈出新;例如,在绘画里,外在的情境都是从宗教传说中来的,通常是用类似的方式重复来重复去的。在这种表现中能看出真正艺术创造,比起发现某种情境来,要深刻得多。

The same is true too of the wealth of circumstances and complications that have been presented to us. In this connection modern art has often enough been praised on the ground that, in comparison with antiquity, it displays an infinitely more fruitful imagination, and in fact in the works of art of the Middle Ages too and the modern world there is the maximum variety and diversity of situations, incidents, events, and fates. But with this external abundance nothing is achieved. In spite of it, we have only a few excellent dramas and epic poems. For the chief thing is not the external march and turn of events, as if these, as events and histories, exhausted the stuff of the work of art, but the ethical and spiritual configuration and the great movements of temperament and character which are disclosed and unveiled through the process of this configuration.

这个道理也适用于许多已经运用过的各种情境和情节。在这方面人们往往为现代艺术吹嘘,说它比起古代艺术来,更能表现出无穷的丰富想象,事实上中世纪和近代的艺术作品也的确表现出最丰富多彩的变化和最多的情境、事迹和结局。但是这种外在情境的丰富并不算什么。尽管有丰富的情境,卓越的戏剧和史诗在现代还是很少。因为艺术的要务不在事迹的外在经过和变化,这些事迹和故事有可能会耗尽艺术作品的内容;艺术的要务在于它的伦理和心灵性的表现,以及通过这种表现过程而揭露出来的心境和性格的巨大波动。

If we glance now at the point from which we must proceed further, we see that, on the one hand, the external and inner specific circumstances, states of affairs, and relations become the situation only through the heart, the passion, which views them and maintains itself in them. On the other hand, as we saw, the situation in its specific character is differentiated into

现在我们且来回顾一下我们已经达到的原则,把它作为进一步研究的出发点,我们一方面可以看到:内在的和外在的有定性的环境、情况和关系要变成艺术所用的情境,只有通过它们所引起的心情或情绪才行得通,另一方面我们也可以看到:情境在定性之中分化为矛盾、障碍、纠

oppositions, hindrances, complications, and transgressions, so that the heart, moved by circumstances, feels itself induced to react of necessity against what disturbs it and what is a barrier against its aims and passions. In this sense the action proper only begins when the opposition contained in the situation appears on the scene. But since the colliding action transgresses an opposing aspect, in this difference it calls up against itself the power lying over against it which has been assailed, and therefore, with action, reaction is immediately linked. At this point only has the Ideal entered into full determinacy and movement. For now there stand in battle against one another two interests, wrested from their harmony, and in reciprocal contradiction they necessarily demand a resolution of their discord. Now this movement, taken as a whole, belongs no more to the province of the situation and its conflicts, but leads to the consideration of what we have described above as "the action proper".

纷以致引起破坏,人心感到为起作用的环境所迫,不得不采取行动去对抗那些阻挠他的目的和情欲的扰乱和阻碍的力量。就这个意义来说,只有当情境所含的矛盾揭露出来时,真正的动作才算开始。但是因为引起冲突的动作破坏了一个对立面,它在这矛盾中也就引起被它袭击的那个和它对立的力量来和它抗衡,因此动作与反动作是密切联系在一起的。只有在这错综的动作与反动作中,艺术理想才能显示它的完满的定性和运动。因为在这种情况之下,两种从和谐中分裂出来的旨趣在互相对立和斗争着,它们的这种互相矛盾就必然要求达到解决。这种运动,作为整体来看,已经不属于情境及其冲突的范围,它引导我们进一步研究上文所提到过的真正的动作。

3. Questions for Discussion

(1) How many types of collisions? What are the causes?

(2) Why does Hegel think the third collision is the most vital one?

(3) Analyze a tragedy that you have read with the theory of collision.

3. 讨论题

(1)冲突有几种类型?它们的起因是什么?

(2)为什么黑格尔认为冲突的第三种类型最重要?

(3)用你读到的冲突理论分析一部悲剧。

Chapter 5

1. Introduction to Matthew Arnold

Matthew Arnold (1822-1888) was an English poet and critic of the Victorian age. He is often considered to be the founding father of academic criticism in English, and the principles for literary criticism he advanced—objectivity, attention to detail, and an exclusive focus on the poem rather than the poet—become the foundation for professional literary criticism, setting the stage for the rise of Formalist criticism. Besides literary criticism, Matthew Arnold also made contribution to cultural criticism, religious criticism and educational theory.

Matthew Arnold was born in Laleham, Middlesex. He attended Rugby School in London, a school run by his father, Thomas Arnold. He went to Balliol College, Oxford in 1841. Recommended by Lord Lansdowne, he gained a position as the inspector of the Royal Education Commission in 1851. Arnold remained a school inspector all his life, traveling widely over Britain and even the European continent, and writing extensively on the state of British education.

Arnold published several books of poetry, *The*

第5章

1. 马修·阿诺德简介

马修·阿诺德(1822—1888)是英国维多利亚时期的诗人和批评家。他被认为是英语学术批评之父。他所提出的文学批评原则:客观、注重细节、只关注诗歌而不是诗人,成为文学批评的基础,为形式主义批评兴起搭起了舞台。除了文学批评之外,马修·阿诺德在文化批评、宗教批评以及教育理论方面也有所建树。

马修·阿诺德出生在米德塞克斯郡,拉勒安姆村。他就读于伦敦拉格比公学,其父托马斯·阿诺德任该校校长。马修·阿诺德于1841年进入牛津大学贝利奥尔学院。1851年,受兰斯顿勋爵举荐,他获得英国皇家教育委员会巡视员的职位。阿诺德终生以此为职业,游走于全英国,甚至欧洲大陆,就英国教育状况大量著文。

阿诺德出版了若干部诗集:《迷

Strayed Reveller (1849), *Empedocles on Etna, and Other Poems* (1851), *Poems* (1853), *Poems: Second Series* (1855), *New Poems* (1867). Arnold was elected Professor of Poetry at Oxford in 1857, and he was the first in this position to deliver his lectures in English rather than in Latin. His poem "Dover Beach" (1851) is most loved by readers.

途的狂欢者》(1849)、《恩培多克勒在埃特纳及其他诗歌》(1851)、《诗集》(1853)、《诗歌二集》(1855)、《新诗集》(1867)。阿诺德于1857年被选为牛津大学诗歌教授,他是首位用英语而不是拉丁语做讲座的教授。他的诗歌《多佛海滩》(1851)深受读者喜爱。

Arnold's criticisms are concerned with culture, religion and literature. The influential ones are *Culture and Anarchy* (1869), *Literature and Dogma* (1873), *On Translating Homer* (1862) and *Essays in Criticism* (1865), etc. Arnold is famous for introducing a methodology of literary criticism through his *Essays in Criticism* (1865, 1888), which influence critics to this day.

阿诺德的批评论著涉及文化、宗教和文学。有影响力的著作有《文化与无政府主义》(1869)、《文学与教条》(1873)、《评荷马史诗的翻译》(1862)、《评论集》(1865)等。阿诺德以其在《评论集》中提出的文学批评方法而著称,此方法至今仍对批评家产生影响。

Culture and Anarchy is Arnold's most famous work of cultural criticism, and one of the most influential statements of the zeitgeist of the Victorian age. In *Culture and Anarchy* Arnold argued for a classical education in the great works of literature and art, to instill a sense of culture and virtue in a population that was rapidly tending towards "anarchy", a term for undisciplined democracy by Arnold.

《文化与无政府主义》是阿诺德最著名的文化批评著作,也是维多利亚时代最具影响力的时代精神表达之一。在《文化与无政府主义》中,阿诺德提出对大众进行古典教育,通过伟大的文学和艺术作品为其灌输文化和道德感,这些大众正迅速滑向"无政府主义",阿诺德用该词指不受约束的民主。

"The Function of Criticism at the Present Time" (1865) is one of the most influential essays written on the role of the critic in identifying and elevating literature.

"当代批评的功能"(1865)论述了批评家在确认和提升文学价值中的作用,是最具影响力的文论之一。

2. Selections from "The Function of Criticism at the Present Time"

2."当代批评的功能"选文

Function of Criticism at the Present Time①

Matthew Arnold

Many objections have been made to a

当代批评的功能

马修·阿诺德

我曾经在翻译荷马著作的评论

① Selected from Matthew Arnold's *Essays in Criticism*, London: Macmillan & Co., 1865.

proposition which, in some remarks of mine on translating Homer, I ventured to put forth; a proposition about criticism, and its importance at the present day. I said: "Of the literature of France and Germany, as of the intellect of Europe in general, the main effort, for now many years, has been a critical effort; the endeavour, in all branches of knowledge, theology, philosophy, history, art, science, to see, the object as in itself it really is." I added, that owing to the operation in English literature of certain causes, "almost the last thing for which one would come to English literature is just that very thing which now Europe most desires—criticism"; and that the power and value of English literature was thereby impaired. More than one rejoinder declared that the importance I here assigned to criticism was excessive, and asserted the inherent superiority of the creative effort of the human spirit over its critical effort. And the other day, having been led by a Mr. Shairp's excellent notice of Wordsworth published in the *North British Review*, to turn again to his biography, I found, in the words of this great man, whom I, for one, must always listen to with the profoundest respect, a sentence passed on the critic's business, which seems to justify every possible disparagement of it. Wordsworth says in one of his letters:

中发表了意见并大胆地做出了一个提议,一个关于批评的提议和它在当下的重要性。那时我说:"许多年来,法国和德国的文学领域正如欧洲的普遍知识界一样,最重要最关键的努力,就是努力于批评,竭力在各个知识领域,神学、哲学、史学、艺术、科学方面,去探索事物的真面目。"我还说:由于英国文学受到某些原因的影响,"英国文学上几乎最不想要的事恰恰就是现在整个欧洲最想要的,那便是批评";随之英国文学的力量和价值也因此受损。不止一个辩论者声称我在此对批评给予的重要性是过分高了,并且断言人类内在精神的创造力是远远超过批评的作用的。受到某位谢普先生发表在《北英评论》杂志上评论华兹华斯的那篇杰出文章的启发,我在那天再次查阅了这位诗人的传记。我发现这个伟人的语言总是令我肃然起敬,每一句看起来都是对批评可能存在的轻视的有力辩护。华兹华斯曾在信中说道:

"The writers in these publications (the Reviews), while they prosecute their inglorious employment, cannot be supposed to be in a state of mind very favourable for being affected by the finer influences of a thing so pure as genuine poetry."

"虽然这些出版物(这些评论性杂志)的作者贬低自己的工作,认为其不够光鲜,所以更不能期待他们会有一种心理状态,就像受到了真正纯粹的诗歌的熏陶一样。"

And a trustworthy reporter of his conversation quotes a more elaborate judgment to the same effect:

对他访谈的一个可靠报道者,为这一评论做了更为详尽的表述:

"Wordsworth holds the critical power very low, infinitely lower than the inventive; and he said today that if the quantity of time consumed in

"华兹华斯低视批评的力量,视其远低于原创力;他今天说,如果把

writing critiques on the works of others were given to original composition, of whatever kind it might be, it would be much better employed; it would make a man find out sooner his own level and it would do infinitely less mischief. A false or malicious criticism may do much injury to the minds of others; a stupid invention, either in prose or verse, is quite harmless."

It is almost too much to expect of poor human nature, that a man capable of producing some effect in one line of literature, should, for the greater good of society, voluntarily doom himself to impotence and obscurity in another. Still less is this to be expected from men addicted to the composition of the "false or malicious criticism" of which Wordsworth speaks. However, everybody would admit that a false or malicious criticism had better never have been written. Everybody, too, would be willing to admit, as a general proposition that the critical faculty is lower than the inventive. But is it true that criticism is really, in itself, a baneful and injurious employment; is it true that all time given to writing critiques on the works of others would be much better employed if it were given to original composition, of whatever kind this may be? Is it true that Johnson had better have gone on producing more *Irenes* instead of writing his *Lives of the Poets*; is it certain that Wordsworth himself was better employed in making his *Ecclesiastical Sonnets* than when he made his celebrated "Preface" so full of criticism, and criticism of the works of others? Wordsworth was himself a great critic, and it is to be sincerely regretted that he has not left us more criticism; Goethe was one of the greatest of critics, and we may sincerely congratulate ourselves that he has left us so much criticism. Without wasting time over the exaggeration which Wordsworth's judgment on criticism clearly contains or over an attempt to trace

消耗在评论他人作品的时间用到自己的创作上,无论是何种创作,都会好得多。至少这将使一个人及早地发现自己的写作水平,使其做出的伤害会小。一篇错误的或是恶意的批评可能会对他人造成很大的心理伤害;一篇愚钝的创作,无论是散文或是诗歌,都是相当无害的。"

几乎不太可能期待一个资质平庸的人,一个能够在文学的某个方面产生一定影响的人,可以为了更加美好的社会,甘愿让自己注定碌碌无为和默默无闻。更不用说去期望那些沉溺于只会写像华兹华斯所说的"错误的或恶意的评论"的人会这样做。然而,每个人都愿意承认一篇错误的或恶意的评论最好还是不要写出来。大家也乐于承认一个普遍的命题,那就是批评能力低于创作才能。但是说批评,就其本身而言,真是一个有害又伤人的职业吗?如果将所有花费在评论其他作品上的时间全部用来去写任何一种文体的原创作品上,那真的是再好不过的吗?约翰逊最好多创作些像《艾琳》这样的作品,而不是去写《英国诗人列传》,真该这样吗?对华兹华斯本人来说,他创作的诗集《教会十四行诗》真的要好于他那著名的充满评论性的《序言》以及对他人作品的评论文吗?华兹华斯他自己就是一位伟大的批评家,我们真的很遗憾他留给我们的评论作品太少了。歌德是最伟大的评论家之一,而我们也真是感到庆幸,他为我们留下了如此之多的批评著作。不要为华兹华斯对批评过分夸张的清晰的判断而浪费时间,也不必试图为这些夸张去寻根究底——我认为追

the causes—not difficult, I think to be traced—which may have led Wordsworth to this exaggeration a critic may with advantage seize an occasion for trying his own conscience, and for asking himself of what real service, at any given moment, the practice of criticism either is or may be made to his own mind and spirit, and to the minds and spirits of others.

The critical power is of lower rank than the creative. True; but in assenting to this proposition, one or two things are to be kept in mind. It is undeniable that the exercise of a creative power, that a free creative activity, is the highest function of man; it is proved to be so by man's finding in it his true happiness. But it is undeniable, also, that men may have the sense of exercising this free creative activity in other ways than in producing great works of literature or art; if it were not so, all but a very few men would be shut out from the true happiness of all men. They may have it in well-doing, they may have it in learning, they may have it even in criticising. This is one thing to be kept in mind. Another is, that the exercise of the creative power in the production of great works of literature or art, however high this exercise of it may rank, is not at all epochs and under all conditions possible; and that therefore labour may be vainly spent in attempting it, which might with more fruit be used in preparing for it, in rendering it possible. This creative power works with elements, with materials; what if it has not those materials, those elements, ready for its use? In that case it must surely wait till they are ready. Now, in literature—I will limit myself to literature, for it is about literature that the question arises—the elements with which the creative power works are ideas; the best ideas on every matter which literature touches, current at the time. At any rate we may lay it down as certain that in modern literature no manifestation

寻这些并不难——那便是,华兹华斯对批评的过分夸张或许是有实际好处的,他抓住了一个审视良知的机会。那么,评论家此时可以扪心自问:他的批评著作到底只是反映他自己的理智和精神,还是也能反映出其他人的理智和精神。

批评能力低于创作才能。的确如此,但是在同意这个说法时,要牢记一两件事情。不可否认,创作才能的运用,自由的创作活动,是人可以使用的最高功能;而人在创作中找到真正的快乐也恰恰证实了这一点。但是同样不可否认的是,除了创作伟大的文学或艺术作品,人在其他方面,也能感受到自己运用了这个自由的创作活动。如果并非如此,那么几乎所有人都会被人类真正的幸福拒之门外。人们可以在积德行善,学习知识,甚至是批评中得到这种幸福感。这一件事要牢记。另一件事是,创作才能产生在伟大的文学或艺术作品上,无论运用得如何高明,都不是在时时刻刻和所有情况下能够出现的。因此,所做的尝试也许会是无用功,但或许在准备中,在使其成为可能中得到更多的果实。有要素和材料,那么创作能力便能奏效;假如没有要素,没有材料,那么准备如何运用它呢?如果那样的话,无疑必须等到万事俱备之时。目前,在文学方面——我仅限于文学方面,因为所提出的问题与文学有关——创造才能得以展示的要素是思想,是当下文学触及的每个事物的最好的思想。无论如何,抛开其他不谈,我们可以确定的是,在当代文学中,没有这些思想的创造才能是无法彰显出其重要

of the creative power not working with these can be very important or fruitful. And I say current at the time, not merely accessible at the time; for creative literary genius does not principally show itself in discovering new ideas, that is rather the business of the philosopher. The grand work of literary genius is a work of synthesis and exposition, not of analysis and discovery; its gift lies in the faculty of being happily inspired by a certain intellectual and spiritual atmosphere, by a certain order of ideas, when it finds itself in them; of dealing divinely with these ideas, presenting them in the most effective and attractive combinations—making beautiful works with them, in short. But it must have the atmosphere, it must find itself amidst the order of ideas, in order to work freely; and these it is not so easy to command. This is why great creative epochs in literature are so rare, this is why there is so much that is unsatisfactory in the productions of many men of real genius; because, for the creation of a master-work of literature two powers must concur, the power of the man and the power of the moment, and the man is not enough without the moment; the creative power has, for its happy exercise, appointed elements, and those elements are not in its own control.

性或者成效性。我说的是当时流行的,而不只是当时可及的;因为富有创造力的文学天赋,主要不是在发现新思想中展现出来,更何况这是哲学家的事。文学天赋的伟大之处是一个综合和阐述的工作,而非分析和发现的工作。这样的天赋就在于:当发现自己被某种智力和精神的氛围,某种思想秩序所激发的时候,则会快乐,并领悟这些思想,用最有效、最有魅力的组合来呈现它们——简而言之,就是用它们制造美的作品。但是,为了自由地创作,意味着必须要有这样的氛围,必须能在这个思想秩序中发现自己;而做到这些是非常不易的。这就是为什么在文学上伟大的创新十分稀有,这就是为什么在真正有天赋的人的作品中,差强人意的也不少;因为,对于一部杰出文学作品的创作,两股力量必须并存,人的力量和时机的力量,没有时机,光靠人的力量是不够的;为了愉快地运用这种能力,创作力量要有指定的元素,而那些元素并不在它自己的掌控之中。

Nay, they are more within the control of the critical power. It is the business of the critical power, as I said in the words already quoted, "in all branches of knowledge, theology, philosophy, history, art, science, to see the object as in itself it really is." Thus it tends, at last, to make an intellectual situation of which the creative power can profitably avail itself. It tends to establish an order of ideas, if not absolutely true, yet true by comparison with that which it displaces; to make the best ideas prevail. Presently these new ideas reach society, the touch of truth is the touch of

反之,这些元素大多都在批评力量的掌控之中。这就是批评力量的事情,正如我已经提出的,"在各个知识领域,神学、哲学、史学、艺术、科学中去探索事物的真面目"。如此一来,批评力量最终可能制造出一个完全有利于创造力量的智力环境。它可能会建立一个思想秩序,即使不绝对准确,但与它所替代的相比还是准确的,能够使得最好的思想盛行。如今,这些新思想融入了社会,真理源

life, and there is a stir and growth everywhere; out of this stir and growth come the creative epochs of literature.

Or to narrow our range, and quit these considerations of the general march of genius and of society—considerations which are apt to become too abstract and impalpable—every one can see that a poet, for instance, ought to know life and the world before dealing with them in poetry; and life and the world being in modern times very complex things, the creation of a modern poet, to be worth much, implies a great critical effort before it; else it must be a comparatively poor, barren and short-lived affair. This is why Byron's poetry had so little endurance in it, and Goethe's so much; both Byron and Goethe had a great productive power, but Goethe's was nourished by a great critical effort providing the true materials for it, and Byron's was not; Goethe knew life and the world, the poet's necessary subjects, much more comprehensively and thoroughly than Byron. He knew a great deal more of them, and he knew them much more as they really are.

It has long seemed to me that the burst of creative activity in our literature, through the first quarter of this century, had about it in fact something premature; and that from this cause its productions are doomed, most of them, in spite of the sanguine hopes which accompanied and do still accompany them, to prove hardly more lasting than the productions of far less splendid epochs. And this prematureness comes from its having proceeded without having its proper data, without sufficient materials to work with. In other words, the English poetry of the first quarter of this century, with plenty of energy, plenty of creative force, did not know enough. This makes Byron so empty of matter, Shelley so incoherent, Wordsworth even, profound as he is, yet so wanting in completeness

于生活,到处都有传播和发展,正是这样的传播和发展,迎来了文学创作的时代。

或是为了缩小范围和停止对天赋和社会的大体进程的思考——即容易变得太抽象又难以理解的思考——每个人都知道,比方说,诗人在诗歌创作前应先了解生活和世界;现代生活和世界是非常复杂的,现代诗人的创作,要有很大价值得话,就意味着创作之前的批评努力,否则它肯定是一个相当贫乏、空洞又短暂的事。这就是为什么拜伦的诗歌经不住考验,而歌德的却能;拜伦和歌德都有极好的创作能力,但是歌德的作品蕴含着一个伟大的批评力,为诗歌本身提供了真实素材,而拜伦的则不是。歌德比拜伦更加全面彻底地了解生活和世界,这也是诗人必须了解的课题。他太了解生活和世界了,比它们的真面目知道的还要多。

在我看来,我们的文学中爆发的创作活动,在 19 世纪的头 25 年里,事实上总是有些早产的东西,从这个原因看,这个时代的大部分作品注定要失败,尽管我们满怀希望并一路伴随,仍旧无法证明它们能够比远不及辉煌时代的作品更加持久。而这样的早产来源于在前进过程中,没有适当的资料,没有充足的材料去研究。换言之,本世纪的头 25 年的英国诗歌,有着丰富的活力,大量的创造力,却不足够了解生活和世界。这导致了拜伦的诗歌如此空虚,雪莱的如此语无伦次,华兹华斯还算深刻,仍需完整和多样性。华兹华斯不大喜欢

and variety. Wordsworth cared little for books, and disparaged Goethe. I admire Wordsworth, as he is, so much that I cannot wish him different; and it is vain, no doubt to imagine such a man different from what he is, to suppose that he could have been different. But surely the one thing wanting to make Wordsworth an even greater poet than he is—his thought richer, and his influence of wider application—was that he should have read more books, among them, no doubt, those of that Goethe whom he disparaged without reading him.

But to speak of books and reading may easily lead to a misunderstanding here. It was not really books and reading that lacked to our poetry at this epoch; Shelley had plenty of reading; Coleridge had immense reading. Pindar① and Sophocles—as we all say so glibly and often with so little discernment of the real import of what we are saying—had not many books; Shakespeare was no deep reader. True; but in the Greece of Pindar and Sophocles, in the England of Shakespeare, the poet lived in a current of ideas in the highest degree animating and nourishing to the creative power; society was, in the fullest measure, permeated by fresh thought, intelligent and alive. And this state of things is the true basis for the creative power's exercise, in this it finds its data, its materials, truly ready for its hand; all the books and reading in the world are only valuable as they are helps to this. Even when this does not actually exist, books and reading may enable a man to construct a kind of semblance of it in his own mind, a world of knowledge and intelligence in which he may live and work. This is by no means an equivalent to the artist for the nationally diffused life and thought of the epochs of Sophocles or

书,又蔑视歌德。我十分钦佩华兹华斯,因为他就是他,以至于我不能期望他有所不同,设想如此一个人不同于他本身或是假想他可能是不同的无疑是徒劳的。但确定的是,想要使得华兹华斯成为一个比他现在还要伟大的诗人——他要有更丰富的思想,更广泛的影响——那就是他本应该读更多的书,在这些书中,当然也有他蔑视的不读的歌德的作品。

但是说到书和阅读,很容易引起误解。在这个时代,我们的诗歌缺少的不完全是书和阅读;雪莱和柯尔律治都博览群书。我们总是轻易地说品达和索福克勒斯没有读过那么多书,却经常辨别不出我们这样说的真正含义;莎士比亚并不是一个读书多的人。的确如此;但就像品达和索福克勒斯生活过的希腊,像莎士比亚生活过的英国,诗人都是生活在激发和培养创造力的思想洪流之中。总的来说,整个社会遍布新鲜的思想,智慧又富有生气。这个状态才是发挥创造力的真正基础,在这里,可以找到所需的数据和材料。只有当所有的书和阅读有助于培养和鼓励创造力的时候,它们才会弥足珍贵。即使这个状态实际上不存在,书和阅读也可能使一个人在他心里构建出一种类似的东西,一个知识与智慧并存,可以生活和工作的世界。但是这个世界绝对不等同于索福克勒斯和莎士比亚这些艺术家对全民族普及他们生活观和思想的那个时代的世界;

① 品达(Pindar,约公元前518年—公元前438年),古希腊抒情诗人。他被后世的学者认为是九大抒情诗人之首。

Shakespeare; but, besides that it may be a means of preparation for such epochs, it does really constitute, if many share in it, a quickening and sustaining atmosphere of great value. Such an atmosphere the many-sided learning and the long and widely combined critical effort of Germany formed for Goethe, when he lived and worked. There was no national glow of life and thought there as in the Athens of Pericles① or the England of Elizabeth. That was the poet's weakness. But there was a sort of equivalent for it in the complete culture and unfettered thinking of a large body of Germans. That was his strength. In the England of the first quarter of this century there was neither a national glow of life and thought, such as we had in the age of Elizabeth, nor yet a culture and a force of learning and criticism such as were to be found in Germany. Therefore the creative power of poetry wanted, for success in the highest sense, materials and a basis; a thorough interpretation of the world was necessarily denied to it.

At first sight it seems strange that out of the immense stir of the French Revolution② and its age should not have come a crop of works of genius equal to that which came out of the stir of the great productive time of Greece, or out of that of the Renascence, with its powerful episode The Reformation③. But the truth is that the stir of the French Revolution took a character which essentially distinguished it from such movements as these. These were, in the main, disinterestedly intellectual and spiritual movements; movements in

但是,此外它可能会为这样的时代的到来做好准备,如果在这个世界里有许多思想和生活观分享,就一定会建造出一个具有重大价值的生机勃勃的氛围。这便是一个巨大的价值。当歌德在德国生活和工作的时候,就是这样一个博识多学,又有着长期广泛的批评力的氛围才造就了他。在那里并没有像伯利克里的雅典或者伊丽莎白的英国那样,有着全民族的生活和思想上的光辉。那就是诗人的弱点。但是对它而言,在大量德国人的完整文化和无拘束的思想中,还是有相同之处的。那就是他的优势。在这个世纪前 25 年的英国,既没有像我们说的伊丽莎白时代的全民族的思想和生活的光辉,也没有在德国发现的文化和知识批评的力量。因此,为了取得最大意义的成功,诗歌的创造力需要材料和基础;否则便不能彻底地解释世界了。

初看之下好像很奇怪,法国革命和它的那个时代所引起的巨大的轰动竟没有出现一批天才所写的作品,不敌于希腊的高产时期或是文艺复兴时期,以及强有力的插曲的宗教改革所带来的轰动。但事实是法国革命的轰动带有一个与其他运动本质不同的性质。这些运动大体上是无偏私的智力和精神的运动;人的精神在这些运动中,在自我和不断提高的自我活动中寻找满足。法国革命带

① 伯利克里(Pericles,约公元前 495 年—公元前 429 年),古雅典民主派政治家,活跃于雅典的黄金时代。

② French Revolution:法国大革命(1789—1799)。法国资产阶级革命,致使统治法国多个世纪的君主封建制度在三年之内土崩瓦解。

③ The Reformation:宗教改革,特指基督教在 16 世纪至 17 世纪期间所进行的一次自下而上的宗教改革运动。

which the human spirit looked for its satisfaction in itself and in the increased play of its own activity. The French Revolution took a political, practical character. The movement, which went on in France under the old régime, from 1700 to 1789, was far more really akin than that of the Revolution itself to the movement of the Renascence; the France of Voltaire① and Rousseau② told far more powerfully upon the mind of Europe than the France of the Revolution. Goethe reproached this last expressly with having "thrown quiet culture back." Nay, and the true key to how much in our Byron, even in our Wordsworth is this! —that they had their source in a great movement of feeling, not in a great movement of mind. The French Revolution, however—that object of so much blind love and so much blind hatred—found undoubtedly its motive-power in the intelligence of men, and not in their practical sense; this is what distinguishes it from the English Revolution of Charles the First's time. This is what makes it a more spiritual event than our Revolution, an event of much more powerful and world-wide interest, though practically less successful; it appeals to an order of ideas which are universal, certain, permanent. 1789 asked of a thing, Is it rational? 1642 asked of a thing, Is it legal? Or, when it went furthest, is it according to conscience? This is the English fashion, a fashion to be treated, within its own sphere with the highest respect; for its success, within its own sphere, has been prodigious. But what is law in one place is not law in another; what is law here today is not law even here tomorrow; and as for conscience, what is binding on one man's conscience is not binding on another's. The old woman who threw her stool at the

有政治的、实际的性质。这场运动，从1700年到1789年，在法国的旧的政权体制下进行着，远比革命本身更相似于文艺复兴；伏尔泰和卢梭的法国比起革命的法国更加强有力的号召了欧洲的精神。歌德曾清楚地斥责过革命，因为革命"让我们的文化停滞不前"。不仅如此，我们的拜伦，甚至是华兹华斯的创作的多少，真正的关键在于这个——他们的创作来源是一场伟大的感情运动，而非伟大的精神运动。无论如何，法国革命——是如此盲目的爱和盲目的仇恨的对象——毋庸置疑地找到了它的动力，是在人的智力之中，不在他们的实践感中；这就将它与查理一世时期的英国革命区分开来。这就是使得它比起我们的革命更具有精神的事件原因，一场足以吸引全球的强有力的事件，尽管实践证明并没有那么成功；它呼吁了一个普遍的、明确的、永恒的思想秩序。1789年的革命提问，这是合理的吗？1642年的革命问道，这是合法的吗？或者说当它往后走得更远的时候，这是凭良心说话吗？这就是英国的做派传统，在它自己的范围要被十分尊重地对待；因为在它自己的范围内已经有了惊人的成功。但是一个地方的法律不适用于另一个地方；一样的地方，今天的法律在明天就什么都不是了；至于良心，能约束一个人的良心对另一个人就不管用了。一个老女人在爱丁堡的圣贾尔斯教堂，把她的凳子扔到了

① 伏尔泰(Voltaire,1694-1778)，18世纪法国资产阶级启蒙运动倡导者。
② 卢梭(Rousseau,1712-1778)，19世纪法国伟大的启蒙思想家、哲学家、教育家、文学家。18世纪法国大革命的思想先驱。

head of the surpliced minister in St. Giles's Church at Edinburgh obeyed an impulse to which millions of the human race may be permitted to remain strangers. But the prescriptions of reason are absolute, unchanging of universal validity; to count by tens is the easiest way of counting—that is a proposition of which every one, from here to the Antipodes, feels the force; at least I should say so if we did not live in a country where it is not impossible that any morning we may find a letter in the *Times* declaring that a decimal coinage is an absurdity. That a whole nation should have been penetrated with an enthusiasm for pure reason, and with an ardent zeal for making its prescriptions triumph is a very remarkable thing, when we consider how little of mind or anything so worthy and quickening as mind, comes into the motives which alone in general, impel great masses of men. In spite of the extravagant direction given to this enthusiasm, in spite of the crimes and follies in which it lost itself, the French Revolution derives from the force, truth, and universality of the ideas which it took for its law and from the passion with which it could inspire a multitude for these ideas, a unique and still living power; it is—it will probably long remain—the greatest, the most animating event in history. And as no sincere passion for the things of the mind, even though it turn out in many respects an unfortunate passion, is ever quite thrown away and quite barren of good, France has reaped from hers one fruit—the natural and legitimate fruit though not precisely the grand fruit she expected: she is the country in Europe where the people is most alive.

But the mania for giving an immediate political and practical application to all these fine ideas of the reason was fatal. Here an Englishman is in his element: on this theme we can all go on for hours. And all we are in the habit of saying on it has

穿着白色法袍的牧师的头上,是被冲动驱使,而数百万人却难以理解。但是理性的分析解释却是绝对的,不变的,普遍有效性的;用十进位法计数是最简单的——对于从这里到世界另一头的每一个人来说,那都会放之四海而皆准是一个普遍认同的命题;至少我应该这样说:我们绝不可能住在这样一个国家里,有一天早上人们发现在《泰晤士报》上的一封信声称十进位货币制是荒谬的。当我们考虑到思想或任何事是如此的有价值和鼓舞人心的,总之就是带有动机的并激励着大多数人,那么全民族本应该为了纯粹的理性而满怀热情,并且怀着一份热诚,使分析解释大获成功,这真是一件卓越非凡的事情。尽管这份热情有些过分的趋势,尽管在犯罪和罪恶之中迷失了自己,法国大革命源自于有力量的、真理的、普适性的思想,它相信它的法律并且从这些思想中能够找到鼓舞群众的热情,一种独一无二的仍然富有生命力的力量;法国大革命是——很可能长期都是——史上最伟大、最富有生机的事件了。尽管法国革命在许多方面都证明了其不幸的热情,但是思想上有真正热情的事情还是被保留住了,也算是有益处的。法国大革命已经收获了一份果实——自然的,合法的,尽管不是她所完全期待的那样丰厚的果实:因为她是整个欧洲的人民最富有生命力的国家了。

但是狂热地把所有理性的优秀思想直接运用到政治和实际中去也是致命的。在这方面,一个英国人是在行的:在这个主题上我们可以讨论几个小时。并且我们都习惯于说的

undoubtedly a great deal of truth. Ideas cannot be too much prized in and for themselves, cannot be too much lived with; but to transport them abruptly into the world of politics and practice, violently to revolutionise this world to their bidding—that is quite another thing. There is the world of ideas and there is the world of practice; the French are often for suppressing the one and the English the other; but neither is to be suppressed. A member of the House of Commons said to me the other day: "That a thing is an anomaly, I consider to be no objection to it whatever." I venture to think he was wrong; that a thing is an anomaly is an objection to it, but absolutely and in the sphere of ideas: it is not necessarily, under such and such circumstances, or at such and such a moment, an objection to it in the sphere of politics and practice. Joubert① has said beautifully: "C'est la force et le droit qui règlent toutes choses dans le monde, la force en attendant le droit." (Force and right are the governors of this world; force till right is ready.) Force till right is ready; and till right is ready, force, the existing order of things, is justified, is the legitimate ruler. But right is something moral, and implies inward recognition, free assent of the will; we are not ready for right—right, so far as we are concerned, is not ready—until we have attained this sense of seeing it and willing it. The way in which for us it may change and transform force, the existing order of things, and become, in its turn, the legitimate ruler of the world, should depend on the way in which, when our time comes, we see it and will it. Therefore for other people enamoured of their own newly discerned right, to attempt to impose it upon us as ours, and violently to substitute their right for our force, is an

那些无疑都是真理。我们不能过度从思想本身和为思想本身来推崇思想，也不能全靠思想而活着；但是唐突地把思想硬放到政治和实际的世界当中，暴力地命令彻底改变这个世界——那就是另一回事了。有思想的世界，也有实际的世界；法国人经常压制一个，英国人就压制另一个；但是两者都不能被压制的。一位下议院的官员有一天曾对我说："那样一个事是异常的，我认为没有任何异议。"我冒昧地揣测他说的好像是错的；因为是异常的就是对它有异议，但是显然，在思想的范畴里：在一定的情况下或是在一定的时间内，在政治和实际的范畴中，异议是不必要的。儒贝尔说得好："C'est la force et le droit qui règlent toutes choses dans le monde, la force en attendant le droit."（力量和权利统治着全世界；权利在握才有力量。）权利在握才有力量；那么在权利准备好之前，力量，即是事物现存的秩序，是合乎情理的，也是合法的统治者。但是权利是道德层面的东西，是指意志的内心认识和自由认同；我们还没有做好准备拥有权利——权利，就我们而言，还差得多——直到我们取得对权利的认识和决心。对于我们来说，可以转变力量的方式，即改变事物的现存秩序，才可以成为世界合法的统治者，当我们的时代到来时，它应当取决于我们认识和控制权利的方式了。因此对于其他迷恋于他们自己最新认识到权利的人们来说，企图将他们

---

① 约瑟夫·儒贝尔（Joseph Joubert，1754-1824），法国散文家，以死后发表的文集《随想录》（*Pensées*，1850）著称，引文出自《随想录》第二卷，第102页。

act of tyranny, and to be resisted. It sets at nought the second great half of our maxim, force till right is ready. This was the grand error of the French Revolution; and its movement of ideas, by quitting the intellectual sphere and rushing furiously into the political sphere, ran, indeed, a prodigious and memorable course, but produced no such intellectual fruit as the movement of ideas of the Renascence, and created, in opposition to itself, what I may call an epoch of concentration①. The great force of that epoch of concentration was England; and the great voice of that epoch of concentration was Burke②. It is the fashion to treat Burke's writings on the French Revolution as superannuated and conquered by the event; as the eloquent but unphilosophical tirades of bigotry and prejudice. I will not deny that they are often disfigured by the violence and passion of the moment, and that in some directions Burke's view was bounded, and his observation therefore at fault. But on the whole, and for those who can make the needful corrections, what distinguishes these writings is their profound, permanent, fruitful, philosophical truth. They contain the true philosophy of an epoch of concentration, dissipate the heavy atmosphere which its own nature is apt to engender round it, and make its resistance rational instead of mechanical.

…

If I have insisted so much on the course which criticism must take where politics and religion are concerned, it is because, where these burning matters are in question, it is most likely to go astray. I have wished, above all, to insist on the attitude which criticism should adopt towards things

认识的权利强加于我们,并且以暴力的方式取代我们的力量,这是一种残暴的行为,势必遭到反抗。这种情况,使得我们格言的第二大半部分——权力在握才有力量——成为泡影。这是法国革命的最大错误;它的思想运动,舍弃了智力范围,猛烈地冲进政治领域之中,的确经历了一段惊人又值得纪念的路,但是没有产生像文艺复兴运动思想的智慧果实,相反,却创造了一个我们称之为的凝聚期。这个凝聚期的伟大力量就是英国;而这个时期伟大的发言人就是伯克。时下认为伯克的关于法国革命的作品被这件大事所征服而显得过时了;是有说服力但又存在顽固和偏见的非哲学性的长篇大论。我不否认,他的作品经常会被那时的狂热和暴力搞得面目全非,而且在一些方面伯克的观点也是受限的,因此他的观察可以说是错的。但是大体上,为了那些必要的修正,这些作品的突出表现是深奥,永久,富有成效性和哲学性的真理。它们包含了凝聚期的真正哲学,驱散了由于自然本身而造成的沉重气氛,使得英国的抵抗不再是呆板的而是理性的。

……

如果我一定坚持,批评一定要经历与政治和宗教相关的过程,那是因为这些急于处理的事情很可能要误入歧途了。首先,我希望坚持这个态度——批评应当采纳的是对待普通

① 马修·阿诺德所谓的凝聚期(an epoch of concentration)指集中、专注的时代。

② 埃德蒙·伯克(Edmund Burk,1729-1797),爱尔兰政治家,演说家,政治理论家,他对于法国大革命的批判和反思使得他成为辉格党保守派的主要人物。

in general; on its right tone and temper of mind. But then comes another question as to the subject-matter which literary criticisms should not seek. Here, in general, its course is determined for it by the idea which is the law of its being; the idea of a disinterested endeavour to learn and propagate the best that is known and thought in the world, and thus to establish a current of fresh and true ideas. By the very nature of things, as England is not all the world, much of the best that is known and thought in the world cannot be of English growth, must be foreign; by the nature of things, again, it is just this that we are least likely to know, while English thought is streaming in upon us from all sides, and takes excellent care that we shall not be ignorant of its existence. The English critic of literature, therefore, must dwell much on foreign thought, and with particular heed on any part of it, which, while significant and fruitful in itself, is for any reason specially likely to escape him. Again, judging is often spoken of as the critic's one business, and so in some sense it is; but the judgement which almost insensibly forms itself in a fair and clear mind, along with fresh knowledge, is the valuable one; and thus knowledge, and ever fresh knowledge, must be the critic's great concern for himself. And it is by communicating fresh knowledge, and letting his own judgment pass along with it—but insensibly, and in the second place, not the first, as a sort of companion and clue, not as an abstract lawgiver—that the critic will generally do most good to his readers. Sometimes, no doubt, for the sake of establishing an author's place in literature, and his relation to a central standard (and if this is not done, how are we to get at our best in the world?) criticism may have to deal with a subject-matter so familiar that fresh knowledge is out of the question, and then it must be all judgment; an enunciation and detailed

事物的态度,用它正确的语气与平和的心态。但是另一个问题来了,关于文学批评不应该追寻的内容与素材。在此,一般来说它的过程取决于它所存在的规律,一个被认为是世界上最好的思想,然后要公正无私地努力学习和宣传这个思想,从而建立真实、新鲜的一股思潮。因为英国不是全世界,按照事物的本质来看,在世界上被认为是最好的那部分肯定是在国外;再说,正是这一点我们知道的最少,虽然英国思想在各方面包围着我们,但是一定要注意不应忽视它的存在。因此,英国文学批评应当多琢磨外国的思想,尤其是留心那些其本身是有意义和成果的,但很可能被忽视的部分。批评家的事就是经常提出评判来,在某种意义上正是这样的;但评判是有价值的,几乎不知不觉地形成于一种公平又清晰的思想并带来了新知识;因此知识,那些新的知识才是批评家最该关心的事。通过传递新知识,然后自己再提出评判——但不知不觉中,在第二位而非第一位的,批评家的评判能作为一种指南和线索,而不是一个抽象的立法者——那样才是批评家对读者做得最好的事了。毫无疑问,有时为了确立作家在文学中的地位,就要把他的批评与典范批评作品作比较(如果不这样做,我们又如何获得世界上最好的呢?),可能要处理再熟悉不过的内容和素材,新知识就不再是问题了,然后一定是提出评判;阐明详细的应用原则。最好的保护措施就是绝不让自己变得抽象深奥,要对自己讲述的真理保持一个清晰又生动的意识,一旦这个意识消失了,就意味着事情

application of principles. Here the great safeguard is never to let oneself become abstract, always to retain an intimate and lively consciousness of the truth of what one is saying, and, the moment this fails us, to be sure that something is wrong. Still under all circumstances, this mere judgment and application of principles is, in itself, not the most satisfactory work to the critic; like mathematics, it is tautological, and cannot well give us, like fresh learning, the sense of creative activity.

But stop, some one will say; all this talk is of no practical use to us whatever; this criticism of yours is not what we have in our minds when we speak of criticism; when we speak of critics and criticism, we mean critics and criticism of the current English literature of the day; when you offer to tell criticism its function, it is to this criticism that we expect you to address yourself. I am sorry for it, for I am afraid I must disappoint these expectations. I am bound by my own definition of criticism: a disinterested endeavour to learn and propagate the best that is known and thought in the world. How much of current English literature comes into this "best that is known and thought in the world"? Not very much I fear; certainly less, at this moment, than of the current literature of France or Germany. Well, then, am I to alter my definition of criticism, in order to meet the requirements of a number of practising English critics, who, after all, are free in their choice of a business? That would be making criticism lend itself just to one of those alien practical considerations, which, I have said, are so fatal to it. One may say, indeed, to those who have to deal with the mass—so much better disregarded—of current English literature, that they may at all events endeavour, in dealing with this, to try it, so far as they can, by the standard of the best that it known and thought in the world; one may say, that

不对了。但是在所有情况下,对批评家来讲,仅仅去评判和提出应用原则并不是他们最满意的工作;就像数学,反复阐述,并不能很好地给我们新鲜的知识和创造性活动的快感。

但有些人会反驳:我所谈论的无论如何是没有实际意义的,当我们提起批评时你的批评不是我们所想的,当我们提到批评家和批评时,我们说的是当今英国文学的批评家和批评,当你提到批评的功能时,我们希望你还是对批评的功能有所阐述。对于这个质疑我很遗憾,因为我恐怕会使这些人的期待落空了。我只受我自己定义的批评概念约束:一个被认为是世界上最好的思想,就是要公正无私地努力学习和宣传这个思想。当代英国文学有多少能成为这个"被认为是世界上最好的思想?"恐怕不多;当然比现在的法国或德国当代文学少得多。那么,为了满足大量从事英语批评工作的人的要求,我应该改变我对批评的定义吗?毕竟,他们在选择职业上是自由的。那将会使批评只适合于那些性质不同的实际情况了,而这,正如我之前说的,对批评是致命的。的确对于那些不得不处理的——虽然更好的是忽视它——大量的当代英国文学的问题,有人会说,无论如何,他们也要努力尝试处理这个,到目前为止,被视为全世界公认最好的典范;为了成为这样的典范,有人还说每一位批评家应当

to get anywhere near this standard, every critic should try and possess one great literature, at least, besides his own; and the more unlike his own, the better. But, after all, the criticism I am really concerned with—the criticism which alone can much help us for the future, the criticism which, throughout Europe, is at the present day meant, when so much stress is laid on the importance of criticism and the critical spirit—is a criticism which regards Europe as being, for intellectual and spiritual purposes, one great confederation, bound to a joint action and working to a common result; and whose members have, for their proper outfit, a knowledge of Greek, Roman, and Eastern antiquity, and of one another. Special, local, and temporary advantages being put out of account, that modern nation will in the intellectual and spiritual sphere make most progress, which most thoroughly carries out this program. And what is that but saying that we too, all of us, as individuals, the more thoroughly we carry it out, shall make the more progress?

拥有,除了他自己的民族文学以外,至少还要一个伟大民族的文学,并且是与自己的越不同越好。但是,毕竟我现在真正关心的批评,即是当巨大的压力落在批评之重要性和批评精神上的时候,它能帮助到我们的将来,同样也是整个欧洲目前所指的——为了达到理智和精神的目标,这个批评视欧洲为一个重大的联盟,它的成员满腹经纶,有着希腊、罗马、古老东方的文化知识以及互相传授的知识,必定要一致努力实现共同目标。个别的、地方性的、暂时的优势是没有价值的,现代国家只有全面开展这个计划,才会在理智和精神领域取得最大的进步。难道所说的不也正是我们所有人的吗? 作为个体,我们开展得越全面,是不是取得的进步就越大呢?

There is so much inviting us! —What are we to take? What will nourish us in growth towards perfection? That is the question which, with the immense field of life and of literature lying before him, the critic has to answer; for himself first, and afterwards for others. In this idea of the critic's business the essays brought together in the following pages have had their origin; in this idea, widely different as are their subjects, they have, perhaps, their unity.

有好多事情等着我们呢! ——我们要选择什么? 什么能使我们成长到接近完美? 使用摆在面前的广阔的生活和文学的领域,这个问题就是批评家不得不回答的;先是回答自己,然后是其他人的。在以下各页收集的短文来自于批评家的这种思想;用这种思想,虽然与他们的主题非常不同,但是他们也是有一致性的。

I conclude with what I said at the beginning: to have the sense of creative activity is the great happiness and the great proof of being alive, and it is not denied to criticism to have it; but then criticism must be sincere, simple, flexible, ardent, ever widening its knowledge. Then it may have, is no contemptible measure, a joyful sense of

我用开头谈的来做总结:体验创造性活动就是活着的最大幸福和最好的依据,不可否认批评也有这种感觉;但是批评一定要真诚的、简单的、灵活的、激烈的,并且能扩展知识面的。批评不需要任何卑劣的手段,

creative activity; a sense which a man of insight and conscience will prefer to what he might derive from a poor, starved, fragmentary, inadequate creation. And at some epochs no other creation is possible.

Still, in full measure, the sense of creative activity belongs only to genuine creation; in literature we must never forget that. But what true man of letters ever can forget it? It is no such common matter for a gifted nature to come into possession of a current of true and living ideas, and to produce amidst the inspiration of them, that we are likely to underrate it. The epochs of Aeschylus and Shakespeare make us feel their pre-eminence. In an epoch like those is, no doubt, the true life of literature; there is the promised land, toward which criticism can only beckon. That promised land it will not be ours to enter it, to have saluted it from afar, is already, perhaps, the best distinction among contemporaries, it will certainly be the best title to esteem with posterity.

3. Questions for Discussion

(1) What is the author's opinion of creation and criticism?

(2) How does society impose an effect on creation and criticism?

(3) What is your opinion about criticism?

它可以有创造性活动的愉悦感,这种感觉便是一个有洞察力和良心的人更倾向于从一个贫乏的、干瘪的、不完整的、不充分的创造中获得。并且在某些时代,也只有这样的创作。

尽管如此,创作的最大乐趣只属于真正的创作。在文学中我们不应忘记这一点。但是什么样真正的学者会忘记它呢?有才华的人并不是每一天都有真实的、生气勃勃的思想,并被这种思想鼓舞而创作出可以被我们正确地评价为作品的东西来。埃斯库罗斯和莎士比亚的时代使我们感觉到他们的杰出。像这样的时代,无疑才是文学真正的生活。那里是希望之乡,只有评论家能被召到那里去。我们没有福分到希望之乡去,从远方向它行礼,大概就是在同时代人当中最好的荣誉了,当然它也是最好的头衔,必将博得后人的尊敬。

3. 讨论题

(1)作者对于创作和批评的看法是什么?

(2)社会是如何对创作和批评产生影响的?

(3)你对于批评的看法是什么?

Chapter 6

第 6 章

1. Introduction to Nietzsche

Friedrich Wilhelm Nietzsche (1844-1990) was a German philosopher, essayist, and cultural critic. His writings on truth, morality, language, aesthetics, cultural theory, history, nihilism, power, consciousness, and the meaning of existence have exerted an enormous influence on Western philosophy and intellectual history.

Nietzsche was born in Röcken, where his father was a Lutheran minister. His father died in 1849, and the family relocated to Naumburg, where he grew up in a household comprising his mother, grandmother, two aunts, and his younger sister. In 1864, he attended the University of Bonn for two semesters and then transferred to the University of Leipzig. He was strongly influenced by the writings of philosopher Arthur Schopenhauer (1788—1860). During his time in Leipzig, he began a friendship with composer Richard Wagner (1813—1883). In 1869, at age 24, he was called to a chair in classical philology at Basel, the youngest ever appointed to that post. In the Basel years, Nietzsche published his first book *The Birth*

1. 尼采简介

弗里德里希·威廉·尼采(1844—1900)是德国哲学家、散文家和文化批评家。他的著作涉猎真理、道德、语言、美学、文化理论、历史、虚无主义、权力、意识和存在的意义,对西方哲学和思想史产生了巨大的影响。

尼采出生在吕肯,父亲是此地的路德教牧师。1849 年,父亲去世后,尼采跟随一家女眷:母亲、祖母、两个姑妈及小妹搬到瑙姆堡,在此长大成人。1864 年,他进入波恩大学学习,两学期后转入莱比锡大学。他深受哲学家亚瑟·叔本华(1788—1860)作品的影响。在莱比锡期间,他与作曲家理查德·瓦格纳(1813—1883)结为好友。1869 年,24 岁时,他被任命为巴塞尔大学古典哲学教授,是此职位上被任命的最年轻的教授。在巴塞尔大学期间,尼采出版了他的第一部著作《悲剧的诞生》(1872),散文集《不合时宜的考察》

of Tragedy (1872), a collection of essays *Untimely Meditations* (1873—1876) and the book *Human, All-too-human* (1878) which ended his friendship with Wagner.

(1873—1876),著作《人性的,太人性的》(1878),该著作终结了他与瓦格纳的友谊。

Nietzsche's health, always fragile, forced him to take leave from Basel in 1876—1877. Nietzsche's health did not measurably improve during the leave, and by 1879, he was forced to resign his professorship altogether. Nietzsche suffered a collapse in 1889 while living in Turin, Italy. The last decade of his life was spent in a state of mental incapacitation. He died in Weimar in 1900.

尼采向来体弱多病,孱弱的身体迫使他于 1876—1877 年离开巴塞尔大学。离职期间,尼采的身体并未明显改善,到了 1879 年,他被迫完全辞掉教授职位。1889 年,居住在意大利都灵期间,尼采精神崩溃。他生命的最后十年,一直处于精神失常状态。1990 年,他在魏玛去世。

Nietzsche's productive years were in the 1880s after his leaving Basel. Nietzsche published a book almost every year thereafter. These works are *Daybreak* (1881), *The Gay Science* (1882), *Thus Spoke Zarathustra* (1885), *Beyond Good and Evil* (1886), *On the Genealogy of Morality* (1887), *Twilight of the Idols* (1888), *The Wagner Case* (1888), *The Antichrist* (1888) and *Ecce Homo* (1888), ect.

尼采的丰产之年是在 19 世纪 80 年代,他离开巴塞尔大学之后。此后每年,尼采都出版一本著作。这些著作是《曙光》(1881)、《快乐的科学》(1882)、《查拉图斯特拉如是说》(1885)、《善恶的彼岸》(1886)、《道德的系谱》(1887)、《偶像的黄昏》(1888)、《瓦格纳事件》(1888)、《反基督》(1888)《看哪,这人!》(1888)等。

In these works of the 1880s, Nietzsche developed the central points of his philosophy. One of these was his famous statement that "God is dead," a rejection of Christianity as a meaningful force in contemporary life. Others were his endorsement of self-perfection through creative drive and a "will to power," and his concept of a "super-man".

在 19 世纪 80 年代的作品中,尼采形成了他的哲学中的核心要点。其中最著名的一句话是"上帝已死",在他所处的时代,发出反对基督教的强音。此外,他倡导人类通过创造力、"权力意志"和"超人"理念实现自我完善。

In *The Birth of Tragedy*, Nietzsche expresses the notion that tragedy is composed of two fundamental elements: the Apollonian and the Dionysian. The Apollonian is related to the Greek god Apollo, who is used as a symbol for measured restraint and harmony. The Dionysian is from the Greek god Dionysus, used a symbol of unbridled passion. For Nietzsche, Apollo represents the plastic / visual arts of painting, sculpture and epic

在《悲剧的诞生》中,尼采提出,悲剧由两个基本要素构成:日神精神和酒神精神。日神精神与希腊之神阿波罗相关,被用作为节制与和谐的象征。酒神精神源自希腊之神狄奥尼索斯,象征不受约束的激情。对于尼采而言,阿波罗代表造型/视觉艺术,如绘画、雕塑、史诗;而狄奥尼

poetry; Dionysus, by contrast, represents the non-visual art of music. The Apollonian and the Dionysian are creative / art tendencies or powers in man and these art tendencies are associated with dream and intoxication. For Nietzsche, artists, in the first instance, are "imitators" either of Apollonian dreams or Dionysian ecstasies.

Nietzsche thinks that the works of Aeschylus and Sophocles represent the summit of artistic creation, the true realization of tragedy, for they keep the delicate balance of the Dionysian and Apollonian. He points out that it is with Euripides that tragedy begins its death. Nietzsche objects to Euripides' utilization of Socratic rationalism in his tragedies, claiming that the infusion of ethics and reason robs tragedy of its foundation, namely the balance of the Dionysian and Apollonian.

索斯代表非视觉艺术,如音乐。日神精神和酒神精神是人的创造/艺术倾向或创造力,这些艺术倾向与梦和醉有关。尼采认为艺术家首先是模仿者,他们要么是日神之梦的模仿者,要么是酒神之醉的模仿者。

尼采认为,埃斯库罗斯和索福克勒斯的作品代表艺术创作的巅峰,是悲剧的典范,因为他们的作品达到日神精神和酒神精神的精妙平衡。他指出,悲剧到欧里庇得斯那里开始走向死亡。尼采反对欧里庇得斯将苏格拉底的理性主义用于悲剧,提出伦理和理性的融合吞噬了悲剧的基础,即酒神精神与日神精神的平衡。

2. Selections from *The Birth of Tragedy*

2.《悲剧的诞生》选文

The Birth of Tragedy①

Friedrich Wilhelm Nietzsche

1

We will have achieved much for the study of aesthetics when we come, not merely to a logical understanding, but also to the immediately certain apprehension of the fact that the further development of art is bound up with the duality of the Apollonian and the Dionysian, just as reproduction depends upon the duality of the sexes,

悲剧的诞生

弗里德里希·威廉·尼采

1

当我们不仅仅从逻辑理解出发,而且从事实的直观性出发,来了解艺术的持续发展是与日神和酒神的二元性密切相关的,我们就会在美学研究方面收获更多。正如生育依赖于性的二元性那样,其中的冲突是联系不断的,而和谐则只是偶尔的。我们

① Selected from *The Birth of Tragedy*, translated by Ian Johnston, Arlington: Richer Resources Publications, 2009. Ian Johnston 的几个译本在网上可以免费获得,但经过对比发现译者一直在修改译本,多数情况是不同版本会有一些文字变化,但意思没有太大区别,个别情况是先译版本中的某些错误在后一版本中有纠正。本节选文参考了多个版本,有一定取舍。

their continuing strife and only periodically occurring reconciliation. We take these names from the Greeks who gave a clear voice to the profound secret teachings of their contemplative art, not in ideas, but in the powerfully clear forms of their world of God.

With those two gods of art, Apollo and Dionysus, we connect our recognition that in the Greek world there exists a huge contrast, in origin and purposes, between visual (plastic) arts, the Apollonian, and the non-visual art of music, the Dionysian. Both very different drives go hand in hand, for the most part in open conflict with each other and simultaneously provoking each other to always new and more powerful offspring, in order to perpetuate for themselves the contest of opposites which the common word "Art" only seems to bridge, until they finally, through a marvelous metaphysical act of the Greek "will", they appear paired up each other and, as this pair, produce Attic① tragedy, just as much a Dionysian as an Apollonian work of art.②

In order to get closer to these two instinctual drives, let us think of them next as the separate artistic worlds of dreams and of intoxication, physiological phenomena between which we can observe an opposition corresponding to the one between the Apollonian and the Dionysian.

According to the idea of Lucretius③, the marvelous divine shapes first appeared to the mind of man in a dream. It was in a dream that the great artist saw the delightful anatomy of superhuman

从希腊人那里借用这些名称,希腊人不是用理念,而是用他们神话世界里的鲜明形象,使得他们沉思艺术的深厚秘籍得以发出声音,让人们了解。

我们的认识是同日神和酒神这两位艺术之神相联系的。在希腊世界里,从起源和目的来说,在造型视觉艺术日神和非视觉音乐艺术酒神之间存在着巨大的对立。两种非常不同的本能彼此共存,并且多半又彼此公开冲突,同时激起对方的更有力的新生,以求在这新生中永远保持着对立面的竞争,“艺术”这个普通的单词像一座桥一样来连接这种对立。直到他们最终通过希腊“意志”这个非凡的超自然行为相互结合起来,而这种结合产生了阿提卡悲剧,酒神和日神结合起来的艺术作品。

为了使我们更近地认识这两种本能,让我们把它们想象成梦和醉两个分开的艺术世界。在这些生理现象之间我们可以观察到一种相应的对立,如日神和酒神因素之间一样。

根据卢克莱修的见解,非凡的神的形象首先出现在人们的梦里,而伟大的艺术家正是在梦里看到了超人优美的骨骼。探寻诗歌创作秘籍的希腊诗人也会回忆起梦,并且给出了

① Attic:(古希腊雅典城邦)阿提卡的;雅典式的;雅典文化的。

② 日神阿波罗的属性代表造型艺术的精美,酒神狄奥尼索斯的属性代表音乐艺术的兴奋。

③ 卢克莱修(约公元前 99 年—约公元前 55 年),罗马共和国末期的诗人和哲学家,以哲理长诗《物性论》(*De Rerum Natura*)著称于世。承认世界的可知性,认为感觉是事物流射出来的影像作用于人的感官的结果,是一切认识的基础和来源,驳斥了怀疑论。认为幸福在于摆脱对神和死亡的恐惧,得到精神的安宁和心情的恬静。

existence, and the Hellenic poet, questioned about the secrets of poetic creativity, would have recalled the dream and given an explanation exactly similar to the one Hans Sachs provides in *Die Meistersinger*.

My friend, that is precisely the poet's work—
To figure out his dreams, mark them down.
Believe me, the truest illusion of mankind
Is revealed to him in dreams:
All poetic art and poeticizing
Is nothing but interpreting true dreams.

The beautiful appearance of the world of dreams, in whose creation each man is a complete artist is the precondition of all plastic art, indeed, as we shall see, an important half of poetry. We enjoy the form with an immediate understanding, all shapes speak to us; nothing is indifferent and unnecessary.

For all the very intense life of these dream realities, we nevertheless have the thoroughly disagreeable sense of their illusory quality. At least that is my experience. For their frequency, even normality, I can point to many witnesses and the utterances of poets. Even the philosophical man has the presentiment that this reality in which we live and have our being is an illusion, that under it lies hidden a second quite different reality. And Schopenhauer① specifically designates the ability to recognize at certain times that human beings and all things are mere phantoms or dream pictures as the trademark of philosophical ability.

Now, just as the philosopher behaves in relation to the reality of existence, so the

同汉斯·萨克斯在《名歌手》中那样非常接近的解释：

我的朋友，那正是诗人的使命——
解释并记下他的梦。
相信我，人类最真实的幻想
是在梦中向他透露的。
一切诗学和诗艺
都是在解释梦境。

梦境的美丽外观是一切造型艺术的前提，实际上，正如我们将要看到的，也是诗歌重要的一部分。而在创造梦境方面，每个人都是全面的艺术家。我们享受这种心领神会的感觉，每一种模型都在向我们倾诉，没有什么无关紧要、多余的东西。

即使在梦的现实生活最活跃时，我们仍然对它们虚幻的品质非常不满。至少这是我的经验，我可以提供许多证据和诗人名言来证明它们的活跃性，甚至是常态。就连哲学家也有这种预感：在我们生活和存在于其中的这个现实之下隐藏着另外一个完全不同的现实。因此这种表象的现实就是一种幻觉。叔本华明确指出那种在某些时候能够识别出人类和万物只是幻影或是梦幻中的画面的能力是哲学家能力的一种标志。

正如哲学家面对存在的现实那样，感性的艺术家面对梦的现实。他

① 亚瑟·叔本华(Arthur Schopenhauer,1788-1860),德国著名哲学家,开创了唯意志主义及生命哲学学派,代表作有《作为意志与表象的世界》(*Die Welt als Wille und Vorstellung*,1819;英译名(1) *The World as Will and Idea*;英译名(2) *The World as Will and Representation*)、《论意志的自由》(*On the Freedom of the Will*,1839)等。叔本华认为艺术品具有一种超时间的本质,而音乐同时具备超时间和超空间的本质,所以音乐不只是对理念的复制,它还更接近意志其本身。

artistically excitable man behaves in relation to the reality of dreams. He looks at them precisely and with pleasure, for from these pictures he fashions his interpretation of life; from these events he rehearses his life. This is not merely a case of agreeable and friendly images which he experiences with a complete understanding. They also include what is serious, cloudy, sad, dark, sudden scruples, teasing accidents, nervous expectations, in short, the entire "divine comedy" ①of life, including the *Inferno*②—all this moves past him, not just like a shadow play—for he lives and suffers in the midst of these scenes, yet also not without that fleeting sensation of illusion. And perhaps several people remember, like me, amid the dangers and terrors of a dream, successfully cheering themselves up by shouting: "It is a dream! I want to dream it some more!" I have also heard accounts of some people who had the ability to set out the causality of one and the same dream over three or more consecutive nights. These facts are clear evidence showing that our innermost beings, the secret underground in all of us, experiences its dreams with deep enjoyment and a sense of delightful necessity.

陶醉于梦的现实,并从这些画面中来阐释生活的意义,来演练他的生活。这不仅仅是一种他清楚地经历过的愉快亲切的意象,它还包含了严肃、忧愁、悲伤、黑暗、突然的不安、命运的捉弄以及紧张的期待。总而言之,生活的整部"神曲",包括"地狱"一起他都经历过了,不是像皮影戏那样,而是他生活和经历在这些场景里,还有那种幻觉稍纵即逝的感觉。也许一些人记得,就像我一样,当身处危险和恐惧的梦中时,会鼓励自己,结果喊出声来:"这是一个梦!我要把它梦下去!"我还听说过有人会一连三四夜做同一个连贯的梦。事实清楚地证明我们内在的本质,我们所有人内心深处的秘密就是我们都带着强烈的喜悦和愉快的必要性经历和感受着梦。

The Greeks expressed this joyful necessity of the dream experience in their god Apollo, who, as god of all the plastic arts, is at the same time the god of prophecy. In accordance with the root meaning of his association with brightness, he is the god of light. He also rules over the beautiful appearance of the inner fantasy world. The higher

希腊人在他们的日神身上表达了这种梦的经验的愉快的必要性。日神作为一切造型艺术的神,同时也是预言之神。根据他和光明联系的根源,他也是光明之神。他也统治着内心幻想世界的美丽外观。更高的真理,与日常现实粗略的理解相对比

① 《神曲》(*Divina Commedia*),意大利诗人但丁的史诗,创作于1307年至1321年,全诗分为《地狱》、(Inferno)、《炼狱》(Purgatory)、《天堂》(Paradise)三部,每部33首,最前面还增加一首序诗,一共100首。它被认为是欧洲乃至世界最伟大的文学作品之一。

② 地狱形似一个上宽下窄的漏斗,共9层。第一层是林勃,生于基督之前,未能接受洗礼的古代异教徒,在这里等候上帝的审判。在其余8层,罪人的灵魂按生前所犯的罪孽(贪色、饕餮、贪婪、愤怒、信奉邪教、强暴、欺诈、背叛),分别接受不同的严酷刑罚。

truth, the perfection of this condition in contrast to the sketchy understanding of our daily reality, as well as the deep consciousness of a healing and helping nature in sleep and dreaming, is at the same time the symbolic analogy to the capacity to prophesy the truth, as well as to art in general, through which life is made possible and worth living. But also that delicate line which the dream image may not cross so that it does not work its effect pathologically—otherwise the illusion would deceive us as crude reality)—that line must not be absent from the image of Apollo, that boundary of moderation, that freedom from more ecstatic excitement, that fully wise calm of the god of images. His eye must be "sun-like", in keeping with his origin; even when he is angry and gazes with displeasure, the consecration of the beautiful illusion rests on him.

And so concerning Apollo one could endorse in an eccentric way, what Schopenhauer says of the man trapped in the veil of Maja①: "As on the stormy sea which extends without limit on all sides, howling mountainous waves rise up and sink and a sailor sits in a row boat, trusting the weak craft, so, in the midst of a world of torments, the solitary man sits peacefully, supported by and trusting in the principium individuationis②(the principle of individuality)" (*World as Will and Idea*, Vol. I, p. 416). Yes, we could say of Apollo that the imperturbable trust in that principle and the calm sitting still of the man caught up in it attained its loftiest expression in him, and we may even designate Apollo himself as the marvelous divine image of the principium individuationis, from whose gestures and gaze all the joy and wisdom of

的这种状态的完美性,以及在睡梦中起治愈和帮助本质作用的深刻的意识同时也是预言真理能力的象征性的相似物,一般来说,对艺术也是如此。正是这样,人生才成为可能并值得一过。但是梦象可能无法越过那纤弱的界限以免引起病理作用。否则,幻觉就会用粗糙的现实欺骗我们——在日神的形象中同样不可或缺,适度的克制,免受强烈的刺激,日神形象的完全智慧和镇定。他的眼睛必须像太阳一样保持他的本源;即使在他生气和怒视的时候,仍不失那美丽光辉的尊严。

因此,奇怪的是,叔本华关于藏身在摩耶之幕下的人所说的,也可适用于日神。《作为意志和表象的世界》第一卷,416 页写道:"波涛汹涌的大海无边无际,翻卷着咆哮的巨浪,水手坐在小舟上,托身于一叶扁舟;同样的,隐士平静地置身于苦难世界之中,信赖个体化原理的支持。"那么,关于日神我们也可以说,在他身上,对这一原理的坚定信任和置身其中的镇定精神,得到了最崇高的体现,我们甚至可以把日神作为个体化原理的非凡的神圣形象。日神的举止和凝视向我们传达了幻觉的全部喜悦、智慧和美丽。

① Maja:印度哲学的"摩耶",叔本华在《作为意志和表象的世界》中指幻相、表象。

② the principium individuationis(the principle of individuality):个体化原理,源于叔本华所著《作为意志和表象的世界》。

illusion, together with its beauty, speaks to us.

In the same place Schopenhauer also described for us the monstrous horror which seizes a man when he suddenly doubts the ways of comprehending illusion, when the sense of a foundation, in any one of its forms, appears to suffer a breakdown. If we add to this horror the ecstatic rapture, which rises up out of the same collapse of the principium individuationis from the innermost depths of human beings, yes, from the innermost depths of nature, then we have a glimpse into the essence of the Dionysian, which is presented to us most closely through the analogy to intoxication.

在同一处,叔本华也向我们描述了一种巨大的惊骇,当人突然怀疑理解幻觉的方式时,当这种牢固的感觉以任何一种形式崩溃时,这种惊骇就淹没了他。如果我们再给这种惊骇增加个体化原理崩溃之时从人的内心深处即本性中升起的狂喜,我们就瞥见了酒神的本质,把它比拟为醉是最贴切的。

Either through the influence of narcotic drink, of which all primitive men and peoples speak in their hymns, or through the powerful coming on of spring, which drives joyfully through all of nature, that Dionysian excitement arises; as its power increases, the subjective fades into complete forgetfulness of self. In the German Middle Ages, under the same power of Dionysus, constantly growing hordes waltzed from place to place, singing and dancing; in that St. John's and St. Vitus's dancing we recognize the Bacchic① chorus of the Greeks once again, with its precursors in Asia Minor②, right back to Babylon and the orgiastic Sacaea (a riotous Babylonian festival).

抑或是由于原始人群和民族的颂诗里说到的那种麻醉饮料的威力,又或是源于春天那种使万物复苏、欣欣向荣的春之力,酒神的激情就苏醒了。随着激情的高涨,主观逐渐进入一种浑然忘我之境。在德国中世纪,在酒神之力的驱使下,人们汇集成群,载歌载舞,巡游各地。在圣约翰节和圣维托斯节的歌舞者身上,我们又一次目睹了古希腊酒神歌队及小亚细亚的历史,乃至巴比伦和崇尚秘仪(一种巴比伦式的狂欢节)的萨克亚人。

There are man who, from a lack of experience or out of apathy, turn mockingly or pityingly away from such phenomena as from a "sickness of the people", with a sense of their own health. These poor people naturally do not have any sense of how deathly and ghost-like this very "health" of theirs sounds, when the glowing life of the Dionysian throng roars past them. Under the magic of the

有一些人由于缺乏阅历或是冷漠,因此,只关心自己的身体健康,而嘲讽或是怜悯地避开这种现象,犹如避开一种"民间疾病"。这些可怜虫当然没有想到,当酒神歌队的炽烈生活在他们身边沸腾之时,他们的健康会怎样地惨如尸色,恍如幽灵。在酒

① Bacchic: 酒神的;喧闹的;醉酒的
② Asia Minor: 小亚细亚

Dionysian, not only does the bond between man and man lock itself in place once more, but also nature itself, no matter how alienated, hostile, or subjugated, rejoices again in her festival of reconciliation with her prodigal son, man. The earth freely offers up her gifts and the beasts of prey from the rocks and the desert approach in peace. The wagon of Dionysus is covered with flowers and wreaths; under his yolk stride panthers and tigers.

神的魔力之下,不仅人与人之间的关系更加密切了,而且疏远、敌意、被奴役的大自然也再次和她的浪子人类欢庆她们和解的日子。大地无私地奉献它的礼物,石崖荒漠中的猛兽也驯良地前来。酒神的车辇满载着百卉花环,由虎豹拉着前行。

If someone were to transform Beethoven's *Ode to Joy* into a painting and not restrain his imagination when millions of people sink dramatically into the dust, then we could come close to the Dionysian. Now is the slave a free man; now all the stiff, hostile barriers break apart, those things which necessity and arbitrary power or "saucy fashion" have established between men. Now, with the gospel of world harmony, every man feels himself not only united with his neighbor, reconciled and fused together, but also as if the veil of Maja had been ripped apart, with only scraps fluttering around before the mysterious original unity. Singing and dancing, man expresses himself as a member of a higher community: he has forgotten how to walk and talk and is on the verge of flying up into the air as he dances. The enchantment speaks out in his gestures. Just as the animals speak and the earth gives milk and honey, so now something supernatural echoes out of him. He feels himself a god. He now moves in a lofty ecstasy, as he saw the gods move in his dream. The man is no longer an artist. He has become a work of art. The artistic power of all of nature, the rhapsodic satisfaction of the primordial unity, reveals itself here in the intoxicated performance. The finest clay, the most expensive marble—man—is here worked and chiseled, and the cry of

如果有人能够把贝多芬的《欢乐颂》化作一幅画,并且继续狂想着数百万人戏剧性地落入尘埃,那么他就接近酒神的境界了。此刻奴隶也成了自由人。那些横隔在人与人之间的贫困、专断或是"粗俗之风"也土崩瓦解了。此刻在世界和谐福音中,每个人不仅感到他和邻居的团结、和解、融洽,甚至融为一体了。仿佛摩耶之幕也被撕掉了,只剩下碎片飘浮在神秘的原始实体之前。人们载歌载舞地表达着自己成了较高团体的一员,他已经忘记了如何行走和讲话,并在跳舞时欲飞向天空。他的行为举止表明他已经着魔了。就像此刻野兽开口说话,大地流出牛奶和蜂蜜一样,超自然的奇迹也发生在人类身上。他感觉自己就是神,他现在傲慢地、欣喜若狂地飘移犹如他在梦境里看到众神的飘移。人不再是艺术家了,他已经变成了艺术品:整个大自然的艺术能力达到了一种最高的原始团结的巅峰满足,以陶醉的形式表现出来了。人,这世界上高贵的黏土,最昂贵的大理石,在这里被捏制

the Eleusinian mysteries[1] rings out to the chisel blows of the Dionysian world artist: "Do you fall down, you millions? World, do you have a sense of your creator?"

10

It is an incontestable tradition that Greek tragedy in its oldest form had as its subject only the suffering of Dionysus and that for a long time later the individually present stage heroes were simply Dionysus. But with the same certainty we can assert that right up to the time of Euripides Dionysus never ceased being the tragic hero, that all the famous figures of the Greek theatre, like Prometheus[2], Oedipus[3], and so on, are only masks of that primordial hero, Dionysus. The fact that behind all these masks stands a divinity, that is the single fundamental reason for the frequently admired characteristic "ideality" of those well-known figures.

Someone, I don't know who, made the claim that all individuals, as individuals, are comic and thus untragic, and from that we might gather that the Greeks in general could not tolerate individuals on the tragic stage. In fact, they seem to have felt this way: that Platonic distinction between and evaluation of the "idea" in contrast to the "idol" in connection with likenesses lies deeply grounded in the nature of the Greeks. But for us to make use of Plato's terminology, we would have to talk of the tragic figures of the Greek stage in something like

和雕琢,而应和着酒神的宇宙艺术家的斧凿声,厄琉息斯秘仪呼喊道:"苍生啊,你们颓然倒下了吗?宇宙啊,你感觉到那创造者了吗?"

10

这是一个无可争辩的传统:希腊悲剧在其最古老的形式中仅仅以酒神的受苦为主题,并且在那之后舞台上的主角都只是酒神。但是,同样确信的是在欧里庇得斯之前,酒神一直都是悲剧主角。希腊戏剧中所有著名角色,比如:普罗米修斯、俄狄浦斯等等,都只是酒神最原始的面具。事实是在所有的面具之下藏着一位神,这就是那些著名角色之所以经常具有如此让人羡慕的"理想"性的主要原因。

我不知道谁曾经声称所有个人作为个人都是喜剧性的,因此,也就是非悲剧性的。由此我们可以推断希腊人总体来说是不能容忍个人登上悲剧舞台的。事实上,他们似乎有这样的感觉:柏拉图对"理念"和"偶像"摹本的区别和评价一般来说是如何深深地根植于希腊人的本性之中的。但是我们为了利用柏拉图的术语,我们得这样来讲述希腊舞台悲剧形象:真正的酒神以多种形象出现,

① Eleusinian mysteries:厄琉息斯秘仪。酒神祭是古希腊民间信仰的一种仪式,在神话传说上,它与厄琉息斯地母祭的秘仪有密切关系,两者都与古希腊农业生产有关。

② 普罗米修斯(Prometheus),在希腊神话中,是最具智慧的神明之一,最早的提坦巨神(Titans)后代,名字有"先见之明"(Forethought)的意思。提坦十二神之一伊阿佩托斯(Iapetus)与名望女神克吕墨涅(Clymene)的儿子。普罗米修斯不仅创造了人类,还为人类带来了火,并传授知识。

③ 俄狄浦斯(Oedipus),希腊神话中忒拜(Thebe)的国王拉伊奥斯(Laius)和王后约卡斯塔(Jocasta)的儿子,他在不知情的情况下,杀死了自己的父亲并娶了自己的母亲。

the following terms: the one truly real Dionysus appears in a multiplicity of shapes, in the mask of a struggling hero and, as it were, bound up in the net of the individual will. So now the god made manifest talks and acts in such a way that he looks like an erring, striving, suffering individual: the fact that he generally appears with this epic definition and clarity is the effect of Apollo, the interpreter of dreams, who indicates to the chorus its Dionysian state by that metaphorical appearance.

In reality, however, that hero is the suffering Dionysus of the mysteries, that god who experiences the suffering of the individual in himself, the god about whom the amazing myths tell how he, as a child, was dismembered by the Titans and now in this condition is venerated as Zagreus①. Through this is revealed the idea that this dismemberment, the essentially Dionysian suffering, is like a transformation into air, water, earth, and fire, that we also have to look upon the condition of individuation as the source and basis for all suffering, as something in itself reprehensible. From the smile of this Dionysus arose the Olympian gods, from his tears arose mankind. In that existence as dismembered god Dionysus has the dual nature of a cruelly savage daemon and a lenient, gentle master.

The initiates in the Eleusinian mysteries hoped for a rebirth of Dionysus, which we now can understand as a premonition of the end of individuation: the initiates' thundering song of jubilation cried out to this approaching third Dionysus. And only with this hope was there a ray of joy on the face of the fragmented world, torn apart into individuals, as myth reveals in the

在斗争英雄的面具之下,注定陷入个人意志之网。因此,现在这位神的言行举止如同一位犯了错误,挣扎着、受苦着的个人:事实是这位神明以史诗似的明确性和清晰性出现,这些都是释梦者日神阿波罗的功劳,它用比喻的现象向歌队暗示了酒神的状态。

然而,那位英雄实际上是神秘的受苦酒神,那位受苦的神明在它自己身上经历着个体化痛苦。一个神奇的神话讲述了他在幼年时怎样被提坦众神肢解,现在,他又被尊称为扎格列欧斯。这表明,这种肢解,本来意义上酒神的受苦,即转化为空气、水、土地和火。因此,我们必须把个体化状态作为一切受苦的根源和始因,作为本身应受谴责的事。从这位酒神的微笑中产生了奥林匹斯众神,从他的眼泪中产生了人类。在那种存在中,作为被肢解了的神,酒神具有了双重天性:一个残酷野蛮的恶魔和一位温和仁慈的君主。

新入会的古希腊秘仪寄希望于酒神的新生,这些我们现在可以理解成是个体化终结的预感:新入会的秘仪们向正在降生的第三个酒神表示狂热的欢呼歌唱。只有有了这个希望,这个支离破碎的、分裂为个体的世界的面孔上才有了一线的快乐。

① 据古希腊神话,第一个酒神狄俄尼索斯(the first Dionysus)是宙斯(Zeus)和其女儿珀尔塞福涅(Persephone)的私生子。赫拉(Hera)嫉妒,命泰坦神族把他肢解。雅典娜(Athena)保护了他的心脏并还给宙斯。宙斯吞下这颗心脏与塞墨勒(Semele)产一子,名为酒神扎格列欧斯,以纪念死者狄俄尼索斯。

picture of Demeter① sunk in eternal sorrow, who rejoices again for the first time when someone says to her that she might be able once again to give birth to Dionysus. In these established views we already have assembled all the components of a profound and pessimistic world view, together with the mysterious teachings of tragedy: the basic acknowledgement of the unity of all existing things, the observation that individuation is the ultimate foundation of all evil, art the joyful hope, that the spell of individuation is there for us to break, as a premonition of a re-established unity.

正如德墨忒耳神话所启示的那样,她沉沦在永久的悲伤里时,当她听说她可能再次生育酒神时,她才再一次重新快乐起来。在上述观点中,我们已经形成了一种深厚而又悲观的世界观,连同这些悲剧神秘的教学:认识到万物根本上浑然一体,观察到个体化是万恶之源,艺术是快乐的希望,个体化的魅惑是让我们去打破的,作为一个重建统一体的预感。

It has been pointed out earlier that the *Homeric Epic*② is the poetry of Olympian culture, with which it sang its own song of victory over the terrors of the fight against the Titans. Now, under the overwhelming influence of tragic poetry, the Homeric myths were newly reborn and show in this metamorphosis that since then the Olympian culture has also been overcome by an even deeper world view. The defiant Titan Prometheus reported to his Olympian torturer that for the first time his rule was threatened by the highest danger, unless he quickly joined forces with him. In Aeschylus we acknowledge the union of the frightened Zeus, worried about his end, with the Titan.

之前已经指出,荷马史诗是奥林匹斯文化的诗篇,它歌唱了奥林匹斯文化对提坦战争恐吓的胜利。现在,在悲剧诗歌的巨大影响之下,荷马神话获得重生,在这个重生的变化中奥林匹斯文化也受到了更深刻的世界观的压制。大胆的提坦神普罗米修斯向折磨他的奥林匹斯神预告,除非奥林匹斯神尽快地和他联盟,否则,奥林匹斯神的统治将会受到巨大的威胁。从埃斯库罗斯那里我们知道了惊恐的、担心他的末日的宙斯最终与这位提坦神联盟了。

Thus the earlier age of the Titans is belatedly brought back from Tartarus into the light once more. The philosophy of wild and naked nature looks with the open countenance of truth at the myths of the Homeric world dancing past it: before the flashing eyes of this goddess, those myths grow

于是提坦的年轻时代又一次从塔尔塔罗斯地狱复起,再次看到光明。狂野裸露的自然界哲学,带着真理的未加掩饰的面容,直视荷马世界飘逸着经过的神话。在这位女神一闪而过的眼神之前,这些神话慢慢地

① 德墨忒耳(Demeter),希腊神话中司掌农业的谷物女神,亦被称为丰饶女神。

② 《荷马史诗》(*Homeric Epic*)是古希腊盲诗人荷马创造的两部长篇史诗《伊利亚特》和《奥德赛》的统称。《伊利亚特》和《奥德赛》的主题分别是在特洛伊战争中,阿喀琉斯与阿伽门农间的争端,以及特洛伊沦陷后,奥德修斯返回伊萨卡岛上的王国,与妻子珀涅罗珀团聚的故事。《荷马史诗》是早期英雄时代的大幅全景,也是艺术上的绝妙之作,它以整个希腊及其四周的汪洋大海为主要背景,充分展现了自由主义的情景,并为日后希腊人的道德观念(进而为整个西方社会的道德观念),立下了典范。

pale and tremble—until the mighty fist of the Dionysian artist forces them into the service of the new divinity. The Dionysian truth takes over the entire realm of myth as the symbol of its knowledge and speaks of this knowledge, partly in the public culture of tragedy and partly in the secret celebrations of dramatic mystery ceremonies, but always in the disguise of the old myths. What power was it which liberated Prometheus from his vultures and transformed the myth into a vehicle of Dionysian wisdom? It was the Herculean power of music, which attained its highest manifestation in tragedy and knew how to interpret myth with a new significance in the most profound manner, something we have already described before as the most powerful capacity of music.

For it is the lot of every myth gradually to creep into the crevice of an assumed historical reality and to become analyzed as a unique fact in answer to the historical demands of some later time or other. The Greek were already fully on their way to labeling cleverly and arbitrarily the completely mythical dreams of their youth as a historical, pragmatic, and youthful history. For this is the way religions tend to die out, namely, when the mythical pre-conditions of a religion, under the strict, rational eyes of an orthodox dogmatism, become systematized as a closed totality of historical events and people begin anxiously defending the credibility of their myths but resisting every naturally continuing life and further growth of those same myths and when the feeling for the myth dies out and in its place the claim to put religion on a historical footing steps forward.

The newly born genius of Dionysian music now seized these dying myths, and in its hands myth blossomed again, with colors which it had never shown before, with a scent which stirred up a longing premonition of a metaphysical world. After

变得苍白和颤抖,直到酒神艺术家的铁拳迫使他们服务于新的神灵。酒神的真理占据了整个神话王国,把它作为自己知识的象征,并且赞扬这种知识,部分在悲剧的公众文化之中,部分在戏剧性秘仪礼节上的典礼里,但总是在古老神话的外衣之下。是什么力量把普罗米修斯从秃鹰魔爪之下解救出来,并把这个神话变成酒神智慧的龙辇?是音乐的赫拉克勒斯般的力量啊!它在悲剧中达到了最高的表现,而且知道如何从一个有新意的、更为深刻的方式去解释神话;这种方式就是我们之前已经描述过的音乐的最强能力。

因为这是每个神话的命运:逐渐蔓延成一种假定的历史事实,而被后人当作一种特有的历史事实来分析。希腊人已经对他们全部的青年历史做了机智、任性的标记,把它们标记为一种实用史学的青年史。因为这就是宗教趋于灭亡的方式:在正统教条主义严格而又理智的目光下,一种宗教的神话前提作为历史事件的总和而系统化,人们也开始焦急地捍卫他们的神话威信,但是却抵制这些神话的每一个自然地生存和发展;当人们对神话的感觉消亡时,就把宗教置于历史的足迹之上。

新生的酒神音乐天才现在抓住了这些即将灭亡的神话,在酒神手上,这些神话又再次繁荣起来了,呈现出了前所未有的色彩,激发出了一

this last flourishing, myth collapsed, its leaves grew pale, and soon the mocking Lucians of antiquity grabbed up the flowers, scattered around by all winds, colorless and withered. Through tragedy myth attains its most profound content, its most expressive form. It lifts itself up again, like a wounded hero, and all the remaining strength and wise tranquilly of a dying man burn in its eyes with its final powerful light.

种强烈的形而上学世界的情感。在此短暂的繁荣之后,神话再次衰弱,枝叶枯萎;很快玩世不恭的古人鲁奇安之流抓住了这些随风飘落、褪色而凋零的花瓣。借助悲剧神话达到了它最深刻的内容和最传神的形式。神话再次站立,犹如一位受伤的英雄,而全部剩余的精力和临终者明智的沉静在神话的眼中燃起了它最后的力量之光。

What did you want, you presumptuous Euripides, when you sought to force this dying man once more into your cheerful service? He died under your powerful hands. And now you used a counterfeit, masked myth, which knew only how to dress itself up with the old splendor, like Hercules' monkey. And as myth died with you, so with you died the genius of music as well. Although you liked to plunder with greedy hands all the gardens of music, even so you achieved only a counterfeit, masked music. And because you abandoned Dionysus, you were then abandoned also by Apollo. Even though you hunted out all the passions from their beds and charmed them into your circle, even though you sharpened and filed a really sophisticated dialectic for the speeches of your heroes —nevertheless your heroes have only counterfeit, masked passions and speak only a counterfeit, masked language.

专横的欧里庇得斯,当你企图强迫这位临终者再次为你欣然服务时,你究竟想要什么?他死于你粗暴的手掌下。而现在你需要一位伪装的冒牌神话——它只知道用以前的辉煌装扮自己,就像赫拉克勒斯的猴子那样。并且如同神话对你来说已经死去一样,你已经失去了音乐的天赋。尽管你喜欢贪婪地掠夺音乐乐园,即便如此,你得到的也仅仅是一种伪装的冒牌音乐。而且由于你遗弃了酒神,日神也因此遗弃了你。即使你从它们的领地上试图获取所有的热情,并且使其着迷于你的领地;即使你为你的英雄们磨砺好一种诡辩的辩证法台词——然而你的英雄们只有伪装的冒充的热情,只讲虚伪的冒充的话语。

12

Before we designate this other spectator by name, let's linger here a moment to call to mind for ourselves that impression of the duality and incommensurability at the heart of Aeschylean①

12

在指出另一个观众的名字之前,让我们稍息片刻来回顾一下我们之前谈到的关于埃斯库罗斯悲剧之本质中的二元性和不可兼容性的印象。

① 埃斯库罗斯(Aeschylus,约公元前 525 年—公元前 456 年),古希腊悲剧作家,代表作有《被缚的普罗米修斯》、《阿伽门农》、《善好者》等。索福克勒斯(Sophocle,约公元前 496 年—公元前 406 年),古希腊悲剧作家,代表作有《安提戈涅》、《俄狄浦斯王》等。欧里庇得斯(Euripides,约公元前 485 或 480 年—公元前 406 年),古希腊悲剧作家,代表作有《美狄亚》、《希波吕托斯》等。

tragedy, something we described earlier. Let us think about our own surprise at and unease with the chorus and the tragic hero of those tragedies, both of which we did not know how to reconcile with what we are used to any more than with the tradition—until we again recognized that duality itself as the origin and essence of Greek tragedy, as the expression of two artistic drives woven together, the Apollonian and the Dionysian.

To cut that primordial and all-powerful Dionysian element out of tragedy and to rebuild tragedy as a pure, new, and un-Dionysian art, morality, and world view—that has now revealed itself to us very clearly as the tendency of Euripides. Near the end of his life, Euripides himself proposed as emphatically as possible for his contemporaries the question about the value and meaning of this tendency in a myth. Should the Dionysian exist at all? Should we not eradicate it forcefully from Greek soil? Of course we should, the poet says to us, if only it were possible, but the god Dionysus is too powerful. The most sensible opponent, like Pentheus in the *Bacchae*, is unexpectedly charmed by Dionysus and runs from in this enchanted state to his own destruction.

The judgment of the two old men, Cadmus and Tiresias, seems also to be the judgment of the aged poet: the thinking of the cleverest individual does not throw away that old folk tradition, that eternally propagating reverence for Dionysus; indeed, where such amazing powers are concerned, it is appropriate at least to demonstrate a diplomatically prudent show of joining in. But even with that, it is still possible that the god might take offence at such lukewarm participation and in the end transform the diplomat into a dragon—as happens here with Cadmus.

The poet tells us this, a poet who fought throughout his long life against Dionysus with heroic force—only to conclude his life with a

让我们想想我们自己对于此种悲剧的歌队和悲剧英雄的诧异，我们不知道这两种是如何与我们的习惯达成和解的，就像同传统一样难以协调——直到我们重新发现那作为希腊悲剧的起源和本质的二元性本身，它是日神和酒神两种彼此交织的艺术表现。

从悲剧中去除掉那原始的全能的酒神因素，并且重新建立在一种单纯的、全新的、非酒神艺术、道德观和世界观基础之上——那就是现在已经给我们暴露的非常清楚的欧里庇得斯的意图。在欧里庇得斯晚年的时候，在一部神话剧里，他向他的同时代人尽可能地强烈提出这种倾向的价值和意义。酒神因素应该存在吗？难道我们不应该把它强行从希腊土壤里铲除掉吗？诗人告诉我们，当然应该，倘若我们能够做到的话，但是酒神太强大了。最聪明的对手，如《酒神伴侣》中的彭透斯，也意外地被酒神迷住了，并以此迷醉状态走向灭亡。

卡德摩斯和提瑞西阿斯二位老人的判断看上去似乎也是这位老诗人的判断：最聪明的人的思考不能摒弃古老的民间传统——对酒神永久的尊敬。实际上比较合宜的做法是对如此神奇的力量显示出一种外交式谨慎的合作。但是即便如此，酒神可能依然会对这种冷淡的合作感到恼怒，而最终把外交官——在这里是卡德摩斯——变成了一条龙。

这是一位诗人告诉我们的，他终其一生的英勇力量对抗酒神，却是最终以颂扬敌手和自杀结束自己的生

glorification of his opponent and a suicide, like a man suffering from vertigo who, in order to escape the dreadful dizziness, which he can no longer endure, throws himself off a tower. That tragedy is a protest against the practicality of his artistic program, and it had already succeeded! A miracle had taken place: just when the poet recanted, his program had already triumphed. Dionysus had already been chased off the tragic stage, and by a daemonic power speaking out from Euripides. But Euripides was, in a certain sense, only a mask: the divinity which spoke out of him was not Dionysus, and not Apollo, but an entirely new-born daemon called Socrates.

This is the new opposition: the Dionysian and the Socratic. And from this contrast, Greek tragedy perished as a work of art. No matter how much Euripides might now seek to console us with his retraction, he was unsuccessful: the most magnificent temple lay in ruins. What use to us are the laments of the destroyer and his awareness that it had been the most beautiful of all temples? And even if Euripides himself, as a punishment, has been turned into a dragon by the artistic critics of all ages—who can be satisfied with this paltry compensation?

Let us get closer now to this Socratic project, with which Euripides fought against and conquered Aeschylean tragedy.

What purpose (that's the question we need to ask at this point) could Euripides' intention to ground drama solely on the un-Dionysian have generally had, if we assume its implementation had the very highest ideals? What form of drama still remained, if it was not to be born from the womb of music, in that mysterious half-light of the Dionysian? All it could be was dramatic epic, an Apollonian art form, in which the tragic effect is naturally unattainable.

命,就像一个眩晕的人仅仅为了逃避可怕的难以忍受的天旋地转,而从高塔上跳了下来。这部悲剧是对他的倾向之可行性的一个抗议;可是它毕竟已经实行了啊!一个奇迹已经发生了:就在诗人刚刚放弃他的倾向之时,这倾向已经获胜了。酒神已经被欧里庇得斯之口的魔力逐出了舞台。但是从某种意义上说欧里庇得斯也仅仅是副面具,借他之口说话的神祇不是酒神,也不是日神,而是一个全新的、名叫苏格拉底的精灵。

这是新的对立:酒神精神和苏格拉底精神的对立。希腊悲剧作为艺术作品就毁灭于这种对立之中。现在无论欧里庇得斯怎样用他的悔改来安慰我们都不成功:最富丽堂皇的庙宇毁于一旦。破坏者的悔恨痛惜及其意识到它是所有庙宇中最漂亮的庙宇,对我们来说又有什么用呢?作为惩罚,即使欧里庇得斯自己被所有年代的艺术批评家变成了一条龙——谁又会对这微不足道的补偿感到满意呢?

让我们进一步考察一下苏格拉底倾向,这正是欧里庇得斯借此来对抗和征服埃斯库罗斯悲剧的。

欧里庇得斯意图把戏剧仅仅建立在非酒神基础之上,如果我们假设这一意图得到了最高理想的执行,他的目的究竟是什么?(此时我们需要提出此问题。)如若戏剧不是孕育于音乐的怀抱,诞生于酒神那神秘的暗光之中,那么戏剧还保留了哪些形式?只有戏剧化的史诗罢了,一种日神的艺术形式;在此种形式下,悲剧效果自然是无法达到了。

This is not a matter of the content of the represented events. Indeed, I could assert that in Goethe's proposed *Nausikaa* it would have been impossible to make the suicide of that idyllic being—which was to be carried out in the fifth act—grippingly tragic, for the power of the Apollonian epic is so extraordinary that right before our very eyes it magically transforms the most horrific things through that joy in and redemption through appearances. The poet of the dramatic epic cannot completely fuse with his pictures, any more than the epic rhapsodist can: it is still a matter of calm, tranquil contemplation, looking with open eyes, a state which sees the images in front of it. The actor in this dramatized epic still remains, in the most profound sense, a rhapsodist; the consecration of the inner dream lies upon all his actions, so that he is never completely an actor.

How is Euripides' work related with respected to this ideal of Apollonian drama? It is just like the relationship of the solemn rhapsodist of the olden times to the younger attitude, whose nature is described in Plato's *Ion*① as follows: "When I say something sad, my eyes fill with tears. But if what I say is horrifying and terrible, then the hairs on my head stand on end from fright, and my heart beats loudly." Here we no longer see the epic dissolution of being in appearances, the disinterested coolness of the real actor, who remains, particularly in his most intense activity, totally appearance and delight in appearances. Euripides is the actor with the beating heart, with his hair standing on end. He designs his work as a Socratic thinker, and he carries it out as a passionate actor.

Euripides is a pure artist neither in planning his work nor in carrying it out. Thus, the

这并不是事件内容的问题。实际上,我可以断言,在歌德所构思的《瑙西卡》中,不可能使那种田园诗般的人物的自杀引起悲剧效果(这一幕预定在第五幕中出现)。日神史诗的力量如此之大,以至于就在我们的眼前他神奇般地把最恐惧的事情通过喜悦和外观的救赎而改变了。戏剧化史诗的诗人如同史诗朗诵者那样,很少同他的形象完全融为一体:他依然镇定安静地思考、观看着眼前的形象。这种戏剧化史诗中的演员从某种更深刻的意义上来说依然是一位吟诵者;内在梦境的庄严气氛隐藏在他的所有动作之中,以至于他从来不完全是一位演员。

欧里庇得斯的戏剧和日神戏剧的这种理想关系如何?就像那老一辈严肃的吟诵者与年轻吟诵者的关系一样,在柏拉图的《伊安篇》里,这样描述这个青年的性情:"我在朗诵悲伤的事迹时,就泪眼蒙眬。但当我朗诵恐怖事迹时,就毛骨悚然,心惊肉跳。"在此,我们再也看不到对于外观的史诗式的陶醉,再也看不到真正演员的无动于衷的冷静,真正的演员达到最高演艺时,完全成为外观及其以外观为乐。欧里庇得斯是一位心脏悸动、毛骨悚然的演员。他作为苏格拉底式的思想家设计作品,并像一位激情的演员那样去演出。

欧里庇得斯在设计作品和演出

① 《伊安篇》(*Ion*)是柏拉图较早的一篇对话录。它通过苏格拉底与诵诗人伊安的对话,探讨了诗人文艺才能产生的原因,是诗人凭借专门的技艺还是凭借灵感来创作的。柏拉图通过与伊安的辩论得出诗人是凭借灵感来创作的结论,并描述了灵感产生时的状态,这对后世产生了深远的影响。

Euripidean drama is simultaneously a cool and fiery thing, equally capable of freezing or burning. It is impossible for it to attain the Apollonian effect of the epic, while, on the other hand, it has divorced itself as much as possible from the Dionysian elements, and now, in order to work at all, it needs new ways to arouse people, methods which can no longer lie within either of the two individual artistic drives of the Apollonian and the Dionysian. These method of arousing people are detached paradoxical ideas, substituted for Apollonian objects of contemplation, and fiery emotional effects, substituted for Dionysian enchantment. The fiery effects are, to be sure, imitated with the highest degree of realism, but the ideas and emotional effects are not in the slightest imbued with the spirit of art.

作品中都不是一位纯粹的艺术家。因此,欧里庇得斯的戏剧同时兼有冷和热,既可冻结又可燃烧。它一方面不可能达到史诗的日神效果,而另一方面又尽可能地摆脱酒神因素。现在为了产生效果,就需要新的方法引起人们的注意,而这种方法不再在日神和酒神的两种个体化艺术冲动的范围。这些引起人们注意的方法是与矛盾论相分离的,代替了日神理性的沉思和酒神炽烈情感的魔力。这种炽烈情感的效果确实是对现实的最高程度的模仿,但是理性和情感效果却丝毫都没有进入艺术氛围。

If we have recognized this much, that Euripides was not at all successful in basing his drama solely on Apollonian principles, that, by contrast, his un-Dionysian tendencies led him astray into an inartistic naturalism, we will now able to move closer to the essential quality of Socratic aesthetics, whose most important law runs something like this: “Everything must be understandable in order to be beautiful,” a corollary to the Socratic saying, “Only the knowledgeable person is virtuous.” With this canon in hand, Euripides assessed all the individual features and justified them according to this principle: the language, the characters, the dramatic construction, the choral music.

如果我们已经发现欧里庇得斯把他的戏剧仅仅建立在日神基础上是不成功的,相比之下,他的非酒神倾向使他误入非艺术的自然主义的歧途。我们现在可以接近审美苏格拉底主义的实质了,其最重要的原则大致如此“理解然后美”,和苏格拉底的“知识即美德”的原则遥相呼应。欧里庇得斯手持这一教规来衡量戏剧的各种成分——语言、性格、戏剧结构、歌队音乐。

What we habitually assess so frequently in Euripides as a poetical deficiency and a backward step, in comparison with Sophoclean tragedy, is for the most part the product of that emphatic critical process, that daring intelligence. Let the Euripidean prologue serve for us as an example of what that rationalistic method produces. Nothing can be more offensive to our stage techniques than

在与索福克勒斯的悲剧作比较时,我们通常把欧里庇得斯的作品看作诗的缺陷和倒退的东西,多半是那种深入的批判过程和大胆的理解的产物。让我们以欧里庇得斯的开场白为例来看这种理性主义方法的产品,再也没有比欧里庇得斯的戏剧开场白更违背我们舞台技巧的东西了。

the prologue in a Euripidean play. That a single person should step forward at the beginning of a work and explain who he is, what has gone on before the action starts, what has happened up to this point, and, indeed, what will occur in the unfolding of the work, that would strike a modern poetical dramatist as a wanton, inexcusable abandonment of the effect of suspense. If we, in fact, know everything which is going to happen, who will want to sit around waiting to see that it really does happen? For here there is nothing like the stimulating relationship between a prophetic dream and a real event which occurs later. Euripides thought quite differently about the matter.

The effect of tragedy never depended on epic suspense, on the tempting uncertainty about what would happen now and later. It depended far more on those great rhetorical-lyrical scenes in which the passion and dialectic of the main hero swelled up into a wide and powerful torrent. Everything was preparing for pathos, not for action, and what did not prepare the way for pathos was considered disposable. But the most serious barrier to the delighted devotion to such scenes is any part the spectator found missing, a gap in the network of the previous events. As long as the listener still has to figure out what this or that person means, what gives rise to this or that conflict in motives or purposes, then his full immersion in the suffering and action of the main characters, his breathless sympathy with and fear for them, is not yet possible. The Aeschylean-Sophoclean tragedies made use of the most elegant artistic methods to provide the spectators in the opening scenes, as if by chance, all those necessary clues to understanding everything, a technique in which their noble artistry proves its worth by allowing the necessary features to appear, so to speak, as something masked and accidental.

在一出戏的开头,总有一个人登场自报家门,说明剧情的来龙去脉,迄今发生过什么,甚至随着剧情发展会发生什么。这会使一位现代剧作家感到非常吃惊,认为这种抛弃了悬念效果的做法是无法原谅的。实际上,如果我们知道了即将发生的一切,谁还愿意坐在那里等着看它真的发生呢?在这里任何事情都如在预言的梦里发生的那样,也总是在同一个后来真实发生的事实相吻合。可是,欧里庇得斯对此却有不同的想法。

悲剧的效果从来不是靠史诗的悬念,不是靠对现在和即将发生的事情的诱人的不确定性。而是依靠重大的修辞抒情场面,在其中,主角的激情和雄辩激起波澜壮阔的洪流。一切都是为同情而准备的,不是为了动作;而且凡不是为同情而准备的方法都应遭到摒弃。但是最严重地妨碍一位观众兴致勃勃地欣赏这种场景的,便是他不知道某一个环节,剧情前史的织物上有一个漏洞。只要这位观众一直在琢磨这或那个漏洞到底为何物,这种那种动机和目的的冲突有何前因,那么他就没有全身心地投入到主角的苦难和行为,那他就不可能产生那种同呼吸共命运的共鸣。埃斯库罗斯和索福克勒斯的悲剧运用了最巧妙的艺术手法,在开场白里面就给观众提供了所有帮助理解戏剧的线索,好像在无意中告知观众的。这是显示了大家的风范,仿佛遮掩了必然的形式,而使之作为偶然的东西流露出来。

But for all that, Euripides believed he noticed that during those first scenes the spectator was oddly disturbed having to figure out the simple arithmetic of the previous events, so that the poetical beauties and the pathos of the exposition were lost on him. Therefore Euripides set up the prologue even before the exposition and put it in the mouth of a person whom people could trust—often a divinity had to more or less guarantee the outcome of the tragedy for the public and take away all doubts about the reality of the myth, in a manner similar to the way in which Descartes① was able to establish the reality of the empirical world only through an appeal to the truthfulness of God and his inability to lie. At the end of his drama, Euripides once again made use of this same divine truthfulness in order to confirm his hero's future for the public. This is the function of the notorious deus ex machina②. Between the epic prologue and epilogue lay the lyrical, dramatic present, the essential "drama".

尽管如此,欧里庇得斯仍然相信他发现在头几场里,观众格外焦虑地要了解之前事迹的情况,以致忽略了诗歌的美和正文的激情。因此,欧里庇得斯在正文前安排了开场白,而且借一个人们可以信赖的人物之口说出来——通常是一位神灵出场,他必须或多或少地向观众担保悲剧的结果,消除人们对神话的真实性的所有怀疑。这种方法跟笛卡儿认为只有通过诉诸神的诚实,才能建立经验世界的真实性的方法。在戏剧的结尾,欧里庇得斯再次利用这种神的诚实,以便向观众确认他的英雄人物的归宿。这就是声名狼藉的机械降神的使命。在史诗的序言和尾声之间,呈现着戏剧的精华之所在。

So Euripides as a poet is, above all, the echo of his conscious knowledge, and it is precisely this which confers upon him such a memorable place in the history of Greek art.

因此,欧里庇得斯作为一位诗人,首先是他的自觉认识的回声;而正是这一点使他在希腊艺术史上占据了一个非常显著的地位。

In view of his critically productive creativity it must have often struck him that he had to bring alive in drama the opening of Anaxagoras'③ text, the first lines of which go as follows: "In the beginning everything was confused, but then came reason and created order." And if, among

由于他的批判性的创造活动,使他认为他必须把阿那克萨戈拉著作开头的话灵活地运用于戏剧,开头几句是这么说的:"泰初万物混沌,然后出现理性,创立秩序。"阿那克萨戈拉以其"理性"而立身于哲学家之

① 笛卡儿(Descartes,1596—1650),法国著名的哲学家、物理学家、数学家、神学家,对现代数学的发展做出了重要的贡献,因将几何坐标体系公式化而被认为是解析几何之父。他是二元唯心主义者的代表,留下名言"我思故我在"(I think, therefore I am.),提出了"普遍怀疑"的主张,是欧洲近代资产阶级哲学的奠基人之一,黑格尔称他为"现代哲学之父"。

② Deus ex Machina:机械将神。欧里庇得斯往往在剧情的纠纷难以解决的场合,运用舞台机器,降下一个扮神仙的角色,来解决困难。

③ 阿那克萨戈拉(Anaxagoras,公元前500年—公元前428年),古希腊哲学家,原子唯物论的思想先驱。他主张地球是一个圆柱体,相信天体和地球的性质大体上是同样的,否认天体是神圣的并主张"精神"(nous)是生命世界的变化及动力来源。

philosophers, Anaxagoras, with his concept of nous (mind), seems like the first sober man among nothing but drunkards, so Euripides might have conceptualized his relationship to the other poets with a similar image. So long as the single creator of order and ruler of all, the mind, was still excluded from artistic creativity, everything was still mixed up in a chaotic primordial pudding. That's how Euripides must have judged the matter; that's how he, as the first "sober" poet, must have passed sentence on the "drunken" poets.

中,犹如第一个清醒者身处一群醉汉之中。因此,欧里庇得斯可能用一种相近的意象来理解他同其他诗人的关系。只要万物的创造者和统治者"理性"依然被排除于艺术创造活动之外,万物就始终处于混乱的原始混沌状态。因此,欧里庇得斯必须做出判断,也是他作为第一个"清醒的"诗人批判那些"醉醺醺"的诗人。

What Sophocles said about Aeschylus—that he does what's right, without being aware of it—was certainly not said in any Euripidean sense. Euripides would have conceded only that Aeschylus created improperly because he created without any conscious awareness. Even the god-like Plato speaks of the creative capability of poets and how this is not a conscious understanding, but for the most part only ironically, and he draws a comparison with the talent of prophets and dream interpreters, since the poet is not able to write until he has lost his conscious mind and reason no longer resides in him. Euripides undertook the task, as Plato did, too, of showing the world the opposite of the "irrational" poet. His basic aesthetic principle, "Everything must be conscious in order to be beautiful" is, as I have mentioned, the corollary of the Socratic saying, "Everything must be conscious in order to be good." ①

索福克勒斯说,埃斯库罗斯做了正确的事,却没有意识到。但欧里庇得斯却肯定不会这么认为的。欧里庇得斯认为正因为埃斯库罗斯是无意识做的,所以他才做了不正确的事。连神圣的柏拉图在谈及诗人的创造力时,也因为这不是一种有意识的领悟,就多半用一种嘲讽的口吻谈论,把这同预言者和释梦者作比较;似乎诗人在失去意识和理性之前是无法创作的。欧里庇得斯像柏拉图那样,承担起了给世人指出"非理性"诗人的对立面的任务。正如我们之前已经提到过了,他的基本审美原则是"理解然后美",正如苏格拉底所说的"知识即美德"。

With this in mind, we are entitled to assess Euripides as the poet of aesthetic Socratism. Socrates, however, was that second spectator, who did not understand the older tragedy and therefore did not value it. With Socrates as his ally, Euripides dared to be the herald of a new artistic creativity. If the older tragedy perished from this

头脑中有了这些原则之后,我们就有权把欧里庇得斯当作审美苏格拉底主义的诗人来评价了。然而,苏格拉底却是那第二个观众,它不理解较早的悲剧也不能给予评价。有了苏格拉底的联盟,欧里庇得斯敢于成

① 此处两个引文英译文与本节前面出现的两个引文文字不尽相同,但意思相近,作为审美原则"理解然后美"、"知识即美德"已被国内学界广泛接受,故中译文采用同一文字,不做变化。

development, then aesthetic Socratism is the murdering principle. But insofar as the fight was directed against the Dionysian of the older art, we recognize in Socrates the enemy of Dionysus, the new Orpheus①, who roused himself against Dionysus, and who, although destined to be torn apart by the maenads② of the Athenian Court of Justice, nevertheless compelled the overpowering god himself to run away. Dionysus, as before, when he fled from Lycurgus, king of the Edoni, saved himself in the depths of the sea, that is, in the mysterious floods of a secret cult which would gradually overrun the entire world.

为新艺术创造力的先驱。如果古悲剧在这些新艺术中消亡,那么审美苏格拉底主义就是一种谋杀原则。但是就这场斗争针对古老艺术的酒神因素而言,我们认识到了酒神的敌人苏格拉底,以及起反抗酒神的新俄耳浦斯。尽管他注定会被雅典法庭的酒神的女祭司们撕成碎片,但他无论如何还是把这位非常强大的神灵赶跑了。以前当酒神从伊多尼国王莱克格斯那里逃走时,也是藏身于大海深处,即藏身于一种逐渐席卷全世界的秘仪崇拜的神秘洪水之中。

17

Dionysian art also wishes to convince us of the eternal delight in existence: only we are to seek this delight, not in appearances, but behind them. We are to recognize how everything which comes into being must be ready for painful destruction. We are forced to gaze directly into the terror of individual existence—and nonetheless are not to become paralyzed: a metaphysical consolation tears us momentarily out of the hustle and bustle of changing forms. For a short time we really are the primordial essence itself and feel its unbridled lust for and joy in existence. The struggle, the torment, the destruction of appearances now seem to us necessary, on account of the excess of innumerable forms of existence pressing and punching themselves into life and of the exuberant fecundity of the world will. We are transfixed by the raging barbs of this torment in the very moment when we become, as it were, one with the immeasurable primordial delight in existence and when, in

17

酒神艺术也希望使我们相信存在的永恒乐趣:只有我们不在表象寻找乐趣时,我们才能在表象的背后找到这种乐趣。我们认识到了存在着的一切必须准备着痛苦的衰亡,我们被迫正视个体生存的恐惧——但是无论如何也不会吓瘫:一种超自然的安慰使我们暂时逃离于这变换多端的繁乱世界。我们暂时真的成为原始生灵的本身,感觉到它的不可遏制的生存欲望和快乐;现在我们才觉得由于无数竞相生存的生命形态的过剩,那么斗争、痛苦以及表象的毁灭对我们来说就是必需的。就在我们仿佛与无限原始的生存狂喜合为一体时,当我们陶醉于酒神的狂喜之时,我们会被痛苦的利刺击中;我们感觉到了这种坚不可摧的、永恒的喜悦本质。尽管有恐惧和怜悯之情,我们依然是幸运的生者,不是作为个

① 俄耳浦斯(Orpheus),他的父亲是太阳神阿波罗,母亲是司管文艺的缪斯女神卡利俄帕(Muse Calliope),具有非凡的艺术才能。由于他不敬重酒神,被酒神手下的女祭司们(Maenads)杀害并将他的尸体撕得粉碎抛到荒郊野外。

② maenads:酒神的女祭司们,性情狂暴,又被称为狂女。

Dionysian rapture, we sense the indestructible and eternal nature of this joy. In spite of fear and compassion, we are fortunate vital beings, not as individuals, but as the one force of Life, with whose procreative joy we have been fused.

体,而是众生一体,我们与它的生产欢乐紧密相连。

The story of how Greek tragedy arose tells us now with clear certainty how the Greeks' tragic work of art really was born out of the spirit of music. With this idea we think we have, for the first time, done justice to the original and astonishing meaning of the chorus. At the same time, however, we must concede that the significance of the tragic myth established previously was never conceptually and transparently clear to the Greek poets, to say nothing of the Greek philosophers. Their heroes speak to a certain extent more superficially than they act; the myth really does not find its adequate objectification in the spoken word.

希腊悲剧如何产生的故事现在清楚确定地告诉我们,希腊的悲剧艺术作品是如何诞生于音乐精神的。由于这一思想,我们认为我们第一次公正地理解了歌队的起源及其令人吃惊的原本意义。然而,同时我们必须承认希腊诗人从来没有明确清楚地理解之前建立的悲剧神话的重大意义,更不要说希腊哲学家了。希腊诗人们的主角的谈论在某种程度上比他们的行为更为肤浅;神话在他们所说的话里根本得不到体现。

The structure of the scenes and the vivid images reveal a deeper wisdom than the poet himself can grasp in words and ideas. We can make the same observation about Shakespeare, whose Hamlet, for example, similarly speaks in a more superficial manner than he acts, so that we derive the doctrine of Hamlet we discussed earlier, not from the words, but from the deeper view and review of the totality of the work. With respect to Greek tragedy, which, of course, comes to us only as a drama of words, I have even suggested that the incongruity between myth and word can easily seduce us into considering it shallower and more empty of meaning than it is and thus also into assuming a more superficial effect than it must have had according to the testimony of the ancients, for we easily forget that what the poet as a wordsmith could not achieve, the attainment of the highest intellectualization and idealization of myth, he could have achieved successfully at any moment as a creative musician!

剧情的结构和生动的形象比诗人本人的台词和想法更为深刻。我们可以对莎士比亚做同样的观察,比如说他的戏剧里面的人物哈姆雷特,在相似的意义上,他说的话比他的行为肤浅,因此,我们推出了我们之前讨论过了的哈姆雷特的教规不是出自于他的台词,而是来源于作品的更深刻的观察和对作品的全局回顾。关于希腊悲剧,我们现在当然只能读到剧本,我甚至已经建议过神话和台词之间的不一致很容易迷惑我们,使我们以为它比它实际上的样子肤浅空洞,因此,根据古人的证词而假定它的效果更为肤浅。因为,我们很容易地忘记了达到神话的最高理智化和理想化的境界,诗人用言语是难以企及的,他作为创造的音乐家却随时可以做到。

Admittedly we are almost forced to recreate through scholarship the extraordinary power of the musical effects in order to experience something of that incomparable consolation necessarily characteristic of true tragedy. But we would experience this superior musical power for what it is only if we ourselves were Greeks; whereas, considering the entire development of Greek music in comparison to the music we know and are familiar with, so infinitely richer by comparison, we believe that we are hearing youthful songs of musical genius, sung with only a timid sense of their power. The Greeks are, as the Egyptian priests say, eternal children and, even in tragic art, only children who do not know what a sublime toy has arisen under their hands, something which will be destroyed.

公认地通过学术的深入研究,我们几乎被强迫重新创造音乐效果的非凡力量,以便于体验到真正的悲剧所固有的那种无与伦比的慰藉。但是,除非我们是希腊人,我们才能体验到音乐原本的超然力量;然而,考虑到整个希腊音乐的发展及其我们所知道和熟悉的音乐的对比,听起来我们也只是像年轻的音乐天才那样怀着羞涩的信心去歌唱。如埃及牧师所说,希腊人永远是孩子,甚至在悲剧艺术方面也是孩子,因为只有孩子不知道在他们手中制造和毁坏了一种多么高贵的玩具。

That struggle of the spirit of music for pictorial and mythic revelation, which becomes increasingly intense from the beginning of the lyric right up to Attic tragedy, suddenly breaks apart, right after it first attained full luxuriant bloom and, so to speak, disappears from the surface of Hellenic art, although the Dionysian world view born out of this struggle lives on in the mysteries and, in the most amazing transformations and degenerations, never stops attracting more serious natures to it. Is it not possible that one day it will rise from its mystic depths as art once more?

音乐精神追求形象和神话的启示,这种追求从最早的抒情诗到古希腊雅典悲剧,在刚刚达到其鼎盛时期时,突然中断。可谓是从希腊艺术的表层消失了。虽然从这种追求中产生的酒神世界观在秘仪中保存了下来,但是却发生了巨大的形质变化。尽管如此,它却从未停止吸引庄重的本质。它会不会某一天再次作为艺术从它神秘的深渊中升起来呢?

At this point we are concerned with the question whether the power whose opposition broke tragedy has sufficient force for all time to hinder the artistic reawakening of tragedy and the tragic world view. If the old tragedy was derailed by the dialectical drive for knowledge and for the optimism of science, we might have to infer from this fact an eternal struggle between the theoretical and the tragic world view, and only after the spirit of science is taken right to its limits and its claim to universal validity destroyed by the proof of those

现在我们要考虑一下这个问题:打破悲剧的那种反对力量,是否在任何时候都强大得足以阻碍悲剧艺术及其悲剧世界观的复苏。如果说古老的悲剧被辩证的知识冲动和科学乐观主义冲动引向了歧途,那么我们可以从这一事实推断出在理论世界观和悲剧世界观之间存在着永恒的斗争。只有当科学精神达到了它的极限,它所自称的普遍有效性被这些

limits would it be possible to hope for a rebirth of tragedy. For a symbol of such a cultural form, we would have to set up Socrates the player of music, in the sense talked about earlier. By this confrontation I understand with respect to the spirit of science that belief, which first came to light in the person of Socrates, that nature can be rationally understood and that knowledge has a universal healing power.

极限所打破,这才有可能希望悲剧的重生。按照我们之前讲过的意义,用音乐的苏格拉底来象征这样的文化形式。与此相反,关于科学精神,我理解为最早出现于苏格拉底人格之中那种可以理性理解大自然和那种可以治愈一切的知识的信念。

Anyone who remembers the most immediate consequences of this restless, forward-driving spirit of science will immediately recall how it destroyed myth and how, through this destruction, poetry was driven out of its naturally ideal soil as something which from now on was without a home. If we have correctly ascribed to music the power to be able to bring about out of itself a rebirth of myth, then we will also have to seek out the spirit of science on the path where it has its hostile encounter with the myth-creating power of music. This occurred in the development of the new Attic dithyramb, whose music no longer expressed the inner essence, the will itself, but only gave back an inadequate appearance in an imitation delivered through ideas. From such inwardly degenerate music those with a true musical nature turned away with the same aversion which they had shown when confronted by the art-killing attitude of Socrates.

任何一个记得那种草率的、向前的科学精神的后果的人马上就会回忆起科学精神是如何毁灭神话的,而通过这种毁灭,诗歌又是如何被驱逐出它那自然理想的土壤,从此无家可归。如果我们认为音乐具有从自身再生出神话的能力,那么我们也必须找到科学精神走在反对音乐这种创造神话能力的道路上。这一点体现在新希腊酒神赞美歌中,它的音乐已经不再表达内在的本质、自身的意志,而是以概念为中介进行模仿,呈现出了不合格的表象。对于这种已经退化的音乐,真正的音乐天性已经厌弃它了,就如同厌弃苏格拉底毁灭艺术倾向一样。

The instinct of Aristophanes, which had such a sure grasp, was certainly right when he linked together Socrates himself, the tragedies of Euripides, and the music of the new writers of dithyrambs, hating each of them equally and smelling in all three phenomena the characteristics of a degenerate culture. Through that newer dithyramb, music was, in an outrageous manner, turned into a mimetic demonstration of appearances, for example, a battle, a storm at sea, and in the process was certainly robbed of all its power to create myths. For when music seeks to

阿里斯托芬的可靠直觉确实是对的,他对苏格拉底本人、欧里庇得斯的悲剧和酒神赞美歌的新诗人都怀有同样的厌恶之情,并且在这三种现象中嗅到了一种堕落文化的特征。通过新酒神赞美歌,音乐以粗暴的方式把诸如战争、海里的风暴等变成一种现象的临摹,这种过程完全剥夺了它创造神话的能力。因为当音乐仅是引起我们沉溺于去寻找人生和自然的一个事件与音乐的某种节奏形

arouse our indulgence only by compelling us to look for external analogies between an event in life and nature and certain rhythmic figures and characteristic musical sounds, when our understanding is supposed to be satisfied with the recognition of these analogies, then we are dragged down into a mood in which a conception of the mythic is impossible, for myth desires to be vividly felt as a single instance of universality and truth staring into the infinite.

Truly Dionysian music confronts us as such a universal mirror of the world will: that vivid event reflected in this mirror widens out at once for our feelings into the image of an eternal truth. By contrast, in the sound painting of the newer dithyramb such a vivid event is immediately stripped of every mythic character. Now the music has become a feeble copy of the phenomenon and, in the process, infinitely poorer than the phenomenon itself. Through this impoverishment the phenomenon itself is even lowered in our feelings, so that now, for example, a battle imitated in this kind of music exhausts itself in marches, trumpet calls, and so forth, and our imagination is held back by these very superficialities.

Painting with music is thus in every respect the opposite to the myth-creating power of true music: through the former a phenomenon becomes even more impoverished than it is; whereas, through Dionysian music the individual phenomenon becomes richer and widens into a world picture. It was a powerful victory of the non-Dionysian spirit when, in the development of the newer dithyramb, it alienated music from itself and forced it down to be the slave of appearances. Euripides, who, in a higher sense, must be considered a thoroughly unmusical nature, is for this very reason an ardent supporter of the newer dithyrambic music and uses all its stock effects and

态或特定音响之间的表面相似之处，当我们的假定只是为满足于认识这些类比事物时，那么我们就陷入了无法理解神话的心境。因为神话渴望被作为普遍和无限中的一个个体而被鲜明地感觉到。

真正的酒神音乐如同一面普遍的世界意志的镜子置于我们面前：每一件事实都会清楚地投射到这面镜子上，我们立即感觉到了它扩展成为一种永恒真理的镜像。相比之下，在新酒神赞美歌的音响画面中，这样清楚的事实就会立刻失去了任何神话的特征。现在音乐已经变成了一种现象的粗劣临摹，因而远比现象本身贫乏。由于这些贫乏现象本身在我们的感觉中显得更为低下了。以致现在，比如说，如此用音乐临摹的战争就仅仅消耗殆尽于这些嘈杂声和军号声之中了，而我们的想象力也被禁锢在这些非常肤浅的表面现象上了。

因此，音响图画在任何方面都同真正的音乐的创造神话的能力相对立，它使现象比现象本身更为贫乏；相反，酒神音乐却丰富了个体现象，使之扩展为世界画面。这是非酒神精神获得的巨大成功，它通过新酒神的赞美歌的发展而使音乐和自身疏远，把音乐降为表象的奴隶。在更高意义上来说，欧里庇得斯具有一种非常彻底的非音乐本质，正是因为此原因，他是新酒神赞美歌的热忱追随者，并且以一个强盗的慷慨使用着这种音乐的全部戏剧效果和文体。

styles with the open-handedness of a thief.

From another perspective we see the force of this un-Dionysian spirit in action directing its effects against myth, when we turn our gaze toward the way in which the presentation of character and the psychological complexities increase alarmingly in the tragedies of Sophocles. The character can no longer be allowed to broaden out into an eternal type, but, by contrast, must come across as an individual because of the artistic qualifications and shading and the most delicate clarity of every line, so that the spectator generally no longer experiences the myth but the commanding naturalism of the artist, his power of imitation.

当我们注意到索福克勒斯悲剧中性格呈现和心理复杂性的刻画在不断增加时,从另一个角度我们看到了这种非酒神精神在反对神话行动中的力量了。性格不能再扩展成永恒的典型了,相反应该以个体来体现,由于人为的细节描写和色调渲染,通过一切线条的细致刻画以便于让观众一般不再感受到神话,而是体验到艺术家威严的自然主义及其他的模仿能力。

Here, we also become aware of the victory of appearances over the universal and of the delight in the particular, like an anatomical specimen, as it were. Already we breathe the air of a theoretical world, which values the scientific insight higher than the artistic reflection of a universal principle. The movement along the line of increasingly typical characteristics quickly goes further. While Sophocles still paints whole characters and yokes their sophisticated development to myth, Euripides already paints only large individual character traits, which are capable of expressing themselves in violent passions. In the newer Attic comedy there are only masks with one expression, silly old men, deceived pimps, and mischievous slaves in an inexhaustible repetition.

在这里,我们也注意到了现象对于普遍性的胜利以及特别的开心,就像解剖标本那样。我们已经呼吸到一个理论世界的气息了,在这里科学认识高于世界原则的艺术反映。刻画性格的运动进展在迅速地前进。索福克勒斯却依然在刻画完整的性格,并把他们深奥微妙的发展和神话联系起来;欧里庇得斯已经仅仅刻画重大的性格特征,那种能够在激情时刻表现自己的性格特征。从新的希腊喜剧中,就只有一种表情面具,不厌其烦地反复刻画糊涂的老人、受骗的皮条客以及恶作剧的奴隶等。

Where now has the myth-building spirit of music gone? What is still left for music now is music either of excitement or of memory, that is, either a means of stimulating jaded and worn out nerves or sound painting. As far as the first is concerned, the text is largely irrelevant. Already in Euripides, when his heroes or chorus first start to sing, things get really out of hand. What must it have been like with his impertinent successors?

音乐创造神话的精神如今去了哪里?音乐如今留下来的不是兴奋,便是回忆。即音乐不是刺激迟钝疲惫的神经就是音响图画。至于前者,音乐和歌词基本上不相干。在欧里庇得斯那里,当他的主角或是歌队开始歌唱时,事情就已经开始不可收拾了。那么他的后继者们会搞成什么样呢?

However, the new un-Dionysian spirit manifests itself with the utmost clarity in the conclusions of the newer plays. In the old tragedy, the metaphysical consolation was there to feel at the conclusion. Without that, the delight in tragedy generally cannot be explained. The sound of reconciliation from another world echoes most purely perhaps in *Oedipus at Colonus*. Now, once the genius of music flew away from tragedy, tragedy is, in the strict sense of the term, dead: for out of what are people now supposed to be able to create that metaphysical consolation?

Consequently, people looked for an earthly solution to tragic dissonance. After the hero was sufficiently tortured by fate, he received a well-earned reward in an impressive marriage, in divine tributes. The hero became a gladiator, to whom people occasionally gave his freedom, after he had been well beaten and was covered with wounds. The deus ex machina moved in to replace metaphysical consolation. I don't wish to claim that the tragic world view was completely destroyed everywhere by the surging spirit of the un-Dionysian: we know only that it must have fled out of art into the underworld, so to speak, degenerating into a secret cult.

But over the widest surface area of Hellenic existence raged the consuming wind of that spirit which announces itself in that form of "Greek serenity" to which I have already referred earlier, as an impotent, unproductive delight in existence. This cheerfulness is the opposite of the marvelous "naivete" of the older Greeks, which we must see, in accordance with its given characteristics, as the flowering of Apollonian culture, blossoming out of a dark abyss, as the victory over suffering and the wisdom of suffering, which the Hellenic will gains through its ability to mirror beauty.

The noblest form of that other form of "Greek serenity", the Alexandrian, is the cheerfulness of

然而,把新的非酒神精神表现得淋漓尽致是新戏剧的结局。在古悲剧中,在结尾总会感觉到那种超自然的慰藉。没有它,悲剧中的喜悦一般就无法解释。在《俄狄浦斯在科罗诺斯》一剧中,来自于另一个世界的和解之声最单纯地回响着。现在音乐的天才已经从悲剧中消失,那也就意味着悲剧已经死去:因为人们离开了悲剧,还能从哪儿再创造出那种超自然的慰藉呢?

结果,人们就寻找悲剧冲突的世俗解决。在主角受尽命运的折磨之后,他得到了他应得的报酬,以大团圆或是宠荣加身而结束。悲剧英雄变成了格斗士,在他受尽折磨遍体鳞伤之后,人们偶尔给他自由。机械降神取代了超自然的慰藉。我不想说悲剧世界观被蜂拥而来的非酒神精神完全毁灭了。我们只知道它肯定逃出了艺术领域,而进入了一种地狱似的黑暗社会,堕落成了一种秘仪崇拜。

但是,在希腊民族广大的地区表面,到处弥漫着非酒神精神,以"希腊的乐天"的形式出现,我之前已经谈到了,这是一种无力的不再生产的生存欲望。这种高兴是同古希腊人美好的"纯真无邪"截然对立的。按照既有的特征,后者应当被作为从黑暗深渊中开出的日神文化的花朵,希腊意志借助美的反映而获取的对于痛苦和痛苦智慧的胜利。

另一种"希腊的乐天",即亚历山大的乐天的最高贵形式,是理论家的

the theoretical man. It manifests the same characteristic features I have just derived out of the spirit of the un-Dionysian—it fights against Dionysian wisdom and art; it strives to dissolve myth; in place of a metaphysical consolation, it sets an earthy consonance, indeed, a deus ex machina of its own, namely, the god of machines and crucibles, that is, the forces of nature spirits, recognized and used in the service of a higher egoism; it believes in correcting the world through knowledge, in a life guided by science, and thus is really in a position to confine the individual man within the narrowest circle of soluble problems, inside which he can cheerfully say to life: "I want you. You are worth knowing."

乐天,它显示了我刚才从非酒神精神推断出的那些特征:它反对酒神智慧和艺术;它竭力消除神话;它用了一种机械降神的方式取代了超自然的慰藉,即机械降神自己,称为机关和熔炉之神。也即被认识和应用来为高度的利己主义服务的自然精神力量;它相信知识能改造世界,科学可以指导人生。就这样把个体局限到可以解决的任务这个最狭窄的范围内,在其中他可以兴奋地对人生说:"我需要你,你值得认识。"

3. Questions for Discussion

(1) What is Nietzsche's definition of art?

(2) What is the distinction between the two art worlds of dreams and intoxication?

(3) What caused the death of the Greek tragedy?

3. 讨论题

(1)尼采对艺术的定义是什么?

(2)梦境和迷醉两种艺术世界的区别是什么?

(3)什么造成了希腊悲剧的死亡?

Chapter 7

第7章

1. Introduction to Sigmund Freud

1. 弗洛伊德简介

Sigmund Freud (1856-1939) was an Austrian neurologist and the founder of psychoanalysis, who created an entirely new approach to the understanding of the human personality. He is regarded as one of the most influential and controversial minds of the 20th century.

西格蒙德·弗洛伊德(1856—1939)是奥地利精神病医生,精神分析的创始人,他创造了全新的理解人格的方法。他被认为是20世纪最有影响,也最有争议的思想家之一。

Sigmund Freud was born in a Jewish merchant family in the Austrian town of Freiberg, Moravia (now Pribor in the Czech Republic). When he was four years old, his family moved to Vienna. In 1873, Freud began to study medicine at the University of Vienna. After graduation, he worked at the Vienna General Hospital. In 1885, Freud went to Paris as a student of the neurologist Jean Charcot (1825—1893). On his return to Vienna the following year, Freud set up in private practice, specialising in nervous and brain disorders. In 1902, Freud was appointed Professor of Neuropathology at the University of Vienna, a post he held until 1938. In 1910, the International Psychoanalytic Association was founded with Carl Jung, a close associate of Freud's, as the president. In 1938, shortly after the Nazis annexed

弗洛伊德出生在奥匈帝国的摩拉维亚省弗赖堡镇(今捷克共和国的普日博尔市)的一个犹太商人家庭。他四岁时,全家搬到维也纳。1873年,弗洛伊德在维也纳大学学习医学。毕业后他在维也纳综合医院任职。1885年,弗洛伊德到巴黎跟随神经学家让·沙可(1825—1893)学习。次年回到维也纳后,弗洛伊德开办了私人诊所,专治神经和大脑紊乱症。1902年,弗洛伊德被任命为维也纳大学神经病理学教授,他在此职位工作到1938年。1910年,国际精神分析协会创立,弗洛伊德最亲密的同行荣格担任主席。1938年,纳粹吞并奥地利不久,弗洛伊德与妻子和女儿安娜

Austria, Freud left Vienna for London with his wife and daughter Anna. He died of cancer in 1939.

逃离维也纳来到伦敦。1939年,弗洛伊德死于癌症。

Freud wrote more than 50 books. The famous ones are *Studies on Hysteria* (1895) corporate with Josef Breuer, *The Interpretation of Dreams* (1900), *The Psychopathology of Everyday Life* (1901), *Three Essays on the Theory of Sexuality* (1905), *Totem and Taboo* (1913), *On Narcissism* (1914), *Beyond the Pleasure Principle* (1920), *The Ego and the Id* (1923), *The Future of an Illusion* (1927), *Civilization and Its Discontents* (1929), *Moses and Monotheism* (1939) and *An Outline of Psycho-Analysis* (1940).

弗洛伊德一生写有50多部著作,其中最著名的有:与约瑟夫·布鲁尔合著的《歇斯底里症研究》(1895)、《梦的解析》(1900)、《日常生活之精神病学》(1901)、《性学三论》(1905)、《图腾与禁忌》(1913)、《论自恋》(1914)、《超越快乐原则》(1920)、《自我与本我》(1923)、《幻象之未来》(1927)、《文明及其不满》(1929)、《摩西与一神论》(1939)、《精神分析概要》(1940)等。

The concept of the unconscious is central to Freud's account of the mind. Freud states explicitly that the concept of the unconscious is based on the theory of repression. According to Freud, there are three levels of consciousness: conscious, preconscious and unconscious.

无意识概念是弗洛伊德心理研究论著中的核心概念。弗洛伊德明确指出,无意识概念是基于压抑理论的。弗洛伊德将意识划分为三个层次:意识、前意识和潜意识。

According to Freud's structural theory of the mind, the id, the ego and the superego function at different levels of consciousness. The id is the unconscious reservoir of drives, which are constantly active. Ruled by the pleasure principle, the id demands immediate satisfaction of its urges, regardless of undesirable effects.

根据弗洛伊德的心理结构理论,本我、自我和超我在意识的不同层次发生作用。本我是无意识驱动力的源泉,驱动力经常处于活跃状态。在享乐原则支配下,本我不顾一切地要求所有的需要得到即刻的满足。

The ego operates mainly at conscious and preconscious levels, although it also contains unconscious elements because both the ego and the superego evolved from the id. Ruled by the reality principle, the ego takes care of the id urges as soon as the adequate circumstance is found. Inappropriate desires are not satisfied but repressed.

自我主要在意识和前意识层面活动,尽管它也包括无意识成分,因为自我和超我都源自本我。在现实原则支配下,自我在合适的条件下,满足本我的需求。不合适的欲望不能得到满足,并受到压制。

Only partially conscious, the superego serves as a censor on the ego functions and comprises the individual's ideals derived from the values of his family and society, being the source of guilty feelings and fear of punishment.

超我只有部分属于意识,是自我运作过程中的监管者,代表与家庭和社会的价值观相吻合的个人理想,是内疚感和畏惧感之源。

The interpretation of dreams is based on those

弗洛伊德对梦的分析是建立在

theories about the unconscious. Freud deems that dream is a satisfaction of repressed desires in a disguised form which mostly connects with sex. Many wishes of man are reduced to appear in a compromised way of dream as the result of the fact that they are intolerant of social morals and thus repressed by the conscious.

For Freud, dream and literature share many similarities. Firstly, both of them originate from desires repressed in the childhood. By virtue of fantasy and literary creation respectively, the dreamer and the writer make it possible to satisfy their own desires. Secondly, they deviate from the reality in some way. Freud holds that the fundamental drive of artistic creation is the instinctive desires repressed by artists themselves. In this sense, their creative activities, therefore, is quite similar to the daydream or fantasy of the ordinary people. Artists realize the aspirations—honor, power, women and so on—by building their own imaginary world. Therefore, artists are daydreamers, and the process of artistic creation, likewise, is daydreaming.

他的无意识理论基础上的。他认为,梦是一种以伪装形式出现的被压抑的欲望的满足,这种欲望大多与性有关。由于人的许多愿望得不到社会道德的认可,被排斥在意识层面之外,只好以迂回曲折的方式出现在梦中。

在弗洛伊德看来,梦和文学作品之间有很多相似性。首先,梦和文学作品都源于儿童时期受到压抑的欲望。做梦者通过他的梦幻,作家通过他的文学创作,使各自的欲望满足成为可能。其次,梦和文学作品都是对现实的某种脱离。弗洛伊德认为,艺术创造原动力是艺术家被压抑的种种本能欲望。在这个意义上,艺术家的艺术创作活动和普通人的白日梦或幻想非常接近。艺术家在自己虚构的艺术世界中实现他从前的梦想:荣誉、权力和女人等等。因此,艺术家犹如白日梦者,艺术创作仿佛是白日做梦。

2. Full Text of "Creative Writers and Daydreaming"

2.《创作家与白日梦》全文

Creative Writers and Daydreaming①

Sigmund Freud

We Laymen have always been intensely curious to know—like the cardinal who put a

创作家与白日梦

西格蒙德·弗洛伊德

我们这些门外汉总是急切地想了解——正如那位向亚利欧斯多提

① Selected from *The Standard Edition of the Psychological Works of Sigmund Freud*, Vol. 9, edited and translated by James Strachey, in collaboration with Anna Freud, assisted by Alix Strachey and Alan Tyson, London: the Hogarth Press, 1956-1974.

similar question to Ariosto①—from what sources that strange being, the creative writer, draws his material, and how he manages to make such an impression on us with it and to arouse in us emotions of which, perhaps, we had not even thought ourselves capable. Our interest is only heightened the more by the fact that, if we ask him, the writer himself gives us no explanation, or none that is satisfactory; and it is not at all weakened by our knowledge that not even the clearest insight into the determinants of his choice of material and into the nature of the art of creating imaginative form will ever help to make creative writers of us.

出类似问题的红衣主教一样——不可思议的创作家是从什么源头发掘了创作素材,又是如何加工组织这些素材,以至于使我们产生如此深刻的影响,在我们的心中激发起连我们自己都不曾料想的情感。假如我们向作家讨教,他本人也难以说清,即使解释了也不会令我们满意。正因为如此,便使我们对此产生了更加浓厚的兴趣,即使我们都彻底了解了作家是怎样选取素材的,了解创造想象形式的艺术的真谛,也不可能帮助我们把自己修炼成为创作家。

If we could at least discover in ourselves or in people like ourselves an activity which was in some way akin to creative writing! An examination of it would then give us a hope of obtaining the beginnings of an explanation of the creative work of writers. And, indeed, there is some prospect of this being possible. After all, creative writers themselves like to lessen the distance between their kind and the common run of humanity; they so often assure us that every man is a poet at heart and that the last poet will not perish till the last man does.

如果我们至少能在自己身上或者和我们相似的人身上发现一种与文学创作在某种程度上相似的能动性,那该多么令人欣慰。检查这种能动性将使我们有希望对作家的创作做出解释。的确,这种可能性是有的。毕竟,作家本身也希望减少他们和普通人间的差距。因此他们通常让我们相信每一个人内心深处都是诗人,只要有人,就有诗人。

Should we not look for the first traces of imaginative activity as early as in childhood? The child's best-loved and most intense occupation is with his play or games. Might we not say that every child at play behaves like a creative writer, in that he creates a world of his own, or, rather, rearranges the things of his world in a new way which pleases him? It would be wrong to think he does not take that world seriously; on the contrary, he takes his play very seriously and he expends

我们是否该到童年时代寻找想象力能动性的最初轨迹?孩子最喜欢和专注的就是他的游戏和玩耍。我们是否应该说每一个孩子玩游戏时都像一个创作家,因为他创造的是他自己的世界,或者说是按照他自己的喜好重新安排他世界中的事物。认为孩子没有认真对待自己创造的世界是不正确的。相反,他非常认真

① 鲁多维奇·亚利欧斯多(Ludovico Ariosto,1474-1533)是意大利作家,将其诗作《疯狂奥兰多》(*Orlando Furioso*,1516))献给红衣主教伊波里托·德埃斯特(Ippolito d'Este)后,红衣主教问他:"鲁多维奇,你是从哪儿找到这么多故事的?"

large amounts of emotion on it. The opposite of play is not what is serious but what is real. In spite of all the emotion with which he cathects his world of play, the child distinguishes it quite well from reality; and he likes to link his imagined objects and situations to the tangible and visible things of the real world. This linking is all that differentiates the child's "play" from "fantasying".

The creative writer does the same as the child at play. He creates a world of fantasy which he takes very seriously—that is, which he invests with large amounts of emotion—while separating it sharply from reality. Language has preserved this relationship between children's play and poetic creation. It gives the name of Spiel① (play) to those forms of imaginative writing which require to be linked to tangible objects and which are capable of representation. It speaks of a Lustspiel or Trauerspiel (comedy or tragedy) and describes those who carry out the representation as Schauspieler (players). The unreality of the writer's imaginative world, however, has very important consequences for the technique of his art; for many things which, if they were real, could give no enjoyment, can do so in the play of fantasy, and many excitements which, in themselves, are actually distressing, can become a source of pleasure for the hearers and spectators at the performance of a writer's work.

There is another consideration for the sake of which we will dwell a moment longer on this contrast between reality and play. When the child has grown up and has ceased to play, and after he has been laboring for decades to envisage the realities of life with proper seriousness, he may one day find himself in a mental situation which once more undoes the contrast between play and reality. As an adult he can look back on the intense

地对待他的世界而且在里面投入了大量的感情。游戏的所谓的反不是所谓的严肃而是真实的。尽管他集中精力关注自己的世界,孩子却是将这个世界与现实严格区分开来。他喜欢将自己想象的物体同有形的、可见的现实世界相连。这个链接就是孩子的游戏与想象的区别。

创作家与玩要中的孩子做着相同的事情。他创造一个幻想世界并认真对待它——也就是说,他为它投入大量的情感——同时又将它与现实明确分离。语言保留了孩子的游戏和诗人创作之间的关系。这种富有想象力的创作形式被称为"Spiel"(游戏),这种创作形式与现实世界里的事物相联系,并具有表现能力。作品被称作"Lustspiel"(喜剧)和"Trauerspiel"(悲剧),将那些从事表演的人称为"Schauspieler"(演员)。但是,创作者幻想世界的非真实性对他的艺术技巧具有很重要的影响。因为很多事物如果是真实的就无法给人以享受,但是以想象喜剧的形式却可以。许多兴奋的事情,他们本身实际上是令人悲伤的,但在作家的作品上演之际,却能变成听众和观众的快乐源泉。

出于另一种考虑,我们在现实性和游戏间的对比上还要多花一些时间。当孩子长大不再玩游戏时,在他经过几年努力从而严肃地面对现实之后,他可能有一天发现自己不再将现实与想象对立了。作为一个成人,他可以回望童年玩游戏时的严肃模样。如果把今天表面上严肃的工作

① Spiel:[德文] 戏剧。

seriousness with which he once carried on his games in childhood, and, by equating his ostensibly serious occupations of today with his childhood games, he can throw off the too heavy burden imposed on him by life and win the high yield of pleasure afforded by humor.

当成童年时代的游戏,那么他就可以摆脱生活施加给他的沉重压力,并通过幽默的方式获得大量的快乐。

As people grow up, then, they cease to play, and they seem to give up the yield of pleasure which they gained from playing. But whoever understands the human mind knows that hardly anything is harder for a man than to give up a pleasure which he has once experienced. Actually, we can never give anything up; we only exchange one thing for another. What appears to be a renunciation is really the formation of a substitute or surrogate. In the same way, the growing child, when he stops playing, gives up nothing but the link with real objects; instead of playing, he now fantasies. He builds castles in the air and creates what are called daydreams. I believe that most people construct fantasies at times in their lives. This is a fact which has long been overlooked and whose importance has therefore not been sufficiently appreciated.

长大后,人们就不玩耍了。他们似乎放弃从游戏中获得快乐。但任何了解人性的人都知道人是不可能放弃曾经经历过的快乐的。事实上,我们从不会放弃任何东西;我们只是把一物换成另一物。表面上看起来放弃的东西只是一种替代形式。同样的,成长中的孩子不再玩耍时,他放弃的只是现实事物之间的联系,他现在不是玩耍,而是幻想。他凭空建造城堡并创造一些我们称之为梦的东西。我相信大部分人偶尔会幻想。这是一个长期被忽略的事实,因此幻想的重要性目前还未被意识到。

People's fantasies are less easy to observe than the play of children. The child, it is true, plays by himself or forms a closed psychical system with other children for the purposes of a game; but even though he may not play his game in front of the grown-ups, he does not, on the other hand, conceal it from them. The adult, on the contrary, is ashamed of his fantasies and hides them from other people. He cherishes his fantasies as his most intimate possessions, and as a rule he would rather confess his misdeeds than tell anyone his fantasies. It may come about that for that reason he believes he is the only person who invents such fantasies and has no idea that creations of this kind are widespread among other people. This difference in the behavior of a person who plays and a person

成人的幻想比孩子的游戏要难观察得多。的确,孩子独自玩耍或者为了游戏的缘故和其他孩子形成一种亲密的心理系统,但是尽管孩子不在大人面前玩游戏,他也不会向大人隐瞒。相反,成人以自己的幻想为耻,因此会将幻想隐藏起来。成人将幻想作为自己最私密的财产。一般来说,成人宁愿坦诚自己的错误行为而不愿告诉任何人自己的幻想。因此,他会认为自己是唯一一个有此类幻想的人,却不知道幻想在其他人身上也是很常见的。一个人在游戏和幻想时行为上的差异可以用两个动机来解释,然而这两种动机却是相互

who fantasies is accounted for by the motives of these two activities, which are nevertheless adjuncts to each other.

依存的。

A child's play is determined by wishes: in point of fact by a single wish—one that helps in his upbringing—the wish to be big and grown up. He is always playing at being "grown up", and in his games he imitates what he knows about the lives of his elders. He has no reason to conceal this wish. With the adult, the case is different. On the one hand, he knows that he is expected not to go on playing or fantasying any longer, but to act in the real world; on the other hand, some of the wishes which give rise to his fantasies are of a kind which it is essential to conceal. Thus he is ashamed of his fantasies as being childish and as being impermissible.

孩子的游戏是由其愿望决定的。事实上也是他唯一的愿望——这个愿望在他成长过程中起着重大作用——也就是长大。孩子总是玩长大的游戏,在他的游戏中模仿自己熟悉的大人的行为。他没有理由去隐瞒这个愿望。而成人却不同。一方面,他知道自己不应该继续玩游戏或者幻想,而是在现实世界中行动起来;另一方面,他意识到把会引起幻想的那些愿望隐藏起来至关重要。如此一来,他就为那些孩子气的、不被许可的幻想感到羞愧。

But, you will ask, if people make such a mystery of their fantasying, how is it that we know such a lot about it? Well, there is a class of human beings upon whom, not a god, indeed, but a stern goddess—Necessity—has allotted the task of telling what they suffer and what things give them happiness. These are the victims of nervous illness, who are obliged to tell their fantasies, among other things, to the doctor by whom they expect to be cured by mental treatment. This is our best source of knowledge, and we have since found good reason to suppose that our patients tell us nothing that we might not also hear from healthy people.

你会问,既然人们将自己的幻想隐藏,那我们又是如何了解这么多呢?事情是这样的,世上有一类人,不是上帝,而是一位严厉的女神——必要性——让他们讲述自己经历的痛苦和使之愉快的事物。这些人就是精神疾病的受害者,他们不得不向医生讲述自己的幻想,从而希望得到精神上的治疗。这是我们知识的最佳来源。我们有充足的理由相信如果病人对我们守口如瓶,那么我们从健康人那里也无从得知。

Let us make ourselves acquainted with a few of the characteristics of fantasying. We may lay it down that a happy person never fantasies, only an unsatisfied one. The motive forces of fantasies are unsatisfied wishes, and every single fantasy is the fulfillment of a wish, a correction of unsatisfying reality. These motivating wishes vary according to the sex, character, and circumstances of the person who is having the fantasy; but they fall naturally into two main groups. They are either ambitious

现在让我们来认识一下幻想的一些特点。我们可以断言幸福的人不会有幻想,只有那些愿望难以满足的人才去幻想。幻想的动力是未被满足的愿望,每一个幻想都是对愿望的满足和对不尽如人意的现实的补偿。这些充足动力的愿望根据性别、性格和幻想着的人所处的环境不同而变化。大致上分为两类。要么是野心的愿望从而提高幻想者的地位,

wishes, which serve to elevate the subject's personality; or they are erotic ones. In young women the erotic wishes predominate almost exclusively, for their ambition is as a rule absorbed by erotic trends. In young men egoistic and ambitious wishes come to the fore clearly enough alongside of erotic ones. But we will not lay stress on the opposition between the two trends; we would rather emphasize the fact that they are often united. Just as, in many altarpieces, the portrait of the donor is to be seen in a corner of the picture, so, in the majority of ambitious fantasies, we can discover in some corner or other the lady for whom the creator of the fantasy performs all his heroic deeds and at whose feet all his triumphs are laid. Here, as you see, there are strong enough motives for concealment; the well-brought-up young woman is only allowed a minimum of erotic desire, and the young man has to learn to suppress the excess of self-regard which he brings with him from the spoilt days of his childhood, so that he may find his place in a society which is full of other individuals making equally strong demands.

要么是性幻想。年轻女性主要是性幻想,因为她们的野心通常被性欲同化。年轻男性的自我和野心幻想和性幻想并驾齐驱。我们不去讨论之间的对立。我们宁愿强调两者之间的联合。正如在许多祭祀装饰品上,对捐赠者的描写可以在绘画的角落里看到。因此在大部分的野心幻想中,我们可以发现幻想者为某个女性展现他所有的英雄行为并把所有的胜利果实堆在她的脚下。正如你所见,有足够的隐藏动机。受过良好教育的年轻女性只允许少量的性欲,而且年轻男性也要学会压制对自身利益的过分关注,这种过分关注是他在童年时代受宠爱的日子里养成的——以便在其他也有着同样强烈要求的人际社会中找到可以的自己的位置。

We must not suppose that the products of this imaginative activity—the various fantasies, castles in the air and daydreams—are stereotyped or unalterable. On the contrary, they fit themselves into the subject's shifting impressions of life, change with every change in his situation, and receive from every fresh active impression what might be called a "date-mark". The relation of a fantasy to time is in general very important. We may say that it hovers, as it were, between three times—the three moments of time which our ideation involves. Mental work is linked to some current impression, some provoking occasion in the present which has been able to arouse one of the subject's major wishes. From there it harks back to a memory of an earlier experience (usually an infantile one) in which this wish was fulfilled; and

我们不应该认为想象活动的产物——各种幻想、空中楼阁和白日梦——是已经定型或者不可改变的。相反,他们适应主题的转移,并根据情况的变化做出相应变化,并从每个新鲜活泼的印象中去接受称为日戳的印象。一般来说,幻想与时间的关系是至关重要的。我们可以说幻想似乎徘徊在三种时间之间——我们的想象经历的三种时刻。心理活动和某些现时的印象相关联。目前某些惊人的场合能够引起主体的主要愿望。心理活动由此而退回到对早年经历的记忆(通常是童年时代的经历),在这个时期该重大愿望曾得到满足,于是在幻想中便创造了一个与

it now creates a situation relating to the future which represents a fulfillment of the wish. What it thus creates is a daydream or fantasy, which carries about it traces of its origin from the occasion which provoked it and from the memory. Thus past, present and future are strung together, as it were, on the thread of the wish that runs through them.

未来相联系的场景来表现愿望的满足情况。心理活动如此创造出来的东西叫做白日梦或者幻想，其根源在于刺激其产生的事件和某段经历的记忆。这样，过去、现在和未来就串联在一起了，愿望这根轴线贯穿其中。

A very ordinary example may serve to make what I have said clear. Let us take the case of a poor orphan boy to whom you have given the address of some employer where he may perhaps find a job. On his way there he may indulge in a daydream appropriate to the situation from which it arises. The content of his fantasy will perhaps be something like this. He is given a job, finds favor with his new employer, makes himself indispensable in the business, is taken into his employer's family, marries the charming young daughter of the house, and then himself becomes a director of the business, first as his employer's partner and then as his successor. In this fantasy, the dreamer has regained what he possessed in his happy childhood—the protecting house, the loving parents and the first objects of his affectionate feelings. You will see from this example the way in which the wish makes use of an occasion in the present to construct, on the pattern of the past, a picture of the future.

一个很普通的例子可以证明我刚才所说的。我们以一个穷孤儿为例，你把可能雇佣他干活的雇主地址给他。在去的路上，他可能沉浸于与之相关的白日梦中。幻想的内容可能如下：他找到一份工作，深得雇主的喜爱，自己在这份工作中扮演着至关重要的位置，还被带到雇主的家里，和雇主美丽的女儿结婚，自己变成了主管，刚开始是雇主的合作伙伴，最终成为他的继承人。在这个幻想中，幻想着重拾童年时代的快乐——庇护他的家庭，慈爱的父母以及他最初一见钟情的妙龄佳人。你可以从这个案例中发现愿望如何用在过去结构的基础上，然后利用当前情境构建未来图景。

There is a great deal more that could be said about fantasies; but I will only allude as briefly as possible to certain points. If fantasies become over-luxuriant and over-powerful, the conditions are laid for an onset of neurosis or psychosis. Fantasies, moreover, are the immediate mental precursors of the distressing symptoms complained of by our patients. Here a broad bypath branches off into pathology.

关于幻想还有很多例子，但是我将尽可能扼要地说明其中几点。如果幻想变得过于丰富多彩、强烈无比的话，那么神经症和精神病就处于待发作状态。而且，幻想是我们的病人经常抱怨的苦恼病状的直接心理预兆。它像一条宽敞的岔道伸向病理学范畴。

I cannot pass over the relation of fantasies to dreams. Our dreams at night are nothing else than fantasies like these, as we can demonstrate from

在此我不能略过而不谈幻想与梦之间的关系。其实我们在夜里所

the interpretation of dreams. Language, in its unrivaled wisdom, long ago decided the question of the essential nature of dreams by giving the name of daydreams to the airy creations of fantasy. If the meaning of our dreams usually remains obscure to us in spite of this pointer, it is because of the circumstance that at night there also arise in us wishes of which we are ashamed; these we must conceal from ourselves, and they have consequently been repressed, pushed into the unconscious. Repressed wishes of this sort and their derivatives are only allowed to come to expression in a very distorted form. When scientific work had succeeded in elucidating this factor of dream distortion, it was no longer difficult to recognize that night dreams are wish-fulfillments in just the same way as daydreams—the fantasies which we all know so well.

So much for fantasies. And now for the creative writer. May we really attempt to compare the imaginative writer with the "dreamer in broad daylight", and his creations with daydreams? Here we must begin by making an initial distinction. We must separate writers who, like the ancient authors of epics and tragedies, take over their material ready-made, from writers who seem to originate their own material. We will keep to the latter kind, and, for the purposes of our comparison, we will choose not the writers most highly esteemed by the critics, but the less pretentious authors of novels, romances and short stories, who nevertheless have the widest and most eager circle of readers of both sexes. One feature above all cannot fail to strike us about the creations of these story-writers: each of them has a hero who is the center of interest, for whom the writer tries to win our sympathy by every possible means and whom he seems to place under the protection of a special providence. If, at the end of one chapter of my story, I leave the hero unconscious and bleeding from severe wounds, I

做的梦就属上述幻想,这一点我们可以通过梦之诠释来证实。语言早就以其无与伦比的智慧对梦的本质问题下了定论,把漫无边际的幻想创造命名为白日梦。如果我们梦境通常模糊不清的话,那是因为夜间的环境使我们产生了一些令自己感到羞愧的愿望,而这些愿望我们又必须对自己隐瞒,所以它们受到压抑,被推进潜意识之中。这种受压抑的愿望及其派生物,只得以一种极其歪曲的形式表现出来。当科学工作已经成功地解释造成梦变形的因素时,就不难看出夜间的梦与白日梦——即我们非常了解的幻想一样,都是愿望的满足。

关于幻想就说这些,现在谈谈创作家。我们真的可以将富有想象力的创作者和"大白天做梦者"相提并论吗?创作家的作品可以和白日梦相比吗?这里首先对此做出初步的区分。我们必须把那些接手现有资料的作家,比如史诗和悲剧的作者,和原创作家区分开来。我们在比较时主要针对后一类作家。我们不选择那些被批评家高度赞扬的作家,而是选择那些名气不是很大,作品却受广大男女读者欢迎的长篇小说、传奇文学、短篇小说的作家。这些小说家的作品中最惊人特点就是:它们都有一个主人公作为兴趣中心,作者试图使用一切方法让主人公赢得读者的同情,这个主人公似乎受到某种特殊的保护。如果在小说的某一章节末尾,我让主人公处于无意识状态并且受重伤流血不止,那么在下一章节的开头肯定是主人公被细心照料并

am sure to find him at the beginning of the next being carefully nursed and on the way to recovery; and if the first volume closes with the ship he is in going down in a storm at sea, I am certain, at the opening of the second volume, to read of his miraculous rescue—a rescue without which the story could not proceed. The feeling of security with which I follow the hero through his perilous adventures is the same as the feeling with which a hero in real life throws himself into the water to save a drowning man or exposes himself to the enemy's fire in order to storm a battery. It is the true heroic feeling, which one of our best writers has expressed in an inimitable phrase: "Nothing can happen to me!" It seems to me, however, that through this revealing characteristic of invulnerability we can immediately recognize His Majesty the Ego, the hero alike of every daydream and of every story.

逐渐康复。如果小说第一卷末尾,主人公乘坐的轮船在风暴中沉了,那么在下一卷的开篇必然是主人公被神奇获救。没有主人公的获救,小说就无法继续。这种跟随主人公冒险的感觉和现实生活中主人公为救落水者挺身而出或者为了阻止一场战争而直面敌人的炮火的感觉是一样的。这是一种真正的英雄的感觉。我们以为最优秀的作家曾用一句无比精彩的话表达过:我不会有事。而正是通过这种刀枪不入、英雄不死的启示性特征,我们似乎可以立即认出每场白日梦和每篇小说里的主角如出一辙,都是一个至高无上的自我。

Other typical features of these egocentric stories point to the same kinship. The fact that all the women in the novel invariably fall in love with the hero can hardly be looked on as a portrayal of reality, but it is easily understood as a necessary constituent of a daydream. The same is true of the fact that the other characters in the story are sharply divided into good and bad, in defiance of the variety of human characters that are to be observed in real life. The "good" are the helpers, while the "bad" ones are the enemies and rivals, of the ego which has become the hero of the story.

这些自我中心小说表现出了类似性。小说中,所有女性都爱上同一个男主人公,这一点很难说是对现实的描写,但是,作为白日梦必要的构成因素却很容易被理解。同样,作者无视现实生活中人物性格的多样性,而是将人物简单地划分为好人和坏人。好人是自我的助手,而坏人是自我的敌人和竞争对手。这个自我就是故事的主角。

We are perfectly aware that very many imaginative writings are far removed from the model of the naive day-dream; and yet I cannot suppress the suspicion that even the most extreme deviations from that model could be linked with it through an uninterrupted series of transitional cases. It has struck me that in many of what are known as "psychological" novels only one person—once again the hero—is described from within. The

我们十分清楚,许多富于想象的作品和天真的白日梦相距甚远。但我仍不能放弃这种推测:即使偏离白日梦模式最远的作品也可以通过不间断的、一系列的过渡事件与白日梦相联系。我注意到,所谓的心理小说,其中只有一个人——主人公——的心理活动被描写。作者好像坐在

author sits inside his mind, as it were, and looks at the other characters from outside. The psychological novel in general no doubt owes its special nature to the inclination of the modern writer to split up his ego, by self-observation, into many part-egos, and, in consequence, to personify the conflicting currents of his own mental life in several heroes. Certain novels, which might be described as "eccentric", seem to stand in quite special contrast to the type of the day-dream. In these, the person who is introduced as the hero plays only a very small active part; he sees the actions and sufferings of other people pass before him like a spectator. Many of Zola's later works belong to this category. But I must point out that the psychological analysis of individuals who are not creative writers, and who diverge in some respects from the so-called norm, has shown us analogous variations of the daydream, in which the ego contents itself with the role of spectator.

主人公的脑袋里,从外部看其他人物。一般来说心理小说将这种特点归因于现代作家倾向于凭借自我观察,将他的主人公分成许多部分自我,结果是作家将自己心理生活中相冲突的几个倾向在几个主角身上体现出来。另外,某些小说,或许可以称之为怪癖小说,似乎与白日梦类型形成非常特殊的对比。在这些小说中,那些作为主人公的人物只是小说中的一小部分。他像旁观者一样看着别人的行为和遭受的痛苦。许多左拉的晚期作品就属于这一范畴。但是我必须指出的是:通过对那些非创作作家和不同于所谓正常人的人群分析,心理小说为我们展示了各种各样的白日梦。在这些小说中,自我以一种旁观者的身份得到满足。

If our comparison of the imaginative writer with the daydreamer, and of poetical creation with the daydream, is to be of any value, it must, above all, show itself in some way or other fruitful. Let us, for instance, try to apply to these authors' works the thesis we laid down earlier concerning the relation between fantasy and the three periods of time and the wish which runs through them; and, with its help, let us try to study the connections that exist between the life of the writer and his works. No one has known, as a rule, what expectations to frame in approaching this problem; and often the connection has been thought of in much too simple terms. In the light of the insight we have gained from fantasies, we ought to expect the following state of affairs. A strong experience in the present awakens in the creative writer a memory of an earlier experience (usually belonging to his childhood) from which there now proceeds a wish which finds its fulfilment in the creative work. The

如果我们将富有想象力的作家与白日梦,诗意的作品与白日梦之间作对比有什么价值的话,那么它必须有某些方面的结果。譬如,我们试着将我们前面提到的关于幻想、三个时间和贯穿三个时间的愿望之间的关系命题运用于这些作者的作品,借助于此,我们试着研究一下作者的生活与其作品之间的联系。一般来说,无人知晓在研究这个问题时应设想什么样的预期结果,而且人们常常把这种联系看得过于简单。借助于我们对幻想研究的结果,我们应该预料事态:现时的强烈经验唤醒创作者早期的记忆(通常属于孩童时代的记忆),由此产生一个在其作品中可以得到满足的愿望。其作品本身能够显示出近期的诱发事件和旧时的记忆。

work itself exhibits elements of the recent provoking occasion as well as of the old memory.

Do not be alarmed at the complexity of this formula. I suspect that in fact it will prove to be too exiguous a pattern. Nevertheless, it may contain a first approach to the true state of affairs; and, from some experiments I have made, I am inclined to think that this way of looking at creative writings may turn out not unfruitful. You will not forget that the stress it lays on childhood memories in the writer's life—a stress which may perhaps seem puzzling—is ultimately derived from the assumption that a piece of creative writing, like a daydream, is a continuation of, and a substitute for, what was once the play of childhood.

不要被这个程式的复杂吓到。我想事实上它是个极其细小的结构。然而,它或许包含着弄清事实真相的第一步。从以往的实验来看,我倾向于认为这种看待创作的方法不可能没有功效。你不会忘记儿童时代的压力——这个压力可能有点令人困惑——最终来自于创作如白日梦一样是孩童时代游戏的继续或者替代。

We must not neglect, however, to go back to the kind of imaginative works which we have to recognize, not as original creations, but as the re-fashioning of ready-made and familiar material. Even here, the writer keeps a certain amount of independence, which can express itself in the choice of material and in changes in it which are often quite extensive. Insofar as the material is already at hand, however, it is derived from the popular treasure-house of myths, legends and fairy tales. The study of constructions of folk-psychology such as these is far from being complete, but it is extremely probable that myths, for instance, are distorted vestiges of the wishful fantasies of whole nations, the secular dreams of youthful humanity.

然而,回到那些作品中我们不能忘记——它们不是原创作品却让人们熟悉的故事重新受到欢迎。即使在这类作品中,作者也拥有相当大的自主权,这种自主权可以在材料选择和广泛的变化中表现出来。就现成的故事来说,这类作品来源于神话、传奇及童话故事。这些民族心理结构研究还远远不够充分,但那时极有可能像神话这类传说是整个民族愿望的幻想,也是人类早期尚未宗教化的梦幻歪曲后的残迹。

You will say that, although I have put the creative writer first in the title of my paper, I have told you far less about him than about fantasies. I am aware of that, and I must try to excuse it by pointing to the present state of our knowledge. All I have been able to do is to throw out some encouragements and suggestions which, starting from the study of fantasies, lead on to the problem of the writer's choice of his literary material. As for the other problem—by what means the creative

你可能会说虽然在标题中我将创作家放在幻想之前,但是我所讲述的有关创作家的内容远不及幻想那么多。我意识到这一点,但我这么做是有理由的,因为我们现在所拥有的知识还很有限。我所能做的就是:基于对幻想的研究提出鼓励和一些能引导出作家选择文学材料问题的建议。至于其他问题——创作者的

writer achieves the emotional effects in us that are aroused by his creations—we have as yet not touched on it at all. But I should like at least to point out to you the path that leads from our discussion of fantasies to the problems of poetical effects.

You will remember how I have said that the daydreamer carefully conceals his fantasies from other people because he feels he has reasons for being ashamed of them. I should now add that even if he were to communicate them to us he could give us no pleasure by his disclosures. Such fantasies, when we learn them, repel us or at least leave us cold. But when a creative writer presents his plays to us or tells us what we are inclined to take to be his personal daydreams, we experience a great pleasure, and one which probably arises from the confluence of many sources. How the writer accomplishes this is his innermost secret; the essential arspoetica① lies in the technique of overcoming the feeling of repulsion in us which is undoubtedly connected with the barriers that rise between each single ego and the others. We can guess two of the methods used by this technique. The writer softens the character of his egoistic daydreams by altering and disguising it, and he bribes us by the purely formal—that is, aesthetic—yield of pleasure which he offers us in the presentation of his fantasies. We give the name of an incentive bonus, or a fore-pleasure, to a yield of pleasure such as this, which is offered to us so as to make possible the release of still greater pleasure arising from deeper psychical sources. In my opinion, all the aesthetic pleasure which a creative writer affords us has the character of a force-pleasure of this kind, and our actual enjoyment of an imaginative work proceeds from a liberation of tensions in our minds. It may even be that not a

作品如何引起我们的情感共鸣——我们目前还没有涉及。但是我至少应该向你们指出引导我由幻想的讨论到诗意效果问题的道路。

你会记得我说过,白日梦患者谨慎地将自己的幻想隐藏起来不让别人知道,因为他觉得以这些幻想为耻。现在我应该补充一点,即使他告诉我们自己的幻想,但在讲述的过程中他丝毫没有愉悦感。我们知道这些幻想时会产生反感,或者至少会扫兴。但是,当创作家向我们呈现他的戏剧或是那些我们会认为是作者自己的白日梦时,我们却能获得愉悦感。这种快乐极有可能是由许多来源汇集而成。作者如何做到这点的是一个秘密。诗艺的本质在于克服我们的冲动,这种冲动无疑与单个自我和其他人的自我之间的障碍有关。我们可以猜想使用这种技巧中的两种方法。作者通过改变和掩饰利己主义的白日梦以软化他们的利己性质。他通过纯形式的——审美——快感来收买我们这些读者。我们将这类快乐命名为"额外刺激"或者"前期快感"。作者向我们提供这种快乐是为了有可能从更深的精神源泉中释放出更大的快乐。在我看来,所有创作者提供的审美愉悦感都有此类的前期快感的性质。我们对一部富有想象力作品的欣赏来源于思想中的压力释放。更有可能的是这种显著效果是由于作者使我们能够在不自责和不羞耻的情况下享受我们自己的白日梦。这就带我们

① Arspoetica:[拉丁语] 诗艺。

little of this effect is due to the writer's enabling us thenceforward to enjoy our own daydreams without self-reproach or shame. This brings us to the threshold of new, interesting and complicated inquiries; but also, at least for the moment, to the end of our discussion.

走向新的、刺激的、复杂难懂的调查工作难题上了,但至少是目前,它也把我们带到了我们讨论的终点。

3. Questions for Discussion

(1) How do you understand the relation between creative writers and daydream?

(2) Why do people conceal their daydreams?

(3) What methods do the creative writers use to make readers experience their daydreams without repulsion?

3. 讨论题

(1)如何理解创作家与白日梦之间的关系?

(2)为什么人们总习惯于对自己的白日梦避而不谈?

(3)创作家们运用了哪些方法使读者能够毫无反感地分享和体验他们的白日梦?

Chapter 8

第 8 章

1. Introduction to Carl Gustav Jung

1. 荣格简介

Carl Gustav Jung (1875-1961) was a Swiss psychiatrist and founder of the school of analytical psychology. He proposed and developed the concepts of the extroverted and introverted personality, archetypes, and the collective unconscious. His works have been influential not only in psychology, but in religion and literature as well.

Jung was born in Kesswill, Switzerland. Jung was the only child of a Protestant clergyman for years, and had a much younger sister. Jung was a quiet and observant child and he spent hours observing the roles of the adults around him, which no doubt shaped his later career and work. Jung's childhood was further influenced by the complexities of his parents. His father, Paul, developed a failing belief in the power of religion as he grew older. Jung's mother, Emilie, was haunted by mental illness and, when her boy was just three, left the family to live temporarily in a psychiatric hospital.

From 1895 to 1900 Jung learned medical

卡尔·古斯塔夫·荣格(1875—1961)是瑞士心理学家,分析心理学的创立者。他提出并发展了很多概念,如外向性格和内向性格、原型、集体无意识。他的著作不仅在心理学领域,而且在宗教、文学领域都深有影响。

荣格出生在瑞士的凯斯威尔,父亲是一位新教牧师。荣格有一个比他小很多的妹妹,多年来他都是家中唯一的孩子,性格安静,善于观察。他花大量的时间观察周围成年人的角色,这无疑有益于他以后的事业和著作。荣格的童年还受到他父母复杂状况的影响。他的父亲保罗随着年龄的增长,对宗教力量失去了信念。他的母亲埃米利有精神病,在荣格 3 岁时,曾在精神病医院住院治疗过一段时间。

1895 年至 1900 年,荣格在巴塞

science in Basel University and then worked as an assistant physician at the Burgholzli psychiatric hospital in Zurich. Jung used Word Association Test, a research technique to explore the complexes in the personal unconscious and published the book *Studies in Word Association* (1906). He found groups of repressed psychic content for which he invented the now famous word "complex". In 1905 he worked as a lecturer in psychiatry in Zurich University. Between 1907 and 1912 he and Freud worked closely together. They together set up the International Psychoanalytical Association in 1910, Jung being the president. Many believed that Jung would continue Freud's psychoanalysis, but this did not occur. Viewpoints and temperament ended their collaboration and, eventually their friendship. The publication of *Psychological Types* (1921) set the differences between Jung's position and that of Freud.

尔大学学习医学，之后在苏黎世的伯格尔茨利精神病院做助理医师。荣格使用词语联想测验这一研究技术来探索人的无意识中的情结，发表了《词语联想研究》(1906)一书。现在广为人知的"情结"一词为荣格所创，用于概括聚集成丛的压抑的心理内容。1905 年，他任苏黎世大学精神病学讲师。1907 至 1912 年，荣格和弗洛伊德合作紧密。1910 年，他们共同建立了国际心理分析协会，荣格任第一届主席。很多人认为荣格将继承弗洛伊德的精神分析，但事实并非如此。观点与性格上的差异最终导致两人合作的终止，甚至友谊的终结。《心理类型学》(1921)的出版明确显示出荣格与弗洛伊德不同的观点立场。

Jung had rich knowledge in the symbolism of complex mystical traditions such as Gnosticism, Alchemy, Kabala, and he studied Hinduism and Buddhism closely. He published extensively on his findings, authoring some 200 works on his theories, including *Modern Man in Search of a Soul* (1933), *Psychology and Religion: The Terry Lectures Series* (1938), *Psychology and Alchemy* (1944), *The Undiscovered Self* (1957) and his autobiography *Memories, Dreams, Reflections* (1961). The authorized anthology of Jung is the 20-volume *The Collected Works of C. G. Jung*.

荣格对诺斯替教、炼金术、犹太神秘哲学等传统的象征手法很熟悉，他还悉心研究过印度教和佛教。他发表了大量的研究结果，有约 200 篇/部的理论文章和著作，其中包括《寻求灵魂的现代人》(1933)、《心理学与宗教——泰利讲座》(1938)、《心理学与炼金术》(1944)、《未发现的自我》(1957)及其自传《回忆、梦想、思考》(1961)。荣格的主要作品都汇编在 20 卷的《荣格全集》中。

Jung conceives of the psyche, or one's total personality, as composed of a conscious and unconscious realm. The unconscious realm he split into the personal unconscious and the collective unconscious. The personal unconscious is largely composed of repressed elements from one's personal history, while the collective unconscious is composed of instincts and archetypes which are

荣格认为，心灵或整体人格是由意识和无意识领域构成的。他将无意识领域划分为个人无意识和集体无意识。个人无意识主要是由个人被压抑的经验构成的，而集体无意识则由人类共有的各种本能和原型构成。集体无意识被认为是人类古老智慧的巨大宝库。

common to all human beings. The collective unconscious can be considered as an immense depository of ancient wisdom.

Archetypes are forms or symbols that are manifested by all people in all cultures. According to Jung, especially important archetypes are the persona, the shadow, the anima/animus, the self, the mother, the child, and the wise old man. Jung views the persona, the shadow, the anima and animus, and the self as particularly important parts of the personality.

原型是所有人类和所有文化中表现出的形象或象征。荣格认为人格面具、阴影、阿尼玛/阿尼姆斯、自我、母亲、孩子和智慧老人是一些尤为重要的原型。荣格认为人格面具、阴影、阿尼玛/阿尼姆斯和自我在人格系统中最为重要。

The persona is the mask we wear to make a particular impression on others and it may reveal or conceal our real nature. The shadow is the dark or negative side of the personality. The anima is said to represent the feminine in men and the animus is the comparable counterpart in the female psyche.

人格面具是我们用以示人的面具,它可能显露或掩盖我们的本性。阴影是人格中阴暗或消极的一面。阿尼玛是男人心灵中女性的一面,阿尼姆斯是女人心灵中男性的一面。

Individuation means becoming a single, homogeneous being, and it also implies becoming one's own self with incomparable uniqueness.

个体化意味着成为一个单一的、同质的存在,它也意味着成为具有无与伦比的独特性的自己。

2. Selections from *The Archetypes and the Collective Unconscious*

2.《原型与集体无意识》选文

Conscious, Unconscious and Individuation①

Carl Gustav Jung

意识、无意识与个体化

卡尔·古斯塔夫·荣格

The relation between the conscious and the unconscious on the one hand, and the individuation process on the other, are problems that arise almost regularly during the later stages of analytical treatment. By "analytical" I mean a procedure that takes account of the existence of the unconscious.

在分析治疗的后期阶段中,意识、无意识与个体化过程之间的关系问题定期出现。我用"分析"一词意指一个解释无意识存在的过程。这些问题并不会出现在一个基于暗示

① Selected from *The Archetypes and the Collective Unconscious*, 2nd Edition, London: Routledge, 1991. "Conscious, Unconscious and Individuation" was originally written in English as "The Meaning of Individuation", the introductory chapter of *The Integration of the Personality*, New York: Farrar & Reinhart, 1939.

These problems do not arise in a procedure based on suggestion. A few preliminary words may not be out of place in order to explain what is meant by "individuation".

I use the term "individuation" to denote the process by which a person becomes a psychological "individual", that is, a separate, indivisible unity or "whole". It is generally assumed that consciousness is the whole of the psychological individual. But knowledge of the phenomena that can only be explained on the hypothesis of unconscious psychic processes makes it doubtful whether the ego and its contents are in fact identical with the "whole". If unconscious processes exist at all, they must surely belong to the totality of the individual, even though they are not components of the conscious ego. If they were part of the ego they would necessarily be conscious, because everything that is directly related to the ego is conscious. Consciousness can even be equated with the relation between the ego and the psychic contents. But unconscious phenomena are so little related to the ego that most people do not hesitate to deny their existence outright. Nevertheless, they manifest themselves in an individual's behaviour. An attentive observer can detect them without difficulty, while the observed person remains quite unaware of the fact that he is betraying his most secret thoughts or even things he has never thought consciously. It is, however, a great prejudice to suppose that something we have never thought consciously does not exist in the psyche. There is plenty of evidence to show that consciousness is very far from covering the psyche in its totality. Many things occur semiconsciously, and a great many more remain entirely unconscious. Thorough investigation of the phenomena of dual and multiple personalities, for instance, has brought to light a mass of material with observations

的过程之中。为了解释什么是"个体化",几句预备性的话是必需的。

我用"个体化"来指代一个人成为心理上独立个体这一过程。换言之,心理上独立个体就是一个独立的、不可分的统一体或者"整体"。人们通常假定意识就是整个心理个体。但是现象知识只能用无意识心理过程假设来解释,这就使得自我及其内容是否与整体相一致变得可疑。如果无意识过程确实存在,那么尽管它们不是有意识自我的组成部分,它们肯定也是属于个体化整体。如果它们是自我的一部分,那么它们必然是有意识的,因为与自我有直接关系的一切事物都是有意识的。意识甚至等同于自我与心理内容的关系,而无意识现象与自我关系甚少,以至于大部分人直接否定了它们的存在。然而,它们表现在个体行为中。一位细心的观察者很容易就能发现它们。而被观察者已经暴露了最私密的想法或者他从未有意识地想过某事,但他们对此却浑然不觉。会认为我们从未想过的东西就不存在于我们的心理中,这是极大的偏见。许多证据证明意识远没有涵盖全部的心理。许多事情的发生都是半意识的,更多数是无意识的。比如,对双重或者多重人格的全面观察已然发现,大量材料都已证明了这一点。(这里读者可以参考皮埃尔·雅内、西奥多·弗洛努瓦、莫顿·普林斯等人的著作。)

to prove this point. (I would refer the reader to the writings of Pierre Janet①, Théodore Flournoy②, Morton Prince③, and others.)

The Importance of such phenomena has made a deep impression on medical psychology, because they give rise to all sorts of psychic and physiological symptoms. In these circumstances, the assumption that the ego expresses the totality of the psyche has become untenable. It is, on the contrary, evident that the whole must necessarily include not only consciousness but the illimitable field of unconscious occurrences as well, and that the ego can be no more than the centre of the field of consciousness.

无意识的重要性已然给医学心理学留下了深刻的印象。因为它们引起了所有心理和生理上的症状。在这种背景下,自我代表了心理全部的假说已经没有说服力了。相反,整体不仅包括意识也包括无意识的广阔领域,而自我不再是意识领域的核心,这已成为不容置疑的事实。

You will naturally ask whether the unconscious possesses a centre too. I would hardly venture to assume that there is in the unconscious a ruling principle analogous to the ego. As a matter of fact, everything points to the contrary. If there were such a centre, we could expect almost regular signs of its existence. Cases of dual personality would then be frequent occurrences instead of rare curiosities. As a rule, unconscious phenomena manifest themselves in fairly chaotic and unsystematic forms. Dreams, for instance, show no apparent order and no tendency to systematization, as they would have to do if there were a personal consciousness at the back of them. The philosophers Carus and von Hartmann④ treat the unconscious as a metaphysical principle, a sort of universal mind, without any trace of personality or ego-consciousness, and similarly Schopenhauer's "Will" is without an ego. Modern psychologists, too, regard the unconscious as an egoless function below the threshold of

读者自然会问无意识是否也有一个中心。我不会冒险去假设无意识中有一个与自我相似的支配原则。事实上,一切事实都证明没有。如果有这样一个中心,我们便可以期待显示其存在的规律性迹象。这样的话,双重人格案例将不再是凤毛麟角。一般来说,无意识现象以混乱、无秩序的形式显示出来。比如,梦并没有系统化的秩序和趋势,因为如果他们背后有意识做支撑,他们就必须显示出来。哲学家加鲁斯和冯·哈特曼把无意识视为一个形而上学的准则,一种普世心理,没有任何的人格或者自我意识痕迹,正如叔本华所说的"意志"没有自我一样。现代心理学家同样把无意识认为是一种意识阈限之下的一种功能,它不具有自我性。与哲学家不同的是他们倾向于从意识中获得潜意识功能。雅内认为

---

① 考皮埃尔·雅内(Pierre Janet,1859-1947),法国心理学家、哲学家。
② 西奥多·弗洛努瓦(Théodore Flournoy,1854-1920),瑞士心理学家。
③ 莫顿·普林斯(Morton Prince,1854-1929),美国神经学医师。
④ 冯·哈特曼(Karl Robert Eduard von Hartmann,1842-1906),德国哲学家。

consciousness. Unlike the philosophers, they tend to derive its subliminal functions from the conscious mind. Janet thinks that there is a certain weakness of consciousness which is unable to hold all the psychic processes together. Freud, on the other hand, favours the idea of conscious factors that suppress certain incompatible tendencies. Much can be said for both theories, since there are numerous cases where a weakness of consciousness actually cause certain contents to fall below the threshold, or where disagreeable contents are repressed. It is obvious that such careful observers as Janet and Freud would not have constructed theories deriving the unconscious mainly from conscious sources had they been able to discover traces of an independent personality or of autonomous will in the manifestations of the unconscious.

意识有一个弱点,这使得它不能统一所有的心理过程。另一方面,弗洛伊德支持意识因素抑制某些不可兼容趋势这一观点。两个理论都有其合理成分。有很多案例能够证明,要么意识的某一弱点导致特定成分陷入门阀之下,要么不合意的内容被压制。很明显,像雅内、弗洛伊德这样细致的观察者如果在无意识表象中发现独立个性或自由意志的迹象,他们是不会构建出无意识主要衍生自意识源泉的理论。

If it were true that the unconscious consists of nothing but contents accidentally deprived of consciousness but otherwise indistinguishable from the conscious material, then one could identify the ego more or less with the totality of the psyche. But actually the situation is not quite so simple. Both theories are based mainly on observations in the field of neurosis. Neither Janet nor Freud had any specifically psychiatric experience. If they had, they would surely have been struck by the fact that the unconscious displays contents that are utterly different from conscious ones, so strange, indeed, that nobody can understand them, neither the patient himself nor his doctors. The patient is inundated by a flood of thoughts that are as strange to him as they are to a normal person. That is why we call him "crazy": we cannot understand his ideas. We understand something only if we have the necessary premises for doing so. But here the premises are just as remote from our consciousness as they were from the mind of the patient before he went mad. Otherwise he would never have become

如果构成无意识的确实是仅仅为偶然得自于意识的内容,与意识材料并无区别,人们就可以或多或少地把自我等同于心理的整体性。事实上,问题远非如此简单。两个理论主要是基于对神经衰弱症的观察。雅内和弗洛伊德都没有精神病。如果他们有这方面的经历,他们就会惊讶于无意识与意识所显示的内容大不相同这个事实。无意识是如此的陌生,以至于无论病人还是医生都不能理解。患者被思想洪水淹没,这股思想洪水对病人和其他正常人来说都是陌生的。这就是我们称病人为疯子的原因:我们都不能理解他的想法。只有我们有理解某事的必要前提时,我们才能够懂得它。但是现在这个前提正如病人在变疯之前一样,离我们的意识非常遥远。否则,病人是不会变疯的。

insane.

There is, in fact, no field directly known to us from which we could derive certain pathological ideas. It is not a question of more or less normal contents that became unconscious just by accident. They are, on the contrary, products whose nature is at first completely baffling. They differ in every respect from neurotic material, which cannot be said to be at all bizarre. The material of a neurosis is understandable in human terms, but that of a psychosis is not.

This peculiar psychotic material cannot be derived from the conscious mind, because the latter lacks the premises which would help to explain the strangeness of the ideas. Neurotic contents can be integrated without appreciable injury to the ego, but psychotic ideas cannot. They remain inaccessible, and ego-consciousness is more or less swamped by them. They even show a distinct tendency to draw the ego into their "system".

Such cases indicate that under certain conditions the unconscious is capable of taking over the role of the ego. The consequence of this exchange is insanity and confusion, because the unconscious is not a second personality with organized and centralized functions but in all probability a decentralized congeries of psychic processes. However, nothing produced by the human mind lies absolutely outside the psychic realm. Even the craziest idea must correspond to something in the psyche. We cannot suppose that certain minds contain elements that do not exist at all in other minds. Nor can we assume that the unconscious is capable of becoming autonomous only in certain people, namely in those predisposed to insanity. It is very much more likely that the tendency to autonomy is a more or less general peculiarity of the unconscious. Mental disorder is, in a sense, only one outstanding example of a

事实上,没有一个领域我们是可以直接获得病态学思想的。这并不是偶然造成一个或多或少的正常内容变成无意识的问题。相反,一开始它们就是让人无法理解的东西。病态与精神衰弱症有很大的不同。神经病的材料根本不能算是古怪的。从人类角度来说,神经病症的案例是可以理解的,但是精神病的材料则是不可以的。

因为有意识的头脑缺少帮助解释思想奇特性的前提,所以精神病材料不能得自于它。神经病的内容可以在不对自我造成伤害的情况下得到融合,但是精神病的内容却不行。它们始终令人难以理解,自我意识或多或少被它们淹没。它们甚至显示出把自我吸入它们的系统的明显趋势。

这些案例说明在特定条件下无意识可以代替自我。这样交换的结果是疯癫与混乱,因为无意识并不是具有组织和集中功能的第二人格,而可能是心理过程的一个去中心化的聚集体。但是,没有什么是由人脑产生却绝对独立于心理王国之外的。即使是最疯狂的想法也都必然与心理之中的某物相符。我们不能认为某些头脑含有的成分,其他头脑就不存在。我们也不能认为无意识仅能在某些人中变的自主,即在那些有疯狂倾向的人中。更有可能的是,自主趋势是无意识或多或少的普遍特性。一定程度上,心理混乱是隐性但依然是普遍状况的显著例证。这种自主趋势首先表明它本身处于种种情绪状态之中,正常人的情绪状态也包括

hidden but none the less general condition. This tendency to autonomy shows itself above all in affective states, including those of normal people. When in a state of violent affect one says or does things which exceed the ordinary. Not much is needed: love and hate, joy and grief, are often enough to make the ego and the unconscious change places. Very strange ideas indeed can take possession of otherwise healthy people on such occasions. Groups, communities, and even whole nations can be seized in this way by psychic epidemics.

在内。当处于极度情绪时,一个人的言行会超出正常人。不需要太多情绪:爱与恨,喜与悲就足以让自我和无意识调换位置。在这种情绪下,非常奇怪的想法的确会控制正常人。团体、社区,甚至整个民族都可以被心理流行病支配。

The autonomy of the unconscious therefore begins where emotions are generated. Emotions are instinctive, involuntary reactions which upset the rational order of consciousness by their elemental outbursts. Affects are not "made" or willfully produced; they simply happen. In a state of affect a trait of character sometimes appears which is strange even to the person concerned, or hidden contents may irrupt involuntarily. The more violent an affect the closer it comes to the pathological, to a condition in which the ego-consciousness is thrust aside by autonomous contents that were unconscious before. So long as the unconscious is in a dormant condition, it seems as if there were absolutely nothing in this hidden region. Hence we are continually surprised when something unknown suddenly appears "from nowhere." Afterwards, of course, the psychologist comes along and shows that things had to happen as they did for this or that reason. But who could have said so beforehand?

因此,无意识自主始于情绪滋生之处。情绪是本能的、无意识的反应,这些反应的自然爆发颠覆了意识的理性秩序。情感并非是人为制造或生产的,它们就这样自然地发生了。在某种情感状态下,性格特征有时就被暴露出来,甚至连本人对这些性格特征都感到陌生,或者说是隐藏的内容无意识地闯了进来。这种情感越是强烈,它就越接近病态,在这种状态下自我意识被以前无意识的自主内容推到一边。如果无意识一直处于静止状态,这块被隐藏的领域就像什么也没有发生似的。因此,当一个陌生的东西突然出现时,我们时常感到惊讶。当然,后来心理学家就出现了,他们解释说这些事物由于这些或者那些原因必须出现。但事先谁能这样说呢?

We call the unconscious "nothing," and yet it is a reality in potentia. The thought we shall think, the deed we shall do, even the fate we shall lament tomorrow, all lie unconscious in our today. The unknown in us which the affect uncovers was always there and sooner or later would have presented itself to consciousness. Hence we must

我们称无意识为"零",但它实际上却是一种潜在的事实。我们将要思考的想法,将要采取的行动,甚至是明天将要哀悼的命运,今天都无意识地存在着。经情感揭露的未知事物一直存在,这些未知事物迟早会通

always reckon with the presence of things not yet discovered. These, as I have said, may be unknown quirks of character. But possibilities of future development may also come to light in this way, perhaps in just such an outburst of affect which sometimes radically alters the whole situation. The unconscious has a Janus-face: on one side its contents point back to a preconscious, prehistoric world of instinct, while on the other side it potentially anticipates the future—precisely because of the instinctive readiness for action of the factors that determine man's fate. If we had complete knowledge of the ground plan lying dormant in an individual from the beginning, his fate would be in large measure predictable.

Now, to then extent that unconscious tendencies—be they backward-looking images or forward-looking anticipations—appear in dreams, dreams have been regarded, in all previous ages, less as historical regressions than as anticipations of the future, and rightly so. For everything that will be happens on the basis of what has been, and of what—consciously or unconsciously—still exists as a memory-trace. In so far as no man is born totally new, but continually repeats the stage of development last reached by the species, he contains unconsciously, as an a prior datum, the entire psychic structure developed both upwards and downwards by his ancestors in the course of the ages. That is what gives the unconscious its characteristic "historical" aspect, but it is at the same time the sine qua non① for shaping the future. For this reason it is often very difficult to decide whether an autonomous manifestation of the unconscious should be interpreted as an effect (and therefore historical) or as an aim (and therefore

过意识展现出来。因此我们必须对尚未被发现的事物做出估算。正如我上面提到的,可能是性格中不为人知的怪癖。但是,未来发展的可能性也可能通过这种方式暴露出来。也许正是情感突然爆发改变了整个情势。无意识有两面性:一方面,它的内容指向前意识的、史前的本能世界;另一方面,它潜在地期待未来——恰好因为本能为决定人类命运的行为做准备。如果我们从一开始就能够完全了解潜藏在个体中的基本计划,那么个体的命运很大程度上就可以预测了。

现在,就无意识趋势——无论它们是向后看的意象还是向前看的预期——出现在梦中的程度而言,梦在过去一切时代始终被视为与其说是历史的回归,还不如说是对未来的期待;的确如此。因为未来一切发生的基础是已然存在之物,是——有意识或无意识——依旧作为记忆痕迹而存在的事物。没有人是全新地诞生出来的,而是在不断重复着他们前辈最后达到的阶段。正如推理数据一样,他无意识地含有其祖先随时代的发展向前、向后发展出来的整个心理结构。这就是无意识为什么会有历史性的一面,但同时历史性也是塑造未来的必要条件。也就是因为这一点,人们很难决定无意识自主具体化应该被解释成影响(因此是历史的)还是目的(因此是目的论的和预期的)。意识不考虑祖传前提,也不会考虑这一先验条件对个体命运形成

① sine qua non:[拉丁语] 必要条件。

teleological and anticipatory). The conscious mind thinks as a rule without regard to ancestral preconditions and without taking into account the influence this a priori factor has on the shaping of the individual's fate. Whereas we think in periods of years, the unconscious thinks and lives in terms of millennia. So when something happens that seems to us an unexampled novelty, it is generally a very old story indeed. We still forget, like children, what happened yesterday. We are still living in a wonderful new world where man thinks himself astonishingly new and "modern". This is unmistakable proof of the youthfulness of human consciousness, which has not yet grown aware of its historical antecedents.

As a matter of fact, the "normal" person convinces me far more of the autonomy of the unconscious than does the insane person. Psychiatric theory can always take refuge behind real or alleged organic disorders of the brain and thus detract from the importance of the unconscious. But such a view is no longer applicable when it comes to normal humanity. What one sees happening in the world is not just a "shadowy vestige of activities that were once conscious", but the expression of a living psychic condition that still exists and always will exist. Were that not so, one might well be astonished. But it is precisely those who give least credence to the autonomy of the unconscious who are the most surprised by it. Because of its youthfulness and vulnerability, our consciousness tends to make light of the unconscious. This is understandable enough, for a young man should not let himself be overawed by the authority of his parents if he wants to start something on his own account. Historically as well as individually, our consciousness has developed out of the darkness and somnolence of primordial unconsciousness. There were psychic processes and

的影响。然而,我们以年为周期进行思考,无意识却以千年为周期存在着。因此,某些对我们来说新奇的事物,其实已经是老生常谈了。我们就像孩子一样,忘记了昨天发生的事情。我们仍然生活在一个新奇的世界里,在这里人们认为自己是全新的而且是现代的。这是人类意识年轻的明显证据,人类意识目前还没有意识到历史前提。

事实上,正常人比精神病人更让我相信无意识的自主性。神经病学理论总是借着大脑或真或神经的混乱,从而贬低无意识的重要性。但是当面对正常人的时候,这种观点就不成立了。人们所见的事物并不只是无意识活动的朦胧的残余。而是活生生的心理状态的表达,这种心理状态现在存在并将永远存在。如果事实不是这样的话,人们或许会惊讶。准确地说,最为惊讶的应该是那些最不相信无意识自主性的人。意识年轻敏感,所以它经常轻视无意识。这是可以理解的,如果一个年轻人想靠自己有所作为就不会被父母的权威吓倒。无论从历史还是个人角度来说,我们的意识已经走出了原始无意识的黑暗与梦幻。在自我意识存在很早之前已经有心理过程和心理功能。早在人能说"我知道思考"之前,就已经有了"思考"。

functions long before any ego-consciousness existed. "Thinking" existed long before man was able to say: "I am conscious of thinking".

The primitive "perils of the soul" consist mainly of dangers to consciousness. Fascination, bewitchment, "loss of soul," possession, etc. are obviously phenomena of the dissociation and suppression of consciousness caused by unconscious contents. Even civilized man is not yet entirely free of the darkness of primeval times. The unconscious is the mother of consciousness. Where there is mother there is also a father, yet he seems to be unknown. Consciousness, in the pride of its youth, may deny its father, but it cannot deny its mother. That would be too unnatural, for one can see in every child how hesitantly and slowly its ego-consciousness evolves out of a fragmentary consciousness lasting for single moments only, and how these islands gradually emerge from the total darkness of mere instinctuality.

原始的"灵魂的危险"主要是由意识的危险构成。着迷、陶醉、灵魂丧失、着魔等很明显都是由无意识内容引起的意识分离和压抑。甚至文明人也没有完全摆脱原始时代的黑暗。无意识是意识之母。有母亲就必然有父亲。但是父亲目前仍是未知状态。意识正年轻气盛,有可能否定父亲的存在,但是不可能否定母亲。不然,那就太奇怪了。我们可以从每一个孩子身上看到自我意识如何从短暂的意识碎片中缓慢发展起来,自我意识的小岛又如何在本能的黑暗中凸现出来。

Consciousness grows out of an unconscious psyche which is older than it, and which goes on functioning together with it or even in spite of it. Although there are numerous cases of conscious contents becoming unconscious again (through being repressed, for instance), the unconscious as a whole is far from being a mere remnant of consciousness. Or are the psychic functions of animals remnants of consciousness?

意识发展来源于比它本身要早得多的无意识心理。同时无意识和意识共同起作用,甚至无意识会单独起作用。虽然很多意识内容转变成无意识(比如,通过压抑的方式),无意识作为一个整体远不止是意识的剩余。或者说动物的心理功能是意识的剩余?

As I have said, there is little hope of our finding in the unconscious an order equivalent to that of the ego. It certainly does not look as if we were likely to discover an unconscious ego-personality, something in the nature of a Pythagorean "counter-earth". Nevertheless, we cannot overlook the fact that, just as consciousness arises from the unconscious, the ego-centre, too, crystallizes out of a dark depth in which it was somehow contained in potentia. Just as a human

正如我所说的,在无意识中找到与自我同样的秩序,这种可能性很小。看起来我们肯定不可能发现一个无意识的自我人格,即某种具有毕达哥拉斯的"反地球"性质的东西。然而,我们不忽视这样一个事实,正如意识由无意识发展而来,自我中心来自于某种具有潜能的黑暗中心。正如人类母亲只能生出人类婴儿一

mother can only produce a human child, whose deepest nature lay hidden during its potential existence within her, so we are practically compelled to believe that the unconscious cannot be an entirely chaotic accumulation of instincts and images. There must be something to hold it together and give expression to the whole. Its centre cannot possibly be the ego, since the ego was born out of it into consciousness and turns its back on the unconscious, seeking to shut it out as much as possible. Or can it be that the unconscious loses its centre with the birth of the ego? In that case we would expect the ego to be far superior to the unconscious in influence and importance. The unconscious would then follow meekly in the footsteps of the conscious, and that would be just what we wish.

样,当胚胎在母体中孕育时,孩子最本质的东西潜伏着,所以我们几乎被迫相信无意识不可能是本能和意象的无序的累积物。一定有东西将它聚在一起并表现其整体。无意识中心不可能是自我,因为自我由无意识发展而来又发展成为意识,最终抛弃无意识,力图最大限度地将它排除。或可能会随着自我的产生无意识就失去中心?在那种情况下,我们就会料想在影响力和重要性上自我远远超越无意识。于是无意识就会温顺地追随意识的脚步,这也就是我们所希望的。

Unfortunately, the facts show the exact opposite: consciousness succumbs all too easily to unconscious influences, and these are often truer and wiser than our conscious thinking. Also, it frequently happens that unconscious motives overrule our conscious decisions, especially in matters of vital importance. Indeed, the fate of the individual is largely dependent on unconscious factors. Careful investigation shows how very much our conscious decisions depend on the undisturbed functioning of memory. But memory often suffers from the disturbing interference of unconscious contents. Moreover, it functions as a rule automatically. Ordinarily it uses the bridges of association, but often in such an extraordinary way that another thorough investigation of the whole process of memory-reproduction is needed in order to find out how certain memories managed to reach consciousness at all. And sometimes these bridges cannot be found. In such cases it is impossible to dismiss the hypothesis of the spontaneous activity of the unconscious. Another example is intuition,

不幸的是,事实恰恰相反,意识很容易屈服于无意识的影响,而且无意识思考要比有意识思考更为真实、聪明。通常是无意识动机支配我们的意识决定,尤其在至关重要的问题上。的确,个体的命运很大程度上取决于无意识因素。仔细的调查表明我们的意识决定在多大程度上依赖于记忆不受干扰。但是记忆经常遭受无意识内容干扰。而且,无意识自动起着规则作用,通常以联想为桥梁。这种连接方式如此不同寻常以至于弄明白了某个记忆是如何连接意识的,这需要对记忆再加工的整个过程重新做一个全面调查。有时候,这种关系很难发现。在这种情况下,我们就无法排除无意识自主活动的假说。另一个例子是直觉。直觉主要依靠性质极为复杂的无意识过程。因为这一特殊性,我已然把直觉定义为“经由无意识的知觉”。

which is chiefly dependent on unconscious processes of a very complex nature. Because of this peculiarity, I have defined intuition as "perception via the unconscious".

Normally the unconscious collaborates with the conscious without friction or disturbance, so that one is not even aware of its existence. But when an individual or a social group deviates too far from their instinctual foundations, they then experience the full impact of unconscious forces. The collaboration of the unconscious is intelligent and purposive, and even when it acts in opposition to consciousness its expression is still compensatory in an intelligent way, as if it were trying to restore the lost balance.

无意识与意识的合作彼此之间没有摩擦和干扰,所以人们都意识不到它的存在。但是,当一个人或社会团体行为方式过于偏离无意识本能基础,他们就能感受到无意识的影响力。无意识合作是智慧的、有目的的,甚至当它和意识相反时,也能用一种明智的方式弥补,好像在力图修复无意识与意识的平衡关系。

There are dreams and visions of such an impressive character that some people refuse to admit that they could have originated in an unconscious psyche. They prefer to assume that such phenomena derive from a sort of "super consciousness". Such people make a distinction between a quasi-physiological or instinctive unconscious and a psychic sphere or layer "above" consciousness, which they style the "super conscious". As a matter of fact, this psyche, which in Indian philosophy is called the "higher" consciousness, corresponds to what we in the West call the "unconscious". Certain dreams, visions, and mystical experiences do, however, suggest the existence of a consciousness in the unconscious. But, if we assume a consciousness in the unconscious, we are at once faced with the difficulty that no consciousness can exist without a subject, that is, an ego to which the contents are related. Consciousness needs a centre, an ego to which something is conscious. We know of no other kind of consciousness, nor can we imagine a consciousness without an ego. There can be no consciousness when there is no one to say: "I am

梦境和幻象给人如此深刻的印象,以至于有些人拒绝承认它们根源于无意识心理。人们更倾向于认为这种现象来源于一种超意识。这些人把准生理学或者本能无意识与意识之上的心理范畴或层面严格划分开来。他们称后者为超级意识。事实上,这种心理在印度哲学中被称为更高意识,也就是我们西方人所说的无意识。然而,某种梦境、幻象和神秘经验的确表明无意识中意识的存在。但是,如果我们承认无意识中有意识的存在,那么我们就要面临一个问题:没有意识能够脱离主题而独立存在。也就是和内容相关的自我。我们不知道其他意识,也不能想象无自我的意识。如果没有人说:"我知道自己在做什么",那么也就不可能有意识。

conscious."

It is unprofitable to speculate about things we cannot know. I therefore refrain from making assertions that go beyond the bounds of science. It was never possible for me to discover in the unconscious anything like a personality comparable with the ego. But although a "second ego" cannot be discovered (except in the rare cases of dual personality), the manifestations of the unconscious do at least show traces of personalities. A single example is the dream, where a number of real or imaginary people represent the dream-thoughts. In nearly all the important types of dissociation, the manifestations of the unconscious assume a strikingly personal form. Careful examination of the behaviour and mental content of these personifications, however, reveals their fragmentary character. They seem to represent complexes that have split off from a greater whole, and are the very reverse of a personal centre of the unconscious.

思考一个我们不可能知道的事物没有益处。因此,我克制做出科学以外的言论。在无意识中找到可以和自我相比拟的人格之类的东西是不可能的。虽然无法发现第二自我(除非在双重人格这种罕见案例中),但是无意识的表现至少显示了人格之痕。举一个简单的例子:梦中许多真实的或者想象出来的人物代表着梦中思想。几乎所有重要的分离类型,无意识的表现都呈现一种显著的个人形式。然而,仔细观察这些人格化的行为和心理内容,可以发现他们零碎的特点。他们好像代表着从更大的整体上分裂出来的复合体,是无意识个性化中心的反面。

I have always been greatly impressed by the character of dissociated fragments as personalities. Hence I have often asked myself whether we are not justified in assuming that, if such fragments have personality, the whole from which they were broken off must have personality to an even higher degree. The inference seemed logical, since it does not depend on whether the fragments are large or small. Why, then, should not the whole have personality too? Personality need not imply consciousness. It can just as easily be dormant or dreaming.

人格分裂碎片使我印象深刻。如果碎片具有人格,那么它们所脱离的那个整体则具有更高程度的人格,我常常问自己这样的想法是否有逻辑性。这碎片究竟是大还是小。这一推理似乎是有逻辑的,因为他不取决于碎片是大还是小。那么为什么整体不具有人格呢?人格没有必要包含意识,它很可能就处于休眠或者梦境中。

The general aspect of unconscious manifestations is in the main chaotic and irrational, despite certain symptoms of intelligence and purposiveness. The unconscious produces dreams, visions, fantasies, emotions, grotesque idea, and so forth. This is exactly what we would expect a dreaming personality to do. It seems to be a personality that was never awake and was never

尽管有着智力和目的的某些症候,但一般大体上无意识表现的是混乱的,不理性的。无意识产生梦境、幻象、幻想、情绪、古怪的想法等等。这就是我们指望一个休眠人格做的事情。人格看起来像从未苏醒,从来都意识不到它正过的生活及自身的

conscious of the life it had lived and of its own continuity. The only question is whether the hypothesis of a dormant and hidden personality is possible or not. It may be that all of the personality to be found in the unconscious is contained in the fragmentary personifications mentioned before. Since this is very possible, all my conjectures would be in vain—unless there were evidence of much less fragmentary and more complete personalities, even though they are hidden.

连续性。唯一的问题是潜伏的、休眠的人格这一假设是否有可能。有可能所有在无意识中发现的人格都包含在之前提到的人格碎片中。既然这完全有可能,那么我的一切推测都是徒劳的,除非有证据证明更少不完整人格和更多的完整人格,即使它们处于潜藏状态。

I am convinced that such evidence exists. Unfortunately, the material to prove this belongs to the subtleties of psychological analysis. It is therefore not exactly easy to give the reader a simple and convincing idea of it.

我深信存在这种证据。不幸的是,证明这一点的材料属于心理分析的微妙之处。所以要为读者提供一个简单又有说服力的解释是极为困难的。

I shall begin with a brief statement: in the unconscious of every man there is hidden a feminine personality, and in that of every woman a masculine personality.

我将从一个简短的陈述开始:每一个男性潜意识中潜藏着一个女性人格,同样,女性潜意识中也潜藏着男性人格。

It is a well-known fact that sex is determined by a majority of male or female genes, as the case may be. But the minority of genes belonging to the other sex does not simply disappear. A man therefore has in him a feminine side, an unconscious feminine figure—a fact of which he is generally quite unaware. I may take it as known that I have called this figure the "anima", and its counterpart in a woman the "animus". In order not to repeat myself, I must refer the reader to the literature. This figure frequently appears in dreams, where one can observe all the attributes I have mentioned in earlier publications.

众所周知,性别是由雌性或雄性基因中的多数来定,视情况而定。但是基因中属于另一性别的少数并没有消失。因此,每个男人身上有女性的一面,是一种无意识女性形象——他本身并没有意识到这一事实。我可以让大家都知道我称这个形象为"阿尼玛",称女性身上的男性形象为"阿尼姆斯"。为了避免重复,我必须建议读者阅读文献。这一形象经常出现在梦中,人们可以在我先前的著述中观察到那些特点。

Another, no less important and clearly defined figure is the "shadow". Like the anima, it appears either in projection on suitable persons, or personified as such in dreams. The shadow coincides with the "personal" unconscious (which corresponds to Freud's conception of the unconscious). Again like the anima, this figure has

另一个同等重要和清晰定义的形象是"阴影"。像阿尼玛一样,它或者显现为合适人选身上的投射,或者像这样具体化出现在梦中。阴影与"个人"无意识一致(相当于弗洛伊德的无意识概念)。再次和阿尼玛相

often been portrayed by poets and writers. I would mention the Faust-Mephistopheles① relationship and E. T. A. Hoffmann's② tale *The Devil's Elixir* as two especially typical descriptions. The shadow personifies everything that the subject refuses to acknowledge about himself and yet is always thrusting itself upon him directly or indirectly—for instance, inferior traits of character and other incompatible tendencies.

似的是,这一形象经常被诗人和作家描写。我在此仅提两个特别典型的描写:浮士德—靡菲斯特和霍夫曼的《魔鬼的迷魂汤》。阴影体现的是主体拒绝承认的一切,但又总是或直接或间接地将其强加于己——比如:性格的低级特征及其他不合谐的趋势。

The fact that the unconscious spontaneously personifies certain affectively toned contents in dreams is the reason why I have taken over these personifications in my terminology and formulated them as names.

无意识自发地将梦中的某些为情感所调和的内容人格化,也就是为什么我把这些人格化的表现纳入我的术语之中,并把它们陈述为概念的名称。

Besides these figures there are still a few others, less frequent and less striking, which have likewise undergone poetic as well as mythological formulation. I would mention, for instance, the figure of the hero and of the wise old man, to name only two of the best known.

除了这些形象外,还有其他形象,它们不如这些形象常见和突出。它们也有诗意的、神话的描述。我将特别提到两个最有名的例子,比如英雄形象和智慧老人。

All these figures irrupt autonomously into consciousness as soon as it gets into a pathological state. With regard to the anima, I would particularly like to draw attention to the case described by Nelken. Now the remarkable thing is that these figures show the most striking connections with the poetic, religious, or mythological formulations, though these connections are in no way factual. That is to say, they are spontaneous products of analogy. One such case even led to the charge of plagiarism: the French writer Benoit③ gave a description of the anima and her classic myth in his book *L'Atlantide*④, which is an exact parallel of

一旦意识进入病态状态,所有这些形象会自主地闯进意识之中。关于阿尼玛,我特别希望大家关注尼尔金所描述的病例。现在一个惊人的事情就是这些形象与诗学、宗教、神学陈述有很大的关系,虽然这些关系绝不是事实。也就是说,他们是类推的自发产物。这方面的例子甚至还引发了抄袭的指控:法国作家博努瓦在他的《大西洋岛》中描写了阿尼玛及其神话,而《大西洋岛》与瑞德哈格德的《她》俨然相同。法律诉讼并

① Mephistopheles:靡菲斯特,歌德(Goethe)所著《浮士德》(*Faust*,1808)中的魔鬼。

② 霍夫曼(E. T. A. Hoffmann,1776-1822),德国浪漫主义作家、法学家、作曲家。其作品多神秘怪诞,以夸张手法对现实进行讽刺和揭露,代表作是《魔鬼的迷魂汤》(*The Devil's Elixir*,1815)。

③ 彼埃尔·博努瓦 (Pierre Benoit, 1886-1962),法国小说家。

④ *L'Atlantide*:博努瓦的小说《大西洋岛》,出版于 1919 年。

Rider Haggard's[①] *She*. The lawsuit proved unsuccessful; Benoit had never heard of *She*. (It might, in the last analysis, have been an instance of cryptomnesic[②] deception, which is often extremely difficult to rule out.) The distinctly "historical" aspect of the anima and her condensation with the figures of the sister, wife, mother, and daughter, plus the associated incest motif, can be found in Goethe ("You were in times gone by my wife or sister"), as well as in the anima figure of the regina or femina alba in alchemy. The English alchemist Eirenaeus Philalethes ("lover of truth"), writing about 1645, remarks that the "Queen" was the King's "sister, mother, or wife." The same idea can be found, ornately elaborated, in Nelken's patient and in a whole series of cases observed by me, where I was able to rule out with certainty any possibility of literary influence. For the rest, the anima complex is one of the oldest features of Latin alchemy.

未成功。博努瓦从未听过《她》。(归根到底,这可能是潜在记忆欺骗的例子,而潜在记忆欺骗通常是极难消除的。)阿尼玛显著的历史性和妹妹、妻子、母亲、女儿形象的高度浓缩及相关乱伦主题可以在歌德("你最终从我妻子或妹妹身边走过")和点金术中的"女王"或者"雌性脑白质"等阿尼玛形象之中找到。英国炼金术士艾瑞纽斯·费拉勒德斯("真理的爱人")在1645年写道:女王是国王的妹妹、妈妈或者妻子。虽然经过华丽的阐释,在尼尔金的病人和我的一系列观察案例中可以发现同样的观点。在我的案例中,我能够绝对排除文献影响。至于其他,阿尼玛情结是拉丁炼金术诗人作品中最古老的特点之一。

When one studies the archetypal personalities and their behaviour with the help of the dreams, fantasies, and delusions of patients, one is profoundly impressed by their manifold and unmistakable connections with mythological ideas completely unknown to the layman. They form a species of singular beings whom one would like to endow with ego-consciousness; indeed, they all most seem capable of it. And yet this idea is not borne out by the facts. There is nothing in their behaviour to suggest that they have an ego-consciousness as we know it. They show, on the contrary, all the marks of fragmentary personalities. They are masklike, wraithlike, without problems, lacking self-reflection, with no conflicts, no doubts, no sufferings; like gods, perhaps, who

当人们借助患者的梦、幻想和妄想研究原型人格时,原型人格与外行人不被理解的神学思想之间多重的、明显的联系会给他们留下深刻印象。它们形成一种人们希望付之以自我意识的奇特存在。事实上,它们几乎都能够这样。但是这个想法与事实并不相符。正如我们所知,原型人格行为没有任何迹象显示它们有自我意识。相反,人格行为显示了人格碎片标记。它们像面具、幽灵,没有问题,缺少自我反省,没有矛盾,没有疑问,也没有痛苦。也许像没有人生观的诸神一般,比如《相应部》的梵天,

---

① 莱特·哈葛德(Rider Haggard,1856-1925),英国小说家,1887年发表非洲冒险小说《她》(*She*)。

② cryptomnesic:潜在记忆

have no philosophy, such as the Brahma①-gods of the *Samyutta-nikaya*, whose erroneous views needed correction by the Buddha. Unlike other contents, they always remain strangers in the world of consciousness, unwelcome intruders saturating the atmosphere with uncanny forebodings or even with the fear of madness.

If we examine their content, i.e., the fantasy material constituting their phenomenology, we find countless archaic and "historical" associations and images of an archetypal nature. This peculiar fact permits us to draw conclusions about the "localization" of anima and animus in the psychic structure. They evidently live and function in the deeper layers of the unconscious, especially in that phylogenetic substratum which I have called the collective unconscious. This localization explains a good deal of their strangeness: they bring into our ephemeral consciousness an unknown psychic life belonging to a remote past. It is the mind of our unknown ancestors, their way of thinking and feeling, their way of experiencing life and the world, gods and men. The existence of these archaic strata is presumably the source of man's belief in reincarnations and in memories of "previous existences". Just as the human body is a museum, so to speak, of its phylogenetic history, so too is the psyche. We have no reason to suppose that the specific structure of the psyche is the only thing in the world that has no history outside its individual manifestations. Even the conscious mind cannot be denied a history reaching back at least five thousand years. It is only our ego-consciousness that has forever a new beginning and an early end. The unconscious psyche is not only immensely old, it is also capable of growing into an

其错误百出的观点需要佛陀予以纠正。与其他内容不同,他们是意识世界里的陌生人,不受欢迎的入侵者,具有神秘的预示力或者甚至是令人恐惧的疯狂。

如果我们考察它们的内容,即构成它们的现象学的幻想材料,我们发现无数古代的、历史的联想和原型本质的意象。这一特殊的事实让我们得出阿尼玛和阿尼姆斯处在心理结构中这一结论。显然它们在无意识深层存在并起作用。尤其出现在我们称之为集体无意识的系统发育层中。这个在地化理论中对它们的不可思议做出了诸多解释:它们把属于遥远过去的未知心理生活引入我们短暂的意识之中。它是不为我们所知的祖先的思维方式,它们思考和感受生活的方式,它们体验生活、观察世界及上帝和人类的方式。也许这些远古层面的存在就是人类对复活的信仰以及早先祖先的存在的记忆源泉。打个比方,正如人类身体是其系统历史的博物馆,心理也是这样。我们没有理由假设心理结构是世界上唯一一个在其个体表现之外没有历史的事物。我们甚至不能否认意识心理的历史可以回溯至少到五千年,唯有我们的自我意识中一直有新的起点和早到的终点。无意识心理不仅古老而且能够发展到很久以后。它塑造人类,仅仅是人类身体的一部分,在人类个体身上虽然短暂,但在集体身上却历史悠久。

① Brahma:梵天,印度教主神之一。

equally remote future. It moulds the human species and is just as much a part of it as the human body, which, though ephemeral in the individual, is collectively of immense age.

The anima and animus live in a world quite different from the world outside—in a world where the pulse of time beats infinitely slowly, where the birth and death of individuals count for little. No wonder their nature is strange, so strange that their irruption into consciousness often amounts to a psychosis. They undoubtedly belong to the material that comes to light in schizophrenia.

What I have said about the collective unconscious may give you a more or less adequate idea of what I mean by this term. If we now turn back to the problem of individuation, we shall see ourselves faced with a rather extraordinary task: the psyche consists of two incongruous halves which together should form a whole. One is inclined to think that ego-consciousness is capable of assimilating the unconscious, at least one hopes that such a solution is possible. But unfortunately the unconscious really is unconscious; in other words, it is unknown. And how can you assimilate something unknown? Even if you can form a fairly complete picture of the anima and animus, this does not mean that you have plumbed the depths of the unconscious. One hopes to control the unconscious, but the past masters in the art of self-control, the yogis, attain perfection in samādhi①, a state of ecstasy, which so far as we know is equivalent to a state of unconsciousness. It makes no difference whether they call our unconscious a "universal consciousness"; the fact remains that in their case the unconscious has swallowed up ego-consciousness. They do not realize that a "universal

阿尼玛和阿尼姆斯存在的世界和外在世界不同,在这里时间过得很慢,个体的生与死没有太大的意义。怪不得它们本质很奇特,如此奇特以至于它们闯入意识,往往造成精神病。毫无疑问,它们属于在精神分裂症中显露出来的材料。

我前面提到的集体无意识可能让你对这个概念有了大致的了解。如果现在我们回到个性化问题上,我们就会看到我们面临着艰巨的任务:心理包含着两个不协调的部分,合在一起变成了整体。人们倾向于认为自我意识能同化无意识,至少人们希望这样的解决方案是有可能的。不幸的是,无意识事实上就是无意识,换句话说,无意识是未被感知的。你如何同化一个未知的东西?即使你能形成关于阿尼玛和阿尼姆斯的完整画面,这也并不意味着你已经探测了无意识的最深处。人们希望控制无意识,然而掌握自我控制艺术的往昔大师们,瑜伽修行者,通过三摩地达到的完美状态,一种狂喜的状态,就我们了解而言,只相当于一种无意识状态。他们是否称我们的无意识为普适意识并不会产生任何差异。事实是,在那种情况下,无意识吞噬了自我意识,他们没有意识到普世意识在术语上是个矛盾体。因为排除、

① samādhi:定,也叫三摩地,是瑜伽修行者追求的最终目的。是一种在纯粹且无束缚的感觉中安定下来的状态。

consciousness" is a contradiction in terms, since exclusion, selection, and discrimination are the root and essence of everything that lays claim to the name "consciousness". "Universal consciousness" is logically identical with unconsciousness. It is nevertheless true that a correct application of the methods described in the Pāli Canon① or in the Yoga-sūtra induces a remarkable extension of consciousness. But, with increasing extension, the contents of consciousness lose in clarity of detail. In the end, consciousness becomes all-embracing, but nebulous; an infinite number of things merge into an indefinite whole, a state in which subject and object are almost completely identical. This is all very beautiful, but scarcely to be recommended anywhere north of the Tropic of Cancer.

筛选和区隔是可以要求意识之名的一切根源和本质。普世意识在逻辑上等同于无意识。然而,事实的真相是巴利经文或者瑜伽经文所描述方法的正确应用会导致意识的大幅延伸。但是,意识的内容随着延伸的加剧,失去了细节的透明。最终变得包罗万象,但却模糊一团;无限多的东西融进一个模糊的整体之中,即出现一种主体与客体几乎完全等同的状态。尽管非常漂亮,却几乎没有在北回归线以北的任何地方得到推荐。

For this reason we must look for a different solution. We believe in ego-consciousness and in what we call reality. The realities of a northern climate are somehow so convincing that we feel very much better off when we do not forget them. For us it makes sense to concern ourselves with reality. Our European ego-consciousness is therefore inclined to swallow up the unconscious, and if this should not prove feasible we try to suppress it. But if we understand anything of the unconscious, we know that it cannot be swallowed. We also know that it is dangerous to suppress it, because the unconscious is life and this life turns against us if suppressed, as happens in neurosis.

因为这个原因,我们必须寻找不同的解决方法。我们相信自我意识和我们所谓的现实。北方的气候让人如此深信,以至于记住它会让我们感到舒适。对于我们而言,让我们关心现实是有意义的。所以我们欧洲人的自我意识往往会吞噬无意识,如果这个不可行,我们就努力压制它。但是如果我们理解无意识,我们就会明白它不能被吞噬。同样我们也知道压制无意识是危险的,因为无意识是有生命的,如果它被压制。这一生命就会反击,比如像神经病那样。

Conscious and unconscious do not make a whole when one of them is suppressed and injured by the other. If they must contend, let it at least be a fair fight with equal rights on both sides. Both are aspects of life. Consciousness should defend its reason and protect itself, and the chaotic life of the

当意识和无意识一方压制另一方或者一方遭到另一方迫害时,那么它们就无法形成一个整体。如果它们必须竞争的话,至少要以双方平等的权利公平战斗。它们是生命的两方面。意识应该捍卫它的理性并保护

① Pāli Canon:巴利文大藏经。

unconscious should be given the chance of having its way too—as much of it as we can stand. This means open conflict and open collaboration at once. That, evidently, is the way human life should be. It is the old game of hammer and anvil: between them the patient iron is forged into an indestructible whole, an "individual".

自己,无意识的无秩序生活也应该享有走自己路的机会——在我们容忍的范围内尽可能多的机会。这就意味着同时进行公开冲突和公开合作。很明显,人类生活应该就是那样的。它是锤子和铁砧的老游戏了:在它们中间,有耐心的铁被打造成坚不可摧的整体,也就是个体。

This, roughly, is what I mean by the individuation process. As the name shows, it is a process or course of development arising out of the conflict between the two fundamental psychic facts. I have described the problems of this conflict, at least in their essentials, in my essay "The Relations between the Ego and the Unconscious". A special chapter, however, is the symbolism of the process, which is of the utmost importance for understanding the final stages of the encounter between conscious and unconscious, in practice as well as in theory. My investigations during these last years have been devoted mainly to this theme. It turned out, to my own great astonishment, that the symbol formation has the closest affinities with alchemical ideas, and especially with the conceptions of the "uniting symbol", which yield highly significant parallels. Naturally these are processes which have no meaning in the initial stages of psychological treatment. On the other hand, more difficult cases, such as cases of unresolved transference, develop these symbols. Knowledge of them is of inestimable importance in treating cases of this kind, especially when dealing with cultured patients.

这大体上就是我所说的个体化过程。正如名字所示,它是由两个基本心理事实矛盾冲突引起的发展过程或道路。"自我和无意识关系"一文中,我已经描述过这一冲突问题,至少在他们的本质上。有一章专门是过程象征主义,那对理解意识和无意识在实例中和理论上碰撞最终阶段有重大意义。我最近几年的研究主要致力于这一主题。令我吃惊的是,结果显示象征的形成与炼金思想关系最为紧密,特别是与统一象征概念的关系,它们产生了非常有意义的可比拟之物。很自然,这些过程在心理治疗的初期阶段没有任何意义。在另一方面,更困难的案例发展了这些象征,比如未解决的移情案例。对这一点的了解在治疗此类病例中起到不可估量的作用,特别是在治疗学识渊博的病人中。

How the harmonizing of conscious and unconscious data is to be undertaken cannot be indicated in the form of a recipe. It is an irrational life-process which expresses itself in definite symbols. It may be the task of the analyst to stand by this process with all the help he can give. In this

和谐处理意识与无意识资料不能通过开处方的形式予以指示。它是无理性的生命过程。精神分析一生的任务可能是带着他能提供的一切帮助支持这一过程。在这种情况

case, knowledge of the symbols is indispensable, for it is in them that the union of conscious and unconscious contents is consummated. Out of this union emerge new situations and new conscious attitudes. I have therefore called the union of opposites the "transcendent function". This rounding out of the personality into a whole may well be the goal of any psychotherapy that claims to be more than a mere cure of symptoms.

下,象征知识不可或缺,因为意识与无意识内容在象征中达到完美。在这一整体之外出现新的情境和新的意识态度。因此,我称对立统一面的统一为先验功能。像这样把人格发展至整体很可能就是生成不只为纯粹症候治疗的心理治疗的目标。

3. Questions for Discussion

(1) How do you understand Jung's "individuation"?

(2) What are the differences between the personal unconscious and the collective unconscious?

(3) How do you understanding "anima" or "animus"?

3. 讨论题

(1)你如何理解荣格的"个体化"?

(2)个人无意识和集体无意识的区别是什么?

(3)你如何理解"阿尼玛"或"阿尼姆斯"?

Chapter 9

第9章

1. Introduction to Virginia Woolf

Virginia Woolf (1882-1941) was a British author who is considered to be one of the foremost figures of both modernism and feminism in the twentieth century.

Born into a privileged English household, Virginia Woolf was raised by free-thinking parents and in an environment filled with the influences of Victorian literary society. Her father Leslie Stephen was an eminent literary figure, editor, critic and biographer. Her beautiful mother served as a model for several Pre-Raphaelite painters and she was also a nurse and wrote a book on the profession. Virginia's parents had married each other after being widowed with children and the household contained eight children of three marriages. Two of Virginia's half-brothers were educated at Cambridge, but all the girls were taught at home and utilized the family's lush Victorian library. The deaths of her mother in 1895 and her half-sister Stella Duckworth in 1897 led to Virginia's first nervous breakdown. In 1904, after her father died, Virginia had her second nervous breakdown. Her breakdowns and subsequent recurring depressive

1. 弗吉妮亚·伍尔夫简介

弗吉妮亚·伍尔夫(1882—1941)是英国作家,被认为是20世纪现代主义和女权主义先锋人物之一。

弗吉妮亚·伍尔夫出生在英国上层社会家庭,养育她的父母思想自由,家庭环境弥漫着维多利亚文学社会的影响。其父亲莱斯利·斯蒂芬是著名的作家、编辑、批评家和传记家。其母亲极为美丽,曾为多位前拉斐尔派画家做过模特,她还是一位护士,并就此职业写过一本书。弗吉妮亚的父母在结婚前都曾丧偶并带有孩子,整个家庭共有8个来自3个婚姻的孩子。弗吉妮亚的两个同母异父哥哥在剑桥接受过教育,但所有的女孩都在家接受教育,使用家中藏书丰富的维多利亚式的图书馆。1895年弗吉妮亚的母亲去世,1897年她同母异父的姐姐斯黛拉·达克伍斯去世,致使弗吉妮亚第一次精神崩溃。1904年其父去世后,弗吉妮亚第二次

periods were also induced by the sexual abuse by their half-brothers, George and Gerald Duckworth when Virginia and her sister Vanessa were very young, which Virginia Woolf revealed in her autobiographical essays 22 *Hyde Park Gate* (1921) and *A Sketch of the Past* (1939).

精神崩溃。其多次精神崩溃及后反复出现的阶段性抑郁症的另一诱因是弗吉妮亚和姐姐范妮莎年幼时遭受同母异父哥哥乔治和杰拉德·达克伍斯的性侵害,这在弗吉妮亚·伍尔夫的自传性散文《海德公园门22号》(1921)和《往事札记》(1939)中得以揭露。

After the death of their father, Virginia and her sisters Vanessa and brother Adrian sold 22 Hyde Park Gate, and bought a house at 46 Gordon Square in Bloomsbury. There they came to know the Bloomsbury group, a circle of intellectuals and artists. This group tremendously aided Virginia Woolf as a source of support and criticism as she came into her own as a writer. In 1912, Virginia married Leonard Woolf, a member of the Bloomsbury group who resigned from the colonial service and returned from the East. In 1917, the Woolfs bought a printing press and founded the Hogarth Press. They published some of their writings, and the works of Sigmund Freud, Katharine Mansfield and T.S. Eliot. In 1940, the Woolfs' London home was destroyed during the Blitz, the Germans bombing of the city. At the end of that year Woolf suffered another severe bout of depression. On March 28, 1941, at the age of 59, Woolf drowned herself in the River Ouse.

父亲去世后,弗吉妮亚和姐姐范妮莎及弟弟亚德里安卖掉了海德公园门22号的房子,在布卢姆斯伯里戈顿广场46号买了房子。在此他们结识了布卢姆斯伯里小组,一个由知识分子和艺术家组成的圈子。该小组给予弗吉妮亚·伍尔夫巨大的帮助,他们的支持和批评使其成长为一名作家。1912年,弗吉妮亚和布卢姆斯伯里小组中的伦纳德·伍尔夫结婚,他从东方殖民地辞职返回英国。1917年,伍尔夫夫妇买下一台印刷机,创办了霍加斯出版社。他们出版了部分自己的作品,还出版了西格蒙德·弗洛伊德、凯瑟琳·曼斯菲尔德、T.S.艾略特的作品。1940年,伍尔夫家在伦敦的房子在德军轰炸伦敦的大空袭中被毁。那年年底,伍尔夫遭受了又一次严重抑郁袭击。1941年3月28日,时年59岁的伍尔夫在乌斯河结束了自己的生命。

Throughout her career, Woolf spoke regularly at colleges and universities, penned dramatic letters, wrote moving novels and essays, published a long list of short stories and experimented with several forms of biographical writing. Her well-known works are *The Voyage Out* (1915), *The Mark on the Wall* (1919), *Mrs. Dalloway* (1925), *The Common Reader* (1925), *To the Lighthouse* (1927), *Orlando* (1928), *A Room of One's Own* (1929), *The Wave* (1931), *The Years* (1937), *Three Guineas* (1938), *Between the Acts*

在伍尔夫的职业生涯中,她应邀定期到各大学演讲,写下很多戏剧性的书信,创作了很多感人的长篇小说和散文,出版了大量的短篇小说,用多种形式进行传记书写实验。她广为人知的作品有:《远航》(1915)、《墙上的斑点》(1919)、《达洛维夫人》(1925)、《普通读者》(1925)、《到灯塔去》(1927)、《奥兰多》(1928)、《自己的一间房》(1929)、《海浪》(1931)、《岁月》(1937)、《三个基尼

(1941), *Modern Fiction* (1919) and many others.

Woolf was influenced by some radical feminists when she studied German, Greek and Latin at the Ladies' Department of King's College London between 1897 and 1901. In 1928, Woolf took a grassroots approach to informing and inspiring feminism. She addressed undergraduate women at Girton College and at Newnham College, Cambridge with two papers that eventually became *A Room of One's Own*. In this far-reaching essay, Woolf blamed women's absence from history not on their lack of brains and talent but on their poverty. For her 1931 talk "Professions for Women," Woolf studied the history of women's education and employment and argued that unequal opportunities for women negatively affect all of society. She urged women to destroy the "angel in the house," a reference to Coventry Patmore's poem of that title, the quintessential Victorian paean to women who sacrifice themselves to men. Woolf's another well-known feminist work *Three Guineas* examined the difficulties that female writers and intellectuals faced because men held disproportionate legal and economic power, as well as the future of women in education and society, as the societal effects of industrialization and birth control had not yet fully been realized.

2. Selections from *A Room of One's Own*

A Room of One's Own①

Virginia Woolf

One

But, you may say, we asked you to speak

金币》(1938)、《幕间》(1941)、《现代小说》(1919)等。

1897—1901年间,伍尔夫在伦敦国王学院女子系学习德语、希腊语、拉丁语时,受到一些激进女权主义者的影响。1928年,伍尔夫采用从底层做起的方法来传递和激发女权主义思想。她在剑桥大学格顿学院和纽纳姆学院给女性本科生做了两次讲座,这两篇演讲稿最终成为《自己的一间房》。在此影响深远的散文中,伍尔夫谴责女性在历史中的缺席,但这不是因为女性缺少头脑和才智造成的,而是因为她们的贫穷。在1931年的演讲《女性的职业》中,伍尔夫研究了女性教育和就业史,提出女性不能获得均等机会将对整个社会造成负面影响。她激励女性灭除"家中的天使",这是考文垂·帕特莫尔一首诗的标题,一首典型的维多利亚时代献给为男性牺牲自我的女性的赞歌。伍尔夫另一部广为人知的女权主义作品《三个基尼金币》审视了女性作家和知识分子因男性所具有超比例的法律和经济权力而面临的困难,以及因为工业化的影响和未完全实现的生育控制,未来女性在教育和社会中将面临的困难。

2.《自己的一间房》选文

自己的一间房

弗吉妮亚·伍尔夫

第一章

但是,你或许会说,我们请你来

① Selected from *A Room of One's Own*, New York: Harcourt Brace Jovanovich, Inc., 1929.

about women and fiction—what has that got to do with a room of one's own? I will try to explain. When you asked me to speak about women and fiction I sat down on the banks of a river and began to wonder what the words meant. They might mean simply a few remarks about Fanny Burney①; a few more about Jane Austen②; a tribute to the Brontes and a sketch of Haworth Parsonage under snow; some witticisms if possible about Miss Mitford;③ a respectful allusion to George Eliot④; a reference to Mrs. Gaskell⑤ and one would have done. But at second sight the words seemed not so simple. The title women and fiction might mean, and you may have meant it to mean, women and what they are like; or it might mean women and the fiction that they write; or it might mean women and the fiction that is written about them; or it might mean that somehow all three are inextricable mixed together and you want me to consider them in that light. But when I began to consider the subject in this last way, which seemed the most interesting, I soon say that it had one fatal drawback. I should never be able to come to a conclusion. I should never be able to fulfill what is, I understand, the first duty of a lecturer to hand you after an hour's discourse a nugget of pure truth to wrap up between the pages of your notebooks and keep on the mantelpiece for ever... One can only show how one came to hold whatever one does hold. One can only give one's audience the chance of drawing their own conclusions as they observe the limitations, the prejudices, the idiosyncrasies of the speaker. Fiction here is likely to contain more truth than

谈谈女性和小说——这跟自己的一间房有什么关系？我会尽我所能做出解释。当初你们让我谈一谈女性和小说的时候，我在一条河的岸边坐下来开始思索，想弄明白这些话的意思。它们或许仅仅意味着对范妮·伯尼所做出的少许评论，对简·奥斯汀所做的稍多评价，对勃朗特姐妹的赞许以及对白雪皑皑下的霍沃思寓所所作的素描。如果可以的话，还可以打趣一下米特福德小姐，捎带恭维一下乔治·艾略特，谈及盖斯凯尔夫人，这样一来便可万事大吉。但是细细看来，事情又并非如此简单。女性和小说这个标题可能意味着女性本身以及她们像什么样子，这也可能是你们给出这个题目的意图；也可能意味着女性以及她们笔下的小说；还可能意味着女性以及书写她们的小说；又或许意味着由于种种未知的原因，上述三种情况交织缠绕在一起，因此你们想让我以此为出发点来进行思考。但是当我开始以最后一种方式来思考这一话题时，这看起来好像是最为有趣的方式，我很快察觉到它存在一个致命的缺陷。我应该永远无法得出一个结论。我内心明白，自己应该永远不能完成一位演讲者所谓的第一责任，在一个小时的谈话之后交给你们一个纯粹的真理的天然金块，包在你们笔记本的纸页间，永远地存放在壁炉台上……一个人只能够表明，他是如何拥有他确实已经持

① 范妮·伯尼(Fanny Burney,1752-1840),英国女作家。
② 简·奥斯汀(Jane Austen,1775-1855),英国女作家。
③ 米特福德小姐(Mary Russell Mitford, 1787-1817),英国女剧作家、诗人和散文作家。
④ 乔治·艾略特(George Eliot,1819-1880),英国女作家。
⑤ 盖斯凯尔夫人(Mrs. Gaskell,1810-1865),英国小说家。

fact. Therefore I propose, making use of all the liberties and licenses of a novelist, to tell you the story of the two days that preceded my coming here—how, bowed down by the weight of the subject which you have laid upon my shoulders, I pondered it, and made it work in and out of my daily life...

有的任何见解。人们只能给他的听众提供这样一个机会和条件,即当他们意识到演讲者给出的观点中存在局限、偏见和癖性时,他们能够自己得出结论。相对于事实而言,这里的虚构可能包含更多的真相。因而,我打算充分利用一位小说家所拥有的一切自由和特权,把我到达这儿前两天内发生的故事讲给你们听——你们搁在我肩膀上的这个话题压得我喘不过气来,我思索着,让它在我的日常生活内外动起来……

Here then was I (call me Mary Beton, Mary Seton, Mary Carmichael or by any name you please—it is not a matter of any importance) sitting on the banks of a river a week or two ago in fine October weather, lost in thought. That collar I have spoken of, women and fiction, the need of coming to some conclusion on a subject that raises all sorts of prejudices and passions, bowed my head to the ground. To the right and left bushes of some sort, golden and crimson, glowed with the colour, even it seemed burnt with the heat, of fire. On the further bank the willows wept in perpetual lamentation, their hair about their shoulders. The river reflected whatever it chose of sky and bridge and burning tree, and when the undergraduate had oared his boat through the reflections they closed again, completely, as if he had never been. There one might have sat clock round lost in thought. Thought—to call it by a prouder name than it deserved—had let its line down into the stream. It swayed, minute after minute, hither and thither among the reflections and the weeds, letting the water lift it and sink it, until—you know the little tug—the sudden conglomeration of an idea at the end of one's line: and then the cautious hauling of it in, and the careful laying of it out. Alas, laid on the grass how small, how insignificant this thought

于是这就是我自己(称呼我为玛丽·贝顿、玛丽·塞顿、玛丽·卡迈克尔,或者你们愿意叫的任何名字都可以——这些都无关紧要),一两个星期之前,也就是在十月某个天气晴朗的一天,我坐在一条河的岸边,陷入了沉思。我所说的那个衣领,也就是女性与小说这一话题,以及对一个能够唤起各种各样偏见和激情的题目得出某个定论的需要压得我几乎窒息。我的左右两边生长着金黄色和绯红色的灌木,火一般的颜色,鲜艳夺目,就像燃烧的炉火。在更远处的河岸上,柳树在无尽的哀叹中哭泣,柳丝如披发在肩。河水倒映出了它从天空、桥梁和火红的树木中挑选出的所有事物,而当那位大学生划着小船穿过那些倒影后,那些倒影又重新合二为一,融为一体,就像从来不曾分离。在那儿,一个人完全可以坐一整天,畅游在自己的思绪中。思考——这是给它的一个名不副实的高雅称呼——已经把它的钓线垂到水里去了。钓线四下摇摆,一分钟又一分钟地舞动着,在倒影和杂草中扭动着身姿,随着水流的波动而上下

of mine looked; the sort of fish that a good fisherman puts back into the water so that it may grow fatter and be one day worth cooking and eating. I will not trouble you with that thought now, though if you look carefully you may find it for yourselves in the course of what I am going to say.

跳动，到最后——你知道的，就是那么轻轻地一拉——在一个人的钓线底端的想法突然汇聚，然后是谨慎地把它拖上来，又小心地把它展开。唉，铺展在青草上，我的思想看起来是如此渺小，如此微不足道，它就像一条鱼，聪明的渔夫会把它放回水中，再长肥一些，到时值得烹饪享用。现在，如果你们仔细观察的话，可以在我讲话的过程中自己把它找出来的，而我现在不用那个思考来烦扰你们。

But however small it was, it had, nevertheless, the mysterious property of its kind—put back into the mind, it became at once very exciting, and important; and as it darted and sank and flashed hither and thither, set up such a wash and tumult of ideas that it was impossible to sit still. It was thus that I found myself walking with extreme rapidity across a grass plot. Instantly a man's figure rose to intercept me. Nor did I at first understand that the gesticulations of a curious-looking object, in a cut-away coat and evening shirt, were aimed at me. His face expressed horror and indignation. Instinct rather than reason came to my help; he was a Beadle; I was a woman. This was the turf; there was the path. Only Fellows and Scholars are allowed here; the gravel is the place for me. Such thoughts were the work of a moment. As I regained the path the arms of the Beadle sank, his face assumed its usual repose, and though turf is better walking than gravel, no very great harm was done. The only charge I could bring against the Fellows and Scholars of whatever the college might happen to be was that in the protection of their turf, which has been rolled for 300 years in succession, they had sent my little fish into hiding.

…

但无论多么微乎其微，它却有着独一无二的神秘特质——如果放回头脑中，它立刻变得使人异常兴奋，而且重要；当它猛冲下沉、熠熠闪光之时，在思想上形成了惊涛骇浪和喧哗吵闹，因而若想心平气和地坐着几乎不可能。我就是如此，发现自己正急速穿过一块草地。猛然间，一位男性的身影冲出来阻拦了我。我起初并不明白，一个长相离奇古怪、身穿燕尾服和晚礼服衬衣的人做出的手势竟是针对我的。他面露恐惧和愤怒。此时是本能而并非理智跳出来帮助我，他是位教区执事，而我只是个女人。这儿是草坪，而那儿才是小路。这儿只容许研究员和学者，而砾石路才是我该走的地方。这些想法是一下涌上心头的。当我重新在小路上站稳时，教区执事的胳膊也随之放了下来。他的面部也呈现出了平时的安详与凝重。尽管砾石路没有草坪走起来舒服，却也不会造成太大的伤害。针对不管来自哪所大学的研究员和学者们，我所能够提出的唯一指控是：他们的草坪已被践踏长达300年之久，为保护草坪，他们把我的小鱼吓得躲起来了。

……

Two

... Life for both sexes—and I looked at them, shouldering their way along the pavement—is arduous, difficult, a perpetual struggle. It calls for gigantic courage and strength. More than anything, perhaps, creatures of illusion as we are, it calls for confidence in oneself. Without self-confidence we are babes in the cradle. And how can we generate this imponderable quality, which is yet so invaluable, most quickly? By thinking that other people are inferior to oneself. By feeling that one has some innate superiority—it may be wealth, or rank, a straight nose, or the portrait of a grandfather by Romney①—for there is no end to the pathetic devices of the human imagination—over other people. Hence the enormous importance to a patriarch who has to conquer, who has to rule, of feeling that great numbers of people, half the human race indeed, are by nature inferior to himself. It must indeed be one of the great sources of his power... Women have served all these centuries as looking-glasses possessing the magic and delicious power of reflecting the figure of man at twice its natural size. Without that power probably the earth would still be swamp and jungle. The glories of all our wars would be unknown. We should still be scratching the outlines of deer on the remains of mutton bones and bartering flints for sheepskins or whatever simple ornament took our unsophisticated taste. Supermen and Fingers of Destiny would never have existed. The Czar and the Kaiser would never have worn their crowns or lost them. Whatever may be their use in civilised societies, mirrors are essential to all violent and heroic action. That is why Napoleon and Mussolini

第二章

……对于两个性别的人来说——这时我看着他们在人行横道上推来搡去——生活是艰辛的、困难的、是一场永恒的战斗。它需要巨大的勇气和力量。更值得一提的是,可能因为我们是心存幻想的生物,生活更要求我们要对自己满怀信心。若是没有自信,我们无异于摇篮里的婴儿。那么我们如何才能最快地激发出这种无法估量而又极具价值的自信呢? 通过思考别人会逊色于自己。感到自己有别人所不具有的与生俱来的优势——那或许是财富、地位,可能是挺直的鼻梁,也可能是由罗姆尼画的一幅祖父的肖像画——须知人类想象力中的那些可怜的花样是无穷无尽的。如此一来,对一位须征服并统治他人的长者来说,感到数量众多的人——实际上占人类总人数一半的人——天生就逊色于他自己的感觉,也就弥足珍贵了。这种感觉定是他的权力的一个主要源泉……几百年来,女人一直是镜子的化身,该镜子具有把男人的体型以其真实大小两倍的方式给映射出来的奇幻魔力而又令人愉悦的力量。倘若缺失了那种力量,世界可能仍然是一片沼泽和丛林。我们所有战争的光荣就会无人知晓。我们就仍然在羊骨上画着鹿的轮廓,或者是用火石来换取羊皮,又或者是任何迎合我们质朴趣味的简洁饰物。那超人和命运之手也就从未存在过。俄国沙皇与德国皇帝也就会从未戴上或者失去过

① 罗姆尼(George Romney, 1734-1802),英国肖像画家。

both insist so emphatically upon the inferiority of women, for if they were not inferior, they would cease to enlarge. That serves to explain in part the necessity that women so often are to men. And it serves to explain how restless they are under her criticism; how impossible it is for her to say to them this book is bad, this picture is feeble, or whatever it may be, without giving far more pain and rousing far more anger than a man would do who gave the same criticism. For if she begins to tell the truth, the figure in the looking-glass shrinks; his fitness in life is diminished. How is he to go on giving judgment, civilising natives, making laws, writing books, dressing up and speechifying at banquets, unless he can see himself at breakfast and at dinner at least twice the size he really is? So I reflected, crumbling by bread and stirring my coffee and now and again looking at the people in the street. The looking-glass vision is of supreme importance because it charges the vitality; it stimulates the nervous system. Take it away and man may die, like the drug fiend deprived of his cocaine. Under the spell of that illusion, I thought, looking out of the window, half the people on the pavement are striding to work. They put on their hats and coats in the morning under its agreeable rays. They start the day confident, braced, believing themselves desired at Miss Smith's tea party; they say to themselves as they go into the room, I am the superior of half the people here, and it is thus that they speak with that self-confidence, that self-assurance, which have had such profound consequences in public life and lead to such curious notes in the margin of the private mind.

But these contributions to the dangerous and fascinating subject of the psychology of the other sex—it is one, I hope, that you will investigate when you have five hundred a year of your own—

皇冠。在文明社会里,无论镜子用于何途,对于暴力和英雄壮举都是不可或缺的,这便是拿破仑和墨索里尼如此强调女人低级的原因。如果女人不低级,男人便无法自我膨胀,这也在某种程度上解释了为什么男人常常需要女人。因而,男人受到女人批评时会焦躁不安;听到女人说这本书不好或这幅画拙劣之类的话时,会觉得不可思议,与男人做出相同的评价相比较而言,会给他们带来更多的痛苦,激起更多的愤怒。女人开始说真理的时候,镜子中的影像便开始缩小,他在生活中的地位也开始下降。除非男人在吃早餐和晚餐时,将自己看作比实际上至少要大两倍,不然他如何宣布判决,教化本土人,制定法律,著书立说,一身盛装在晚宴上高谈阔论呢?我思忖着,边捏碎面包,边搅动咖啡,时不时看看街上的行人。镜子里的影像至关重要,它掌控生命力,刺激神经系统。若将其拿走,男人便可能会死去,就像瘾君子被夺走了可卡因。望着窗外,我想,在那幻象的吸引下,路上一半的行人为工作奔波。在明媚的晨光下,他们带上帽子,穿上外套,以自信和振奋的精神开始新的一天,相信自己会在史密斯小姐的茶会上大受欢迎。走进房间的时候,他们告诉自己,我优于这儿一半以上的人,因而他们带着一种极度自信讲话,这种自信对他们的公众生活影响深远,在各自脑海空白处留下奇妙的印记。

但是对于另一性别心理这一危险而又吸引人的话题——我还是希望当你们每年拥有自己的五百英镑

were interrupted by the necessity of paying the bill. It came to five shillings and nine pence. I gave the waiter a ten-shilling note and he went to bring me change. There was another ten-shilling note in my purse; I noticed it, because it is a fact that still takes my breath away—the power of my purse to breed ten-shilling notes automatically. I open it and there they are. Society gives me chicken and coffee, bed and lodging, in return for a certain number of pieces of paper which were left me by an aunt, for no other reason than that I share her name.

My aunt, May Beton, I must tell you, died by a fall from her horse when she was riding to take the air in Bombay. The news of my legacy reached me one night about the same time that the act was passed that gave notes to women. A solicitor's letter fell into the post-box and when I opened it I found that she had left me five hundred pounds a year for ever. Of the two—the vote and the money—the money, I own, seemed infinitely the more important. Before that I had made my living by cadging odd jobs from newspapers, by reporting a donkey show here or a wedding there; I had earned a few pounds by addressing envelopes, reading to old ladies, making artificial flowers, teaching the alphabet to small children in a kindergarten. Such were the chief occupations that were open to women before 1918. I need not, I am afraid, describe in any detail the hardness of the work, for you know perhaps women who have done it; nor the difficulty of living on the money when it was earned, for you may have tried. But what still remains with me as a worse infliction than either was the poison of fear and bitterness which those days bred in me. To begin with, always to be doing work that one did not wish to do, and to do it like a slave, flattering and fawning, not always necessarily perhaps, but it seemed necessary and stakes were too great to run

的时候再深入探讨——我这一想法因必须付账而被打断了,账单是五先令九便士。我给了侍者一张十先令的钞票,他去找零给我。钱包里还有十先令,我因注意到这十先令而激动不已,因为我的钱包还有自动生出十先令的功能。我打开钱包,它就在那里。社会为我提供了鸡肉和咖啡,床和住所,以换取一定金额的钱。钱是姑姑留给我的,别无他由,只因我们姓氏相同。

一定要告诉你们,我的姑姑,梅·贝顿是在孟买骑马外出游玩时,从马上跌落而亡。我知道遗产的那天晚上,刚好国会通过赋予妇女选举权的法案。律师给我寄了一封信,打开信,才知道姑姑给我每年都留了五百英镑。选举权和钱相比,属于我的钱似乎更重要。在获得遗产之前,我都是为报社干些零活谋生,报道这里的毛驴秀或那里的婚礼,也通过替人写信、给老妇人阅读、做假花、教幼儿园的小孩子识字母表挣几英镑。这便是 1918 年之前妇女可选择的主要职业。我想,我不必详述工作的艰辛,因为你们可能认识从事这种工作的人,也不用说靠这些钱生活的困难,因为你们或许也尝试过。但是,比这两者更使我痛苦的是,那些日子在我身上产生的恐惧和痛苦。首先,总是在做自己不想做的工作,像奴隶一样工作,谄媚奉承,也许并不需要一直如此,但又似乎是必要的,倘若冒险,赌注未免太大。其次,一个人的才能随着死亡而逐渐消逝(才能虽微不足道,但对拥有者来说却很重要),然后是我的肉体、灵魂,就像春

risks; and then the thought of that one gift which it was death to hide—a small one but dear to the possessor—perishing and with it myself, my soul—all this became like a rust eating away the bloom of the spring, destroying the tree at its heart. However, as I say, my aunt died; and whenever I change a ten-shilling note a little of that rust and corrosion is rubbed off; fear and bitterness go. Indeed, I thought, slipping the silver into my purse, it is remarkable, remembering the bitterness of those days, what a change of temper a fixed income will bring about. No force in the world can take from me my five hundred pounds. Food, house and clothing are mine forever. Therefore not merely do effort and labour cease, but also hatred and bitterness. I need not hate any man; he cannot hurt me. I need not flatter any man; he has nothing to give me. So imperceptibly I found myself adopting a new attitude toward the other half of the human race. It was absurd to blame any class or any sex, as a whole. Great bodies of people are never responsible for what they do. They are driven by instincts which are not within their control. They too, the patriarchs, the professors, had endless difficulties, terrible drawbacks to contend with. Their education had been in some ways as faulty as my own. It had bred in them defects as great. True, they had money and power, but only at the cost of harbouring in their breasts an eagle, a vulture, forever tearing the liver out and plucking at the lungs—the instinct for possession, the rage for acquisition which drives them to desire other people's fields and goods perpetually; to make frontiers and flags; battleships and poison gas; to offer up their own lives and their children's lives. Walk through the Admiralty Arch (I had reached that monument), or any other avenue given up to trophies and cannon, and reflect upon the kind of glory celebrated there. Or watch in the spring

天的花朵被锈菌侵蚀,树木从内部被毁掉。然而,正如我所说,姑姑已经去世了,每当我花掉十先令时,这种锈迹和腐朽便消退一层,恐惧和痛苦也消失了。将银币放入钱包,我想到往日的艰辛痛苦,一笔固定的收入能给一个人的性情带来这么大的改变,确实意义非凡。世界上没有什么能拿走我的五百英镑。食物、房子和衣服永远是我的,因此,我不必再费劲,再辛劳,也没有憎恨和痛苦了。我不必憎恨任何人,他不能伤害我。我无需奉承任何人,他也没有什么能给我。不知不觉地,我发现我对另一性别的人有了新的态度。对于任何阶级或性别,从整体上加以责备是荒谬的。大部分人从不为自己的所作所为负责,他们被不受控制的本能驱使。那些老爷和教授们也有无穷的困难和必须应对的障碍。在某种程度上,他们所受的教育和我一样有缺陷,也给他们带来了严重的缺点。是的,他们是有钱有权,但其代价是,在胸里养着一只鹰、一只秃鹫,不断地撕扯肝脏,啄食肺叶,这便是要占有的本能,要攫取的欲望,驱使着他们无休止地渴望他人的土地和物品,驱使他们划定疆界,插旗占地,制造战舰,研发毒气,甚至献上自己和孩子的生命。走过海军部大楼的拱门(我已经走到这里了),或者其他充满战利品和大炮的道路,回想这里曾经庆祝的光荣;在春日的阳光下,看着股票经纪人和大律师进入室内,去挣钱,挣得越来越多,而事实是,每年五百英镑足以使人在阳光下生活。我想,怀有这种本能是不愉快的。看着坎布里奇公爵的雕像,尤其是三角

sunshine the stockbroker and the great barrister going indoors to make money and more money and more money when it is a fact that five hundred pounds a year will keep one alive in the sunshine. These are unpleasant instincts to harbour, I reflected. They are bred of the conditions of life; of the lack of civilisation, I thought, looking at the statue of the Duke of Cambridge, and in particular at the feathers in his cocked hat, with a fixity that they have scarcely ever received before. And, as I realized these drawbacks, by degrees fear and bitterness modified themselves into pity and toleration; and then in a year or two, pity and toleration went, and the greatest release of all came, which is freedom to think of things in themselves. That building, for example, do I like it or not? Is that picture beautiful or not? Is that in my opinion a good book or bad? Indeed my aunt's legacy unveiled the sky to me, and substituted for the large and imposing figure of a gentleman, which Milton recommended for my perpetual adoration, a view of the open sky.

So thinking, so speculating, I found my way back to my house by the river. Lamps were being lit and an indescribable change had come over London since the morning hour...

Three

It was disappointing not to have brought back in the evening some important statement, some authentic fact. Women are poorer than men because—this or that. Perhaps now it would be better to give up seeking the truth, and receiving on one's head an avalanche of opinion hot as lava, discoloured as dish-water. It would be better to draw the curtains; to shut out distractions; to light the lamp; to narrow the inquiry and to ask the historian, who records not opinions but fact, to describe under what conditions women lived, not

帽檐上的几根羽毛,它们之前应该从未受到这种关注,我想这是生活条件的产物,是文明缺少的产物。在我意识到这种欠缺后,恐惧和痛苦逐渐转化成了遗憾和宽容,而一两年后,遗憾和宽容也逐渐消失,最终完全释然,这才有了思考事物本身的自由。例如,那栋建筑,我是喜欢还是讨厌?那张图片,美还是丑?在我看来,那是一本好书还是坏书?其实,姑姑的遗产为我揭开了一片新的天空,不再是弥尔顿给我建议的,让我永远崇拜高大且气度不凡的绅士形象,而是广阔的天空。

我这么琢磨着,猜测着,回到了我的河边屋里。灯亮着,伦敦从清晨开始便发生着一种难以名状的变化……

第三章

晚上没带回一些重要的论述和可信的事实,真令人失望。出于这样那样的原因,女人总是比男人更可怜。也许现在放弃找寻真理,让头脑接受山崩一般压来的见解更好,那见解炽热如熔岩,浑浊如洗碗水。最好拉上窗帘,祛除杂念,点亮灯光,缩小探究范围,请教记录事实而非意见的历史学家来描述一下女性的生活状况,当然无须贯穿所有时代,只说英

throughout the ages, but in England, say in the time of Elizabeth.

国,比如在伊丽莎白时代。

For it is a perennial puzzle why no woman wrote a word of that extraordinary literature when every other man, it seemed, was capable of song or sonnet. What were the conditions in which women lived, I asked myself; for fiction, imaginative work that is, is not dropped like a pebble upon the ground, as science may be; fiction is like a spider's web, attached ever so lightly perhaps, but still attached to life at all four corners. Often the attachment is scarcely perceptible; Shakespeare's plays, for instance, seem to hang there complete by themselves. But when the web is pulled askew, hooked up at the edge, torn in the middle, one remembers that these webs are not spun in midair by incorporeal creatures, but are the work of suffering human beings, and are attached to grossly material things, like health and money and the houses we live in.

为什么在一半男性似乎都能创作诗歌或十四行诗的时代,却没有一位女性在那非凡文学中写下只言片语,这是长久已存的困惑。我自问,女性生活在什么条件下;小说,也即想象作品,不会像一颗鹅卵石掷而落地,科学倒是可能那样落地;小说就像蜘蛛网,蛛丝或许只是轻轻相连,但仍在四方连接了生命。通常,这种连接不易察觉。譬如,莎士比亚的戏剧好像全然自顾自地悬挂着。不过一旦蛛网受力而歪曲,边缘处被勾住,或中间被扯破,我们就会记起来这些网,并不是非无实体生物在半空织就的,而是苦难深重的人类的作品,附着于极为物质性的东西,如健康、金钱和我们的住所。

I went, therefore, to the shelf where the histories stand and took down one of the latest, Professor Trevelyan's① *History of England*. Once more I looked up "Women", found "position of", and turned to the pages indicated. "Wife-beating," I read, "was a recognized right of man, and was practiced without shame by high as well as low... Similarly," the historian goes on, "the daughter who refused to marry the gentleman of her parents' choice was liable to be locked up, beaten and flung about the room, without any shock being inflicted on public opinion. Marriage was not an affair of personal affection, but of family avarice, particularly in the 'chivalrous' upper classes... Betrothal often took place while one or both of the parties was in the cradle, and marriage when they

因而我走到摆放着史书的书架前,取下一本最新出版的特里威廉教授写的《英格兰史》。我再一次寻找"女人",找到"其地位",并翻到指示页码。我读到,"殴妻","是公认的男性权利,无论地位高低,男人实施家暴毫无愧色……同样,"历史学家继续写到,"拒绝父母包办婚约的女儿往往被关在屋里挨揍,却不会引起公众舆论任何震惊。婚姻并非个人情感之事,而是家庭敛财之道,'崇尚骑士精神的'上层阶级尤其如此……婚姻一方或双方尚在襁褓之中便已由父母订下婚约,才刚脱离保姆照顾就步入婚姻"。那是在1470年左右,

① 特里威廉(George Macaulay Trevelyan, 1876-1962),英国历史学家。

were scarcely out of the nurses' charge." That was about 1470, soon after Chaucer's time. The next reference to the position of women is some two hundred years later, in the time of the Stuarts. "It was still the exception for women of the upper and middle class to choose their own husbands, and when the husband had been assigned, he was lord and master, so far at least as law and custom could make him. Yet even so," Professor Trevelyan concludes, " neither Shakespeare's women nor those of authentic seventeenth-century memoirs ... seem wanting in personality and character." ... Indeed, if woman had no existence save in the fiction written by men, one would imagine her a person of the utmost importance; very various; heroic and mean; splendid and sordid; infinitely beautiful and hideous in the extreme; as great as a man, some think even greater. But this is woman in fiction. In fact, as Professor Trevelyan points out, she was locked up, beaten and flung about the room.

乔叟的时代刚过去不久。书中提及女性地位的下一个参照在大约200年之后的斯图亚特时代。特里威廉教授总结道,"中上阶层女性自由选择夫婿仍属例外,一旦丈夫被指定,他就是户主或主人,至少法律与习俗赋予他们这种角色。即便如此,莎士比亚笔下的女性与真实的17世纪回忆录中的女性都不乏个性与性格。"……确实,如果女人只存在于男人写的虚构作品之中,人们会将她想象成最重要的人;各式各样:既英勇又卑劣,既杰出又污秽,既美艳绝伦又凶神恶煞,伟大之处堪比男人,有人认为更甚于男人。但这只是虚构故事中的女人。而事实上,恰如特里威廉教授所说,女人被关在屋里挨打挨揍。

A very queer, composite being thus emerges. Imaginatively she is of the highest importance; practically she is completely insignificant. She pervades poetry from cover to cover; she is all but absent from history. She dominates the lives of kings and conquerors in fiction; in fact she was the slave of any boy whose parents forced a ring upon her finger. Some of the most inspired words, some of the most profound thoughts in literature fall from her lips; in real life she could hardly read, could scarcely spell, and was the property of her husband.

如此一来,一种非常奇怪的复合人出现了。在想象中,她最为重要,实际上却无足轻重。她自始至终遍布于诗歌之中,却又几乎缺席于历史。在虚构文学作品中,她主宰着国王和征服者的生活。实际上,一旦父母把戒指硬戴在她的手指上,她就是任何男孩的奴隶。她的唇间吐出文学中某些最具灵感、最为深刻的思想。而在实际生活中,她却几乎不识字,不会拼写,而只是其丈夫的财产。

It was certainly an odd monster that one made up by reading the historians first and the poets afterwards—a worm winged like an eagle; the spirit of life and beauty in a kitchen chopping up suet. But these monsters, however amusing to the

通过先读历史,再读诗歌而构想出的女人,当然是一个奇特的怪物——一个长着鹰翅的蠕虫,一个在厨房里剁板油的生命与美的精灵。

imagination, have no existence in fact. What one must do to bring her to life was to think poetically and prosaically at one and the same moment, thus keeping in touch with fact—that she is Mrs. Martin, aged thirty-six, dressed in blue, wearing a black hat and brown shoes; but not losing sight of fiction either—that she is a vessel in which all sorts of spirits and forces are coursing and flashing perpetually. The moment, however, that one tries this method with the Elizabethan woman, one branch of illumination fails; one is held up by the scarcity of facts. One knows nothing detailed, nothing perfectly true and substantial about her. History scarcely mentions her. ... Occasionally an individual woman is mentioned, an Elizabeth or a Mary; a queen or a great lady. But by no possible means could middle-class women with nothing but brains and character at their command have taken part in any one of the great movements which, brought together, constitute the historian's view of the past. Nor shall we find her in any collection of anecdotes. Aubrey① hardly mentions her. She never writes her own life and scarcely keeps a diary; there are only a handful of her letters in existence. She left no plays or poems by which we can judge her. What one wants, I thought—and why does not some brilliant student at Newnham or Girton supply it? —is a mass of information; at what age did she marry; how many children had she as a rule; what was her house like; had she a room to herself; did she do the cooking; would she be likely to have a servant? All these facts lie somewhere, presumably, in parish registers and account books; the life of the average Elizabethan woman must be scattered about somewhere, could one collect it and make a book of it. It would be

尽管想象起来如此有趣,这些怪物并不存在。若要赋予其生命,人们就必须诗情洋溢又平淡无奇地思考。既与事实保持协调——她是马丁太太,36岁,穿蓝色衣服,戴黑色帽子,穿棕色鞋子。与此同时不忘记虚构,也就是说,她是一个容器,体内有各种精神和力量在不断运行着、闪烁着。然而,一旦人们把这个方法运用在伊丽莎白时期的女人身上,由于事实的缺乏,这方面将无法阐述。人们对她的所知,没有一件是详尽的、完全真实的和实质性的。历史对其提及少之又少……有时候会提到个别的女人,她叫伊丽莎白或玛丽,是一个女王或一位贵妇。但是,一个只有脑力与品格再无他物可以自由支配的中产阶级女人,是不可能参与任何伟大运动的。这些运动一起构成了历史学家对过去的见解。我们也不可能在任何轶事集中发现她。奥布里难得提及她。她从不写自传,几乎不写日记。现存的只有几张她的信件。她没有留下任何诗篇与戏剧来让我们对她做出评价。我想,人们所需要的是大量的信息:她什么年龄结婚,她一般来说会有几个孩子,她的房子是什么样子,她有自己的房间吗,她会下厨吗,她会有一个仆人吗——在纽纳姆学院或者格顿学院,怎么没有一个才华横溢的学生提供这些资料呢?所有这些事实一定在教区记事录及账簿上。伊丽莎白时代女人的生活一定散落在某些地方。若能将这些收集起来,能写成一本书。在书架上寻找这些不存在的书时,我想,

① 奥布里(John Aubrey, 1626-1697),英国文物专家、作家。

ambitious beyond my daring, I thought, looking about the shelves for books that were not there, to suggest to the students of those famous colleges that they should re-write history, though I own that it often seems a little queer as it is, unreal, lop-sided; but why should they not add a supplement to history? Calling it, of course, by some inconspicuous name so that women might figure there without impropriety? For one often catches a glimpse of them in the lives of the great, whisking away into the background, concealing, I sometimes think, a wink, a laugh, perhaps a tear.... But what I find deplorable, is that nothing is known about women before the eighteenth century. I have no model in my mind to turn about this way and that. Here am I asking why women did not write poetry in the Elizabethan age, and I am not sure how they were educated; whether they were taught to write; whether they had sitting-rooms to themselves; how many women had children before they were twenty-one; what, in short, they did from eight in the morning till eight at night. They had no money evidently; according to Professor Trevelyan they were married whether they liked it or not before they were out of the nursery, at fifteen or sixteen very likely. It would have been extremely odd, even upon this showing, had one of them suddenly written the plays of Shakespeare, I concluded, and I thought of that old gentleman, who is dead now, but was a bishop, I think, who declared that it was impossible for any woman, past, present, or to come, to have the genius of Shakespeare. He wrote to the papers about it. He also told a lady who applied to him for information that cats do not as a matter of fact go to heaven, though they have, he added, souls of a sort. How much thinking those old gentlemen used to save one! How the borders of ignorance shrank back at their approach! Cats do not go to heaven. Women cannot write the plays of

向这些名牌大学学生建议他们重写历史,是超出我胆量的奢望。尽管我觉得现有的历史有点古怪,不真实,不平衡。但是他们为什么不能给历史增加一个补遗呢?给那补遗一个不引人注目的名字,这是当然的,让妇女可以不违礼法自如地出现其中。这有何不可?须知人们常在伟人传记中瞥见她们,她们匆匆掠过消失于背景之中。有时我想,她们隐藏了一个眼色,一声大笑,也许是一滴泪水……令我哀叹的是,有关18世纪以前的妇女,一切不得而知。我脑海中没有可以顺着思来想去的她们的形象。我要问的是:为什么伊丽莎白时代的女人不写诗歌,而且我也不清楚她们是怎样接受教育的;她们是否会写字;是否有自己的起居室;多少女人在21岁之前就生了孩子;以及,简单来讲就是,她们从早上8点到晚上8点都做些什么。显然,她们没有钱。据特里威廉教授所说,她们还没走出儿童室就嫁人了,不管她们是否愿意。出嫁的年龄可能是在十五、十六岁。因此,我敢说,如果她们当中有谁突然写出了和莎士比亚一样精彩的剧本,反倒十分奇怪。我又想到那位老绅士——已故,但我觉得他生前是位主教——宣称,任何女人,不管是过去的、现在的还是将来的,都不可能拥有莎士比亚的天赋。他在报纸上发文作此论述。对一位向他咨询的女人,他也说道:猫是上不了天堂的,尽管——他补充道——猫也有某种灵魂。这些老绅士用了多少心思来拯救别人啊!他们一到,无知的边界就退缩了!猫上不了天堂,女人写不出莎士比亚的戏剧。

Shakespeare.

Be that as it may, I could not help thinking, as I looked at the works of Shakespeare on the shelf, that the bishop was right at least in this; it would have been impossible, completely and entirely, for any woman to have written the plays of Shakespeare in the age of Shakespeare. Let me imagine, since the facts are so hard to come by, what would have happened had Shakespeare had a wonderfully gifted sister, called Judith, let us say. Shakespeare himself went, very probably—his mother was an heiress—to the grammar school, where he may have learnt Latin—Ovid, Virgil and Horace—and the elements of grammar and logic. He was, it is well known, a wild boy who poached rabbits, perhaps shot a deer, and had, rather sooner than he should have done, to marry a woman in the neighborhood, who bore him a child rather quicker than was right. That escapade sent him to seek his fortune in London. He had, it seemed, a taste for the theatre; he began by holding horses at the stage door. Very soon he got work in the theatre, became a successful actor, and lived at the hub of the universe, meeting everybody, knowing everybody, practicing his art on the boards, exercising his wits in the streets, and even getting access to the palace of the queen. Meanwhile his extraordinarily gifted sister, let us suppose, remained at home. She was as adventurous, as imaginative, as agog to see the world as he was. But she was not sent to school. She had no chance of learning grammar and logic, let alone of reading Horace and Virgil. She picked up a book now and then, one of her brother's perhaps, and read a few pages. But then her parents came in and told her to mend the stockings or mind the stew and not moon about with books and papers. They would have spoken sharply but kindly, for they were substantial people who knew

不管怎样,翻看书架上的莎士比亚作品,我不由会想,那位主教起码在这一点上是对的:莎士比亚时代的女人是完全不可能写出莎士比亚戏剧的。既然事实难以取证,那就容我想象一番。假设莎士比亚有一个天赋过人的妹妹,比如名叫朱迪斯,那会发生什么事情?莎士比亚本人很可能上了文法学校——他的母亲是继承人——并且在学校里学会了拉丁文,读了奥维德、维吉尔和贺拉斯的作品,以及学了语法和逻辑基础知识。众所周知,他年少时桀骜不驯,偷猎过兔子,也许还射杀过鹿,并且过早地娶了一个邻家女子,因为这位女子在未婚前便怀了他的孩子。为此越轨行为,他逃往伦敦以谋出路。他似乎对戏剧特别感兴趣,起初在剧院门口给人们牵马,不久在剧院谋有一职,成为一名成功的演员。他于是居住在这个世界中心的闹市区,什么人都能见到,什么人都认识。他在舞台上实践他的艺术,在街头发挥着他的才智,甚至可以出入女王的宫殿。但与此同时,我们可以设想,他的天才妹妹却只能待在家里。她像他一样喜欢冒险,一样富于想象,一样渴望了解世界。但她没有上过学,她没有机会学习语法和逻辑,更别说去读贺拉斯和维吉尔的作品了。她时不时会拿起一本书读上几页,可能是他哥哥的吧。但一会她父母走了进来,要她去补袜子,或者去看着炖肉,而不是浪费时间读书看报。或许他们言辞有些严厉,但却是好心的。他们是体面人,懂得女人的生活状况,也是爱女心切——事实上,很可

the conditions of life for a woman and loved their daughter—indeed, more likely than not she was the apple of her father's eye. Perhaps she scribbled some pages up in an apple loft on the sly, but was careful to hide them or set fire to them. Soon, however, before she was out of her teens, she was to be betrothed to the son of a neighboring wool-stapler. She cried out that marriage was hateful to her, and for that she was severely beaten by her father. Then he ceased to scold her. He begged her instead not to hurt him, not to shame him in this matter of her marriage. He would give her a chain of beads or a fine petticoat, he said; and there were tears in his eyes. How could she disobey him? How could she break his heart? The force of her own gift alone drove her to it. She made up a small parcel of her belongings, let herself down by a rope one summer's night and took the road to London. She was not seventeen. The birds that sang in the hedge were not more musical than she was. She had the quickest fancy, a gift like her brother's, for the tune of words. Like him, she had a taste for the theatre. She stood at the stage door; she wanted to act, she said. Men laughed in her face. The manager—a fat, loose-lipped man—guffawed. He bellowed something about poodles dancing and women acting—no woman, he said, could possibly be an actress. He hinted—you can imagine what. She could get no training in her craft. Could she even seek her dinner in a tavern or roam the streets at midnight? Yet her genius was for fiction and lusted to feed abundantly upon the lives of men and women and the study of their ways. At last—for she was very young, oddly like Shakespeare the poet in her face, with the same grey eyes and rounded brows—at last Nick Greene the actor-manager took pity on her; she found herself with child by that gentleman and so—who shall measure the heat and violence of the poet's heart when caught and

能她也是父亲的掌上明珠。或许,她在存放苹果的阁楼上涂写过几页,之后又小心翼翼地藏起来,或者烧掉。然而,不久,二十岁不到的她就被许配给一位羊毛商邻里的儿子。她疾呼自己讨厌婚姻,并因此被父亲毒打一顿。之后,他不再斥责她,而是乞求她不要伤害他,不要让这件婚事使他蒙羞。他说,他可以给她一串珍珠项链或者一件漂亮的裙子,眼里还含着泪水。她怎么还忍心违抗呢?她怎能伤他的心呢?但是那股天赋的力量驱使她违抗自己的父亲。一个夏日的夜晚,她把自己的东西收拾了一个包裹,然后顺着一根绳子逃出来,踏上了前往伦敦的旅途。她还未满 17 岁。雀跃在树篱上的小鸟歌声还不及她的动听。对于词语的声调,她有着敏捷的想象力,这是他们兄妹两人共有的天赋。和哥哥一样,她也喜欢戏剧,并且对此颇有见地。她站在剧院门前,她说她想表演,男人们却当面嘲笑她,尤其是那个多嘴的胖经理。他大叫大喊地说什么贵宾狗跳舞,女人的表演——没有女人,他说,有可能成为演员。他暗示什么,你可以去想象一下。她没有受过专业训练,难道她可以去酒馆乞讨,可以在午夜时分还在大街上流浪吗?不,她的天赋在虚构想象上面,那些男男女女的生活是怎样的,就是她所渴望的,就是她想象的源泉。而且,她还非常年轻,她那灰色的眼睛,弯弯的眼眉,像极了她的哥哥莎士比亚。未想,尼克格林先生对她动了恻隐之心;而且她怀上了他的骨肉——谁又能去估量被这副女人的躯体所束缚的那炽热与激烈的诗人之心呢?

tangled in a woman's body? —killed herself one winter's night and lies buried at some crossroads where the omnibuses now stop outside the Elephant and Castle.

That, more or less, is how the story would run, I think, if a woman in Shakespeare's day had had Shakespeare's genius. But for my part, I agree with the deceased bishop, if such he was—it is unthinkable that any woman in Shakespeare's day should have had Shakespeare's genius. For genius like Shakespeare's is not born among labouring, uneducated, servile people. It was not born in England among the Saxons and the Britons. It is not born today among the working classes. How, then, could it have been born among women whose work began, according to Professor Trevelyan, almost before they were out of the nursery, who were forced to it by their parents and held to it by all the power of law and custom? Yet genius of a sort must have existed among women as it must have existed among the working classes. Now and again an Emily Bronte or a Robert Burns blazes out and proves its presence. But certainly it never got itself on to paper. When, however, one reads of a witch being ducked, of a woman possessed by devils, of a wise woman selling herbs, or even of a very remarkable man who had a mother, then I think we are on the track of a lost novelist, a suppressed poet, of some mute and inglorious Jane Austen, some Emily Bronte who dashed her brains out on the moor or mopped and mowed about the highways crazed with the torture that her gift had put her to. Indeed, I would venture to guess that Anon, who wrote so many poems without signing them, was often a woman. It was a woman Edward Fitzgerald①, I

终于一个冬日夜晚,她亲手了结了自己的生命。她被葬在了十字路口的地方,现在就是公共汽车的一个停靠站,正好在“大象与城堡”酒馆的外面。

我想,如果在莎士比亚时代,一个女性拥有莎士比亚的天赋,故事差不多就是如此了。不过,我倒是赞同已故主教的看法,如果他真是主教——确实在莎士比亚的时代有这样的女子也是难以置信的。像莎士比亚这样的天才可不是在劳动的、未接受教育的、做奴仆的人群中诞生出来的。不是在英国的撒克逊和布拉吞人中诞生的,也不是在今天的工人阶级中诞生的。因此又怎么可能诞生在妇女之中呢?按照特里威廉教授的说法,由于父母的逼迫,还有社会的各种习俗法则,她们在走出儿童室之前就已经开始工作,被束缚了。妇女之中必有天才者,正如天才必定存在于工人阶级当中一样。那么,如今某个艾米莉·勃朗特或某个罗伯特·彭斯耀然显现在世,这便证明了天才的存在。但这种天才肯定不会诉诸笔墨。然而当一个人读到一个女巫被人们所回避,一位女性被魔鬼附体,一位智慧的女性在卖香草,又或是一位杰出的男士有母亲时,那我们就寻到了一位迷途的小说家,一位压抑的诗人,一个沉默无闻的简·奥斯汀。又或是艾米莉·勃朗特,她跑到荒野上将自己的头撞破,在路旁做出各种鬼脸扮相,因为她的天赋折磨着她,使她发狂。确实,我想大胆猜

① 爱德华·菲茨杰拉德(Edward Fitzgerald,1809-1883),英国作家,他从波斯文翻译的《鲁拜集》(*Rubaiyat of Omar Khayyam*)成为英国文学名著。

think, suggested who made the ballads and the folk-songs, crooning them to her children, beguiling her spinning with them, on the length of the winter's night.

This may be true or it may be false—who can say? —but what is true in it, so it seemed to me, reviewing the story of Shakespeare's sister as I had made it, is that any woman born with a great gift in the sixteenth century would certainly have gone crazed, shot herself, or ended her days in some lonely cottage outside the village, half witch, half wizard, feared and mocked at. For it needs little skill in psychology to be sure that a highly gifted girl who had tried to use her gift for poetry would have been so thwarted and hindered by other people, so tortured and pulled asunder by her own contrary instincts, that she must have lost her health and sanity to a certainty. No girl could have walked to London and stood at a stage door and forced her way into the presence of actor-managers without doing herself a violence and suffering an anguish which may have been irrational—for chastity may be a fetish invented by certain societies for unknown reasons—but were none the less inevitable. Chastity has then, it has even now, a religious importance in a woman's life, and has so wrapped itself round with nerves and instincts that to cut it free and bring it to the light of day demands courage of the rarest. To have lived a free life in London in the sixteenth century would have meant for a woman who was a poet and playwright a nervous stress and dilemma which might well have killed her. Had she survived, whatever she had written would have been twisted and deformed, issuing from a strained and morbid imagination.

测一下,写了很多的诗却没有吟唱的那些无名氏估计多半是女性。我觉得,这倒是让人很容易想到一个名叫爱德华·菲茨杰拉德的女性,她创作了诗歌和民谣,一边向她的孩子们低声吟唱,照看他们,一边纺纱,用这些民谣诗歌帮助她消磨时间,度过冬季的漫漫长夜。

这亦真亦假,谁又能讲得清楚呢?但是在回顾我所杜撰的莎士比亚妹妹的故事时,我觉得,其中有一点是真实的,即出生于16世纪的任何一位具有了不起的天赋的女性都必然会发狂、自杀,或者在村外的一间茅舍里孤独地了结此生,半是女巫,半是术士,为人们所惧怕又为人们所嘲笑。因为只要略知心理学即可知道,一个试图将其才能用于诗歌创作的极具天赋的姑娘,一定会受到他人的反对和阻挠,也一定会被自己的矛盾本能所折磨和撕裂,结果她必然会丧失健康和心智。没有一个女孩可以走到伦敦,站在剧场门口,闯到演员经理面前,而免于侵犯,不受痛苦——这痛苦是非理性的——因为贞洁也许是某些社会出于一些未知的原因而创造出来的崇拜对象——但这又是难以避免的。贞洁在过去,甚至在现在,依然在妇女的生活中具有宗教价值,并且被神经和本能团团包裹住,以至于想要解放它,并将其置于光天化日之下需要难得的勇气。对于一位女诗人和剧作家来说,要想在16世纪的伦敦过上自由的生活,也就意味着她会遭受精神上的紧张,陷入进退两难的境地,而那种处境完全可以把她逼上绝路。如果她有幸存活下来,不管她写的是

And undoubtedly, I thought, looking at the shelf where there are no plays by women, her work would have gone unsigned. That refuge she would have sought certainly. It was the relic of the sense of chastity that dictated anonymity to women even so late as the nineteenth century. Currer Bell①, George Eliot, George Sand, all the victims of inner strife as their writings prove, sought ineffectively to veil themselves by using the name of a man. Thus they did homage to the convention, which if not implanted by the other sex was liberally encouraged by them, that publicity in women is detestable. Anonymity runs in their blood....

什么,都会被扭曲和变形的,都是来自于她牵强和病态的想象。看着没有女性作品的书架,我想,毫无疑问她们的剧作不会有署名。她们一定是以匿名来为自己寻求庇护所。正是这种贞洁感的余威让妇女迟至 19 世纪仍隐姓埋名。柯勒·贝尔、乔治·艾略特、乔治·桑,她们的作品证明她们是内心冲突的牺牲品,她们都曾无力地寻求用男生的名字来掩护自己。如此说来,她们是对传统表达敬意,这种传统如果不是由另一种性别建立起来的话,也是会被她们极力赞扬的,这种传统认为,女性引起公众注意是很令人厌恶的。匿名流淌在女性的血液中.......

Four

... Aphra Behn② proved that money could be made by writing at the sacrifice, perhaps, of certain agreeable qualities; and so by degrees writing became not merely a sign of folly and a distracted mind, but was of practical importance. A husband might die, or some disaster overtake the family. Hundreds of women began as the eighteenth century drew on to add to their pin money, or to come to the rescue of their families by making translations or writing the innumerable bad novels which have ceased to be recorded even in textbooks, but are to be picked up in the fourpenny boxes in the Charing Cross Road. The extreme activity of mind which showed itself in the later eighteenth century among women—the talking, and

第四章

……阿芙拉·贝恩证明了,如果以牺牲某种令人愉快的品质为代价,写作是可以用来挣钱的;并且久而久之,写作也就不仅仅是愚蠢和精神错乱的迹象,同时也是具有实际重要性的。丈夫可能死去或者家庭突然遭受灾难的袭击。在 18 世纪,数百名妇女开始通过翻译或撰写难以计数的蹩脚小说来填补私房钱或在关键时刻救助家庭,那些小说甚至在教科书里也没有提及,但是仍可在查令十字街的廉价书摊上偶然发现。18 世纪后期,妇女们的思维极度活跃——谈话,聚会,撰写关于莎士比亚的文章,翻译经典作品——这种活跃建立

① 柯勒·贝尔(Currer Bell)是夏洛蒂·勃朗特的化名。她和妹妹艾米莉、安妮于 1846 年出版了一部诗集,名为《柯勒、埃利斯和阿克顿·贝尔的诗集》(*Poems by Currer, Ellis, and Acton Bell*)。

② 阿芙拉·贝恩(Aphra Behn,1640-1689),英国剧作家、小说家、诗人,第一位以写作为生的英国女性。

the meeting, the writing of essays on Shakespeare, the translating of the classics—was founded on the solid fact that women could make money by writing. Money dignifies what is frivolous if unpaid for. It might still be well to sneer at "blue stockings with an itch for scribbling," but it could not be denied that they could put money in their purses. Thus, towards the end of the eighteenth century a change came about which, if I were rewriting history, I should describe more fully and think of greater importance than the Crusades or the Wars of the Roses. The middle-class woman began to write. ... Without those forerunners, Jane Austen and the Brontes and George Eliot could no more have written than Shakespeare could have written without Marlowe, or Marlowe without Chaucer, or Chaucer without those forgotten poets who paved the ways and tamed the natural savagery of the tongue. For masterpieces are not single and solitary births; they are the outcome of many years of thinking in common, of thinking by the body of the people, so that the experience of the mass is behind the single voice. ... All women together ought to let flowers fall upon the tomb of Aphra Behn which is, most scandalously but rather appropriately, in Westminster Abbey, for it was she who earned them the right to speak their minds. It is she—shady and amorphous as she was—who makes it not quite fantastic for me to say to you tonight; Earn five hundred a year by your wits.

...

Six

...

Next I think that you may object that in all this I have made too much of the importance of material things. Even allowing a generous margin for symbolism, that five hundred a year stands for

在一个根深蒂固的事实之上,那就是妇女可以靠写作来谋生。钱使没有报酬便显得微不足道的事情获得了尊严。或许仍然有理由讥笑"渴望涂鸦的女学究",但是不可否认的是,她们的确使钱进入了自己的钱包。因此,在 18 世纪晚期的时候就产生了一些变化,这些变化比十字军东征或玫瑰战争更具意义,倘若我可以重写历史,我应该将其描写得更详尽。这些变化就是,中产阶级的妇女开始写作了……如果没有那些先驱,简・奥斯汀、勃朗特姐妹和乔治・艾略特就不可能写作,就像没有马洛,莎士比亚也不可能写作或者说没有乔叟,马洛也不可能写作,或者如果没有那些铺平道路并使处于自然蛮荒状态的语言得以驯化的已被遗忘的诗人,乔叟也不可能写作。因为杰作并非单一地、孤独地诞生。杰作是多年集思广益的成果,是一群人思考的产物,因而在一人声音背后是群体的经验……所有的女性应该在阿芙拉・贝恩的墓碑上,送上一束鲜花。她葬于威斯敏斯特教堂,这听起来有点儿骇人听闻,但是实际上又是十分恰如其分,正是因为她为女性赢得了说出自己思想的话语权。她身份来历不明,且又多情,但正是她在今晚让我想对你们说,用你的才智一年挣五百英镑,这并非异想天开。

……

第六章

……

接下来,我猜,你们肯定会提出异议,说我太物质化了。事实上,我们得给象征主义留下回旋的余地。

the power to contemplate, that a lock on the door means the power to think for oneself, still you may say that the mind should rise above such things; and that great poets have often been poor men. Let me then quote to you the words of your own Professor of Literature, who knows better than I do what goes to the making of a poet. Sir Arthur Quiller-Coach① writes:

... It is—however dishonouring to us as a nation—certain that, by some fault in our commonwealth, the poor poet has not in these days, nor has had for two hundred years, a dog's chance. Believe me—and I have spent a great part of ten years in watching some three hundred and twenty elementary schools, we may prate of democracy, but actually, a poor child in England has little more hope than had the son of an Athenian slave to be emancipated into that intellectual freedom of which great writings are born.

Nobody could put the point more plainly. ... That is it. Intellectual freedom depends upon material things. Poetry depends upon intellectual freedom. And women have always been poor, not for two hundred years merely, but from the beginning of time. Women have had less intellectual freedom than the sons of Athenian slaves. Women, then, have not had a dog's chance of writing poetry. That is why I have laid so much stress on money and a room of one's own. ...

I told you in the course of this paper that Shakespeare had a sister; but do not look for her in Sir Sidney Lee's② life of the poet. She died

那年薪五百英镑意味着能够深思熟虑,那门上上锁意味着自我思考,那你肯定会说思想比物质崇高,而伟大的诗人往往穷困潦倒。那么让我在这引用你们自己文学老师的话,如何成为一名诗人,他肯定了解得更多。阿瑟·奎勒-库奇爵士写道:

……它——对于我们民族来说,不论是怎样的耻辱——都是不争的事实,由于我们英联邦的某种过错,今天的穷诗人已经没有起码的机会了,而且200年来一直如此。请相信我——我花了10年中大量的时间观察了大约320所小学,我们可以奢谈民主,但实际上,英国的穷孩子就像雅典奴隶的儿子一样没有机会得到智力自由,而只有智力自由才能产生伟大的作品。

谁也不能把这一点说得更清楚了……就是这么回事。智力自由有赖于物质基础,诗歌创作有赖于智力自由。然而,女性历来贫穷,不仅仅是200年来,而是有史以来就贫穷。女人们的智力自由比希腊奴隶的儿子还要少。所以女人连最起码的机会都很少。这就是为何如此强调女人的经济情况和自己的一间房……

在这篇论文里,我告诉过你,莎士比亚有个妹妹,但是不要去西德尼·李爵士写有关莎士比亚的传记

① 阿瑟·奎勒-库奇(Arthur Quiller-Coach,1863-1944),英国诗人、小说家,以编纂《牛津英国诗选》(*The Oxford Book Of English Verse*, 1250-1900,1900)和《牛津歌谣集》(*The Oxford Book of Ballads*,1911))而著称。

② 西德尼·李(Sidney Lee,1859-1926),英国作家,其《莎士比亚传》(*Life of William Shakespeare*)问世于1890年。

young—alas, she never wrote a word. She lies buried where the omnibuses now stop, opposite the Elephant and Castle. Now my belief is that this poet who never wrote a word and was buried at the crossroads still lives. She lives in you and in me, and in many other women who are not here tonight, for they are washing up the dishes and putting the children to bed. But she lives; for great poets do not die; they are continuing presences; they need only the opportunity to walk among us in the flesh. This opportunity, as I think, it is now coming within your power to give her. For my belief is that if we live another century or so—I am taking of the common life which is the real life and not of the little separate lives which we live as individuals—and have five hundred a year each of us and rooms of our own; if we have the habit of freedom and the courage to write exactly what we think; if we escape a little from the common sitting-room and see human beings not always in their relation to each other but in relation to reality; and the sky, too, and the trees or whatever it may be in themselves; if we look past Milton's hogey, for no human being should shut out the view; if we face the fact, for it is a fact, that there is no arm to cling to, but that we go alone and that our relation is to the world of reality and not only to the world of men and women, then the opportunity will come and the dead poet who was Shakespeare's sister will put on the body which she has so often laid down. Drawing her life from the lives of the unknown who were her fore-runners, as her brother did before her, she will be born. As for her coming without that preparation, without that effort on our part, without that determination that when she is born again she shall find it possible to live and write her poetry, that we cannot expect, for that would be impossible. But I maintain that she would come if we worked for her, and that so to work, even in

里寻找她。哎,她英年早逝,也没有写过什么东西。她被埋在公共汽车站下,对面就是“大象与城堡”酒馆。此刻,我相信,这位从未写过什么,被埋在十字路口的诗人依然活着。活在你我心间,活在今晚不在场的所有其他女性(她们正在洗碗,哄孩子入睡)心中。但是她依然活着,因为伟大的诗人不会死去,他们的精神永存,所需的只是一个行走于我们之间的肉体。而我认为,你们有力量赋予她机会。因为我相信,如果我们再活上一个世纪——我所说的是普通生活,即真正的生活,而非我们作为个人的单独生活——我们每个人都会有年薪五百英镑,拥有自己的一间房。如果我们习惯于自由,有勇气精确地书写自己所想;如果我们逃离普通的客厅一点点,不只是注重人与人之间的关系,而是注重人与现实之间的关系;还要观察天空、树木、任何可能的事物本身;如果我越过弥尔顿的幽灵的观点来看,因为任何一个人都不应该遮蔽视野;如果我们面对事实,因为这个事实是,没有可傍的大腕,而我们只能独自行走,我们的关系不只是男人与女人之间的关系,还有人与社会的关系,那么机会就会降临。而莎士比亚的妹妹,这位已经长眠的诗人也就会活在她经常舍弃的那个躯体上。她就会像她的哥哥之前做的那样,从那些无人知晓的前辈的生命中汲取营养,从而使生命得以长存。我们不能期望,她会在没有那种准备、没有像我们那样做出的努力、没有当她重生时定会发现有可能活着和写诗那种决心的情况下到来,因为这是不可能的。不过我坚持认

poverty and obscurity, is worthwhile.

为,如果我们为她而努力,她就会到来,即使是在贫困潦倒和默默无闻之中,这样的努力也是值得的。

3. Questions for Discussion

(1) How do you understand Virginia Woolf's "a room of one's own" and "five hundred pounds a year"?

(2) Do you think the difficulties women faced in Virginia Woolf's time still exist in our time or they are all gone?

(3) What does Virginia Woolf suggest women should do to write works as great as Shakespeare's?

3. 讨论题

(1)你如何理解弗吉妮亚·伍尔夫所说的"自己的一间房"和"一年五百英镑"的含义?

(2)你认为弗吉妮亚·伍尔夫时代的女性面临的困难在我们的时代仍然存在还是已经完全消失了?

(3)弗吉妮亚·伍尔夫告诉女性要写出与莎士比亚作品一样伟大的作品需要怎么做?

Chapter 10

第10章

1. Introduction to T. S. Eliot

T. S. Eliot, in full Thomas Stearns Eliot (1888-1965) was a poet, playwright, literary critic, editor, leader of the Modernist movement in poetry, and winner of the Nobel Prize in Literature in 1948. Eliot exercised a strong influence on Anglo-American culture in the 20th century.

Eliot was born in St. Louis, Missouri in a rich family with roots in England. His father was a successful businessman. His mother was erudite and passionate for literature and wrote poems. From 1898 to 1905, Eliot attended Smith Academy in St. Louis. He attended Harvard University before studying philosophy at the Sorbonne in Paris in 1910, earning a B. A. and M. A. in English Literature. From 1911 to 1914, he was back at Harvard studying Indian philosophy and Sanskrit. In 1914, Eliot settled down in London where he acquainted with Ezra Pound, an American poet. He worked as a teacher at a private school and then a clerk at Lloyds Bank in London. In 1915, Eliot married Vivien Haigh-Wood (1888-1947), a British dancer. In 1922, he founded a literary

1. 艾略特简介

T. S.艾略特,全名托马斯·斯特恩斯·艾略特(1888—1965)是诗人、剧作家、文学批评家、编辑、现代派诗歌运动领袖,1948年诺贝尔文学奖得主。艾略特对20世纪英美文化产生了巨大的影响。

艾略特出生于美国密苏里州的圣路易斯,祖籍英国,家境十分优越。其父亲是一名成功的商人。其母亲博学多才,酷爱文学,曾写过诗歌。1898—1905年间,艾略特在圣路易斯的史密斯学院学习。他在1910年赴巴黎索尔邦大学学习哲学前,在哈佛大学获得英语文学学士和硕士学位。1911—1914年,他重返哈佛大学修读印度哲学和梵文。1914年,艾略特定居伦敦,在此结识了美国诗人庞德。艾略特在伦敦做过私立学校教师和劳埃德银行职员等工作。1915年,艾略特与英国舞蹈演员薇薇安·黑-伍德(1888—1947)结婚。1922年,他创办了文学季刊《标准》。1924年,

quarterly, *The Criterion*. In 1924, Eliot left his bank post to join the publishing house Faber & Faber. In 1926, he became a lecturer at Oxford University. In 1927, He became a British subject, renouncing his American citizenship. Vivien suffered from mental instability and was often sent to the sanitarium. Feeling greatly tired, Eliot lived separately from his wife in 1933. In 1956, Eliot married Valerie Fletcher (1926-2012). In 1965, Eliot died in London and aged 77.

艾略特辞去银行职位,加入费伯-费伯出版社。1926年,他任牛津大学讲师。1927年,艾略特成为英国公民,放弃美国国籍。薇薇安因精神疾病,经常被送入疗养院治疗。1933年,身心疲惫的艾略特与妻子正式分居。1956年,艾略特与瓦莱里·弗岚切(1926—2012)结婚。1965年,艾略特在伦敦逝世,享年77岁。

Eliot started writing poems in 1909. His well-known poems and collections of poems are *The Love Song of J. Alfred Prufrock* (1915), *Poems* (1919), *The Waste Land* (1922), *The Hollow Men* (1925), *Poems* 1909-1925 (1925), *Ash Wednesday* (1930), *Burnt Norton* (1941), *Four Quartets*(1943), and *Collected Poems* (1962). *The Waste Land* is widely regarded as one of the most important poems of the 20th century and a central work of modernist poetry.

艾略特从1909年开始创作诗歌。他广为人知的诗歌和诗集有:《普鲁弗洛克的情歌》(1915)、《诗集》(1919)、《荒原》(1922)、《空心人》(1925)《诗集 1909—1925》(1925)、《圣灰星期三》(1930)、《焦灼的诺顿》(1941)、《四个四重奏》(1943)以及《诗集》(1962)等。《荒原》被公认为是20世纪最重要的诗歌之一和现代诗歌的核心之作。

Eliot was one of the founders of British and American New Criticism. He wrote many critical essays and elaborated his theory of poetry in his critical essays. The influential essays are "Tradition and the Individual Talent" (1917), *The Sacred Wood: Essays on Poetry and Criticism* (1920), "The Function of Criticism" (1923), *Thoughts After Lambeth* (1931), *Essays Ancient and Modern* (1936) and *Notes Towards the Definition of Culture* (1940).

艾略特是英美新批评派的奠基人之一。他著有大量的文学评论文,并在文论中阐述了自己的诗歌理论。有影响力的论著有:《传统与个人才能》(1917)、《圣林:诗歌与批评文集》(1920)、《批评的功能》(1923)、《朗伯斯后的沉思》(1931)、《古典与现代散文》(1936)、《文化定义札记》(1940)等。

Eliot articulated the idea of "objective correlative" in his essay "Hamlet and His Problems" (1919) which was included in *The Sacred Wood*. Eliot defined "objective correlative" as:

艾略特在《哈姆雷特和他的问题》(1919)一文中提出"客观对应物"思想,该文收录在《圣林》中。艾略特对"客观对应物"的定义如下:

The only way of expressing emotion in the form of art is by finding an "objective correlative"; in other words, a set of objects, a situation, a chain of events which shall be the formula of that

以艺术形式表现情感的唯一途径,就是寻找某个"客观对应物",换言之,就是找寻一组物,一个情景,一

particular emotion; such that when the external facts, which must terminate in sensory experience, are given, the emotion is immediately evoked.

The idea of "objective correlative" is closely related to "Impersonal" theory of poetry proposed by Eliot in "Tradition and the Individual Talent".

Eliot raises two points in "Tradition and the Individual Talent": he first redefines "tradition" by emphasizing the importance of history to writing and understanding poetry, and he then argues that poetry should be essentially "impersonal," that is separate and distinct from the personality of its writer. "Impersonal" theory of poetry has laid a theoretic foundation for British and American New Criticism.

Eliot also dedicated himself to the verse dramas and wrote *The Rock* (1934), *Murder in the Cathedral* (1935), *The Family Reunion* (1939), *The Cocktail Party* (1950), and *The Elder Statesman* (1958).

连串的事件,而所有这些都必须是表现情绪的态势,因为,当感官经验终止,外界事实呈现时,那种情绪就即刻被召唤出来。

"客观对应物"思想与"非人格化"诗歌理论有密切的联系,该理论在艾略特的《传统与个人才能》中被提出。

在《传统与个人才能》中,艾略特提出两点:他首先重新定义了"传统",强调历史在诗歌创作和理解中的重要性;其次他提出诗歌本质上应该是"非人格化"的,即诗歌与诗人的人格是分离的和有区别的。"非人格化"诗歌理论为英美新批评派奠定了理论基础。

艾略特也致力于诗剧创作,主要作品有:《岩石》(1934)、《大教堂中的谋杀》(1935)、《家庭聚会》(1939)、《鸡尾酒会》(1950)、《老政治家》(1958)等。

2. Full Text of "Tradition and the Individual Talent"

2.《传统与个人才能》全文

Tradition and the Individual Talent①

T. S. Eliot

I

In English writing we seldom speak of tradition, though we occasionally apply its name in deploring its absence. We cannot refer to "the tradition" or to "a tradition"; at most, we employ

传统与个人才能

T. S. 艾略特

一

在英文著作中,我们很少会谈及传统,尽管我们在因失去传统而感到遗憾时会使用这个词。我们不会提

① Selected from T. S. Eliot's *The Sacred Wood: Essays on Poetry and Criticism*, London: Methuen & Co. Ltd., 1920.

the adjective in saying that the poetry of So-and-so is "traditional" or even "too traditional". Seldom, perhaps, does the word appear except in a phrase of censure. If otherwise, it is vaguely approbative, with the implication, as to the work approved, of some pleasing archaeological reconstruction. You can hardly make the word agreeable to English ears without this comfortable reference to the reassuring science of archaeology.

及"这种传统"或"一种传统";最多用其形容词来说某个人的诗是"传统的",或者甚至是"太拘泥于传统了"。除了在带有谴责意味的语句中,这个词也很少出现。否则,那也只是一种含糊的赞许,言外之意,这部作品之所以被赞许就是因为:它的创作理念类似于考古修复所要遵循的原则,这一点是让人满意的。如果没有以一种自在的口吻提及令人安心的考古学的话,你几乎无法让传统这个词使英国人听起来悦耳。

Certainly, the word is not likely to appear in our appreciations of living or dead writers. Every nation, every race, has not only its own creative, but its own critical turn of mind; and is even more oblivious of the shortcomings and limitations of its critical habits than of those of its creative genius. We know, or think we know, from the enormous mass of critical writing that has appeared in the French language the critical method or habit of the French; we only conclude (we are such unconscious people) that the French are "more critical" than we, and sometimes even plume ourselves a little with the fact, as if the French were the less spontaneous. Perhaps they are; but we might remind ourselves that criticism is as inevitable as breathing, and that we should be none the worse for articulating what passes in our minds when we read a book and feel an emotion about it, for criticizing our own minds in their work of criticism. One of the facts that might come to light in this process is our tendency to insist, when we praise a poet, upon those aspects of his work in which he least resembles anyone else. In these aspects or parts of his work we pretend to find what is individual, what is the peculiar essence of the man. We dwell with satisfaction upon the poet's difference from his predecessors, especially his

当然,我们在鉴赏今日或昔日作家的作品时,这个词不可能会出现。每个国家,每个民族,不仅有它自己的创作,而且还有它自己的批评的气质;但是,把每个国家,每个民族的批评习惯中出现的缺点与局限和它自己创作天才的缺点与局限进行比较,前者更容易被人遗忘。我们从大量的法文批评著作中,知道了或者自认为知道了,法国人的批评方法或者批评习惯;于是,我们就下结论(我们是这样天真的民族),认为法国人比我们"更挑剔",有时候甚至还因此洋洋得意,似乎法国人没有我们来得自然。也许他们就是这样;但是我们也应该要提醒自己:正如人不能没有呼吸一样,批评是必要的;还应该提醒自己:当我们在阅读一本书籍并且有所感触的时候,我们要把头脑里的想法明确地说出来,要评判我们在对别人的作品进行批评时的心理。事实上,在这个过程中,当我们称赞一位诗人时,极有可能倾向于关注他作品中呈现出的与其他人最不同的方方面面。我们自以为在他的作品中的这些方面或部分内容中找到哪

immediate predecessors; we endeavour to find something that can be isolated in order to be enjoyed. Whereas if we approach a poet without this prejudice we shall often find that not only the best, but the most individual parts of his work may be those in which the dead poets, his ancestors, assert their immortality most vigorously. And I do not mean the impressionable period of adolescence, but the period of full maturity.

些是体现他个性的,哪些是他的特质。谈起诗人和前辈、尤其是和他的前一辈之间的不同之处,我们很是满意;我们竭尽全力找出某些能够被孤立的东西来进行欣赏。然而,假如我们对一位诗人进行批评时,不带有这种偏见的话,我们通常会在他的作品中发现,不仅其最好的部分,而且其最具有个性的部分也许都体现了已故诗人以及他的前辈们的杰出成果。我不是指这段易受影响的青春期,而是指这段完全成熟的时期。

Yet if the only form of tradition, of handing down, consisted in following the ways of the immediate generation before us in a blind or timid adherence to its successes, "tradition" should positively be discouraged. We have seen many such simple currents soon lost in the sand; and novelty is better than repetition. Tradition is a matter of much wider significance. It cannot be inherited, and if you want it you must obtain it by great labour. It involves, in the first place, the historical sense, which we may call nearly indispensable to anyone who would continue to be a poet beyond his twenty-fifth year; and the historical sense involves a perception, not only of the pastness of the past, but of its presence; the historical sense compels a man to write not merely with his own generation in his bones, but with a feeling that the whole of the literature of Europe from Homer and within it the whole of the literature of his own country has a simultaneous existence and composes a simultaneous order. This historical sense, which is a sense of the timeless as well as of the temporal and of the timeless and of the temporal together, is what makes a writer traditional. And it is at the same time what makes a writer most acutely conscious of his place in time, of his contemporaneity.

然而,如果认为传承传统的唯一形式就在于盲目、胆怯地去追随上一代的成果的话,那么我们应该果断地摈弃“传统”。我们曾看到许多类似的潮流很快就消失于沙滩中;然而,创新总比一味地重复要好。事实上,传统本身有着更广泛的意义。传统无法被继承,而是需要你付出巨大的努力才能得到。首先,它涉及历史意识。对于年龄在25岁以上的还想成为诗人的任何一个人来说,历史意识对他来说几乎是不可或缺的;此外,历史意识还涉及洞察能力,要求从事文学创作的人不仅要意识到过去的东西发生于过去,还要意识到过去的东西仍影响着当下;这种历史意识促使一个人在进行创作时不能只关注他自己所处的那个时代的背景,还要想到自荷马以来的整个欧洲文学的发展动态与他本国的整个文学发展是同时并存的,并且建立成了一个同时并存的发展秩序。只有具备了这样的历史意识,我们才能把他称为传统作家:他要意识到过去的永恒性,也要意识到当下时代潮流的短暂性,还要意识到这种永恒性和短暂性是同时并存的。同时,正是在这样的历史意识中,一位作家才可以极其敏锐地意识到他在时代中的地位以及他作品所体现的时代性。

No poet, no artist of any art, has his complete meaning alone. His significance, his appreciation is the appreciation of his relation to the dead poets and artists. You cannot value him alone; you must set him, for contrast and comparison, among the dead. I mean this as a principle of aesthetic, not merely historical, criticism. The necessity that he shall conform, that he shall cohere, is not one-sided; what happens when a new work of art is created is something that happens simultaneously to all the works of art which preceded it. The existing monuments form an ideal order among themselves, which is modified by the introduction of the new (the really new) work of art among them. The existing order is complete before the new work arrives; for order to persist after the supervention of novelty, the whole existing order must be, if ever so slightly, altered; and so the relations, proportions, values of each work of art toward the whole are readjusted; and this is conformity between the old and the new. Whoever has approved this idea of order, of the form of European, of English literature, will not find it preposterous that the past should be altered by the present as much as the present is directed by the past. And the poet who is aware of this will be aware of great difficulties and responsibilities.

任何诗人、艺术家都无法单靠自己个人的努力来展现其作品富含的全部意义。他具有怎样的影响力以及对他本人评价如何也就是对他和已故的诗人、艺术家之间的关系的评价。你不能不设条件,单独去衡量他;而是必须把他和前人放在一起,进行对照和比较。我想要表达的是,这不仅仅是历史批评的原则,而且是一种美学批评的原则。他之所以必须要遵循传统,保持一致,不是出于单方面原因的考虑;一件新的艺术作品被创作出来后,不仅它本身发生了变化,同时也给那些在它之前就被创作出来的所有艺术品带来了变化。现存的不朽著作相互之间建立了一个完美的体系,但是这一体系又因新的(真正新的)艺术作品的引进而被打乱。在新作品出现之前,这个现存的体系是完整的;为了不让新著作影响其完整性,整个现存的体系都必须作出相应的调整,即便是非常微小的改变;因此,每件艺术品对于整体的关系、所占的比例、价值都要重新调整;这就是新与旧之间的一致性过程。无论是谁只要是赞同体系这一理念、赞同关于欧洲文学及英国文学的形式的概念的,就不会觉得:这种过去应随着现实而改变正如现实应接受过去的指导的看法是荒谬、可笑的了。要是诗人能够意识到这一点,他也就能够意识到自己要面对的困难以及肩上所承担的责任。

In a peculiar sense, he will be aware also that he must inevitably be judged by the standards of

从某种特殊的意义上来说,他也

the past. I say judged, not amputated, by them; not judged to be as good as, or worse or better than, the dead; and certainly not judged by the canons of dead critics. It is a judgment, a comparison, in which two things are measured by each other. To conform merely would be for the new work not really to conform at all; it would not be new, and would therefore not be a work of art. And we do not quite say that the new is more valuable because it fits in; but its fitting in is a test of its value—a test, it is true, which can only be slowly and cautiously applied, for we are none of us infallible judges of conformity. We say: it appears to conform, and is perhaps individual, or it appears individual, and may conform; but we are hardly likely to find that it is one and not the other.

会意识到自己必须不可避免地要经受过去的种种标准的评判。我说的评判,不是批判;不是要评判他是否跟已故的前辈一样优秀,或者比他们更糟糕又或是更好;当然也不是要用已故的评论家的那些准则对他给予评判,而是两者之间互相衡量的一种评判和比较。如果仅仅遵循传统,新作品反而无法在真正意义上遵循传统;它将不是新作,因此也不是艺术之作。然而,我们也不会因新作品适应时代潮流而认为它更有价值;但是,这种适应是对它的价值的一种考验——这种考验,的确只能谨慎地进行,是一个缓慢的过程,因为我们都会对传统作出错误的评判。我们说,它似乎是遵循传统的,也许又是个人的,或者它看似是个人的,也许是遵循传统的;但是我们不能说它是这个,而不是那个。

To proceed to a more intelligible exposition of the relation of the poet to the past: he can neither take the past as a lump, an indiscriminate bolus, nor can he form himself wholly on one or two private admirations, nor can he form himself wholly upon one preferred period. The first course is inadmissible, the second is an important experience of youth, and the third is a pleasant and highly desirable supplement. The poet must be very conscious of the main current, which does not at all flow invariably through the most distinguished reputations. He must be quite aware of the obvious fact that art never improves, but that the material of art is never quite the same. He must be aware that the mind of Europe—the mind of his own country—a mind which he learns in time to be much more important than his own private mind—is a mind which changes, and that this change is a development which abandons nothing en route,

为了更进一步清楚地说明诗人与过去的关系:他既不能把过去看成是乱糟糟的一团,看成是一颗没有差别的大药丸,也不能完全因为私底下崇拜的一两个作家而自立门户,或者完全因为偏爱某一个时期而自立门户。第一条路是走不通的,第二条路是青少年的一次重要的经历,第三条路是一种愉悦并且十分令人向往的弥补。诗人必须充分意识到主要的潮流,这种潮流并不总是通过名声显赫的作家体现出来的。他必须充分意识到这个显而易见的事实,即艺术从不会改善,但是艺术的题材从来都不是一成不变的。他还必须意识到欧洲人的思想——他本国的思想——一种他必须及时领悟到的思想,这种思想远比他个人的思想重要

which does not superannuate either Shakespeare, or Homer, or the rock drawing of the Magdalenian① draughtsmen. That this development, refinement perhaps, complication certainly, is not, from the point of view of the artist, any improvement. Perhaps not even an improvement from the point of view of the psychologist or not to the extent which we imagine; perhaps only in the end based upon a complication in economics and machinery. But the difference between the present and the past is that the conscious present is an awareness of the past in a way and to an extent which the past's awareness of itself cannot show.

——是一种变化着的思想，并且这种变化是一种发展，一种绝不会在中途抛弃任何东西的发展，它既不会把莎士比亚、荷马的作品，也不会把马格德林文化时期画家的石画看作过时的。这种发展，也许是精致的，当然也是复杂的，但是在艺术家的眼里，这并没有什么改善。也许甚至在心理学家的眼里，这也不是什么改善或者没有达到我们想象中的那种程度；也许到最后却发现这种改善只是基于经济和机械的相互影响。但是，从某种程度上，现在与过去的区别就是我们所意识到的现在包含对过去的一种认识，然而，在一定程度上，过去却不能认识其本身。

Someone said: "The dead writers are remote from us because we know so much more than they did." Precisely, and they are that which we know.

有人说："已故的作家与我们相差甚远，因为我们知道的要比他们多。"准确地说，我们对他们的所作所为了如指掌。

I am alive to a usual objection to what is clearly part of my programme for the métier of poetry. The objection is that the doctrine requires a ridiculous amount of erudition (pedantry), a claim which can be rejected by appeal to the lives of poets in any pantheon. It will even be affirmed that much learning deadens or perverts poetic sensibility. While, however, we persist in believing that a poet ought to know as much as will not encroach upon his necessary receptivity and necessary laziness, it is not desirable to confine knowledge to whatever can be put into a useful shape for examinations, drawing-rooms, or the still more pretentious modes of publicity. Some can absorb knowledge, the more tardy must sweat for it.

我知道，关于诗歌创作我明确地给出的一些要求通常会遭到反对。反对的原因是：这些声明要求博学多闻(卖弄学识)竟然达到了荒唐可笑的地步，为了了解诗人们的生平，即使去恳求任何一座万神殿，这种要求都会被驳回。我们甚至断定博学会减弱或者破坏对诗的敏感度。然而，尽管我们坚信，只要不破坏诗人所必需的接受性和必需的懒惰性，诗人应该博学多才，但是我们不能把知识局限于应付各种考试、客厅应酬、或者是作为当众炫耀的方式。有的人可以当场吸收知识，而反应较慢的

① 马格德林文化(Magdalenian)是指欧洲的旧石器时代晚期文化。年代距今约 1.7 万—1.15 万年。

Shakespeare acquired more essential history from Plutarch① than most men could from the whole British Museum②. What is to be insisted upon is that the poet must develop or procure the consciousness of the past and that he should continue to develop this consciousness throughout his career.

人就必须付出巨大的努力才能接受它。大多数人都是从英国国家博物馆了解历史,与他们相比,莎士比亚从普鲁塔克那里获取的重大历史要更多。我们所要坚持的就是:诗人必须发展或者获得对于过去的意识,并且在他的整个事业生涯中要继续发展这种意识。

What happens is a continual surrender of himself as he is at the moment to something which is more valuable. The progress of an artist is a continual self-sacrifice, a continual extinction of personality.

于是,他要不断地放弃当前的自己,去追求更有价值的东西。一位艺术家的发展就是要不断地牺牲自我,不断地消灭个性。

There remains to define this process of depersonalization③ and its relation to the sense of tradition. It is in this depersonalization that art may be said to approach the condition of science. I shall, therefore, invite you to consider, as a suggestive analogy, the action which takes place when a bit of finely filiated platinum④is introduced into a chamber containing oxygen and sulphur dioxide.

这里仍需说明的是这种诗歌的"非人格化"过程以及它对于传统意识的关系。正是通过"非人格化",艺术才能说的上是几近科学的。因此,我想将下述实验作为一个暗喻,请你们考虑一下:假如我把一条精致的白金丝,放进一个含有氧气和二氧化硫的瓶子里面,它们将会发生什么样的反应。

II

二

Honest criticism and sensitive appreciation are directed not upon the poet but upon the poetry. If we attend to the confused cries of the newspaper

不管是诚恳的批评还是敏感的鉴赏,它们的着眼点不在于诗人,而

---

① 普鲁塔克(Plutarch,公元46年—公元120年),是一位用希腊文写作的罗马传记文学家、散文家,以及柏拉图学派的知识分子。他的传世之作为《希腊罗马名人传》(*Parallel Lives*)和《掌故清谈录》(*Moralia*)。

② 英国国家博物馆,又名不列颠博物馆,成立于1753年,位于英国伦敦新牛津大街北面的大罗素广场。

③ "非人格化"是艾略特著名的文学批评理论,他认为"诗不是放纵感情,而是逃避感情,不是表现个性,而是逃避个性"。(卞之琳译)这就是说,他反对诗歌创作上的主观自我直白表现,主张诗人对个性要做最少的要求,创作主体在从事艺术实践时不宜将自身的个性特征带入文本,而应以消灭个性为旨归。

④ 铂金(简称Pt),是一种天然纯白的白色贵金属,被誉为贵金属之王。艾略特借用金属的化学反应来阐释"非人格化"诗歌理论,这与炼金术有着紧密的关联性。炼金术常出现在玄学派代表诗人约翰·多恩(John Donne, 1572-1631)的神学诗里,这体现了艾略特对玄学派诗歌传统的继承和结合。

critics and the susurrus of popular repetition that follows, we shall hear the names of poets in great numbers; if we seek not Blue-book knowledge but the enjoyment of poetry, and ask for a poem, we shall seldom find it. I have tried to point out the importance of the relation of the poem to other poems by other authors, and suggested the conception of poetry as a living whole of all the poetry that has ever been written. The other aspect of this Impersonal theory of poetry is the relation of the poem to its author. And I hinted, by an analogy, that the mind of the mature poet differs from that of the immature one not precisely in any valuation of "personality", not being necessarily more interesting, or having "more to say", but rather by being a more finely perfected medium in which special, or very varied, feelings are at liberty to enter into new combinations.

在于诗歌本身。如果我们关注报纸上登出的有关批评家们杂七杂八的嚷嚷声以及随之而来的群众的喃喃低语声，我们就可以听到许多诗人的名字；如果我们不是以寻求蓝皮书上的知识为目的，而是为了欣赏诗歌而去寻找一首诗，我们却很难找到这样的诗。在文章的第一部分，我已经试图指出一首诗与其他诗人所写的诗之间有着重要的联系，并且认为诗歌是从古到今所有诗歌的有机整体。“非人格”诗歌理论的另一方面就是谈论诗与作者本人的关系。我通过一个比喻来揭示这样一个道理：成熟诗人与非成熟诗人的差异并不在于谁的诗更“个性化”，更有趣，更耐人寻味，而在于谁的诗可以作为一个较为完美的媒介，通过这种媒介，特殊的或者是多变的情感可以进行新的自由组合。

The analogy was that of the catalyst. When the two gases previously mentioned are mixed in the presence of a filament of platinum, they form sulphurous acid. This combination takes place only if the platinum is present; nevertheless the newly formed acid contains no trace of platinum, and the platinum itself is apparently unaffected; has remained inert, neutral, and unchanged. The mind of the poet is the shred of platinum. It may partly or exclusively operate upon the experience of the man himself; but, the more perfect the artist, the more completely separate in him will be the man who suffers and the mind which creates; the more perfectly will the mind digest and transmute the passions which are its material.

我拿化学上的催化剂做了一个如上所述的比喻。当氧气和二氧化硫与一条白金丝混合时，它们会产生硫酸。只有在白金丝的作用下，才能发生这个化学反应；然而，在新形成的硫酸里却找不到一丝白金的迹象，而且白金本身很显然也未受到丝毫的影响；它是惰性的，保持中性，本身没有发生任何改变。诗人的思想就像是这条白金丝。它也许会对诗人本身的经验产生部分或彻底的影响；但是，一位艺术家越是完美，他身上所体现出来的作为承受者的人和作为创造者的思想分离得越是彻底，思想消化得就越是完美，并且越能将激情转化为创作素材。

The experience, you will notice, the elements which enter the presence of the transforming catalyst, are of two kinds: emotions and feelings.

你会发现，这种经验，影响催化剂发生变化的元素包括两种：即情

The effect of a work of art upon the person who enjoys it is an experience different in kind from any experience not of art. It may be formed out of one emotion, or may be a combination of several; and various feelings, inhering for the writer in particular words or phrases or images, may be added to compose the final result. Or great poetry may be made without the direct use of any emotion whatever: composed out of feelings solely. Canto XV of the *Inferno* (Brunetto Latini①) is a working up of the emotion evident in the situation; but the effect, though single as that of any work of art, is obtained by considerable complexity of detail. The last quatrain gives an image, a feeling attaching to an image, which "came", which did not develop simply out of what precedes, but which was probably in suspension in the poet's mind until the proper combination arrived for it to add itself to. The poet's mind is in fact a receptacle for seizing and storing up numberless feelings, phrases, images, which remain there until all the particles which can unite to form a new compound are present together.

绪和情感。一部艺术作品对鉴赏者会有所影响,这种影响是一种经验,但是,这种经验在本质上却又有别于其他任何非艺术作品的经验。它也许形成于一种情绪,也许是由各种情绪共同组合而成;然而,为了完成一部作品,作者用各种特殊的单词、短语或意象表达各种各样的情感,也许还会把这些情感表达的方式加入到自己的创作中。或者说,即便没有任何情绪的成分包含在内,还是能够创作出伟大的诗歌:单纯地由感情流露的方式组成。在《神曲》地狱篇:第十五首中,在情绪处理方面,很显然是采取了逐渐激发的方式;但是它所激发的效果,虽然跟其他任何一部艺术作品的效果一样简单,却得益于一些相当复杂的细节。诗歌的最后四行描写了一个意象,表达了寄托于该意象的一种情感,这个意象的"出现",不仅以前文作为铺垫,而且有可能它早就停留在诗人的思想中,等到一个可以结合的良机,它便主动地与其结合。事实上,诗人的头脑是一个容器,抓住并储存大量的感情、短语、意象。它们一直在那儿,直到可以结合在一起的粒子形成一个新的复合体,它们就出现了。

If you compare several representative passages of the greatest poetry you see how great is the variety of types of combination, and also how completely any semi-ethical criterion of "sublimity" misses the mark. For it is not the "greatness", the intensity, of the emotions, the components, but the intensity of the artistic process, the pressure, so to speak, under which

假如你从最伟大的诗中挑出几个典型的章节,并将它们进行比较,你会发现结合的方式是多么的丰富,还可以发现任何有关"崇高"的半伦理批评标准都是徒劳。因为诗的价值不在于情绪的强度有多大,不在于这些组成成分,而在于艺术过程的强

① 布鲁内托·拉蒂尼(Brunetto Latini,1220-1295),犯同性恋罪,但他是整个"地狱篇"里最受诗人但丁尊敬的人。

the fusion takes place, that counts. The episode of Paolo and Francesca① employs a definite emotion, but the intensity of the poetry is something quite different from whatever intensity in the supposed experience it may give the impression of. It is no more intense, furthermore, than Canto XXVI, the voyage of Ulysses②, which has not the direct dependence upon an emotion. Great variety is possible in the process of transmutation of emotion: the murder of Agamemnon, or the agony of Othello, gives an artistic effect apparently closer to a possible original than the scenes from Dante. In the *Agamemnon*, the artistic emotion approximates to the emotion of an actual spectator; in *Othello* to the emotion of the protagonist himself. But the difference between art and the event is always absolute; the combination which is the murder of Agamemnon is probably as complex as that which is the voyage of Ulysses. In either case there has been a fusion of elements. *The Ode of Keats*③ contains a number of feelings which have nothing particular to do with the nightingale, but which the nightingale, partly, perhaps, because of its attractive name, and partly because of its reputation, served to bring together.

度,也可以说是在于组合时所产生的压力强度。在保罗与弗兰西斯卡的这段情节中,确实有情绪的成分包含在内,但是诗的强度却大大不同于假设经验所留给我们的印象的强度。并且,它跟第二十六章:尤利西斯的海上漂流的强度是一样的,第二十六章并没有直接依赖于一种情绪。情绪转化的过程也许是多种多样的:阿伽门农被刺杀或者是奥赛罗的痛苦所产生的艺术效果,较之于但丁作品中的场景,可能显得更为逼真。《阿伽门农》所带来的艺术情绪接近于一个目击者的情绪;而《奥赛罗》所带来的艺术情绪则又接近于剧中主人公自己的情绪。但是,艺术与事件之间的差别总是绝对的;阿伽门农被刺杀所用的组合可能跟尤利西斯海上漂流所用的组合一样复杂。这两者的任何一个场景都是由各种因素组合而成的。济慈的《夜莺颂》表达了各种各样的情感,这些情感与夜莺本身毫无特殊联系,但是,这些情感之所以能与夜莺相融合,也许一方面是因为它那引人注目的名字,另一方面是因为它的声誉。

The point of view which I am struggling to attack is perhaps related to the metaphysical

我正进行竭力攻击的观点也许是形而上学的理论:它主张达到灵

① 但丁在《神曲》(*Divina Commedia*)地狱篇(Inferno)第 5 首,也即地狱第二圈,描述了保罗与弗兰西斯卡(Paolo and Francesca)之间动人的爱情悲剧。

② 《神曲》地狱篇第 26 首讲述了尤利西斯(Ulysses)的故事。他是特洛伊战争(Trojan War)的战略家,凭借木马计占领了特洛伊城(Troy)。战争结束后,他没有回家与妻子团圆,却打造一条船,与同伴一同探索世界,在海上漂流了很多年,一直漂流到直布罗陀海峡(the Strait of Gibraltar)。

③ 约翰·济慈(John Keats, 1795-1821),英国浪漫派诗人,代表作有:《夜莺颂》(*Ode to a Nightingale*)、《希腊古瓮颂》(*Ode on a Grecian Urn*)、《秋颂》(*Ode on Melancholy*)等。

theory① of the substantial unity of the soul: for my meaning is, that the poet has, not a "personality" to express, but a particular medium, which is only a medium and not a personality, in which impressions and experiences combine in peculiar and unexpected ways. Impressions and experiences which are important for the man may take no place in the poetry, and those which become important in the poetry may play quite a negligible part in the man, the personality.

I will quote a passage② which is unfamiliar enough to be regarded with fresh attention in the light—or darkness—of these observations:

And now methinks I could e'en chide myself
For doating on her beauty, though her death
Shall be revenged after no common action.
Does the silkworm expend her yellow labours
For thee? For thee does she undo herself?
Are lordships sold to maintain ladyships
For the poor benefit of a bewildering minute?
Why does yon fellow falsify highways,
And put his life between the judge's lips,
To refine such a thing—— keeps horse and men
To beat their valours for her?...

In this passage (as is evident if it is taken in its context) there is a combination of positive and negative emotions: an intensely strong attraction toward beauty and an equally intense fascination by the ugliness which is contrasted with it and which destroys it. This balance of contrasted emotion is in the dramatic situation to which the speech is pertinent, but that situation alone is inadequate to

魂的物质统一。因为,我的意思是,诗人无法表现"个性",只有一种特殊的媒介,而且仅仅是作为媒介,而不是体现个性,通过这种媒介,印象和经验以奇特且出人意料的方式结合起来。对诗人有重要意义的印象和经验,也许在他的诗歌中并没有起到什么作用,在诗歌中具有重要意义的印象和经验,也许在诗人,在个性中所起的作用是微不足道的。

我在这里将引用一节鲜为人知的诗,以一种全新的着眼点对它进行观察:

如今我甚至还在自责
为沉迷于她的美貌,尽管她的死
不是随随便便就可以报复。
蚕儿为何为了你消耗体力
为你?为你而牺牲它自己?
男人又为何为了女人而出卖尊严
只是为了那令人着迷的刹那间?
为什么那家伙要拦路打劫
让自己的命运任由法官裁决
为了美化这件事——还派出人马
为她展现他们的勇猛?……

在这一诗节中(通过上下文就明显可以看出)有正反两种情绪的结合:一种是对美有着极其强烈的吸引力,另一种是对丑有着同样强度的迷恋,它们两两对立,互相抵消。这种对立情绪要在台词得当的戏剧场景中才能达到平衡,单靠场景本身是不足以使其达到平衡的。这好比戏

① 艾略特认为玄学派诗人是把思想和感情统一起来,达到灵魂的物质统一,是统一的感受性典范。
② 摘自西里尔·图尔纳(Cyril Tourneur,约1575-1626)的《复仇者的悲剧》(*The Revenger's Tragedy*)第三幕第五场。

it. This is, so to speak, the structural emotion, provided by the drama. But the whole effect, the dominant tone, is due to the fact that a number of floating feelings, having an affinity to this emotion by no means superficially evident, have combined with it to give us a new art emotion.

剧所带来的结构化的情绪。但是,整体的效果、主要的基调都是因为许多漂浮不定的情感会对这种情绪产生吸引力,表面上这种吸引力表现得并不明显,然而它们一旦结合就会给我们带来一股新的艺术情绪。

It is not in his personal emotions, the emotions provoked by particular events in his life, that the poet is in any way remarkable or interesting. His particular emotions may be simple, or crude, or flat. The emotion in his poetry will be a very complex thing, but not with the complexity of the emotions of people who have very complex or unusual emotions in life. One error, in fact, of eccentricity in poetry is to seek for new human emotions to express; and in this search for novelty in the wrong place it discovers the perverse. The business of the poet is not to find new emotions, but to use the ordinary ones and, in working them up into poetry, to express feelings which are not in actual emotions at all. And emotions which he has never experienced will serve his turn as well as those familiar to him. Consequently, we must believe that "emotion recollected in tranquillity"① is an inexact formula. For it is neither emotion, nor recollection, nor, without distortion of meaning, tranquillity. It is a concentration, and a new thing resulting from the concentration, of a very great number of experiences which to the practical and active person would not seem to be experiences at all; it is a concentration which does not happen consciously or of deliberation. These experiences are not "recollected", and they finally unite in an atmosphere which is "tranquil" only in that it is a

诗人之所以是卓越的或者是令人感兴趣的,并不是因为他的个人情绪,也不是因为那种由生活中的特殊事件而激起的情绪。他的特殊情绪也许是简单的、粗鲁的或是平和的。他诗歌中所体现的情绪是非常复杂的,但是这种复杂性与生活中情绪复杂或情绪异常的那类人的情绪复杂性相比,是有区别的。事实上,诗歌中存在一种古怪的错误,即寻求表达人类情绪的新方式;而就在不当之处寻找新意时发现自己有悖常理。诗人的任务不是寻找新的情绪,而是将普通的情绪融入诗歌创作中,以此来表达实际情绪中根本没有的情感。诗人可以像处理自己熟知的情绪那样去处理那些从未有过的情绪。因此,我们必须坚信"情绪是在宁静中回忆起来的,"这是一个不精确的公式。因为诗歌不是情绪,不是回忆,如果没有歪曲词义的话,也不是宁静。它是一种积累,一种由许许多多的经验累积而成的新东西,这些经验对于实用派和乐观派而言似乎根本算不上是经验;这并不是一种自觉的或者深思熟虑的积累。这些经验都不是"回忆出来"的,它们最终在"宁

① 摘自威廉·华兹华斯(William Wordsworth, 1770-1850),《抒情歌谣集》(*Lyrical Ballads*):"Poetry is the spontaneous overflow of powerful feelings: it takes its origin from emotion recollected in tranquility."

passive attending upon the event. Of course this is not quite the whole story. There is a great deal, in the writing of poetry, which must be conscious and deliberate. In fact, the bad poet is usually unconscious where he ought to be conscious and conscious where he ought to be unconscious. Both errors tend to make him "personal." Poetry is not a turning loose of emotion, but an escape from emotion; it is not the expression of personality, but an escape from personality. But, of course, only those who have personality and emotions know what it means to want to escape from these things.

静"的气氛中结合起来只是因为它是被动地参与到这个事件中来的。当然,诗歌创作并非完全就是这么一回事儿。在诗歌创作过程中,有很多东西需要你自觉地去认真思考。事实上,一位蹩脚的诗人通常是应该在自觉的地方表现得不自觉,不应该自觉的地方却又表现得自觉。这两种错误都有可能使他具备"个性"。诗歌不是放纵情绪,而是回避情绪;不是表现个性,而是回避个性。可是,当然,只有那些有个性和情绪的诗人才明白主张回避个性、回避情绪的意义所在。

III

δ δε νους ισως Θειοτερον τι και απαθες εστιν ①

This essay proposes to halt at the frontier of metaphysics or mysticism, and confine itself to such practical conclusions as can be applied by the responsible person interested in poetry. To divert interest from the poet to the poetry is a laudable aim: for it would conduce to a juster estimation of actual poetry, good and bad. There are many people who appreciate the expression of sincere emotion in verse, and there is a smaller number of people who can appreciate technical excellence. But very few know when there is expression of significant emotion, emotion which has its life in the poem and not in the history of the poet. The emotion of art is impersonal. And the poet cannot reach this impersonality without surrendering himself wholly to the work to be done. And he is not likely to know what is to be done unless he lives in what is not merely the present, but the present

三

灵魂乃天赐,圣洁不动情

这篇论文准备停笔于形而上学或神秘主义的边缘,将其局限于实用的结论,能够被那些对诗歌感兴趣的人所使用。如果能把感兴趣的焦点从诗人身上转移到诗歌身上,这是一个值得赞赏的目标:因为这样有利于对诗歌的好坏作出一个比较公正的评价。有很多人鉴赏的是诗歌中所流露出的真挚情绪,也有少数一部分人能够鉴赏到诗歌中运用到的卓越技巧。但是,当诗中表达了一种意义非凡的情绪时,却几乎没人知道这种包含生命意义的情绪存在于诗歌中,而不是存在于有关诗人的历史中。艺术的情绪是非个性的。诗人如果不能全身心地投入到创作中,他就无法实现个性化。并且,他不知道自己接下来要怎么做,除非他让自己

① 原文为希腊文,见亚里士多德《灵魂轮》(*Doctrine of Soul*),中文为卞之琳译。

moment of the past, unless he is conscious, not of what is dead, but of what is already living.

既活在当下,又活在过去的此时此刻;除非他意识到的不是已经逝去的,而是早就已经存在着的东西。

3. Questions for Discussion

(1) How do you understand "tradition"?

(2) How do you understand " individual talent"?

(3) How do you understand Eliot's "impersonal theory of poetry"?

3. 讨论题

(1)你是如何理解"传统"的?

(2)你是如何理解"个人才能"的?

(3)你是如何理解艾略特的"非人格化"诗歌理论的?

Chapter 11

1. Introduction to Aldo Leopold

Aldo Leopold (1887-1948) was a renowned American scientist and scholar, exceptional teacher, philosopher, and gifted writer. He is considered the father of wildlife ecology of the 20th century.

Leopold was born in Burlington, Iowa. He developed an interest in the natural world at an early age, spending hours observing, journaling, and sketching his surroundings. After graduation from the Yale Forest School in 1909, he joined the U.S. Forest Service and was assigned to Arizona and New Mexico. From 1928 to 1931, funded by American Sporting Arms and Ammunition Manufacturers' Institute, Leopold surveyed the number of hunters in central North, and the results were written in *Report on a Game Survey of the North Central States* (1931). In 1933, he was hired as a professor on Wildlife Management of University of Wisconsin and gave lectures on "Wildlife Management". In 1935, the Leopold family purchased a worn-out farm near Baraboo, Wisconsin, in an area known as the sand counties.

第11章

1. 利奥帕德简介

阿尔多·利奥帕德(1887—1948)是美国著名的科学家、学者,杰出的教师、哲学家和天才作家。他被认为是20世纪野生动物生态学之父。

利奥帕德出生于美国依阿华州柏林顿市。他自幼便对自然界产生了兴趣,花大量的时间观察、记录和描绘周围的环境。1909从耶鲁大学林业学院毕业后,他就职于联邦林业局,被派往亚利桑那州和新墨西哥州工作。1928—1931年间,在美国运动武器和弹药制造商协会的资金支持下,利奥帕德调查了中北部的狩猎人数,调查结果写进《中北部各州狩猎调查报告》(1931)。1933年,他被聘为威斯康星大学的野生动物管理学教授,主讲"野生动物管理"课程。1935利奥帕德一家在威斯康星州邻近巴拉布镇一个被称作"沙乡"的地方购买了一个荒废的农场。在此农场,利奥帕德将自己的生态保护信念

It was here Leopold put into action his conservation beliefs and wrote many of the essays in *A Sand County Almanac*. Leopold was stricken by heart attack and died on April 21, 1948 while fighting a grass fire on a neighbor's farm.

付诸行动,写下了《沙乡年鉴》中的多篇文章。1948 年 4 月 21 日,利奥帕德在邻近农场草场救火时,心脏病突发去世。

Leopold published more than 500 articles, papers, reports, newsletters, and letters. He kept detailed diaries and journals of his Forest Service activity, his travels, hunting and field experience, and observations and activities at his Sand County farm. Leopold's cornerstone book *Game Management* (1933) created a new science that intertwined forestry, agriculture, biology, zoology, ecology, education and communication.

利奥帕德发表了 500 多篇文章、论文、报告、通讯稿和书信等。他保留有详细的日记和日志,记录林业管理活动、游历、狩猎、田野活动以及在沙乡农场的各种观察及活动。利奥帕德的奠基之作《野生动物管理》(1933)一书创造了一门将林业、农业、生物学、动物学、生态学、教育和传媒学交汇融合的新科学。

Leopold is best known for his book *A Sand County Almanac* (1949) by millions of people around the globe. The book, often acclaimed as the 20th thcentury's literary landmark in conservation, melds exceptional poetic prose with keen observations of the natural world. Beyond his descriptions of the natural world, Leopold articulated in this book an innovative idea known as the "land ethic".

利奥帕德的《沙乡年鉴》(1949)一书为全世界成千上百万的人而知。此书常被称作 20 世纪环境保护之作中的里程碑,充满诗意的文字和对自然界的敏锐观察以无与伦比的方式融合在一起。除了对自然界的描述之外,利奥帕德在此书中表达了"土地伦理"这一全新的思想。

Leopold did not define the land ethic with a litany of rights and wrongs in *A Sand County Almanac*. Instead, he presented it as a set of values that naturally grew out of his lifetime of experiences in the outdoors. Leopold wrote that "we can only be ethical in relation to something we can see, understand, feel, love, or otherwise have faith in."

利奥帕德在《沙乡年鉴》中没有用枯燥冗长的对错的方式给土地伦理下定义。相反,他通过自己一生的户外活动经验自然地表达了一套价值观。利奥帕德写道:"在对某种事物的关系上,只有在我们可以看见、了解、感到、热爱,或者对它表示信任时,我们才是道德的。"

Leopold pointed out that, the land ethic simply enlarges the boundaries of the ethical community to include soils, waters, plants, and animals, or collectively: the land. The relationships between people and land are intertwined: care for people cannot be separated from care for the land. A land ethic is a moral code of conduct that grows out of these interconnected caring relationships.

利奥帕德指出,土地伦理只是扩大了道德共同体的界限,它包括土壤、水、植物和动物,或者总称为土地。人与土地的关系是相互交织的:对人的关爱不能脱离对土地的关爱。土地伦理是一种道德行为准则,产生于有内在联系的各种关爱关系之中。

2. Selections from *A Sand County Almanac*

*A Sand County Almanac*①

Aldo Leopold

Marshland Elegy

A dawn wind stirs on the great marsh. With almost imperceptible slowness it rolls a bank of fog across the wide morass. Like the white ghost of a glacier the mists advance, riding over phalanxes of tamarack, sliding across bog meadows bogmeadows heavy with dew. A single silence hangs from horizon to horizon.

Out of some far recess of the sky a tinkling of little bells falls soft upon the listening land. Then again silence. Now comes a baying of some sweet-throated hound, soon the clamor of a responding back. Then a far clear blast of hunting horns, out of the sky into the fog.

High horns, low horns, silence, and finally a pandemonium of trumpets, rattles, croaks, and cries that almost shakes the bog with its nearness, but without yet disclosing whence it comes. At last a glint of sun reveals the approach of a great echelon of birds. On motionless wing they emerge from the lifting mists, sweep a final arc of sky, and settle in clangorous descending spirals to their feeding grounds. A new day has begun on the crane marsh.

A sense of time lies thick and heavy on such a place. Yearly since the ice age it has wakened each spring to the clangor of cranes. The peat layers that comprise the bog are laid down in the basin of an

2.《沙乡年鉴》选文

沙乡年鉴

阿尔多·利奥帕德

沼泽地的哀歌

黎明的风轻拂着巨大的沼泽地。它悄无声息地滚动着一片片迷雾，笼罩在宽阔的沼泽地上。薄雾像冰川上白色的幻影，缓慢地向前推进，弥漫在落叶松方阵之上，滑过沼泽，留下沉重的露水。一种划过天际的寂静笼罩在地平线之间。

远处隐蔽的天空传来一阵清脆的铃声，轻柔地落在倾听的大地。接着又是一阵安静。现在传来轻快的狗吠声，一会便是一阵回应的狗叫声。然后是远处清晰的狩猎号角的声音通过天空穿过雾霭传过来。

号角声时而响亮，时而低沉或是一阵寂静，最后是一阵喧嚣的喇叭声、脚步声、呱呱声和喊叫声，如此近距离地震撼着沼泽地，却仍旧无法辨别这些声音来自何处。最后，闪耀的太阳下呈梯形的雁群出现在天空。它们的翅膀无需扇动，浮现在上升的迷雾中，掠过穹窿似的天空，响亮的鸣叫声穿过天空，螺旋似地降落在它们的觅食之地。鹤泽新的一天就开始了。

在这样的地方有着浓厚的时间观念。自冰河世纪以来，每年都是鹤鸣声唤醒沉睡的春天。沼泽的泥炭

---

① Selected from *A Sand County Almanac*, New York: Oxford University Press, 1949.

ancient lake. The cranes stand, as it were, upon the sodden pages of their own history. These peats are the compressed remains of the mosses that clogged the pools, of the tamaracks that spread over the moss, of the cranes that bugled over the tamaracks since the retreat of the ice sheet. An endless caravan of generations has built of its own bones this bridge into the future, this habitat where the oncoming host again may live and breed and die.

To what end? Out on the bog a crane, gulping some luckless frog, springs his ungainly hulk into the air and flails the morning sun with mighty wings. The tamaracks re-echo with his bugled certitude. He seems to know.

Our ability to perceive quality in nature begins, as in art, with the pretty. It expands through successive stages of the beautiful to values as yet uncaptured by language. The quality of cranes lies, I think, in this higher gamut as yet beyond the reach of words.

This much, though, can be said: our appreciation of the crane grows with the slow unraveling of earthly history. His tribe, we now know, stems out of the remote Eocene. The other members of the fauna in which he originated are long since entombed within the hills. When we hear his call we hear no mere bird. We hear the trumpet in the orchestra of evolution. He is the symbol of our untamable past, of that incredible sweep of millennia which underlies and conditions the daily affairs of birds and men.

And so they live and have their being —these cranes—not in the constricted present, but in the wider reaches of evolutionary time. Their annual return is the ticking of the geological clock. Upon the place of their return they confer a peculiar

层位于古老的湖底。鹤群像往常一样站立着,在那片浸透着历史的篇章上。这些泥炭层是阻塞池塘的苔藓被挤压之后的残留,也有覆盖在苔藓上面的落叶松的残留,还有在冰盖退去后,在落叶松上高歌的鹤的尸骨。一代又一代的旅行队用自己的骨骼建立了这座通向未来的桥梁,未来的主宰者将会再次在这片栖息地生存、繁衍和死去。

结局会是怎样?一只鹤在沼泽之上,狼吞虎咽地享受着一直倒霉的青蛙,笨重的身体跃在空中,用有力的翅膀拍打着早晨的阳光。落叶松发出坚定的吼声回应空中的鹤声。它似乎知道这一切。

同艺术一样,我们感知自然特性的能力是从美的欣赏开始的。它通过日益完善的美的阶段逐渐扩展为无法用言语表达的价值观。我想,从较高的范围来讲,鹤的特性也是难以用言语捕捉的。

即使如此,我们还可以说:我们对鹤的欣赏是随着地质历史的慢慢解开而发展的。如今我们知道,鹤的种族来源于遥远的始新世。它起源的种族里的其他成员自被埋葬在这片山里已经是很久以前的事了。当我们听到了它的鸣叫,我们听到的不仅仅是鸟叫声,更是进化的号角。它代表了我们难以制服的历史和不可思议的辉煌时代,这个时代构成并奠定了鸟类和人类的日常生活基础。

由此可见,这些鹤不仅仅是生存在当下,而且经历了历史进化的长河。它们每年的返回就像是地质钟一样,嘀嘀往前走。它们回来的地方

distinction. Amid the endless mediocrity of the commonplace, a crane marsh holds a paleontological patent of nobility, won in the march of aeons, and revocable only by shotgun. The sadness discernible in some marshes arises, perhaps, from their once having harbored cranes. Now they stand humbled, adrift in history.

因此有了特别的意义。与其他普通的沼泽地相比,一个有着鹤群栖息遗迹的沼泽地势必要蕴含着崇高的古生物研究专利,它成了历史长河中的胜利者,却被猎枪毁掉了这一切。我们看到的一些沼泽地的悲哀,也许就是源于那里曾经是鹤的栖息地。如今它们忍辱负重地矗立着,在历史长河中漂泊着。

Some sense of this quality in cranes seems to have been felt by sportsmen and ornithologists of all ages. Upon such quarry as this the Holy Roman Emperor Frederick loosed his gyrfalcons. Upon such quarry as this once swooped the hawks of Kublai Khan①. Marco Polo tells us: "He derives the highest amusement from sporting with gyrfalcons and hawks. At Changanor the Khan has a great Palace surrounded by a fine plain where are found cranes in great numbers. He causes millet and other grains to be sown in order that the birds may not want."

各个时代的猎人和鸟类学家已经感受到鹤的这种特性。为了得到这样的猎物,神圣罗马帝国皇帝弗雷德里克释放出他的隼,忽必烈汗放出他的鹰去捕捉鹤。马可·波罗告诉我们:"他从隼和鹰的使用中得到最大的乐趣。在察汗淖尔,可汗有一座被美丽的大草原环绕的宫殿,那里有很多鹤。他怕这些鸟没东西吃,命人种了小米和其他谷物给它们。"

The ornithologist Bengt Berg②, seeing cranes as a boy upon the Swedish heaths, forthwith made them his life work. He followed them to Africa and discovered their winter retreat on the White Nile. He says of his first encounter: "It was a spectacle which eclipsed the flight of the roc in *the Thousand and One Nights*."

鸟类学家本特·伯格少年时在瑞士荒地上看到鹤,便决定终生从事鹤的研究工作。他跟随鹤群到非洲,发现鹤群冬天栖息在白尼罗河上。他曾谈到第一次跟随鹤群的感受:"那壮观的景象使《天方夜谭》中飞行的巨鸟队伍黯然失色。"

When the glacier came down out of the north, crunching hills and gouging valleys, some adventuring rampart of the ice climbed the Baraboo Hills and fell back into the outlet gorge of the Wisconsin River. The swollen waters backed up and formed a lake half as long as the state, bordered on the east by cliffs of ice, and fed by the torrents that fell from melting mountains. The shorelines of this old lake are still visible; its bottom is the bottom of

当冰川从北方移动下来时,它们嘎吱嘎吱地移过山丘,碾过峡谷,一些勇猛的冰墙越过巴拉布山,落到威斯康星河谷的出口。涨满的水堵塞而形成了延伸半个洲的湖,东边挨着悬崖的冰层,山上融化的冰水汇成急流又流入河水中。这片古老的湖的边界线依旧可以看见,它的湖底就是巨大的沼泽地的底部。

① 忽必烈(Kublai Khan,1215-1294):中国元朝皇帝,在查干湖的宫殿周围置了一大片肥沃的草原。
② 本特·伯格(Bengt Berg,1885-1967),瑞典鸟类学家。

the great marsh.

The lake rose through the centuries, finally spilling over east of the Baraboo range. There it cut a new channel for the river, and thus drained itself. To the residual lagoons came the cranes, bugling the defeat of the retreating winter, summoning the on-creeping host of living things to their collective task of marsh-building. Floating bogs of sphagnum moss clogged the lowered waters, filled them. Sedge and leather-leaf, tamarack and spruce successively advanced over the bog, anchoring it by their root fabric, sucking out its water, making peat. The lagoons disappeared, but not the cranes. To the moss meadows that replaced the ancient waterways they returned each spring to dance and bugle and rear their gangling sorrel-colored young. These, albeit birds, are not properly called chicks, but *colts*. I cannot explain why. On some dewy June morning watch them gambol over their ancestral pastures at the heels of the roan mare, and you will see for yourself.

One year not long ago a French trapper in buckskins pushed his canoe up one of the moss-clogged creeks that threat the great marsh. At this attempt to invade their miry stronghold the cranes gave vent to loud and ribald laughter. A century or two later Englishmen came in covered wagons. They chopped clearings in the timbered moraines that border the marsh, and in them planted corn and buckwheat. They did not intend, like the Great Kahn at Changanor, to feed the cranes. But the cranes do not question the intent of glaciers, emperors, or pioneers. They ate the grain, and when some irate farmer failed to concede their usufruct in his corn, they trumpeted a warning and sailed across the marsh to another farm.

There was no alfalfa in those days, and the hill-farms made poor hay land, especially in dry years. One dry year someone set a fire in the

几个世纪以来这个湖一直在上升，最终漫过了巴拉不草原的东部。在那里开辟了一条新的水源，这样就可以把水流出去。鹤群来到残留的湖边，吹响着冬季迁徙凯旋的号角，召集它们的同类去完成建构沼泽的集体任务。漂浮的泥炭藓沼泽堵塞在低水位，填满了小湖。莎草、地桂、落叶松和云杉也接连地遍布泥沼，通过它们的根部扎根在沼泽地，从水中吸收养分，再产生泥炭。湖渐渐消失了，而鹤却依然存在着。每年春天鹤群迁徙到取代了古代水路的沼泽边的草地，在那里跳舞、唱歌和养育它们笨拙的红褐色幼崽。它们虽然是鸟类，却不应该被称作小鸟，而是“小驹”。我无法解释为什么。你可以在六月一个露湿的早晨，去看它们在祖先的牧草地上跟着红棕色“母马”跳跃嬉戏，便会明白是为什么了。

不久前的某一年，一个穿着鹿皮衣的法国捕猎者把他的独木舟推到威胁着巨大沼泽地的一条泥沼堵塞的小溪。对于试图侵犯它们泥泞的栖息地的人，鹤群会大声粗俗地嘲笑他们。一或两世纪后，英国人乘着加盖的马车来了。他们在沼泽地边上长满树木的冰碛上开荒，种上玉米和荞麦。他们无意像伟大的可汗在察汗淖尔那样为养鹤而种植。而鹤却不问冰川、皇帝或拓荒者的意图。它们吃掉了谷物，一些恼怒的农民不愿意给予鹤对谷物的拥有权时，它们发出警告之声，飞过沼泽到另一个农场。

那个年代还没有苜蓿草，山里的农场只有少量的干草收成，旱年尤其如此。某个旱年，有人在落叶松林里

tamaracks. The burn grew up quickly to bluejoint grass, which, when cleared of dead trees, made a dependable hay meadow. After that, each August, men appeared to cut hay. In winter, after the cranes had gone South, they drove wagons over the frozen bogs and hauled hay to their farms in the hills. Yearly they plied the marsh with fire and axe, and in two short decades hay meadows dotted the whole expanse.

Each August when the haymakers came to pitch their camps, singing and drinking and lashing their teams with whip and tongue, the cranes whinnied to their colts and retreated to the far fastnesses. "Red shitepokes" the haymakers called them, from the rusty hue which at that season often stains the battleship-gray of crane plumage. After the hay was stacked and the marsh again their own, the cranes returned, to call down out of October skies the migrant flocks from Canada. Together they wheeled over the new cut stubbles and raided the corn until frosts gave the signal for the winter exodus.

These haymeadow days were the Arcadian age① for marsh dwellers. Man and beast, plant and soil lived on and with each other in mutual toleration, to the mutual benefit of all. The marsh might have kept on producing hay and prairie chickens, deer and muskrat, crane-music and cranberries forever.

The new overlords did not understand this. They did not include soil, plants, or birds in their ideas of mutuality. The dividends of such a balanced economy were too modest. They envisaged farms not only around, but in the marsh. An

放了一把火。大火过后迅速地长出了拂子茅草,清理掉死树后,那里便成了可靠的干草草场。自那以后,每年 8 月人们都会去那里割干草。冬天,鹤飞回南方,人们在冰冻的沼泽地上驾着马车,把山里收割的干草运到农场。每年他们用大火和斧头对待这片沼泽地,短短的 20 年干草牧场就遍布于整个广阔的区域。

每年 8 月,干草收割者在那里搭起帐篷,唱着歌、喝着酒,用鞭子鞭打和言语吆喝着他们的马队,鹤对它们的“小驹”发出轻微的嘶声,撤退到自己的阵地。干草收割者称它们为“红色沙丘鹤”,因为在那个季节它们的羽毛会从战舰般的银灰色变成红褐色。等干草都被堆成草垛,沼泽地又变成它们的了,鹤又回到这里,呼唤十月份的天空中正从加拿大迁徙回来的候鸟群。它们一起在新割的残茎上盘旋,袭击地里的玉米,直到霜冻降临,它们才从那里飞走。

这些干草牧场的岁月是沼泽地居住者田园牧歌式的时代。人和牲畜、植物和土地相互包容,为了集体相互的利益在这里共同生存。沼泽地会继续不断地生产干草、草原松鸡、鹿、麝鼠,鹤音乐般的鸣叫以及蔓越橘。

新的土地领主根本不懂这一点。他们的互惠观念中没有土地、植物或者鸟类的存在。那种平衡经济的利益太有限了。他们眼里所设想的农场不仅仅在周围,还包括 在 沼 泽 地

① arcadian:田园牧歌式的。阿卡迪亚(Arcadia)位于伯罗奔尼撒半岛,多里安人(Dorians)入侵希腊时(公元前 1100 年—公元前 1000 年)没被占领。因为与世隔绝而过着牧歌式生活,所以古希腊和古罗马的田园诗将其描绘成世外桃源。

epidemic of ditch-digging and land-booming set in. The marsh was grid-ironed (gridironed) with drainage canals, speckled with new fields and farmsteads.

中。挖沟渠、增加田地的做法迅速传播开来。沼泽被排水的渠道划分成很多格子,一眼望去,星星点点地分布着新开垦的田野和农场。

But crops were poor and beset by frosts, to which the expensive ditches added an aftermath of debt. Farmers moved out. Peat beds dried, shrank, caught fire. Sun-energy out of the Pleistocene shrouded the countryside in acrid smoke. No man raised his voice against the waste, only his nose against the smell. After a dry summer not even the winter snows could extinguish the smoldering marsh. Great pockmarks were burned into field and meadow, the scars reaching down to the sands of the old lake, peat-covered these hundred centuries. Rank weeds sprang out of the ashes, to be followed after a year or two by aspen scrub. The cranes were hard put, their numbers shrinking with the remnants of unburned meadow. For them, the song of the power shovel came near being an elegy. The high priests of progress knew nothing of cranes, and cared less. What is a species more or less among engineers? What good is an undrained marsh anyhow?

但是庄稼的收成很糟糕,且被霜冻包围着,昂贵的沟渠又增添了一笔债务。农民们都离开了。泥炭层干枯且萎缩了,引起了大火。来自更新世的太阳能用腐蚀性的烟雾覆盖着村庄。没有人提出反对浪费资源,只看到人们鼻子对气味的反感。经过一个干燥的夏天,就连冬天的雪都未能熄灭闷着燃烧的沼泽。田野和牧场上留下被燃烧的巨大印记,甚至延伸到老湖的沙地上,因为它曾被泥炭层覆盖了几个世纪。丛生的杂草从灰烬中长了出来,之后的一两年间又长出了山杨树丛。鹤的处境越来越艰难,在那片残余的未被燃烧过的草地上生存,它们的数目在缩减着。对于它们来说,掘土机工作的声音就像是一首挽歌。追求进步的大祭司对鹤一无所知,关心则更少。一个物种的多与少跟工程师有何相关?一个未干涸的沼泽对他们又有何益处?

For a decade or two crops grew poorer, fires deeper, wood-fields larger and cranes scarcer, year by year. Only reflooding, it appeared, could keep the peat from burning. Meanwhile, cranberry growers had, by plugging drainage ditches, reflooded a few spots and obtained good yields. Distant politicians bugled about marginal land, over-production, unemployment relief, conservation. Economists and planners came to look at the marsh. Surveyors, technicians, CCCs①, buzzed about. A

在十到二十年间,一年一年地,庄稼长得越来越差、火烧得越来越深入、林间的空地越来越大,鹤却越来越少。只有重新灌溉渠水,才能阻止泥炭层继续燃烧下去。同时,蔓越橘种植者要堵住排水渠,使一些地方重新灌满水才能获得好的产量。于是,远方的政治家开始大肆鼓吹边际土地、生产过剩、失业救济和自然保护。

① CCC(Civilian Conservation Corps):(美国)民间护林保土队,是美国在 1933—1942 年间,对 19~24 岁的单身救济户失业男性推行的以工代赈计划,提供人力劳动职缺,组织失业的年轻男性到联邦政府、各州与地方政府拥有的农村地带进行自然资源保育工作。

counter-epidemic of reflooding set in. Government bought land, resettled farmers, plugged ditches wholesale. Slowly the bogs are re-wetting. The fire pocks (firepocks) become ponds. Grass fires still burn, but they can no longer burn the wetted soil.

经济学家们和规划者们开始把眼光放到这片沼泽地上。接着勘测员、技术人员、护林保土队便蜂拥而至。一阵重新灌溉水渠的“流行病”开始了。政府购买土地，重新安置农民，大量地堵塞沟渠。渐渐地，沼泽地又恢复了潮湿。火坑变成了池塘。草原的火还在燃烧，但它们再也不能燃烧潮湿的土地。

All this, once the CCC camps were gone, was good for cranes, but not so the thickets of scrub popple that spread inexorably over the old burns, and still less the maze of new roads that inevitably follow governmental conservation. To build a road is so much simpler than to think of what the country really needs. A roadless marsh is seemingly as worthless to the alphabetical conservationist as an undrained one was to the empire-builders. Solitude, was one natural resource still undowered of alphabets, is so far recognized as valuable only by ornithologists and cranes.

所有这一切，一旦护林保土队撤离，是有利于鹤的，但事实上并非如此。灌木丛无情地遍布于被燃烧过的地方，还有在政府自然保卫队的带领下修建的迷宫似的道路。建造一条道路比去思考这个乡村真正需要什么简单得多。一个没有道路的沼泽地对所谓的自然资源保护者来说，就如同一个未排水的沼泽对帝国建筑师一样，是毫无价值的。荒野——一种还未被列入保护的自然资源，只有鸟类学家和鹤意识到它无穷的价值。

Thus always does history, whether of marsh or marketplace, end in paradox. The ultimate value in these marshes is wildness, and the crane is wildness incarnate. But all conservation of wildness is self-defeating, for to cherish we must see and fondle, and when enough have seen and fondled, there is no wilderness left to cherish.

因此，无论是沼泽或是市场的历史，都在自相矛盾中结束。沼泽地最大的价值在于荒野，而鹤则是荒野的化身。但是所有的荒野资源保护总是与自己的原来目的背道而驰。因为我们珍惜资源，我们必须去关心和爱护它，等到我们爱够了之后，才发现已经没有荒野给我们去珍惜了。

Some day, perhaps in the very process of our benefactions, perhaps in the fullness of geological time, the last crane will trumpet his farewell and spiral skyward from the great marsh. High out of the clouds will fall the sound of hunting horns, the baying of the phantom pack, the tinkle of little bells, and then a silence never to be broken, unless perchance in some far pasture of the Milky Way.

有朝一日，或许正当我们做着善行时，或许在地质成熟时期，最后一只鹤将会吹起离别的号角，盘旋着从巨大的沼泽地飞向天空。从遥远的云朵中传来狩猎的号声，猎狗幽怨的吠声，叮当的铃声，然后便是一片死寂。除了在银河上的某个遥远的牧场上偶尔会有些动静。

Thinking like a Mountain

A deep chesty bawl echoes from rimrock to rimrock, rolls down the mountain, and fades into the far blackness of the night. It is an outburst of wild defiant sorrow, and of contempt for all the adversities of the world.

Every living thing (and perhaps many a dead one as well) pays heed to that call. To the deer it is a reminder of the way of all flesh, to the pine a forecast of midnight scuffles and of blood upon the snow, to the coyote a promise of gleanings to come, to the cowman a threat of red ink at the bank, to the hunter a challenge of fang against bullet. Yet behind these obvious and immediate hopes and fears there lies a deeper meaning, known only to the mountain itself. Only the mountain has lived long enough to listen objectively to the howl of a wolf.

Those unable to decipher the hidden meaning know nevertheless that it is there, for it is felt in all wolf country, and distinguishes that country from all other land. It tingles in the spine of all who hear wolves by night, or who scan their tracks by day. Even without sight or sound of wolf, it is implicit in a hundred small events: the midnight whinny of a pack horse, the rattle of rolling rocks, the bound of a fleeing deer, the way shadows lie under the spruces. Only the ineducable tyro can fail to sense the presence or absence of wolves, or the fact that mountains have a secret opinion about them.

My own conviction on this score dates from the day I saw a wolf die. We were eating lunch on a high rimrock, at the foot of which a turbulent river elbowed its way. We saw what we thought was a doe fording the torrent, her breast awash in white water. When she climbed the bank toward us and

像山一样思考

一声深远的、骄傲的嚎叫,回荡在悬崖之中,在山谷中翻滚,消散在茫茫黑夜中。这是狂野般蔑视的悲哀和对世上一切苦难的藐视在情感上的迸发。

每个活着的生命(也许还有一些消逝的)都会留意到这个声音。对于鹿来说,这是死亡的警钟;对于松林来说,这是一场暗夜混战和血腥的预兆;对于郊狼来说,一场从中渔利的好机会即将来临;对于牧牛人来说,是银行赤字的威胁;对于狩猎者来说,是子弹与狼牙的一场较量。然而在眼前这些明显的希望和恐惧之后有更深一层的意义,只有大山自己知道其中的含义。也只有大山永久地屹立在那里,不带情感地倾听野狼的嚎叫。

即使无法辨识这叫声的隐藏含义,也都知道它的存在,因为在整个狼的领地都能感受到它,使得这个区域同其他地方区别开来。夜里听到狼的叫声或是白天搜索狼的踪迹的人,都会被狼的叫声刺痛脊骨。即便没有看到狼或只听到狼的嚎叫,你绝对可以从很多小细节中看出:午夜一群马轻微的嘶声,翻滚的石头的隆隆声,野鹿跳跃逃跑的声音,云杉映射的树影。只有无法感化的新手才对狼的存在与否毫无感觉,才体会不到大山隐藏着的关于狼的认识。

自从我亲眼目睹一条狼的死亡后,我开始确信这一点。当时我们正在一个很高的崖顶上吃午餐,山脚下一条湍流的河蜿蜒而过。我们看到一只母鹿(我们当时这样认为)涉过

shook out her tail, we realized our error: it was a wolf. A half-dozen others, evidently grown pups, sprang from the willows and all joined in a welcoming mêlée of wagging tails and playful maulings. What was literally a pile of wolves writhed and tumbled in the center of an open flat at the foot of our rimrock.

In those days we had never heard of passing up a chance to kill a wolf. In a second we were pumping lead into the pack, but with more excitement than accuracy: how to aim a steep downhill shot is always confusing. When our rifles were empty, the old wolf was down, and a pup was dragging a leg into impassable slide-rocks.

We reached the old wolf in time to watch a fierce green fire dying in her eyes. I realized then, and have known ever since, that there was something new to me in those eyes—something known only to her and to the mountain. I was young then, and full of trigger-itch; I thought that because fewer wolves meant more deer, that no wolves would mean hunters' paradise. But after seeing the green fire die, I sensed that neither the wolf nor the mountain agreed with such a view.

Since then I have lived to see state after state extirpate its wolves. I have watched the face of many a newly wolfless mountain, and seen the south-facing slopes wrinkle with a maze of new deer trails. I have seen every edible bush and seedling browsed, first to anaemic desuetude, and then to death. I have seen every edible tree defoliated to the height of a saddle-horn. Such a mountain looks as if someone had given God a new pruning shears, and forbidden Him all other exercise. In the end the starved bones of the hoped—for deer herd, dead of its own too-much, bleach with the bones of the dead sage, or molder under the high-lined junipers.

急流,水淹没过了她的胸部。当她爬过河畔向我们走来并摇着她的尾巴时,我们意识到自己错了:这是一只狼。另外还有五六只,显然是已经长大的狼崽,从柳树中蹿出来,摇着尾巴互相嬉戏打闹,加入一场欢迎式的战斗。这是一群真真切切的狼,在山脚下一块平坦的空地中间嬉戏扭打着。

那时候没有人会放过杀狼的机会。我们立刻对狼进行扫射,极度兴奋,根本不管有没有打中——我们也不太清楚怎样精准地瞄准陡峭的山下。我们的枪膛打空后,老狼倒下了,小狼拖着腿往封闭的岩石里躲。

随后我们走到老狼的身边,看到老狼眼中曾经凶猛的绿色火焰正在熄灭。从那以后我意识到,于我而言,在那双眼中意味着一些新的含义,一些只有她和大山知道的秘密。那时我还年轻,浑身散发着不动扳机就手痒的冲劲。我以为更少的狼就意味着更多的鹿可以生存,没有狼的地方便是猎人的天堂。但看过那条狼眼中绿色火焰熄灭后,我意识到狼和大山都不会同意这样的观点。

自那以后,我亲眼看着一个州接着一个州消灭了所有的狼。我看到那些狼群灭绝的山的新面貌,那个朝南的斜坡上布满鹿群踏出的迷宫般的小径。我看到所有可吃的灌木丛和树苗都被啃噬过,一开始是变得没有活力被废弃,然后就是枯死。我看到每个可吃的树,从地面到马鞍高度之间的叶子都被吃光。这样的山看起来像是有人给了上帝一把修枝剪,而且还禁止上帝做其他任何事。最终,饥饿的鹿群成群地死去,和那些

I now suspect that just as a deer herd lives in mortal fear of its wolves, so does a mountain live in mortal fear of its deer. And perhaps with better cause, for while a buck pulled down by wolves can be replaced in two or three years, a range pulled down by too many deer may fail of replacement in as many decades.

So also with cows. The cowman who cleans his range of wolves does not realize that he is taking over the wolf's job of trimming the herd to fit the range. He has not learned to think like a mountain. Hence we have dustbowls, and rivers washing the future into the sea.

We all strive for safety, prosperity, comfort, long life, and dullness. The deer strives with his supple legs, the cowman with trap and poison, the statesman with pen, the most of us with machines, votes, and dollars, but it all comes to the same thing: peace in our time. A measure of success in this is all well enough, and perhaps is a requisite to objective thinking, but too much safety seems to yield only danger in the long run. Perhaps this is behind Thoreau's dictum: In wildness is the salvation of the world. Perhaps this is the hidden meaning in the howl of the wolf, long known among mountains, but seldom perceived among men.

The Land Ethic

When god-like Odysseus returned from the wars in Troy, he hanged all on one rope a dozen slave-girls of his household whom he suspected of misbehavior during his absence.

This hanging involved no question of propriety. The girls were property. The disposal of property was then, as now, a matter of expediency, not of right and wrong.

枯死的鼠尾草一起化为白骨,或在高大的够不着的刺柏下腐烂。

我现在怀疑就像鹿群生活在对狼永久的恐惧中一样,大山也生活在对鹿的极度恐惧中。而且我们有理由相信,一只公鹿被狼吃掉后的两到三年内会被新的鹿取代,而被太多的鹿破坏的大山在几十年内都很难恢复它的原貌。

牛群也是如此。牧牛人清理掉他牧场里所有的狼,却没有意识到他是做取代狼调整牧群以达到平衡的工作。他没有学会像山一样思考。就是这样,沙尘暴产生了,洪水把希望卷入了大海里。

我们都在为安全、繁荣、舒适、长寿和长治久安而奋斗。鹿用它灵活的腿,牧牛人用陷阱和毒药,政治家用笔,我们中的大多数用机器、投票和美元斗争着,但我们所要的结果都是一样的:时代的和平。为成功付出的手段已经非常地好了,而且,也许是客观思考所必要的。但是,太过安全似乎隐藏着长远的危险。也许这正是梭罗这一断言的隐含意义:人类的救世主是大自然。也许这是狼嚎叫的所隐晦的含义,一直以来只有山能理解,却很少有人能感受到。

土地伦理

当尊贵的俄底修斯从特洛伊战争中返回家后,他将家里的 12 个女奴全部绞死,因为他怀疑当他不在家时这些女奴有越轨行为。

他对女奴施行的绞刑不会遭到任何质疑。她们是他的个人财产。如现在一样,对财产的处置仅仅是个人的选择,无所谓对与错。

Concepts of right and wrong were not lacking from Odysseus' Greece: witness the fidelity of his wife through the long years before at last his black-prowed galleys clove the wine-dark seas① for home. The ethical structure of that day covered wives, but had not yet been extended to human chattels. During the three thousands years which have since elapsed, ethical criteria have been extended to many fields of conduct, with corresponding shrinkages in those judged by expediency only.

在俄底修斯生活的希腊年代,也当然存在着对与错的观念:俄底修斯乘着黑色船头的大帆船穿过深深的大海回到家前,他妻子在漫长的岁月里对他的忠诚就是一个见证。在那个年代,伦理体系是适用于妻子的,还没有延伸到奴隶身上。在以后的3000年间,伦理标准被扩展到品行的许多方面,只是根据情况有相应的增减。

The Ethical Sequence

This extension of ethics, so far studied only by philosophers, is actually a process in ecological evolution. Its sequences may be described in ecological as well as in philosophical terms. An ethic, ecologically, is a limitation on freedom of action in the struggle for existence. An ethic, philosophically, is a differentiation of social from anti-social conduct. These are two definitions of one thing. The thing has its origin in the tendency of interdependent individuals or groups to evolve modes of co-operation. The ecologist calls these symbioses. Politics and economic are advanced symbioses in which the original free-for-all competition has been replaced, in part, by co-operative mechanisms with an ethical content.

The complexity of co-operative mechanisms has increased with population density, and with the efficiency of tools. It was simpler, for example, to define the anti-social uses of sticks and stones in the days of the mastodons than of bullets and billboards in the age of motors.

The first ethics dealt with the relation between individuals; the Mosaic Decalogue② is an example.

伦理的演变顺序

目前只有哲学家在研究,伦理关系在这方面的扩展事实上是生态演变的一个过程。生态和哲学术语都对伦理的演变顺序作过描述。从生态角度来讲,伦理是对在生存的斗争中行动自由的限制。从哲学角度讲,是社会与反社会行为的区别。这是对这个词的两种定义。伦理起源于互相依赖的个体或群体向合作模式发展的趋势。生态学者称其为共生现象。政治学与经济学是高级的共生,在此,有伦理意义的合作机制已经部分地取代了原始集体的自由竞争。

合作机制已经随着人口的增加和工具的有效应用变得越来越复杂。例如,定义棍棒和石头在乳齿像时代的反社会作用要比定义子弹和广告牌在发动机时代的反社会作用要简单得多。

最初的伦理关系处理得是个体

① wine-dark seas:酒暗海,荷马曾用过此词,意即深深的大海。

② Mosaic Decalogue:摩西十诫。据说是上帝在西奈山山顶亲自传达给摩西的,是上帝对以色列人的告诫。

Later accretions dealt with the relation between the individual and society. The Golden Rule① tries to integrate the individual to society; democracy to integrate social organization to the individual. There is as yet no ethic dealing with man's relation to land and to the animals and plants which grow upon it. Land, like Odysseus' slave-girls, is still property. The land-relation is still strictly economic, entailing privileges but not obligations.

之间的关系，比如摩西十诫。而后随着慢慢的发展涉及个体与社会之间的关系。黄金定律试图将个体统一到社会中；民主则努力将社会体制融合到个体中。迄今为止还没有产生处理人类与土地、与土地上生长的动物和植物之间关系的伦理观。土地，就像俄底修斯的女奴，仍只属于一种财产。人与土地之间的关系仍然是建立在经济基础上的，只会牵涉权益问题而不会尽任何义务。

The extension of ethics to this third element in human environment is, if I read the evidence correctly, an evolutionary possibility and an ecological necessity. It is the third step in a sequence. The first two have already been taken. Individual thinkers since the days of Ezekiel and Isaiah② have asserted that the despoliation of land is not only inexpedient but wrong. Society, however, has not yet affirmed their belief. I regard the present conservation movement as the embryo of such an affirmation.

如果我对这种现象理解正确的话，伦理观在人类环境中第三个元素的扩展是一种演变的可能性和生态的必然性。这是演变顺序中的第三个步骤，前面两步已经完成。自以西结和以赛亚时代以来，一些个体思想家就断言过对土地的掠夺不仅不明智且是错误的行为。然而，社会没有承认他们的信念。我把目前的环境保护运动看作确认这种信念的萌芽期。

An ethic may be regarded as a mode of guidance for meeting ecological situations so new or intricate, or involving such deferred reactions, that the path of social expediency is not discernible to the average individual. Animal instincts are modes of guidance for the individual in meeting such situations. Ethics are possibly a kind of community instinct in-the-making.

伦理可以被看作一种指导模式，以此认识全新或复杂的生态形势，或者参与到这类迟钝的反应中，而普通个体很难辨识清楚社会利益采取的方式。动物的本能是个体认识这些形势的指导模式。伦理也可能是一种正在形成的共同体的本能。

The Community Concept

All ethics so far evolved rest upon a single premise: that the individual is a member of a community of interdependent parts. His instincts

共同体的概念

目前发展的所有伦理都基于一个前提：个体是由互相依存的部分组成的共同体中的一员。他的本能

① The Golden Rule：黄金定律，是与伦理有关的品德，指人应具有同理心。
② Ezekiel and Isaiah：以西结和以赛亚，公元前 6 世纪时希伯来人的先知。

prompt him to compete for his place in that community, but his ethics prompt him also to cooperate (perhaps in order that there may be a place to compete for).

The land ethic simply enlarges the boundaries of the community to include soils, waters, plants, and animals, or collectively: the land.

This sounds simple: do we not already sing our love for and obligation to the land of the free and the home of the brave? Yes, but just what and whom do we love? Certainly not the soil, which we are sending helter-skelter downriver. Certainly not the waters, which we assume have no function except to turn turbines, float barges, and carry off sewage. Certainly not the plants, of which we exterminate whole communities without batting an eye. Certainly not the animals, of which we have already extirpated many of the largest and most beautiful species. A land ethic of course cannot prevent the alteration, management, and use of these "resources", but it does affirm their right to continued existence, and, at least in spots, their continued existence in a natural state.

In short, a land ethic changes the role of *Homo sapiens* from conqueror of the land-community to plain member and citizen of it. It implies respect for his fellow-members, and also respect for the community as such.

In human history, we have learned (I hope) that the conqueror role is eventually self-defeating. Why? Because it is implicit in such a role that the conqueror knows, excathedra, just what makes the community clock tick, and just what and who is valuable, and what and who is worthless, in community life. It always turns out that he knows neither, and this is why his conquests eventually defeat themselves.

促使其为自己在共同体中的一席之地而竞争,而他的伦理观念则促使他去合作(也许那样才能有可以竞争的资格)。

土地伦理只是扩大了共同体的范围,包括土壤、水、植物和动物,或者总称为土地。

这听起来很简单:我们不是已经歌颂过我们对自由之地和勇敢之家的热爱和责任了吗?是的,但我们爱的究竟是什么、又是谁呢?肯定不是土壤,因为我们正在不顾一切地把土壤冲到下游;也肯定不是水,因为在我们看来,水除了转动涡轮、承运船只和带走垃圾以外,没有什么用处;当然也不是植物,我们消灭了共同体中所有的植物也不会眨一下眼睛;也不是动物,我们已经导致了其中许多最大和最美的品种灭绝。当然,土地伦理不能阻止对这些"资源"的改变、管理和利用,但是土地伦理肯定会确认它们继续生存的权利,至少在某些方面,在自然状态下继续生存的权利。

总而言之,土地伦理将人类从土地共同体中征服者的角色转变为共同体中普通的一员和公民。它暗含着对每个成员的尊敬,也包括对这个共同体本身的尊敬。

在人类历史中,我们已经了解到(我希望我们知道)征服者最终都会走向自我毁灭的道路。为什么?因为毫无疑问,征服者就是权威,只有他知道什么使得共同体运行,什么是有价值的人或物,什么是无价值的人或物。结果是他什么都不知道,这也是为什么最终的征服会毁灭他们自己。

In the biotic community, a parallel situation exists. Abraham knew exactly what the land was for: it was to drip milk and honey into Abraham's mouth. At the present moment, the assurance with which we regard this assumption is inverse to the degree of our education.

在生物共同体内存在过类似的情况。亚伯拉罕确切地知道土地意味着什么:土地将牛奶和蜂蜜送到亚伯拉罕一家人的口中。如今,我们看待这个观点的不屑态度与我们的教育程度恰恰成反比。

The ordinary citizen today assumes that science knows what makes the community clock tick; the scientist is equally sure that he does not. He knows that the biotic mechanism is so complex that its workings may never be fully understood.

今天的普通公民认为科学知道什么使得共同体运行,而科学家确信他们根本不知道。科学家知道生物机制是如此的复杂,我们可能永远都不会完全地理解它的运行。

That man is, in fact, only a member of a biotic team is shown by an ecological interpretation of history. Many historical events, hitherto explained solely in terms of human enterprise, were actually biotic interactions between people and land. The characteristics of the land determined the facts quite as potently as the characteristics of the men who lived on it.

事实上,人类只是生物队伍中的一员,这是历史的生态解读所显示的。目前,许多从人类角度去解释的历史事件,其实是人与土地相互影响的结果。土地的特征有力地决定了生活在土地之上的人的特征。

Consider, for example, the settlement of the Mississippi valley. In the years following the Revolution, three groups were contending for its control: the native Indian, the French and English traders, and the American settlers. Historians wonder what would have happened if the English at Detroit had thrown a little more weight into the Indian side of those tipsy scales which decided the outcome of the colonial migration into the cane-lands of Kentucky. It is time now to ponder the fact that the cane-lands, when subjected to the particular mixture of forces represented by the cow, plow, fire, and axe of the pioneer, became bluegrass. What if the plant succession inherent in this dark and bloody ground had, under the impact of these forces, given us some worthless sedge, shrub, or weed? Would Boone and Kenton have

比如,我们来看看密西西比河流域居民的安置。在独立革命后的几年里,土著印第安人、英法商人和美国定居者三股力量为争夺这里的控制权而斗争。历史学家很想知道,如果底特律的英国人稍微将力量倾向印第安人一方,将会发生什么事?这种不稳的局面决定了后来殖民地的移民进入肯塔基州的野藤地。现在是该思考这样的事实了,当时野藤地遭受了拓荒者牛、犁、火和斧子的混合摧残后,逐渐演变成了蓝草地。如果植物本身的演替在这些力量的影响下,在这片黑暗和血腥的土地上只长出了毫无价值的莎草、灌木丛或野草,又会发生什么样的事呢?布恩和肯顿能坚持下来吗?会有大批移民

held out? Would there have been any overflow into Ohio, Indiana, Illinois, and Missouri? Any Louisiana Purchase①? Any transcontinental union of new states? Any Civil War?

Kentucky was one sentence in the drama of history. We are commonly told what the human actors in this drama tried to do, but we are seldom told that their success, or the lack of it, hung in large degree on the reaction of particular soils to the impact of the particular forces exerted by their occupancy. In the case of Kentucky, we do not even know where the bluegrass came from—whether it is a native species, or a stowaway from Europe.

Contrast the cane-lands with what hindsight tells us about the Southwest, where the pioneers were equally brave, resourceful, and persevering. The impact of occupancy here brought no bluegrass, or other plant fitted to withstand the bumps and buffetings of hard use. This region, when grazed by livestock, reverted through a series of more and more worthless grasses, shrubs, and weeds to a condition of unstable equilibrium. Each recession of plant types bred erosion; each increment to erosion bred a further recession of plants. The result today is a progressive and mutual deterioration, not only of plants and soils, but of the animal community subsisting thereon. The early settlers did not expect this: on the ciénegas of New Mexico some even cut ditches to hasten it. So subtle has been its progress that few residents of the region are aware of it. It is quite invisible to the tourist who finds this wrecked landscape colorful and charming (as indeed it is, but it bears scant

涌入俄亥俄、印第安纳、伊利诺斯和密苏里吗?还会发生路易斯安那的购买事件吗? 会有横贯大陆的新州的联合吗? 会发生内战吗?

肯塔基只是历史戏剧中的一句台词。我们一般都会被告知人类在这场戏剧中试图所做的,但却很少有人知道他们的成功与否,很大程度上取决于土地的反应,即土地对这些出于占有目的的特殊力量造成的影响的反应。就拿肯塔基来说,我们甚至都不知道这些蓝草是从哪里来的——它是本地物种还是从欧洲偷运过来的?

将野藤地与后来逐渐显现的西南地区拓荒者同样的勇敢、机智和坚忍相比,他们对这里的占有并没有带来蓝草地或其他能够经受碰撞和猛击的植物。这个地区,由于过度放牧,从越来越多无用的草、灌木丛和野草变成了不稳定的平衡状态。每次各种植物的衰落都会使得土壤流失,而土壤的流失又会造成进一步的植物衰落。现在结果是一种循序渐进的相互衰退,包括植物和土壤,还有勉强维持生存的动物。早期移民没有想到这样的情况:在新墨西哥的沼泽区,一些人甚至挖沟渠加速了水土的流失。这种局势的发展是如此的缓慢以至于当地的居民很少有人能意识到。对于旅游者来说,很难去发现这个被破坏的地区原是多么五彩斑斓和富有魅力(它的确是美丽

① 路易斯安那的购买(Louisiana Purchase)是美国西部领土扩张中的一个重大事件。1803 年,美国从法国以总价 1500 万美元购买面积达两百多万平方公里的路易斯安那,使美国的领土扩大到墨西哥湾。

resemblance to what it was in 1848).

This same landscape was "developed" once before, but with quite different results. The Pueblo Indians settled the Southwest in pre-Colombian times, but they happened not to be equipped with range livestock. Their civilization expired, but not because their land expired.

In India, regions devoid of any sod-forming grass have been settled, apparently without wrecking the land, by the simple expedient of carrying the grass to the cow, rather than vice versa. (Was this the result of some deep wisdom, or was it just good luck? I do not know.)

In short, the plant succession steered the course of history; the pioneer simply demonstrated, for good or ill, what successions inhered in the land. Is history taught in this spirit? It will be, once the concept of land as a community really penetrates our intellectual life.

The Ecological Conscience

Conservation is a state of harmony between men and land. Despite nearly a century of propaganda, conservation still proceeds at a snail's pace; progress still consists largely of letterhead pieties and convention oratory. On the back forty we still slip two steps backward for each forward stride.

The usual answer to this dilemma is "more conservation education". No one will debate this, but is it certain that only the volume of education needs stepping up? Is something lacking in the content as well?

It is difficult to give a fair summary of its content in brief form, but, as I understand it, the content is substantially this: obey the law, vote

和吸引人的,但它与 1848 年的样貌已经没有多少相似之处了)。

这个地区曾经也被"开发"过,却是不同的结果。在哥伦布发现新大陆之前,普布洛印第安人定居在西南地区,然而他们并没有靠放牧生存。如今他们的文明灭绝了,但不是因为土地而灭绝。

印第安人定居在没有草皮的地区,很显然他们没有破坏土地。很简单,他们是将草带给牛而不是让牛去破坏草。(这是深奥智慧的表现,还只是好运呢?我不知道。)

简而言之,植物演替引导着历史的进程。拓荒者只是,好心或是恶意地,证明了什么样的植物在土地上演替。历史是以这样的精神被传播的吗?是的,只要土地的概念被看作共同体的一员,历史就会渗透到我们的精神生活中。

生态学意识

资源保护是人与土地之间一种和谐的状态。尽管宣传了将近一个世纪,资源保护仍以蜗牛的速度缓慢前进着,取得的成果大部分只停留在书面承诺和口头宣传上。在过去的四十年里,我们依然是走一步退两步。

通常解决这种困境的答案是"更多的资源保护教育"。没有人会对此产生异议,但真能肯定只要加大教育的量就可以了?教育的内容没有什么缺陷吗?

我们很难简单地给这个内容做一个合理的总结,但我个人理解的内容实质上是这样的:遵守法律、行使

right, join some organizations, and practice what conservation is profitable on your own land; the government will do the rest.

Is not this formula too easy to accomplish anything worthwhile? It defines no right or wrong, assigns no obligation, calls for no sacrifice, implies no change in the current philosophy of values. In respect of land-use, it urges only enlightened self-interest. Just how far will such education take us? An example will perhaps yield a partial answer.

By 1930 it had become clear to all except the ecologically blind that southwestern Wisconsin's topsoil was slipping seaward. In 1933 the farmers were told that if they would adopt certain remedial practices for five years, the public would donate CCC labor to install them, plus the necessary machinery and materials. The offer was widely accepted, but the practices were widely forgotten when the five-year contract period was up. The farmers continued only those practices that yielded an immediate and visible economic gain for themselves.

This led to the idea that maybe farmers would learn more quickly if they themselves wrote the rules. Accordingly the Wisconsin Legislature in 1937 passed the Soil Conservation District Law. This said to farmers, in effect: *We, the public, will furnish you free technical service and loan you specialized machinery, if you will write your own rules for land-use. Each county may write its own rules, and these will have the force of* law. Nearly all the countries promptly organized to accept the proffered help, but after a decade of operation, no county has yet written a single rule. There has been visible progress in such practices as strip-

投票权、参加组织并在自己的土地上实践哪些资源保护是有益的;其余的事政府会去做的。

这个准则会不会太过简单而达不到任何有价值的效果?它无关对与错,没有规定责任,没有要求牺牲,也没用暗含对现有的哲学价值观做出改变。在土地使用方面,它只激励开明自利。这样的教育会把我们带到多远呢?下面这个例子也许会给出部分答案。

到了 1930 年,除了对生态毫无所知,所有人都很清楚威斯康星州西南部的表土层正在向大海流失。1933 年,农民们被告知,如果他们连续五年采取一些补救方案,政府会派国家资源保护队的成员帮他们安置,还包括必要的机器和材料。提议被广泛地接受了,然而五年合同期满后那些措施又被抛到脑后了。农民们又继续采用那些即时的、有利可图的方式。

这就导致一种观念,认为如果农民自己制定规则,也许他们会学得更快。于是,1937 年威斯康星立法机关通过了土壤保护区法令。实际上这告诉农民:如果你们对土地使用制定自己的规则,政府将会提供免费的技术服务,将专业的机器借给农民。每个县都可以制定自己的规则,这些规则将会拥有法律效力。几乎所有的州都迅速地组织接受了提供的帮助,但是经过十年的运行后,没有一个县制定出自己的规则。当然,在实践过程中也有看得见的进展,比如等

cropping①, pasture renovation, and soil liming, but none in fencing woodlots against grazing, and none in excluding plow and cow from steep slopes. The farmers, in short, have selected those remedial practices which were profitable anyhow, and ignored those which were profitable to the community, but not clearly profitable to themselves. When one asks why no rules have been written, one is told that the community is not yet ready to support them; education must precede rules. But the education actually in progress makes no mention of obligations to land over and above those dictated by self-interest. The net result is that we have more education but less soil, fewer healthy woods, and as many floods as in 1937.

The puzzling aspect of such situation is that the existence of obligations over and above self-interest is taken for granted in such rural community enterprises as the betterment of roads, school, churches, and baseball teams. Their existence is not taken for granted, nor as yet seriously discussed, in bettering the behavior of the water that falls on the land, or in the preserving of the beauty or diversity of the farm landscape. Land-use ethics are still governed wholly by economic self-interest, just as social ethics were a century ago.

To sum up: we asked the farmer to do what he conveniently could to save his soil, and he has done just that, and only that. The farmer who clears the woods off a 75 percent slope, turns his cows into the clearing, and dumps its rainfall, rocks, and soil into the community creek, is still (if otherwise decent) a respected member of society. If he puts lime on his fields and plants his crops on contour, he is still entitled to all the

高植物篱技术、牧场更新和土壤灰化,但是没有防护林地放牧,没有禁止在陡坡上进行犁耕和奶牛的践踏。简单而言,农民选择了有利益的补救措施,而忽视了对共同体有利但对他们自己无利的方法。当有人问为什么没有制定出任何规则,有人会告诉你共同体还没有准备好去支持这些规则,教育必须走在规则之前。但事实上,正在实行的教育中除了被私利支配的义务之外,丝毫没有提到对土地的责任。最终结果便是我们接受的教育越多,土地便越少,健康的树林也越少,而洪水则像 1937 年那时候一样多。

在这种情况下,令人疑惑的是,在自我利益之上的责任理所当然地被看作道路改良、学校、教堂以及棒球队这样的农村共同体建设。改善水流经土地的方式,保护农场的美丽和多样性,这些责任并没有被看成是理所当然的,也没有经过严肃的讨论。就像一个世纪前的社会伦理一样,土地利用伦理仍被自身的经济利益所完全控制。

总而言之,我们要求农民去做一些合宜却又能保护土壤的事,他会照做,而且只会做那一点点。那位砍掉 75 度陡坡上的树木,将他的奶牛赶进林间空地去放牧,将雨水、石块和土壤排进共同体的小河中的农民,仍然是社会上受尊敬的一员(同时也是正派的)。如果他将石灰撒到田里,将

① strip-cropping: 等高植物篱技术,指山丘、坡面上沿等高线按一定的间隔,以线状或条带状密植多年生灌木或草本植物,形成能挡水、挡土的篱笆墙以达到防治水土流失的技术。

privileges and emoluments of his Soil Conservation District. The District is a beautiful piece of social machinery, but it is coughing along on two cylinders because we have been too timid, and too anxious for quick success, to tell the farmer the true magnitude of his obligations. Obligations have no meaning without conscience, and the problem we face is the extension of the social conscience from people to land. No important change in ethics was ever accomplished without any internal change in our intellectual emphasis, loyalties, affections, and convictions. The proof that conservation has not yet touched these foundations of conduct lies in the fact that philosophy and religion have not yet heard of it. In our attempt to make conversation easy, we have made it trivial.

庄家种在等高线上,他仍旧可以享有土壤保护区法令给予的特权和报酬。这个法令是个漂亮的社会机器,但是它随着两个汽缸在咳嗽,因为我们太过胆怯,太急于求成而无法告诉农民责任的真正含义。没有道德理念,责任便失去了它的意义,我们所面临的问题是社会道德从人类到土地的扩展。当我们强调的理智、忠诚、情感和信念这一系列没有发生内部变化时,伦理不可能发生重大变化。哲学和宗教还没有听说过这个伦理观念,证明资源保护还没有触及这些最基本的品行。当我们尝试着让资源保护更加简单时,我们已经把它变得不重要了。

3. Questions for Discussion

(1) What is your understanding of Aldo Leopold's land ethic?

(2) What is your understanding of Aldo Leopold's advocacy of "Thinking like a Mountain"?

(3) Analyze a literary work by adopting ecocritical approach.

3. 讨论题

(1)你如何理解利奥帕德的土地伦理?

(2)你如何理解利奥帕德的"像山一样思考的"主张?

(3)用生态伦理批评方法分析一篇文学作品。

Chapter 12

1. Introduction to Roland Barthes

Roland Barthes (1915-1980) was a French literary critic, literary and social theorist, philosopher and semiologist. Barthes' works extended over many fields and he influenced the development of schools of theory including structuralism, semiology, existentialism, Marxism and post-structuralism.

Roland Barthes was born in the town of Cherbourg in Normandy. His father was a naval officer who was killed in a battle before Roland reached one year of age. Barthes was brought up by his mother, aunt and grandmother. Barthes studied classical letters, grammar, philology and Greek tragedy at the Sorbonne from 1935 to 1939, and during this time, he fell ill to tuberculosis, spending time in sanatoriums, unable to take certain qualifying examinations. In the following years, Barthes taught at many schools. From 1952 to 1959, he worked at the National Centre for Scientific Research, studying lexicology and

第12章

1. 罗兰·巴尔特简介

罗兰·巴尔特(1915—1980)是法国文学批评家、文学与社会理论家、哲学家和符号学家。巴尔特的著作涉及领域广泛,影响了结构主义、符号学、存在主义、马克思主义和后结构主义等理论流派的发展。

罗兰·巴尔特出生于法国诺曼底的瑟堡,父亲是一位海军军官,在他未满一岁时死于海战,此后巴尔特由母亲、姑姑和祖母共同抚养。1935—1939年间,巴尔特在索邦大学主修古典文学、语法、语文学和希腊悲剧,但在此期间,他患上肺结核,在多家疗养院治疗、休养,未能参加多门学业资格考试。之后多年,巴尔特在多所学校教书。1952—1959年,巴尔特在国家科学研究中心工作,研究词汇学和社会学。20世纪60年代,巴尔特专攻符号学和结构主义研究。

sociology. In the 1960s, Barthes explored the fields of semiology and structuralism. By the late 1960s, Barthes had established a reputation. Throughout the 1970s Barthes pursued his literary criticism, developing new ideas of textuality through his works. On February 25, 1980, Barthes was struck by a truck while walking home through the streets of Paris. He succumbed to his injuries, passing away on March 26.

到60年代末,巴尔特已声名鹊起。整个70年代,巴尔特致力于文学批评,在多部作品中阐发与文本性相关的新思想。1980年2月25日,巴尔特在巴黎街道步行回家途中,被卡车撞到。事故对其造成致命伤害,3月26日,巴尔特离开人世。

In his lifetime Barthes published 17 books and numerous articles, many of which were gathered to form collections. The influential works are *Writing Degree Zero* (1953), *Mythologies* (1957), *On Racine* (1963), *Elements of Semiology* (1964), *Criticism and Truth* (1966), *Death of the Author* (1968), *S/Z* (1970), *Empire of Signs* (1970), *New Critical Essays* (1972), *The Pleasure of the Text* (1975), *A Lover's Discourse* (1977), *Camera Lucida* (1980) and many others.

罗兰·巴尔特一生出版了17部著作和发表了大量的文章,多数文章以文集形式出版。影响深远的论著有:《写作的零度》(1953)、《神话学》(1957)、《论拉辛》(1963)、《符号学原理》(1964)、《批评与真理》(1966)、《作者之死》(1968)、《S/Z》(1970)、《符号帝国》(1970)、《新批评论文集》(1972)、《文之悦》(1975)、《恋人絮语》(1977)、《明室——摄影纵横谈》(1980)等。

"The Eiffel Tower" (1964) is an essay written for *The Eiffel Tower*, a collection of photos of the Eiffel Tower taken by photographer André Martin. This essay makes a thorough and marvelous analysis of the Eiffel Tower by using the basic semiological terms and points out various symbolic meanings of the tower. This essay is a typical example of Barthes' effort to put theory of semiology and structuralism into practice. Semiological practice is a way of reading for meanings and an experiment of decoding meaning exhaustively, while it is rather modest on the theoretical level. "The Eiffel Tower" is a successful case of adopting Ferdinand de Saussure's notion of the languistic sign composed of "signifier-signified" to social and cultural analysis by a semiologist and structuralist.

《埃菲尔铁塔》(1964)是罗兰·巴尔特为摄影师安德烈·马丁的摄影集《埃菲尔铁塔》而写的文章。这篇散文采用符号学基本概念对埃菲尔铁塔做了全面而精彩的分析,指出其各种象征意义。该文是巴尔特将符号学原理和结构主义理论运用于实践的优秀范文。符号学实践是一种意义解读法,是一种理论层次上相当谦逊而解读层次上相当细致的实验。《埃菲尔铁塔》是符号学和结构主义者将费尔迪南·德·索绪尔的语言符号"能指—所指"思想推广至社会文化分析的成功案例。

2. Full Text of "The Eiffel Tower"

The Eiffel Tower①

Roland Barthes

Maupassant often lunched at the restaurant in the tower, though he didn't care much for the food: *It's the only place in Paris*, he used to say, *where I don't have to see it*. And it's true that you must take endless precautions, in Paris, not to see the Eiffel Tower; whatever the season, through mist and cloud, on overcast days or in sunshine, in rain—wherever you are, whatever the landscape of roofs, domes, or branches separating you from it, the Tower is there; incorporated into daily life until you can no longer grant it any specific attribute, determined merely to persist, like a rock or the river, it is as literal as a phenomenon of nature whose meaning can be questioned to infinity but whose existence is incontestable. There is virtually no Parisian glance it fails to touch at some time of day; at the moment I begin writing these lines about it, the Tower is there, in front of me, framed by my window; and at the very moment the January night blurs it, apparently trying to make it invisible, to deny its presence, two little lights come on, winking gently as they revolve at its very tip: all this night, too, it will be there, connecting me above Paris to each of my friends that I know are seeing it: with it we all comprise a shifting figure of which it is the steady center: the Tower is friendly.

The Tower is also present to the entire world. First of all as a universal symbol of Paris, it is

2.《埃菲尔铁塔》全文

埃菲尔铁塔

罗兰·巴尔特

莫泊桑经常在埃菲尔铁塔的餐馆用午餐,尽管他并不太喜欢这里的食物。他说:"这是在巴黎唯一看不到铁塔的地方。"确实如此,在巴黎要是想看不见铁塔,你必须绞尽脑汁。无论什么季节,透过雾霭,乌云,阴暗,阳光或雨露;无论你在哪里;无论什么屋顶、穹顶、树枝构成的景致将你们隔开,铁塔始终在那儿。它融入我们的日常生活,直到你无法再赋予它任何其他属性。它坚强不息,像岩石,像河流,它毫不造作,仿如自然界的奇观。我们可以无休止地讨论它的意义,但它的存在却不容争辩。事实上,没有一个巴黎人在一天当中目光不会触及铁塔。此刻,在我开始写几行关于它的文字时,埃菲尔铁塔就在那儿,在我面前,窗户犹如它的画框。这时,一月的夜晚试图笼罩它,意欲使其模糊,否定它的存在。但两小盏灯亮了起来,微微地闪烁,旋转于铁塔的顶端。整个夜晚,它都在那儿,处于巴黎之上,将我和正在注视它的朋友们连接在一起。因为它,我们组成了一幅旋转的画面,而它就是这幅画面的稳定中心。埃菲尔铁塔是友善的。

埃菲尔铁塔也呈现在整个世界

① Selected from *The Eiffel Tower, and Other Mythologies*, translated by Richard Howard, Berkeley: University of California Press, 1997.

everywhere on the globe where Paris is to be stated as an image; from the Midwest to Australia, there is no journey to France which isn't made, somehow, in the Tower's name, no schoolbook, poster, or film about France which fails to propose it as the major sign of a people and of a place: it belongs to the universal language of travel. Further: beyond its strictly Parisian statement, it touches the most general human image-repertoire: its simple, primary shape confers upon it the vocation of an infinite cipher: in turn and according to the appeals of our imagination, the symbol of Paris, of modernity, of communication, of science or of the nineteenth century, rocket, stem, derrick, phallus, lightning rod or insect, confronting the great itineraries of our dreams, it is the inevitable sign; just as there is no Parisian glance which is not compelled to encounter it, there is no fantasy which fails, sooner or later, to acknowledge its form and to be nourished by it; pick up a pencil and let your hand, in other words your thoughts, wander, and it is often the Tower which will appear, reduced to that simple line whose sole mythic function is to join, as the poet says, base and summit, or again, earth and heaven.

This pure—virtually empty—sign—is ineluctable, because it means everything. In order to negate the Eiffel Tower (though the temptation to do so is rare, for this symbol offends nothing in us), you must, like Maupassant, get up on it and, so to speak, identify yourself with it. Like man himself, who is the only one not to know his own glance, the Tower is the only blind point of the total optical system of which it is the center and Paris the circumference. But in this movement which seems to limit it, the Tower acquires a new power: an object when we look at it, it becomes a lookout in its turn when we visit it, and now constitutes as an

面前。首先,它被公认为是巴黎的象征,它广泛地存在于凡是巴黎需要以画面表现出来的地方。从中西部到澳大利亚,任何一场去法国的旅行都是奔着它来的。从某种程度上讲,没有一本教科书、海报或电影这些有关法国的东西不是以埃菲尔铁塔为名将它作为一个民族或一个地方的主要标志:它是旅行中的通用语言。另外,除了严格作为巴黎的象征之外,它还广泛地触及了人类的想象力:它的简单外形激发了我们无尽的天赋想象力。通过我们想象力的呼唤,它成了巴黎的象征,现代化的象征,交流的象征,科学的象征,19世纪的象征,它也是火箭、立柱、铁塔、男性生殖器、避雷针、昆虫的象征。面对梦幻的日程,它是不可回避的标记。正如没有一个巴黎人的目光不会触及它一样。任何一种梦幻或早或晚都会承认它的形式,汲取它的营养。拿起一支铅笔,让你的手,换言之,让你的思想任意纵横,这时铁塔就出现了,它简化成一个简单的线条。它唯一的神话功能就是,正如诗人所说:连接顶与底,或者,天与地。

这个纯粹的——几乎是空的——标志——是不可避免的。因为它意味着一切。为了否定铁塔(尽管这种企图很少见,因为铁塔丝毫不冒犯我们),你必须像莫泊桑一样,登到塔顶与它融为一体。就像人类唯独不能注视自身的目光。铁塔也是整个视觉体系中的唯一盲点——铁塔是中心,巴黎是边围。但是在这场似乎限制它的运动当中,铁塔获取了新生的力量:当我们注视它时,它是一个物体;当我们参观它时,它是一

object, simultaneously extended and collected beneath it, that Paris which just now was looking at it. The Tower is an object which sees, a glance which is seen; it is a complete verb, both active and passive, in which no function, no voice (as we say in grammar, with a piquant ambiguity) is defective. This dialectic is not in the least banal, it makes the Tower a singular monument; for the world ordinarily produces either purely functional organisms (camera or eye) intended to see things but which then afford nothing to sight, what *sees* being mythically linked to what remains hidden (this is the theme of the voyeur), or else spectacles which themselves are blind and are left in the pure passivity of the visible. The Tower (and this is one of its mythic powers) transgresses this separation, this habitual divorce of seeing and being seen, it achieves a sovereign circulation between the two functions; it is a complete object which has, if one may say so, both sexes of sight. This radiant position in the order of perception gives it a prodigious propensity to meaning: the Tower attracts meaning, the way a lightning rod attracts thunderbolts; for all lovers of signification, it plays a glamorous part, that of a pure signifier, i. e., of a form in which men unceasingly put meaning (which they extract at will from their knowledge, their dreams, their history), without this meaning thereby ever being finite and fixed: who can say what the Tower will be for humanity tomorrow? But there can be no doubt it will always be something, and something of humanity itself. Glance, object, symbol, such is the infinite circuit of functions which permits it always to be something other and something much more than the Eiffel Tower.

In order to satisfy this great oneiric function, which makes it into a kind of total monument, the Tower must escape reason. The first condition of

个守望者。它把刚刚还在观望它的巴黎变成了身下既宽广又集中的对象。铁塔是自身能看的一个物体,又是被看的焦点。铁塔是一个完整动词,既可主动又可被动,其任何功能、语态都是完善的(就像在语法上巧妙而双关地所说的那样)。这种辩证法绝不是陈词滥调,它使铁塔成为独一无二的丰碑;因为通常而言世界或产生纯功能有机体(相机或眼睛),它们试图看见事物,但本身绝不出现在视觉里。看见的东西和隐蔽的东西总是神秘地联系着(这是偷窥的主题);或产生一些大场面,它们本身是盲目的,是纯粹的可视物。埃菲尔铁塔(神秘力量之一)违背了这种分离,看与被看的习惯性分离。它在这两种功能之间取得了高效循环。埃菲尔铁塔是一个完整的物体,可以这样说,它有视觉的两种性别。在知觉秩序中,这种光芒四射的位置赋予了它一个奇妙的意义倾向:铁塔吸引着意义,仿如避雷针吸引着雷电;对于一切意义爱好者来说,铁塔扮演着一个有魅力的角色,一个纯粹的角色,也是一种形式的角色,即在这种形式上,人类无休止地附加意义(他们任意从自己的知识、梦想、历史中附加意义),没有这些,意义因此被限定被固定。谁能够说:对于明天的人类而言,铁塔会是什么?但是毫无疑问它一定是某种东西,人类的某种东西。目光、物体、象征,它是各种功能的无限循环,这种循环总是使它成为埃菲尔铁塔之外和超出埃菲尔铁塔的东西。

为了满足使铁塔成为一种完全意义上丰碑的这种伟大功能,铁塔必

this victorious flight is that the Tower be an utterly useless monument. The Tower's inutility has always been obscurely felt to be a scandal, i.e., a truth, one that is precious and inadmissible. Even before it was built, it was blamed for being useless, which, it was believed at the time, was sufficient to condemn it; it was not in the spirit of a period commonly dedicated to rationality and to the empiricism of great bourgeois enterprises to endure the notion of a useless object (unless it was declaratively an *objet* d'art, which was also unthinkable in relation to the Tower); hence Gustave Eiffel①, in his own defense of his project in reply to the Artists' Petition, scrupulously lists all the future uses of the Tower: they are all, as we might expect of an engineer, scientific uses: aerodynamic measurements, studies of the resistance of substances, physiology of the climber, radio-electric research, problems of telecommunication, meteorological observations, etc.. These uses are doubtless incontestable, but they seem quite ridiculous alongside the overwhelming myth of the Tower, of the human meaning which it has assumed throughout the world. This is because here the utilitarian excuses, however ennobled they may be by the myth of Science, are nothing in comparison to the great imaginary function which enables men to be strictly human. Yet, as always, the gratuitous meaning of the work is never avowed directly: it is rationalized under the rubric of use: Eiffel saw his Tower in the form of a serious object, rational, useful; men return it to him in the form of a great baroque dream which quite naturally touches on the borders of the irrational.

须逃离现实。成功逃离现实的第一条件就是铁塔必须成为一个完全无用的丰碑。铁塔的无用性一直晦涩地被感觉是一桩丑闻,也是一个事实,而这恰恰弥足珍贵,是无可否认的。即使在修建之前,人们也谴责铁塔无用。在那个时候,这一点足够对其声讨定罪。那个时代的精神是忠实于理性和资产阶级伟大事业的经验论,那绝不能容忍铁塔的无用性(除非被明确宣布是一件艺术品,但这也不能想象和铁塔有何关系);因此古斯塔夫·埃菲尔在回应艺术家们的质问而捍卫自己的设计时,他小心翼翼地列举了铁塔未来的所有用途:正如一个工程师可能期待的那样,它们都是科学用途:空气动力学测试,物质耐用性研究,攀岩者生理研究,无线电流研究,通讯研究以及气象观察等。这些用途是毋庸置疑的,但比起铁塔的惊人的神话力量,和其在全世界的人文意义,这却是荒谬的。因为无论科学神秘性怎样使这种功利性借口更高尚,但是与铁塔能使人真正成为严格意义上的人类而言的伟大想象性功能相比,它是微不足道的。但是,作品的意外意义从不被直接宣称,它在使用过程中被合理化:埃菲尔视他的铁塔为严肃的、理性的、有用的物体,而人们认为它是伟大的巴洛克式梦幻,这个梦幻十分自然地触碰了非理性边缘。

① 古斯塔夫·埃菲尔(Gustave Eiffel, 1832-1923),法国著名建筑大师、结构工程师、金属结构专家,因设计巴黎的标志性建筑埃菲尔铁塔而闻名于世,被誉为"用铁创造了奇迹的人"。

This double movement is a profound one: architecture is always dream and function, expression of a utopia and instrument of a convenience. Even before the Tower's birth, the nineteenth century (especially in America and in England) had often dreamed of structures whose height would be astonishing, for the century was given to technological feats, and the conquest of the sky once again preyed upon humanity. In 1881, shortly before the Tower, a French architect had elaborated the project of a sun tower; now this project, quite mad technologically, since it relied on masonry and not on steel, also put itself under the warrant of a thoroughly empirical utility; on the one hand, a bonfire placed on top of the structure was to illuminate the darkness of every nook and cranny in Paris by a system of mirrors (a system that was undoubtedly a complex one!), and on the other, the last story of this sun tower (about 1,000 feet, like the Eiffel Tower) was to be reserved for a kind of sunroom, in which invalids would benefit from an air "as pure as in the mountains". And yet, here as in the case of the Tower, the naive utilitarianism of the enterprise is not separate from the oneiric, infinitely powerful function which, actually, inspires its creation: use never does anything but shelter meaning. Hence we might speak, among men, of a true Babel complex: Babel was supposed to serve to communicate with God, and yet Babel is a dream which touches much greater depths than that of the theological project; and just as this great ascensional dream, released from its utilitarian prop, is finally what remains in the countless Babels represented by the painters, as if the function of art were to reveal the profound uselessness of objects, just so the Tower, almost immediately disengaged from the scientific considerations which had authorized its birth (it matters very little here that the Tower should be in

这种双向运动是深刻的：建筑物永远既是梦想又是功能的体现者，既是某种乌托邦的表现，又是一种创造舒适的工具。甚至在铁塔诞生之前，19 世纪（特别是在美国和英国）的人们已经常常在梦想一种具有惊人高度的建筑物了，因为上一世纪对工业技术十分倾倒，于是对天空的征服愿望再一次俘获了人类。1881 年，正好在铁塔建筑之前，一位法国建筑师设计了一个太阳塔。现在看来，这个设计方案从技术上说是相当荒谬的，因为它依赖的是砖石结构而不是钢架结构，并且也以一种纯经验主义的功用性为理由。一方面，在建筑物顶端有烟火装置，它借助一组镜面（这套装置当然十分复杂）来照亮巴黎每一处黑暗的角落；另一方面，这个太阳塔（约一千英尺，与埃菲尔铁塔相仿）设计的最后一道幻想是一种关于日光浴室的，患者可以在室内呼吸到新鲜空气，“就像山中的空气一样纯净”。但是太阳塔的情形也像铁塔一样，建筑事业具有的单纯功利主义与无限强大的梦幻功能是分不开的，实际上鼓舞人们进行这种创造的正是后一动机：实用性除了掩饰意义之外别无所为。因此我们可以在人类中间，看到一种真正的通天塔情结：通天塔本应用于与上帝交流。然而这是一种梦想，它所触及的深度远超过神学构想的深度。摆脱了其功利性支柱的这种宏伟的升天梦想，最终存留在画家表现的无数个通天塔中，似乎艺术的功能只在于揭示物体的深刻的无用性。同样的，铁塔几乎完全认可其存在的科学考虑分离（在这里铁塔和其用途事实上并无多

fact useful), has arisen from a great human dream in which movable and infinite meanings are mingled: it has reconquered the basic uselessness which makes it live in men's imagination. At first, it was sought—so paradoxical is the notion of an empty monument—to make it into a "temple of Science"; but this is only a metaphor; as a matter of fact, the Tower is *nothing*, it achieves a kind of zero degree of the monument; it participates in no rite, in no cult, not even in Art; you cannot visit the Tower as a museum: there is nothing to see inside the Tower. This empty monument nevertheless receives each year twice as many visitors as the Louvre and considerably more than the largest movie house in Paris.

大关系),它产生于人类的一种宏伟的梦想,其中各种可变的和无限的意义混含在一起:铁塔重新克服了那种使其生存于人类想象中的基本无用性。最初,人们企图(因为一个空洞无用的纪念塔的概念是自相矛盾的)使其成为一个"科学庙堂",但它只是一个隐喻,实际上铁塔什么也不是;它达到了纪念塔的某种"零"状态,它不参与任何仪式或礼拜,甚至也不参与艺术。你不可能把铁塔当作一个博物馆去参观:在塔内毫无可看。但这座空的纪念塔每年接待的游客是卢浮宫两倍之多,比巴黎最大电影院的观众人数还多得多。

Then why do we visit the Eiffel Tower? No doubt in order to participate in a dream of which it is (and this is its originality) much more the crystallizer than the true object. The Tower is not a usual spectacle; to enter the Tower, to scale it, to run around its courses, is, in a manner both more elementary and more profound, to accede to a view and to explore the interior of an object (though an openwork one), to transform the touristic rite into an adventure of sight and of the intelligence. It is this double function I should like to speak of briefly, before passing in conclusion to the major symbolic function of the Tower, which is its final meaning.

为什么我们要参观铁塔呢?毫无疑问为了参与它的一个梦想(这也是它的独创之处),相比真正的物件而言,它更是一个梦想结晶体。铁塔不是一个寻常的景观,从一个更基础又更深刻的方式来看,参观它,攀登它,奔跑于它的周围是进入一种视野,探索物体的内在(尽管铁塔是透光的),将旅游习俗转化成目光与智力的探险。我应该简单地说说铁塔的双重功能,然后再总结它的更主要的象征功能,这就是它的最终意义。

The Tower looks at Paris. To visit the Tower is to get oneself up onto the balcony in order to perceive, comprehend, and savor a certain essence of Paris. And here again, the Tower is an original monument. Habitually, belvederes are outlooks upon nature, whose elements—waters, valleys, forests—they assemble beneath them, so that the tourism of the "fine view" infallibly implies a naturist mythology. Whereas the Tower overlooks not nature but the city; and yet, by its very

铁塔注视着巴黎。参观铁塔就是让人登上其露台感受、理解、欣赏巴黎的某种本质。在此铁塔又是一个原始的丰碑。习惯上而言,观望台是对自然的展望,自然的一切元素——水流、山谷、森林——它们都聚集在其下,以至于观光的"美景"必然暗示着自然主义神话。然而铁塔不仅俯瞰自然,它也注目城市。不

position of a visited outlook, the Tower makes the city into a kind of nature; it constitutes the swarming of men into a landscape, it adds to the frequently grim urban myth a romantic dimension, a harmony, a mitigation; by it, starting from it, the city joins up with the great natural themes which are offered to the curiosity of men: the ocean, the storm, the mountains, the snow, the rivers. To visit the Tower, then, is to enter into contact not with a historical Sacred, as is the case for the majority of monuments, but rather with a new nature, that of human space: the Tower is not a trace, a souvenir, in short a culture; but rather an immediate consumption of a humanity made natural by that glance which transforms it into space.

过,铁塔也是被观望的景致,通过这铁塔也使巴黎成了一个自然景观。它把拥挤的人群变成了景观,它给灰暗的城市神话增添了一丝浪漫、一缕和谐、一份宁静。由于它,城市融入了伟大的自然主题,满足了人类的好奇心:海洋、暴风雨、高山、白雪、河流。于是,去参观铁塔,就不是去和历史圣地神交,像参观大多数纪念碑时的情形那样,而是和人类空间的新的大自然亲和。铁塔不是痕迹,不是纪念物,不是文化,简言之,匆匆一瞥使它成了人类自然的直接消费,这一瞥把铁塔转换成了空间。

One might say that for this reason the Tower materializes an imagination which has had its first expression in literature (it is frequently the function of the great books to achieve in advance what technology will merely put into execution). The nineteenth century, fifty years before the Tower, produced indeed two works in which the (perhaps very old) fantasy of a panoramic vision received the guarantee of a major poetic writing (*écriture*); these are, on the one hand, the chapter of *Notre-Dame de Paris* (*The Hunchback of Notre Dame*)① devoted to a bird's-eye view of Paris, and on the other, Michelet's② *Tableau chronologique*. Now, what is admirable in these two great inclusive visions, one of Paris, the other of France, is that Hugo and Michelet clearly understood that to the marvelous mitigation of altitude the panoramic vision added an incomparable power of *intellection*: the bird's-eye view, which each visitor to the Tower can assume in an instant for his own, gives us the

有人会说由于这个原因,铁塔将首次流露在文学上的想象物质化了(它经常是伟大书本的功能,提前实现只能由技术才付诸实践的东西)。在 19 世纪,铁塔出现前的 50 年,确实产生了两部作品,在这两部作品中(也许很古老)全景观的梦幻获得了重要的诗意般写作的保证;一是《巴黎圣母院》中为鸟瞰巴黎而写的一章,另一个是米什莱的《法兰西风光》。在这两部伟大的鸟瞰景致中:一是巴黎,一是法兰西,值得赞叹的是对高度的美妙轻松的感觉给全景增加一种不可比拟的理解力,这点雨果和米什莱都十分清楚。参观铁塔的每一位游客都可以亲自体验一下鸟瞰,它给予了我们不仅仅能感受而且可以阅读的世界,这也是它符合视觉全新的敏感度的原因。在过去,旅

① 《巴黎圣母院》(*The Hunchback of Notre Dame*, 1831),雨果第一部浪漫主义小说。
② 儒勒·米什莱(Jules Michelet, 1798-1874),法国历史学家,他以文学风格的语言来撰写历史著作。

world to read and not only to perceive; this is why it corresponds to a new sensibility of vision; in the past, to travel (we may recall certain—admirable, moreover—promenades of Rousseau①) was to be thrust into the midst of sensation, to perceive only a kind of tidal wave of things; the bird's-eye view, on the contrary, represented by our romantic writers as if they had anticipated both the construction of the Tower and the birth of aviation, permits us to transcend sensation and to see things *in their structure*. Hence it is the advent of a new perception, of an intellectualist mode, which these literatures and these architectures of vision mark out (born in the same century and probably from the same history): Paris and France become under Hugo's pen and Michelet's (and under the glance of the Tower) intelligible objects, yet without—and this is what is new—losing anything of their materiality; a new category appears, that of concrete abstraction; this, moreover, is the meaning which we can give today to the word *structure*; a corpus of intelligent forms.

游(我们可能想到——令人赞赏的卢梭的漫步)就是融入感觉之中,仅仅去感受浪潮般扑面而来的事物;相反,浪漫主义作家笔下的鸟瞰能使我们穿越感知,看清事物内质,浪漫主义作家们好像预料了铁塔的建造和飞行器的诞生。因此,它是新的感知,新的知性模式的到来,这些文学和视觉建筑物标志着(出生于同一世纪,可能来自同一历史):巴黎和法国变成了雨果和米什莱笔下的可理解物,却不会失去它们的物质性——这一点也是新的;一种新的具体的抽象的范畴出现了;此外,这也是今天我们赋予结构一词的意义:结构,即一组富有智力的形式。

Like Monsieur Jourdain② confronted with prose, every visitor to the Tower makes structuralism without knowing it (which does not keep prose and structure from existing all the same); in Paris spread out beneath him, he spontaneously distinguishes separate—because known—points—and yet does not stop linking them, perceiving them within a great functional space; in short, he separates and groups; Paris offers itself to him as an object virtually *prepared*, exposed to the intelligence, but which he must himself construct by a final activity of the mind: nothing less passive than the *overall view* the Tower

就像茹尔丹先生面对散文一样,每个参观铁塔的游客都在毫不知情的情况下创建了结构主义(这并不阻止散文和结构同时存在);巴黎在其身下延伸,他不自觉地区分不同的点——因为众所周知,但又不停地将其联系起来,在一个伟大的功能性空间中感知它。简而言之,游客在进行区分和组合巴黎。事实上,巴黎将自己作为一个精心准备的物体呈现在游客面前,展露出智慧。但游客脑海必须经过最后一番思虑才能构建它。

① 卢梭(Jean Jacques Rousseau,1712-1778),法国启蒙思想家之一。
② 茹尔丹先生(Monsieur Jourdain),法国剧作家莫里哀(Molière,1622-1673)的戏剧《贵人迷》(*The Middle Class Gentleman*,1670)中的主人公。

gives to Paris. This activity of the mind, conveyed by the tourist's modest glance, has a name: decipherment.

What, in fact, is a panorama? An image we attempt to decipher, in which we try to recognize known sites, to identify landmarks. Take some view of Paris taken from the Eiffel Tower; here you make out the hill sloping down from Chaillot, there the Bois de Boulogne①; but where is the Arc de Triomphe②? You don't see it, and this absence compels you to inspect the panorama once again, to look for this point which is missing in your structure; your knowledge (the knowledge you may have of Parisian topography) struggles with your perception, and in a sense, that is what intelligence is: to *reconstitute*, to make memory and sensation cooperate so as to produce in your mind a simulacrum of Paris, of which the elements are in front of you, real, ancestral, but nonetheless disoriented by the total space in which they are given to you, for this space was unknown to you. Hence we approach the complex, dialectical nature of all panoramic vision; on the one hand, it is a euphoric vision, for it can slide slowly, lightly the entire length of a continuous image of Paris, and initially no "accident" manages to interrupt this great layer of mineral and vegetal strata, perceived in the distance in the bliss of altitude; but, on the other hand, this very continuity engages the mind in a certain struggle, it seeks to be deciphered, we must find signs within it, a familiarity proceeding from history and from myth; this is why a panorama can never be consumed as a work of art, the aesthetic interest of a painting ceasing once we try to recognize in it particular points derived from our

没有东西比铁塔目视整个巴黎更为主动了。游客谦虚的一瞥传达的心智活动有一个名称:解读。

究竟何为全景呢?一个我们试图解读的意象,在此我们尽力去辨别已知地址,鉴定地标。让我们以铁塔上看到巴黎的某些景观为例,你可以辨别出这儿是从夏约倾斜而下的山丘,那儿是布洛涅森林;但是哪儿才是巴黎凯旋门呢?你看不见它,这个缺失强迫你再次审视全景,寻找在你结构中消失的这个点;你的知识(关于巴黎地势的知识)和你的感知斗争着,从某种意义上讲,这便是智慧:重新构建,让你的记忆和感知合作以至于在你脑海里产生一个巴黎的幻影,它所有的元素都呈现在你面前,真实的,祖传的,然而在传递给你的整个空间中迷失了方向,因为你对这一空间是未知的。由此我们贴近了全景观复杂辩证的属性,一方面,它是一种欢快的景观,轻快缓慢地流动于巴黎的持续意象中,一开始,没有"意外"来破坏由矿物景象和植物景象构成的伟大场面,这是你从远处居高临下的喜悦中感知的;但是,另一方面,这种持续使心灵又进入某种斗争中,它寻求被解读,我们必须在其中发现标志,来自历史和神话的熟悉性;这也是一个全景不能被当做一件艺术品消费的原因,一旦我们以自身知识试图辨认一幅绘画的特殊点时,这幅画的审美意趣会立即停止;延伸在埃菲尔铁塔脚下的巴黎有一种美

① 布洛涅森林(Bois de Boulogne),巴黎西部的公园,位于塞纳河畔讷伊和布洛涅-比扬古之间,18世纪起向公众开放。

② 巴黎凯旋门(Arc de Triomphe),位于法国巴黎的戴高乐广场中央,香榭丽舍大街的西端。

knowledge; to say that there is a beauty to Paris stretched out at the feet of the Tower is doubtless to acknowledge this euphoria of aerial vision which recognizes nothing other than a nicely connected space; but it is also to mask the quite intellectual effort of the eye before an object which requires to be divided up, identified, reattached to memory; for the bliss of sensation (nothing happier than a lofty outlook) does not suffice to elude the questioning nature of the mind before any image.

是确定无疑的,也就是承认空间视觉带来的欢快性,这种视觉只认可一种完美连接的空间;面对一个要求被分裂、鉴定、重新属于记忆的物体时,这也要掩盖眼光的智力活动;因为感觉的欢快(没有比居高临下的观望更幸福的事了)不足以消除在任何意象前出现的心灵质疑性。

This generally intellectual character of the panoramic vision is further attested by the following phenomenon, which Hugo and Michelet had moreover made into the mainspring of their bird's-eye views: to perceive Paris from above is infallibly to imagine a history; from the top of the Tower, the mind finds itself dreaming of the mutation of the landscape which it has before its eyes; through the astonishment of space, it plunges into the mystery of time, lets itself be affected by a kind of spontaneous anamnesis: it is duration itself which becomes panoramic. Let us put ourselves back (no difficult task) at the level of an average knowledge, an ordinary question put to the panorama of Paris; four great moments immediately leap out to our vision, i.e., to our consciousness. The first is that of prehistory; Paris was then covered by a layer of water, out of which barely emerged a few solid points; set on the Tower's first floor, the visitor would have had his nose level with the waves and would have seen only some scattered islets, the Etoile①, the Pantheon②, a wooded island which was Montmartre and two blue stakes in the distance, the towers of Notre-Dame, then to his left, bordering this huge lake, the slopes of Mont

全景观的普遍智力特征被接下来的景象进一步证明,雨果和米什莱使之成为鸟瞰景观中的主流:从上空感悟巴黎必然想到历史;从塔顶俯瞰时,心灵会幻想在它眼前出现的地形变化;通过空间的奇异性,它陷入了历史迷雾中,放任自己受制于一种自发的回忆:在此过程中它变成全景性。让我们回到(这并非难事)一般知识水平上去,提出一个关于巴黎全景性的普通问题:四个重要的时刻立即出现在我们视觉中,也就是我们的意识中。第一,在前历史时代,巴黎还置身于一片汪洋大海中,水面之上零星出现了几块陆地;站在铁塔的第一层,游客的鼻子和当年的水流恰好齐平,他也只能看见一些零星的小岛,埃杜瓦勒、先贤祠,树木繁盛的是蒙特马尔小岛,远处两个蓝色的立柱,巴黎圣母院塔楼,在他的左边,是靠近大湖边的瓦勒里安山的斜坡;相反,今天将自己置身于显赫高度的游客将会在烟雾缭绕的天气里看见铁塔的最高两层从水面上浮现出来;铁

① 埃杜瓦勒(Etoile)是凯旋门所在之地的名称。

② 先贤祠(le Pantheon),位于巴黎市中心塞纳河左岸的拉丁区,于1791年建成,是永久纪念法国历史名人的圣殿。

Valérien; and conversely, the traveler who chooses to put himself today on the heights of this eminence, in foggy weather, would see emerging the two upper stories of the Tower from a liquid base; this prehistoric relation of the Tower and the water has been, so to speak, symbolically maintained down to our own days, for the Tower is partly built on a thin arm of the Seine filled in (up to the Rue de l'Université) and it still seems to rise from a gesture of the river whose bridges it guards. The second history which lies before the Tower's gaze is the Middle Ages; Cocteau once said that the Tower was the Notre-Dame of the Left Bank; though the Cathedral of Paris is not the highest of the city's monuments (the Invalides, the Pantheon, Sacré-Coeur are higher), it forms with the tower a pair, a symbolic couple, recognized, so to speak, by Tourist folklore, which readily reduces Paris to its Tower and its Cathedral: a symbol articulated on the opposition of the past (the Middle Ages always represent a dense time) and the present, of stone, old as the world, and metal, sign of modernity. The third moment that can be read from the Tower is that of a broad history, undifferentiated since it proceeds from the Monarchy to the Empire, from the Invalides to the Arc de Triomphe: this is strictly the history of France, as it is experienced by French schoolchildren, and of which many episodes, present in every schoolboy memory, touch Paris. Finally, the Tower surveys a fourth history of Paris, the one which is being made now; certain modern monuments (UNESCO, the Radio-Télévision building) are beginning to set signs of the future within its space; the Tower permits harmonizing these unaccommodated substances (glass, metal), these new forms, with the stones and domes of the past; Paris, in its duration, under the Tower's gaze, composes itself like an

塔与水的史前关系可以说象征性地维持到了当下,因为铁塔建立在已填实的塞纳河(直到大学路)的一条细小支流上,它似乎从河流上跃起,保护着每一座桥梁。出现在铁塔面前的第二段历史是中世纪,科可多说过,铁塔是塞纳河左岸的巴黎圣母院,尽管巴黎圣母院不是巴黎古建筑中最高者(荣军院,先贤祠,圣心教堂都比它高),但是它和铁塔组成了象征性的一对,可以说,它为旅游民俗学认可,认为埃菲尔铁塔和巴黎圣母院就是巴黎的浓缩:一个象征,建立于过去(中世纪是一个密集的时间)和现实的对立,石头(同世界一样悠久)和金属(现代化标志)的对立。从铁塔身上看出的第三个历史是一个广泛、难以区分的历史,因为它从君主时代到帝国时代,从荣军院到凯旋门:这才是严格意义上的法兰西历史,就像法国儿童经历的那样,法国的每一段历史都呈现在孩子记忆深处,触及着巴黎。最后,铁塔还注视着巴黎的第四段历史时期,一段正被塑造的历史;一些现代丰碑(联合国教科文大厦,广播大厦)开始在它的空间中树立未来标志:铁塔能够将不合时宜的物质(玻璃,金属)、新的形式和过去的石头、屋顶相协调;在铁塔的注视下,在漫长的历史中,巴黎混合成一块抽象的帆布,在这块帆布上,黑色的椭圆形(从遥远的过去流传下来的)和现代建筑的白色长方形交错并列着。

abstract canvas in which dark oblongs (derived from a very old past) are contiguous with the white rectangles of modern architecture.

Once these points of history and of space are established by the eye, from the top of the Tower, the imagination continues filling out the Parisian panorama, giving it its structure; but what then intervenes are certain human functions; like the devil Asmodeus①, by rising above Paris, the visitor to the Tower has the illusion of raising the enormous lid which covers the private life of millions of human beings; the city then becomes an intimacy whose functions, i.e., whose connections he deciphers; on the great polar axis, perpendicular to the horizontal curve of the river, three zones stacked one after the other, as though along a prone body, three functions of human life: at the top, at the foot of Montmartre, pleasure; at the center, around the Opéra, materiality, business, commerce; toward the bottom, at the foot of the Pantheon, knowledge, study; then, to the right and left, enveloping this vital axis like two protective muffs, two large zones of habitation, one residential, the other blue-collar; still farther, two wooded strips, Boulogne and Vincennes. It has been observed that a kind of very old law incites cities to develop toward the west, in the direction of the setting sun; it is on this side that the wealth of the fine neighborhoods proceeds, the east remaining the site of poverty; the Tower, by its very implantation, seems to follow this movement discreetly; one might say that it accompanies Paris in this westward shift, which our capital does not escape, and that it even invites the city toward its pole of development, to the south and to the west, where the sun is warmer, thereby participating in

一旦从塔顶看到这些历史和空间的点,想象力会继续填满巴黎全景,赋予它结构;但人类的某些功能也会起干扰作用;像从巴黎升起的魔王阿斯莫德,参观铁塔的游客幻想揭开隐藏着成千上万人类私生活的巨大盖子;于是城市变成了游客想解读它的功能,即联系的隐私。在垂直于塞纳河水平面的一条大轴线上,分布着紧密相连的三大区域,好像一个俯卧的人身上,分布着人类生活的三大功能:顶端,也即蒙特马尔地面,是快乐;中间,即歌剧院附近,是物质,商业;末端,即先贤祠脚下,是知识,学问;然后左右两侧,有两大块居民区,像两个保护套覆盖在这条伟大的轴线上,一侧是居民区,另一侧是劳动区;再远一点,有两片绿化带,即布朗宁公园和万赛公园。据观察,一种古老的自然法则促使巴黎向西,即从太阳落山的地方发展;在西区居民财富上升,而东区依旧贫困;铁塔通过这种移植似乎小心翼翼地跟随这一运动;有人说在这向西的运动中铁塔伴随着巴黎,我们的首都也未逃离,铁塔甚至邀请巴黎向极端发展,向南向西,那儿太阳更温暖,参与着使每个城市变成一个居住区的伟大神秘功能:铁塔既无大脑,又无器官,它坐落在偏于巴黎市区一点的地方,铁塔仅仅是目击者,用它微弱的信号,小心翼翼地注视着巴黎空间的整个地理、历史和社会结构。由铁塔的目

① Asmodeus:阿斯莫德,(犹太教鬼魔学中的)魔王。

that great mythic function which makes every city into a living being: neither brain nor organ, situated a little apart from its vital zones, the Tower is merely the witness, the gaze which discreetly fixes, with its slender signal, the whole structure geographical, historical, and social—of Paris space. This deciphering of Paris, performed by the Tower's gaze, is not only an act of the mind, it is also an initiation. To climb the Tower in order to contemplate Paris from it is the equivalent of that first journey, by which the young man from the provinces went up to Paris, in order to conquer the city. At the age of twelve, young Eiffel himself took the diligence from Dijon with his mother and discovered the "magic" of Paris. The city, a kind of superlative capital, summons up that movement of accession to a superior order of pleasures, of values, of arts and luxuries; it is a kind of precious world of which knowledge makes the man, marks an entrance into a true life of passions and responsibilities; it is this myth—no doubt a very old one—which the trip to the Tower still allows us to suggest; for the tourist who climbs the Tower, however mild he may be, Paris laid out before his eyes by an individual and deliberate act of contemplation is still something of the Paris confronted, defied, possessed by Rastignac. Hence, of all the sites visited by the foreigner or the provincial, the Tower is the first obligatory monument; it is a Gateway, it marks the transition to a knowledge: one must sacrifice to the Tower by a rite of inclusion from which, precisely, the Parisian alone can excuse himself, the Tower is indeed the site which allows one to be incorporated into a race, and when it regards Paris, it is the very essence of the capital, it gathers up and proffers to the foreigner who has paid to it his initiational tribute.

光来解释巴黎不仅仅是精神行为,而且也是一个参与仪式。登上铁塔来审视巴黎就仿如是从省城来到巴黎从而想征服它的年轻人的首次旅程。埃菲尔 12 岁的时候和母亲从第戎辛苦来到巴黎时,就发现到了巴黎的神奇魅力。巴黎,作为最高首府,呼唤着一场通向更快乐、更有价值、艺术和繁华境界的运动;这是一个知识造就人类的珍贵世界,并标志着你进入了激情的、有责任的真实生活;登上铁塔让我们想到这无疑是一个古老的神话;登上铁塔的游客,无论他多么温和,经过独特的深思熟虑展现在他面前的巴黎仍是被拉斯帝列所面对、所反抗、所占有的巴黎。因此,凡是外国人和外省人参观的遗址,铁塔是第一个必须被参观的纪念物。它是一座大门,标志着向知识的过渡:一个人必须通过包容仪式来祭奠铁塔,确切说,而仅仅只有巴黎人才能找到借口避开,铁塔实际上是一个能使人融入群体的场所,当它注视巴黎时,它聚集了首都的精华,将其展示给已经支付了参观费用的外国人。

From Paris contemplated, we must now work our way back toward the Tower itself: the Tower which will live its life as an object (before being mobilized as a symbol). Ordinarily, for the tourist, every object is first of all an *inside*, for there is no visit without the exploration of an enclosed space: to visit a church, a museum, a palace is first of all to shut oneself up, to "make the rounds" of an interior, a little in the manner of an owner: every exploration is an appropriation; this tour of the inside corresponds, moreover, to the question raised by the outside: the monument is a riddle, to enter it is to solve, to possess it; here we recognize in the tourist visit that initiational function we have just invoked apropos of the trip to the Tower; the cohort of visitors which is enclosed by a monument and processionally follows its internal meanders before coming back outside is quite like the neophyte who, in order to accede to the initiate's status, is obliged to traverse a dark and unfamiliar route within the initatory edifice. In the religious protocol as in the tourist enterprise, being enclosed is therefore a function of the rite. Here, too, the Tower is a paradoxical object: one cannot be shut up within it since what defines the Tower is its longilineal form and its open structure: How can you be enclosed within emptiness, how can you visit a line? Yet incontestably the Tower is visited: we linger within it, before using it as an observatory. What is happening? What becomes of the great exploratory function of the *inside* when it is applied to this empty and depthless monument which might be said to consist entirely of an exterior substance?

现在我们必须从被审视的巴黎回到铁塔本身,铁塔作为一件物体而活(在成为象征之前)。一般对于游客而言,各物首先都是内在,因为每次旅行都会探索内部空间:参观教堂、博物馆、宫殿首先就是将自己关进去,再有点像个主人的样子围着物体内部绕圈子:每次探索都是一次占有;内在观光和外在提出的问题相呼应:纪念物是一个谜团,进入就是去探索、去占有;在参观过程中我们意识到刚刚提到参观铁塔的仪式性功能;一大群游客聚集在纪念物中,在其内部蜿蜒而行,最终走出纪念物,这就像一个新教徒,为了达到始创地位,他必须在仪式大厦里穿过一条又黑又不熟悉的路径。宗教仪式就像旅游一样,入内是一种仪式功能。然而,铁塔也是一个自相矛盾的物体:人不能被约束其中,因为造就铁塔的是高耸的框架和开放的结构:你怎能受困于空旷之中呢?你怎能参观一根线条呢?但毫无争辩的是铁塔还是被人参观了:在视它为观望台之前人们在其内流连忘返。那时发生什么了呢?当它用于空旷的、深邃的纪念物时,这个纪念物可以说完全是由外在物质构成的,那么内在的伟大探索功能变成什么了呢?

In order to understand how the modern visitor adapts himself to the paradoxical monument which is offered to his imagination, we need merely observe what the Tower gives him, insofar as one sees in it an object and no longer a lookout. On this

为了弄清现代游客是怎样适应于这个提供其想象力、自相矛盾的纪念物,我们只需观察铁塔赋予了它什么?因为人们在其身上看到的只是

point, the Tower's provisions are of two kinds. The first is of a technical order; the Tower offers for consumption a certain number of performances, or, if one prefers, of paradoxes, and the visitor then becomes an engineer by proxy; these are, first of all, the four bases, and especially (for enormity does not astonish) the exaggeratedly oblique insertion of the metal pillars in the mineral mass; this obliquity is curious insofar as it gives birth to an upright form, whose very verticality absorbs its departure in slanting forms, and here there is a kind of agreeable challenge for the visitor; then come the elevators, quite surprising by their obliquity, for the ordinary imagination requires that what rises mechanically slide along a vertical axis; and for anyone who takes the stairs, there is the enlarged spectacle of all the details, plates, beams, bolts, which make the Tower, the surprise of seeing how this rectilinear form, which is consumed in every corner of Paris as a pure line, is composed of countless segments, interlinked, crossed, divergent: an operation of reducing an appearance (the straight line) to its contrary reality (a lacework of broken substances), a kind of demystification provided by simple enlargement of the level of perception, as in those photographs in which the curve of a face, by enlargement, appears to be formed of a thousand tiny squares variously illuminated. Thus the Tower—as—object furnishes its observer, provided he insinuates himself into it, a whole series of paradoxes, the delectable contraction of an appearance and of its contrary reality.

个物体而不是景观。就此而言,铁塔所提供给人的东西有两个方面。一方面是技术上的。铁塔让人消费一定数量的技术效能,或者说一定数量的反常事物,于是参观者就间接地变成了工程师。首先,这里有四块基石,尤其是金属柱子(庞大但并不惊奇)极其夸张地倾斜插入岩石之中;这种倾斜很奇特,它催生了一种垂直的形式,这个垂直承受了倾斜中的分离,这里还有让游客欣悦的挑战;接下来的是电梯,倾斜的让人惊奇,因为一般的想象认为只能沿着垂直的轴线作机械滑行上升;对爬楼梯的人来说,正是钢板、横梁、螺栓等这些所有细节的放大景观构成了铁塔,他们惊奇地发现这个垂直的框架如何由无数交织的、叠加的、散射的碎片构成,这个框架从巴黎各个角度看来都像是一个纯粹的线条:这是一种将其外观(垂直线条)缩减为对立现实(零碎材料组成的网状物)的操作,这是一个单纯放大感知水平的阐释,正如照片中的脸部曲线,通过放大,将会出现由一千个五彩斑斓的细小方块组成。因此,作为对象的铁塔为其观察者,只要他钻进了铁塔,提供了一系列的反常现象,即一种表面与其相反的实际所组成的饶有兴趣的矛盾现象。

The Tower's second provision, as an object, is that, despite its technical singularity, it constitutes a familiar "little world"; from the ground level, a whole humble commerce accompanies its departure: vendors of postcards, souvenirs, knicknacks, balloons, toys, sunglasses, herald a

铁塔提供的第二个方面,是作为物体,尽管它在技术上独具特色,它却构成一个熟悉的"小小世界";从底层起,就有初级商业伴随着旅程的开始:明信片、纪念品、小饰品、气球、玩具、太阳镜等的售卖,预示着一个

commercial life which we rediscover thoroughly installed on the first platform. Now any commerce has a space-taming function; selling, buying, exchanging—it is by these simple gestures that men truly dominate the wildest sites, the most sacred constructions. The myth of the moneylenders driven out of the Temple is actually an ambiguous one, for such commerce testifies to a kind of affectionate familiarity with regard to a monument whose singularity no longer intimidates, and it is by a Christian sentiment (hence to a certain degree a special one) that the spiritual excludes the familiar; in Antiquity, a great religious festival as well as a theatrical representation, a veritable sacred ceremony, in no way prevented the revelation of the most everyday gestures, such as eating or drinking: all pleasures proceeded simultaneously, not by some heedless permissiveness but because the ceremonial was never savage and certainly offered no contradiction to the quotidian. The Tower is not a sacred monument, and no taboo can forbid a commonplace life to develop there, but there can be no question, nonetheless, of a trivial phenomenon here; the installation of a restaurant on the Tower, for instance (food being the object of the most symbolic of trades), is a phenomenon corresponding to a whole meaning of leisure; man always seems disposed—if no constraints appear to stand in his way—to seek out a kind of counterpoint in his pleasures: this is what is called comfort. The Eiffel Tower is a comfortable object, and moreover, it is in this that it is an object either very old (analogous, for instance, to the ancient Circus) or very modern (analogous to certain American institutions such as the drive-in movie, in which one can simultaneously enjoy the film, the car, the food, and the freshness of the night air). Further, by affording its visitor a whole polyphony

商业生活圈,我们看到它重新出现在第一个平台上。现在任何商业都具有征服空间的功能:销售、购买、交换——正是这些简单的行为人们才能真正掌控最野蛮的地域、最神圣的建筑。被驱逐出神庙的放债人的神话实际上是模棱两可的,因为商业证实了对纪念物的饱含深情的熟悉性,纪念物的独特性不再威胁于它,而正是这种基督情感(某种程度上说一种特殊的情感)让心灵排除了熟悉;在古代,一次重大的宗教活动、一次戏剧表演、一项真正的神圣仪式绝不会妨碍日常生活的展示,如吃喝:所有的快乐同时进行,并不是因为疏忽而许可的,而是宗教活动从不会是野蛮的,不会提出和日常生活相矛盾的东西。铁塔不是一个神圣的纪念物,没有禁忌禁止在这儿开展商业活动,然而毫无疑问这儿也有微不足道的东西;例如,铁塔上的一家餐馆就符合休闲的氛围(食物成为很多行业最有象征性的事物);人类似乎总是倾向于在其快乐中寻找对应物——如果没有约束阻挡的话:这被称之为舒适。埃菲尔铁塔是一个让人舒服的物体,正是因为这样它既不是古老的建筑(类似于古代的竞技场)也不是现代的建筑(类似于美国某些设施,比如,露天影院,在这里人们可以同时享受电影、汽车、食物、夜晚的新鲜空气)。此外,铁塔给其游客提供多重快乐,从技术奇观到美味佳肴,还包括了全景,铁塔最终与所有人类的本质功能重聚:自主性;铁塔可以依靠自身存活:人们可以在铁塔上梦想、就餐、观光、理解、感叹、购物;就

of pleasures, from technological wonder to haute cuisine, including the panorama, the Tower ultimately reunites with the essential function of all major human sites: autarchy; the Tower can live on itself: one can dream there, eat there, observe there, understand there, marvel there, shop there; as on an ocean liner (another mythic object that sets children dreaming), one can feel oneself cut off from the world and yet the owner of a world.

像在一艘远洋邮轮上(另一件让儿童幻想的神秘物体),人们感觉自己脱离世界,成为另一个世界的主人。

3. Questions for Discussion

(1) What are the symbolic meanings of the Eiffel Tower analyzed by Roland Barthes?

(2) How do you understand the "uselessness" of the Eiffel Tower?

(3) Try to analyze the symbolic meaning of a building that you know by using semiological terms.

3. 讨论题

(1)罗兰·巴尔特所分析的埃菲尔铁塔的象征含义有哪些?

(2)你如何理解埃菲尔铁塔的"无用性"?

(3)试着运用符号学术语去分析一个你所知的建筑的象征性含义。

Chapter 13

第13章

1. Introduction to Jacques Derrida

1. 雅克·德里达简介

Jacques Derrida (1930-2004) was one of the most well known twentieth century philosophers, and the founder of deconstruction. His thought exerted wide-ranging influence in philosophy, in literary criticism and theory, in art and, in particular, architectural theory, and in political theory.

雅克·德里达(1930—2004)是20世纪最著名的哲学家之一,解构主义之父。他的思想对哲学、文学批评与理论、艺术(尤其是建筑理论)和政治理论均产生了深远的影响。

Jacques Derrida was born in a Jewish family in French-governed Algeria. He either withdrew from, or was forced out of at least two schools during his childhood simply on account of being Jewish. Immediately after World War II, Derrida started to study philosophy. In 1949, he moved to Paris, where he prepared for the entrance exam in philosophy for the prestigious École Normale Supérieure (ENS) and he was eventually accepted to the institution in 1952. Derrida received a grant for studies at Harvard University and he spent the 1956—1957 academic year there. From 1960 to 1964, Derrida taught philosophy at the Sorbonne. In 1964, on the recommendation of Louis Althusser and Jean Hyppolite, Derrida got a permanent

雅克·德里达出生在法属阿尔及利亚的一个犹太人家庭。在少年时代,他至少有两次退学或被迫退学,只因他是犹太人。二战之后,德里达开始学习哲学。1949年,他来到巴黎,准备报考极负盛名的巴黎高等师范学院,1952年,他终于被该校录取。德里达获得到美国哈佛大学学习的基金,在那里他度过了1956—1957学年。1960—1964年,德里达在索邦大学教哲学。1964年,在路易·阿尔都塞和让·伊波里特的推荐下,德里达获得巴黎高等师范学院终身教学职位,他在此职位上一直做到1984年。之后,他成为法国社会

teaching position at the ENS, which he kept till 1984. Then he became full professor at the École des Hautes Études en Sciences Sociales. In 1986 Derrida became Professor of the Humanities at the University of California, Irvine, where he taught until shortly before his death in 2004.

科学高等研究院全职教授。1986年，德里达成为加利福尼亚大学欧文分校的人文教授，执教到2004年他去世前不久。

From the 1960s, Jacques Derrida published numerous books and essays on an immense range of topics and taught and lectured throughout the world. Derrida's fame nearly reached the status of a media star. His representative works are *Writing and Difference* (1967), *Of Grammatology* (1967), *Speech and Phenomena* (1967), *Spurs: Nietzsche's Styles* (1979), *Positions* (1981), *Dissemination* (1981), *Margins of Philosophy* (1982), *Memoires for Paul de Man* (1986), *Glas* (1986), *The Post Card: From Socrates to Freud and Beyond* (1987), *Of Spirit: Heidegger and the Question* (1989), *Specters of Marx* (1993), *Politics of Friendship* (1997), *Adieu: To Emmanuel Levinas* (1999), *Of Hospitality* (2000), *On Touching— Jean-Luc Nancy* (2005) and so on.

从20世纪60年代起，雅克·德里达发表了大量的著作和文章，内容涉及领域广泛，并在世界各地教学、做讲座。德里达的声誉几乎与媒体明星一般。他的代表性作品有《书写与差异》(1967)、《论文字学》(1967)、《言语与现象》(1967)、《马刺——尼采的风格》(1979)、《多重立场》(1981)、《论散播》(1981)、《哲学的边缘》(1982)、《多义的记忆——为保罗·德曼而作》(1986)、《丧钟》(1986)、《明信片》(1987)、《论精神——海德格尔与问题》(1989)、《马克思的幽灵》(1993)、《友爱的政治学》(1997)、《永别了，伊曼努尔·列维纳斯》(1999)、《论好客》(2000)、《触觉——论让·吕克·南希》(2005)等。

Derrida coined the term deconstruction for the critical examination of the fundamental conceptual oppositions inherent in Western philosophy since the time of the ancient Greeks. These oppositions are characteristically "binary" and "hierarchical," involving a pair of terms in which one member of the pair is assumed to be primary or fundamental, the other secondary or derivative, such as mind and body, speech and writing, presence and absence, etc. Deconstruction is generally presented via an analysis of specific texts. It seeks to expose, and then to subvert, the various binary oppositions. Deconstruction has at least two aspects: literary and philosophical. The literary aspect concerns the textual interpretation, where invention is essential

德里达创造了解构这一术语，旨在以批判性姿态审视西方哲学自古希腊以来的那些内在、本质的对立概念。这些对立概念具有"二元对立"和"等级性"特征，即在一对词语中，一个词被认为是主要的、本质的，而另一个词是次要的、派生的，例如，思想和身体、言语和书写、在场和不在场等等。解构一般是通过具体文本分析呈现出来的。它先要揭示，然后颠覆各种二元对立。解构至少包括两个方面：文学的和哲学的。文学方面关注文本阐释，在阐释过程中为发现文本中隐藏的其他意义，发明创

to finding hidden alternative meanings in the text. The philosophical aspect concerns the main target of deconstruction: metaphysics.

Building on theories of the Swiss linguist Ferdinand de Saussure, Derrida coined the term differance, meaning both a difference and an act of deferring, to characterize the way in which linguistic meaning is created rather than given. And meaning is created by the "play" of differences between words—a play that is "limitless", "infinite", and "indefinite". In "Differance", Derrida describes the process of spatial and temporal movement that he claims makes all thought and all reality possible.

"Differance" can be regarded as a good example of Derrida's use of deconstructive strategy. His writing is known for its extreme subtlety, its meticulous attention to detail, and its tenacious pursuit of the logical implications of supposedly "marginal" features of texts.

造是必要的。哲学方面关注解构的主要目标:形而上学。

在瑞士语言学家费尔迪南·德·索绪尔的理论基础上,德里达创造了延异一词,它既指差异,又指进行区别的行为,以显示语言意义是创造出的,而不是指定的。意义是在词语之间对差异的嬉戏而创造出的——嬉戏是"无限的"、"无穷的"、"无定的"。德里达在《延异》中描述了他称之为使所有思想和现实都成为可能的空间和时间的运动。

《延异》一文可以被看成是德里达使用解构策略的一个范例。其写作以极度微妙、关注细枝末节、不懈探求文本中被认为是"边缘性"内容的逻辑意义而著称。

2. Selections from "Differance"

Differance①

Jacques Derrida

The verb "to differ" (différer) seems to differ from itself. On the one hand, it indicates difference as distinction, inequality, or discernibility; on the other, it expresses the interposition of delay, the interval of a spacing and temporalizing that puts off until "later" what is presently denied, the possible that is presently impossible. Sometimes the different and sometimes the deferred correspond (in French) to the verb "to differ". This correlation,

2.《延异》选文

延异

雅克·德里达

动词"相异"(différer)似乎与其本身就相异。一方面,它指差异,意即区别、不等、分辨;另一方面,它又表达了一种延迟的介入,一种时间与空间上的间隔,这种间隔将目前被否认的(可能性)推迟,目前不可能的可能被推迟到未来。在法语中,动词"相异"有时与"延迟"相连接。这样

① Selected from *Speech and Phenomena and Other Essays on Husserl's Theory of Signs*, by Jacques Derrida, translated by David B. Allison, Evanston: Northwestern University Press, 1973.

however, is not simply one between act and object, cause and effect, or primordial and derived.

In the one case "to differ" signifies nonidentity; in the other case it signifies the order of the same. Yet there must be a common, although entirely differant (différante) root within the sphere that relates the two movements of differing to one another. We provisionally give the name differance to this sameness which is not identical: by the silent writing of its *a*, it has the desired advantage of referring to differing, both as spacing/temporalizing and as the movement that structures every dissociation.

As distinct from difference, differance thus points out the irreducibility of temporalizing (which is also temporalization—in transcendental language which is no longer adequate here, this would be called the constitution of primordial temporality—just as the term "spacing" also includes the constitution of primordial spatiality). Differance is not simply active (any more than it is a subjective accomplishment); it rather indicates the middle voice, it precedes and sets up the opposition between passivity and activity. With its a, differance more properly refers to what in classical language would be called the origin or production of differences and the differences between differences, the play (jeu) of differences. Its locus and operation will therefore be seen wherever speech appeals to difference.

Differance is neither a word nor a concept. In it, however, we shall see the juncture rather than the summation—of what has been most decisively inscribed in the thought of what is conveniently called our "epoch": the difference of forces in Nietzsche, Saussure's principle of semiological

一种关联性,不仅仅是简单的行为与客体间的联系,或是因与果,或是原初与引申的关系。

一方面,"相异"指不同一性;一则又可代表同一的顺序。然而在这其中一定有一个共通但完全不同的词根将相异(différante)所代表的两种行为彼此相连。我们暂时先将这种不具有同一性的同一命名为延异:通过无声的书写中的 *a*,延异这个词(相较于原词)就具备了我们所希望的优势,既表达了空间/时间的相异,又将分散的各部分建构起来。

与差异不同,延异便指出了延宕的不可约性(延宕在普遍的语言中也可说是时间化,但在此处不足以适用,此处意为原初的暂时性的组成,就如同"空间化"一词包含了所有原初的空间性的组成)。延异不是单纯的主动,就如同它也不是一个单纯主观履行的行为,它更像是一个中间态,它先于主动被动发生,并且使两者对立起来。通过这个 a,延异比原词更恰当地指出了在古典语言里人们称之为差异之源或者说是造成差异的东西,同时还指涉差异之间的相异之处以及差异的嬉戏(jeu)。因此,延异的位置和作用可见于言语中任何差异存在之处。

延异既非一个单词也非一个概念。然而在其之中,我们应能看见一种结合而不是总和,这种接合深刻于我们常称之为"时代"的思想之中:尼采所说的力量差异,索绪尔的符号

difference①, differing as the possibility of neurone facilitation, impression and delayed effect in Freud, difference as the irreducibility of the trace of the other in Levinas②, and the ontic-ontological difference in Heidegger③.

Reflection on this last determination of difference will lead us to consider differance as the strategic note or connection—relatively or provisionally privileged—which indicates the closure of presence, together with the closure of the conceptual order and denomination, a closure that is effected in the functioning of traces.

I SHALL SPEAK, THEN, OF A LETTER—the first one, if we are to believe the alphabet and most of the speculations that have concerned themselves with it.

I shall speak then of the letter *a*, this first letter which it seemed necessary to introduce now and then in writing the word "difference". This seemed necessary in the course of writing about writing, and of writing within a writing whose different strokes all pass, in certain respects, through a gross spelling mistake, through a violation of the rules governing writing, violating the law that governs writing and regulates its conventions of propriety. In fact or theory we can always erase or lessen this spelling mistake, and, in each case, while these are analytically different from one another but for practical purposes the same, find it grave, unseemly, or, indeed, supposing the greatest ingenuousness, amusing. Whether or not we care to quietly overlook this

学差异原则，弗洛伊德学说中相异使得神经建导、印象与延迟效应成为可能，列维纳斯的差异作为他者踪迹的不可约性，以及海德格尔的存在的体论中的差异性。

反思此处对于差异的终极考量将会引领我们去思考，将延异作为策略上的笔记或联系，它相对地或说临时地较为特别，表明存在的封闭性，同时表明概念上的顺序和命名的封闭，且这种封闭受到踪迹作用的影响。

我就此要谈谈一个字母。如果我们字母表，以及对字母表所作的众多思考是可信的话，我就来谈谈第一个字母。

我要谈谈字母 a 。这第一个字母，似乎有必要悄悄地从各处潜入"差异"一词的书写中。这种潜入要发生在关于文字的书写过程中和文字内部的书写过程中。这种文字的不同轨迹就此表明它们自身在某个明确的点上，同一种粗略的拼写错误相交叉、同规范书写并使书写得体的规章法度中的差错相交叉。人们总是能够，在实际上或判断上抹去或减少差错，根据每次分析过的情景，尽管这种情景大体一致，发现它是严重的和不得体的，也即是说——根据最诚挚的设想——好笑的。这样，即使人们试图默默地忽略这样的逾规行为，人们对这种逾规行为的兴趣还是

① 索绪尔(Saussure)认为在语言中只有差异，不存在绝对项，语言中各种要素的意义不在其自身，而在于与其他要素之间的差异。

② 列维纳斯(E. Levinas)是20世纪法国著名哲学家，他从存在的思考出发，把哲学与基督教、犹太教教义融会贯通，构建出一种伦理哲学。

③ "延异"同海德格尔的"存在"很像，它是其存在论(ontology)区分的一个结果，但德里达认为，延异比存在论区分或存在的真理"更古老"。

infraction, the attention we give it beforehand will allow us to recognize, as though prescribed by some mute irony, the inaudible but displaced character of this literal permutation. We can always act as though this makes no difference. I must say from the start that my account serves less to justify this silent spelling mistake, or still less to excuse it, than to aggravate its obtrusive character.

On the other hand, I must be excused if I refer, at least implicitly, to one or another of the texts that I have ventured to publish. Precisely what I would like to attempt to some extent (although this is in principle and in its highest degree impossible, due to essential de jure reasons) is to bring together an assemblage of the different ways I have been able to utilize—or, rather, have allowed to be imposed on me—what I will provisionally call the word or concept of differance in its new spelling. It is literally neither a word nor a concept, as we shall see. I insist on the word "assemblage" here for two reasons: on the one hand, it is not a matter of describing a history, of recounting the steps, text by text, context by context, each time showing which scheme has been able to impose this graphic disorder, although this could have been done as well; rather, we are concerned with the general system of all these schemata. On the other hand, the word "assemblage" seems more apt for suggesting that the kind of bringing together proposed here has the structure of an interlacing, a weaving, or a web, which would allow the different threads and different lines of sense or force to separate again, as well as being ready to bind others together.

In a quite preliminary way, we now recall that this particular graphic intervention was conceived in the writing—up of a question about writing; it was not made simply to shock the reader or grammarian. Now, in point of fact, it happens that this graphic

可以被事先看作和指定为缄默的反语法、无声的误置的文字耗损的规定。人们似乎总是认为这点无关紧要。此时此地,我应当声明,今天的演讲不是对拼写中的缄默差错进行辩护,更不是为此而认错,而是对某种持续加剧的嬉戏进行辩解。

另一方面,如果我谈及了,至少是暗暗地,我以前莽撞地发表的文本,我请求原谅。这的确是因为,在某种程度上,(即使在理论上,归根结底,这是不可能的),我试图在某种程度上造成几种不同方法的聚合,根据这些方法,我能够利用——或不得已而为之——我临时性地称作词的或概念的,新拼写的延异。尽管如我们所见,延异从字面上而言,既非一个词,也非一个概念。我坚持使用"聚合"这一词有两个原因:一方面,它不是对一种历史的描述,不是逐个地说明文本、语境,每一次都显示其结构能造成书写的混乱,虽然这也能做到,更明确地说,我们关注的是这些结构的一般系统。另一方面,"聚合"这个词似乎更适于暗示这里所提出的聚拢在一起,这种具有编织,或结网功能的结构,它允许把不同意义或力量的线加以区别,同时准备着把其他的线扎在一起。

现在,我们用一种非常初级的方法来回顾一下,这个特殊的书写介入是在关于书写问题的记述中引起的,它不只是为了惊动读者或语法学家。

difference (the *a* instead of the *e*), this marked difference between two apparently vocalic notations, between vowels, remains purely graphic: it is written or read, but it is not heard. It cannot be heard, and we shall see in what respects it is also beyond the order of understanding. It is put forward by a silent mark, by a tacit monument, or, one might even say, by a pyramid—keeping in mind not only the capital form of the printed letter but also that passage from Hegel's *Encyclopaedia* where he compares the body of the sign to an Egyptian pyramid. The *a* of differance, therefore, is not heard; it remains silent, secret, and discreet, like a tomb.

我实际上想说的是,这种书写形式的差异(a 代替 e),这两个元音符号外观上的显著差异,这两种元音间的差异,正巧仍旧是纯粹的书写形式上的:它被辨识出来,或被书写出来,但不能被听出来;它不能通过声音来领悟,而且我们将会明白它也绕过一般性的理解顺序的原因。一个默默的记号,一个缄默的标石,我甚至要说,一个金字塔,提供了这种差异——之所以说成金字塔,是我不仅仅考虑到了这个字母的大写印刷体形式,还考虑到了黑格尔在《哲学全书》中将符号系统比作埃及的金字塔。延异中的 a 是听不见的;它保持沉默、隐秘、谨慎,坟墓一般。

It is a tomb that (provided one knows how to decipher its legend) is not far from signaling the death of the king.

它是一个坟墓(如果人们知道如何解释它的传说),与一个标志着国王死亡的坟墓相去不远。

It is a tomb that cannot even be made to resonate. For I cannot even let you know, by my talk, now being spoken before the Societe Francaise de Philosophic, which difference I am talking about at the very moment I speak of it. I can only talk about this graphic difference by keeping to a very indirect speech about writing, and on the condition that I specify each time that I am referring to difference with an *e* or differance with an *a*. All of which is not going to simplify matters today, and will give us all a great deal of trouble when we want to understand one another. In any event, when I do specify which difference I mean—when I say "with an *e*" or "with an *a*"—this will refer irreducibly to a written text, a text governing my talk, a text that I keep in front of me, that I will read, and toward which I shall have to try to lead your hands and eyes. We cannot refrain here from going by way of a written text, from ordering ourselves by the disorder that is

它是一个不能引起共鸣的坟墓,因为我甚至无法让你通过我目前在法国哲学学会所作的演讲让你们知晓,当我谈论差异的时候我正在谈论的是哪种差异。我可以仅仅通过一种论及书写的十分间接的话语来谈及这种书写差异;或者在我每次确定了我谈论的是带有一个"e"的差异,还是带有一个"a"的延异的状况下来谈及这种书写差异。这都不会简化今天的问题,而会给我们所有的人带来大量的烦恼,如果我们至少是想彼此理解的话。在任何情况下,我的口头表述——当我说"带 e"或是"带 a"的时候——就会不可避免地谈及一个关注我的话语的文字文本,就会谈及我握在我面前、我要读的、我一定要尽力将你们的手、你们的眼睛引向它的文本。不经过一个文字文本,

produced therein—and this is what matters to me first of all.

Doubtless this pyramidal silence of the graphic difference between the *e* and the *a* can function only within the system of phonetic writing and within a language or grammar historically tied to phonetic writing and to the whole culture which is inseparable from it. But I will say that it is just this—this silence that functions only within what is called phonetic writing—that points out or reminds us in a very opportune way that, contrary to an enormous prejudice, there is no phonetic writing. There is no purely and strictly phonetic writing. What is called phonetic writing can only function—in principle and de jure, and not due to some factual and technical inadequacy—by incorporating nonphonetic " signs " (punctuation, spacing, etc.); but when we examine their structure and necessity, we will quickly see that they are ill described by the concept of signs. Saussure had only to remind us that the play of difference was the functional condition, the condition of possibility, for every sign; and it is itself silent. The difference between two phonemes, which enables them to exist and to operate, is inaudible. The inaudible opens the two present phonemes to hearing, as they present themselves. If, then, there is no purely phonetic writing, it is because there is no purely phonetic phone. The difference that brings out phonemes and lets them be heard and understood (entendre) itself remains inaudible.

It will perhaps be objected that, for the same reasons, the graphic difference itself sinks into darkness, that it never constitutes the fullness of a sensible term, but draws out an invisible connection, the mark of an inapparent relation between two spectacles. That is no doubt true. Indeed, since from this point of view the difference

我们就既不能引起、也不能避免文本内所产生的混乱秩序——这一点对我来说至关重要。

毫无疑问,“e”和“a”之间金字塔般沉默的书写差异,仅仅在语音书写系统内,在历史的与语音书写和其密不可分的整个文化相关的某种语言或语法内发生作用。但是,我想说,这点本身——只是在所谓的语音文字内起作用的沉默——十分及时地向我们表明、提醒我们,同广泛的偏见相反,并不存在着语音文字、不存在纯粹的和严格意义上的语音文字。所谓的语音文字,按理说,就本质而言,且不仅仅由于经验和技术的匮乏,它只能通过承认它系统的非语音“符号”(标点、间隙等等)来起作用。对这些非语音符号的必要性和结构的考察很快表明,它们几乎无法承受符号本身这一概念。差异的嬉戏,如索绪尔提醒我们的,是每一个符号的功能和可能性的条件,它本身也是一种沉默的嬉戏。这两个音素间的差异使它们能够存在并且运作。这种差异是听不见的。这种听不见的差异使这两个出现的音素变得可以听见,就像是它们在自我呈现。那么如果没有纯粹的语音书写,就是因为没有纯粹的语音。这种差异显示出音素并且使之被听见和被理解,其本身依然是听不见的。

因为同样的原因,人们会反对说,书写差异本身会消失在黑暗中,它决不能理解为一个完全概念,而是扩充了某种隐秘关系、两种景观间不明显关系的特征。信然。但是,根据这种观点,差异,它被标记在“e”和

between the *e* and the *a* marked in "differance" eludes vision and hearing, this happily suggests that we must here let ourselves be referred to an order that no longer refers to sensibility. But we are not referred to intelligibility either, to an ideality not fortuitously associated with the objectivity of theorem or understanding. We must be referred to an order, then, that resists philosophy's founding opposition between the sensible and the intelligible. The order that resists this opposition, that resists it because it sustains it, is designated in a movement of differance (with an *a*) between two differences or between two letters. This differance belongs neither to the voice nor to writing in the ordinary sense, and it takes place, like the strange space that will assemble us here for the course of an hour, between speech and writing and beyond the tranquil familiarity that binds us to one and to the other, reassuring us sometimes in the illusion that they are two separate things.

Now, how am I to speak of the *a* of differance? It is clear that it cannot be exposed. We can expose only what, at a certain moment, can become present, manifest; what can be shown, presented as a present, a being-present in its truth, the truth of a present or the presence of a present. However, if differance is (I also cross out the "is") what makes the presentation of being-present possible, it never presents itself as such. It is never given in the present or to anyone. Holding back and not exposing itself, it goes beyond the order of truth on this specific point and in this determined way, yet is not itself concealed, as if it were something, a mysterious being, in the occult zone of a nonknowing. Any exposition would expose it to disappearing as a disappearance. It would risk appearing, thus disappearing.

Thus, the detours, phrases, and syntax that I shall often have to resort to will resemble—will

"a"之间的"differance"中,排除了视、听,这或许会愉快地暗示,在此我们应被允许谈及一种不属于感性的秩序,但它也不属于智性,不属于与理论或理解的客观性无偶然关联的想象力。就此,我们应当让我们自己谈及一种秩序,这种秩序抵制感性和智性间的对立,也即哲学的基本对立。这种抵制对立的秩序,抵制它是因为它搬走了它(有一个a),是在两种差异间,或两个字母间的延异的活动中被宣告的。此延异既不属于通常意义上的声音,也不属于通常意义上的文字,它犹如使我们在此一起待一个小时的奇特空间一样,位于声音和文字之间:它超越了使我们和他人连为一体的安闲亲密,并不时使充满幻觉的我们相信它们互不投机。

为谈及延异中的a,我要做什么?不言而喻,延异不能被暴露。人们只能暴露特定时刻的在场者、现形者;只能暴露那些显示、表现为在场的东西;只能暴露真实的在场者,真实在场的或真实在场者的在场。现在,如果延异是(我也划掉"是")可能使在场者现身之物的话,它也绝不会如此显现。它绝不可能被提供给在场、或任何人。延异以固定的方式封存着自身,而非暴露自身,它在某个精确点上越过了真理的法则,但又不掩饰自己,好像它是无确定边界的洞穴中某个神秘的事物。在每一次暴露中,延异都暴露为作为消失的消失,它在显现与消失间冒险。

如此这般,以至于我求助的这些

sometimes be practically indiscernible from—those of negative theology. Already we had to note that differance is not, does not exist, and is not any sort of being-present (on). And we will have to point out everything that it is not, and, consequently, that it has neither existence nor essence. It belongs to no category of being, present or absent. And yet what is thus denoted as differance is not theological, not even in the most negative order of negative theology. The latter, as we know, is always occupied with letting a supraessential reality go beyond the finite categories of essence and existence, that is, of presence, and always hastens to remind us that, if we deny the predicate of existence to God, it is in order to recognize him as a superior, inconceivable, and ineffable mode of being. Here there is no question of such a move, as will be confirmed as we go along. Not only is differance irreducible to every ontological or theological—onto-theological—reappropriation, but it opens up the very space in which onto-theology—philosophy—produces its system and its history. It thus encompasses and irrevocably surpasses ontotheology or philosophy.

For the same reason, I do not know where to begin to mark out this assemblage, this graph, of differance. Precisely what is in question here is the requirement that there be a de jure commencement, an absolute point of departure, a responsibility arising from a principle. The problem of writing opens by questioning the arche. Thus what I put forth here will not be developed simply as a philosophical discourse that operates on the basis of a principle, of postulates, axioms, and definitions and that moves according to the discursive line of a rational order. In marking out differance, everything is a matter of strategy and risk. It is a question of strategy because no

迂回、短语和句式,就类似于否定神学的这些方面,偶尔甚至到了与否定神学无以区分的地步。我们已经表明了延异不是,不存在,不是任何形式的在场-存在者;我们随着也会表明延异不是什么,也即是说,什么都不是。结果,它既没有存在也没有本质。它不是来自于存在者的范畴,不论是在场的还是缺席的。然而,我们描绘的延异的某些方面不是神学的,甚至不属于最为否定的否定神学。否定神学时时关注的是同超本质性的脱离,这种超本质性超乎了有限的本质和存在范畴,也即超乎了在场的范畴,并总是赶紧提醒我们,拒绝给予上帝存在的断言,这仅仅是为了承认他优越的、非凡的、不可言喻的存在模式。这样一种进展在此不容置疑,这也会慢慢地得到证实。延异不仅不可化减为任何本体的或神学的——本体神学的——占有,而且,作为一种本体神学——哲学——生产其系统及历史的空间,它包含着并不可以改变地优于本体神学和哲学。

因为相同的原因,我并不知道从哪里开始写出延异这个聚合,这个图形。因为对恰当起点的寻求,对绝对的出发点,对主要责任的寻求,都是值得怀疑的。书写的疑问性正是通过质疑而显现的。我在此将要提议的东西不会简单地发展成哲学话语,而哲学话语是通过原理、公论、公理、定论来活动的,是沿着理性的线性秩序的话语系列来行进的。在对延异的描写中,一切都是策略性的、冒险性的。策略性的是因为呈现于文字领域之外的超越性真理都无法神学

transcendent truth present outside the sphere of writing can theologically command the totality of this field. It is hazardous because this strategy is not simply one in the sense that we say that strategy orients the tactics according to a final aim, a telos or the theme of a domination, a mastery or an ultimate reappropriation of movement and field. In the end, it is a strategy without finality. We might call it blind tactics or empirical errance, if the value of empiricism did not itself derive all its meaning from its opposition to philosophical responsibility. If there is a certain errance in the tracing-out of differance, it no longer follows the line of logico-philosophical speech or that of its integral and symmetrical opposite, logico-empirical speech. The concept of play (jeu) remains beyond this opposition; on the eve and aftermath of philosophy, it designates the unity of chance and necessity in an endless calculus.

By decision and, as it were, by the rules of the game, then, turning this thought around, let us introduce ourselves to the thought of differance by way of the theme of strategy or stratagem. By this merely strategic justification, I want to emphasize that the efficacy of this thematics of differance very well may, and even one day must, be sublated, i. e., lend itself, if not to its own replacement, at least to its involvement in a series of events which in fact it never commanded. This also means that it is not a theological thematics.

I will say, first of all, that differance, which is neither a word nor a concept, seemed to me to be strategically the theme most proper to think out, if not master (thought being here, perhaps, held in a certain necessary relation with the structional limits of mastery), in what is most characteristic of our "epoch". I start off, then, strategically, from the place and time in which "we" are, even though my opening is not justifiable in the final account,

式地控制这整个领域。冒险的原因是这种策略不单单是这个意义上的策略,即通过一个最终的目标,一个目的或一个控制主题,一种主宰,以及对这个领域的进展的最后占用,从而调整方案的策略。最终,这是一个无终极性的策略,可以称之为盲目的策略,如果经验主义价值本身并未获得同哲学义务相对的全部意义的话,它还可以被称之为漫游经验,如果在延异的踪迹中有某种漫游的话,这种漫游不再遵循哲学的逻辑话语线索,也不遵循一种对称和内在的反向的经验—逻辑话语线索。嬉戏(jeu)概念使自身超越了这种对立,它处在哲学的前夕且超越了哲学,它表明了无尽的运算中必然和偶然的统一。

同样,如果你们愿意,依据决定并作为一种游戏规则,我们将这些主张推翻,就会通过策略主题而被导入延异的思维中。通过这种仅有的策略上的理由,我想强调延异主题功能可以在某一天恰当地,的确也应该,被替代,如果不是参与它自己的替代,至少它应该使自己卷入事实上它从来不会统治过的链条中。就此,再次说明,延异不是神学的。

首先,我要说延异既非一个词也非一个概念,对我来说,延异从策略上说最宜于思考,如果不是控制,延异是有关我们"时代"的最为不可减约之物,此处的思考同结构性的控制界线保持着必要的关系。因此,从策略上来说,即使归根到底,我的起点也并非无可非议,但我仍将从"我们"身处其间的时间和地点着手,因为

and though it is always on the basis of differance and its "history" that we can claim to know who and where "we" are and what the limits of an "epoch" can be.

Although "differance" is neither a word nor a concept, let us nonetheless attempt a simple and approximative semantic analysis which will bring us in view of what is at stake (en vue de l'enjeu).

We do know that the verb "to differ" (différer) (the Latin verb "differre") has two seemingly quite distinct meanings; in the *Littré* dictionary, for example, they are the subject of two separate articles. In this sense, the Latin differre is not the simple translation of the Greek diapherein; this fact will not be without consequence for us in tying our discussion to a particular language, one that passes for being less philosophical, less primordially philosophical, than the other. For the distribution of sense in the Greek "diapherein" does not carry one of the two themes of the Latin differre, namely, the action of postponing until later, of taking into account, the taking-account of time and forces in an operation that implies an economic reckoning, a detour, a respite, a delay, a reserve, a representation—all the concepts that I will sum up here in a word I have never used but which could be added to this series: temporalizing. "To differ" in this sense is to temporalize, to resort, consciously or unconsciously, to the temporal and temporalizing mediation of a detour that suspends the accomplishment or fulfillment of "desire" or "ill", or carries desire or will out in a way that annuls or tempers their effect. We shall see, later, in what respects this temporalizing is also a temporalization and spacing, is space's becoming-temporal and time's becoming-spatial, is "primordial constitution" of space and time, as metaphysics or transcendental phenomenology would call it in the language that is here criticized

正是以延异及其"历史"为基础,我们才据说能知道"我们"是谁,我们在哪儿,一个"时代"的界线可能是什么。

尽管延异既非一个词,也非一个概念,我们还是想进行一番简要和大略的语义分析,这种分析将会让我们发现症结之所在。

我们知道动词"相异"(différer)(拉丁动词 differre)有两个看起来十分不同的意义。比如在利特雷法文词典中,它们是两篇不同文章的对象。在这个意义上,拉丁语 differre 不是简单地对希腊语 diapherein 的翻译,这对我们来说并非无关紧要,它将我们的话语同一种特殊语言连接起来,同一种较之其他语言而言不甚哲学化、本质上不甚哲学化的语言联系起来。因为希腊语 diapherein 中的意义配置同拉丁语 differre 的两种主旨的其中一种并不一致,这种主旨即是推迟行为、考虑行为、考虑时间和活动力量的行为,这种活动暗示着经济估算、迂回、延迟、接替、持存、再现——我将用一个从未用过的,但可以刻写在这条链上的词来概括上述这些概念:延宕。动词"相异"在这个意义上就是延宕,是在暂时性和延宕性的迂回中的有意无意的追索,这种迂回推迟了"欲望"或"意志"的满足和实现,并以一种取消或缓和其效果的方式来平等地影响这种推迟。后面,我们将会明白,这种延宕如何也是一种时间化和间隔化;如何是一种空间的时间化和时间的空间化;如何是时间空间的"原初性构造";如形而上学和超验现象学所说的,它又是如何地在语言中被批判和被置换的。

and displaced.

The other sense of "to differ" ("différer") is the most common and most identifiable, the sense of not being identical, of being other, of being discernible, etc. And in "different", whether referring to the alterity of dissimilarity or the alterity of allergy or of polemics, it is necessary that interval, distance, spacing occur among the different elements and occur actively, dynamically, and with a certain perseverance in repetition.

But the word "difference" (with an *e*) could never refer to differing as temporalizing or to difference as polemos. It is this loss of sense that the word differance (with an *a*) will have to schematically compensate for. Differance can refer to the whole complex of its meanings at once, for it is immediately and irreducibly multivalent, something which will be important for the discourse I am trying to develop. It refers to this whole complex of meanings not only when it is supported by a language or interpretive context (like any signification), but it already does so somehow of itself. Or at least it does so more easily by itself than does any other word: here the *a* comes more immediately from the present participle "different" and brings us closer to the action of "differing" that is in progress, even before it has produced the effect that is constituted as different or resulted in difference (with an *e*). Within a conceptual system and in terms of classical requirements, differance could be said to designate the productive and primordial constituting causality, the process of scission and division whose differings and differences would be the constituted products or effects. But while bringing us closer to the infinitive and active core of differing, "differance" with an *a* neutralizes what the infinitive denotes as simply active, in the same way that "parlance" does not signify the simple fact of speaking, of speaking to

动词"相异"(différer)的另一种意义更常见也更容易确定：非同一性,他者性,可辨识性,等等。在讨论"差异"时,不论它是一个完全不同的他性问题,还是一个敏感和辩论性的他性问题,空隙、距离、间隔,都应在两个他者元素间产生,都应以锲而不舍的重复方式产生。

但是,"差异"一词(有一个 e),绝不会指延宕的差异或辩论的差异。这样,延异(有一个 a)一词对这种意义的缺失进行总体的补偿,因为延异可以同时指涉全部的意义,它具有直接和无可减约的多义性,它对我现在正在试着展开的论述非常重要。据其多义性,这个词,理所当然地同任何意义一样,应遵从它出现于其中的话语,它的解释性语境;但是,它以某种方式,或至少较之任何其他的词而言更容易如此地做到了：这里的 a 直接来自现在分词(different),并且使我们更接近进行中的"相异"行为,甚至在它已经产生构成相异或造成差异(有一个 e)的效果之前。在一个概念系统内,出于传统的要求,可以说延异标明了具有生产性和原初构成性的因果关系,分离和割分的进程,其相异(differings)和差异(differences)将构成生产和后果。但是,在使我们接近 differing 的动词原形和主动态的核心时,"延异"有个 a 便把原形动词所表示的简单主动态变成了中性语态,就如我们语言中的"parlance"并非简单地指讲话,或某人讲,或听别人讲。所谓回应也不是做出反应的行为。我们应当考虑到,

or being spoken to. Nor is resonance the act of resonating. Here in the usage of our language we must consider that the ending "-ance" is undecided between active and passive. And we shall see why what is designated by "differance" is neither simply active nor simply passive, that it announces or rather recalls something like the middle voice, that it speaks of an operation which is not an operation, which cannot be thought of either as a passion or as an action of a subject upon an object, as starting from an agent or from a patient, or on the basis of, or in view of, any of these terms. But philosophy has perhaps commenced by distributing the middle voice, expressing a certain intransitiveness, into the active and the passive voice, and has itself been constituted in this repression.

How are differance as temporalizing and differance as spacing conjoined?

Let us begin with the problem of signs and writing—since we are already in the midst of it. We ordinarily say that a sign is put in place of the thing itself, the present thing—"thing" holding here for the sense as well as the referent. Signs represent the present in its absence; they take the place of the present. When we cannot take hold of or show the thing, let us say the present, the being-present, when the present does not present itself, then we signify, we go through the detour of signs. We take up or give signs; we make signs. The sign would thus be a deferred presence. Whether it is a question of verbal or written signs, monetary signs, electoral delegates, or political representatives, the movement of signs defers the moment of encountering the thing itself, the moment at which we could lay hold of it, consume or expend it, touch it, see it, have a present intuition of it. What I am describing here is the structure of signs as classically determined, in order to define—through

在我们语言的使用中,尾缀"-ance"在主动和被动之间无法确定。我们也会明白,自称为延异之物为何既非单单是主动的,也非单单是被动的,为何它表明或者更恰当地说回忆了类似中间态的东西,为何宣称一个不是活动的活动,一个既不被看作某种激情,也不能看作主体对客体发挥作用的活动——这个活动不是以主动和受动范畴为基础;不以这些术语为基础,也不靠近任何这类术语。对于这种中间态而言,某种非过渡性,可能就是哲学一开始对主动态和被动态的划分,哲学也因此通过这种压抑而形成自身。

延异作为延宕化,延异作为间距化,它们怎样连接在一起?

我们就从文字和符号问题着手——因为我们已在那儿了。符号通常说成是对事物本身的替代,对在场事物的替代。"事物"在此同等地代表意义或所指,符号再现了缺席的在场者,它替代了在场者。当我们无法理解或表明事物,无法陈述在场者、在场之在时,当在场者无法呈现时,我们就通过迂回的符号表意,我们拿来或给予符号。我们用符号表意。在这个意义上,符号是延搁的在场。不论我们关心的是口头符号还是文字符号,是货币符号还是选举代表和政治代表,符号的流通延搁了我们遭遇事物本身的瞬间,我们使事物归我们拥有的瞬间,我们消费物或耗费物、触摸物、凝视物、直觉物的在场的瞬间。我在此为了界定符号而作的描述是在符号的全部陈腐特性中

a commonplace characterization of its traits—signification as the differance of temporalizing. Now this classical determination presupposes that the sign (which defers presence) is conceivable only on the basis of the presence that it defers and in view of the deferred presence one intends to reappropriate. Following this classical semiology, the substitution of the sign for the thing itself is both secondary and provisional: it is second in order after an original and lost presence, a presence from which the sign would be derived. It is provisional with respect to this final and missing presence, in view of which the sign would serve as a movement of mediation.

In attempting to examine these secondary and provisional aspects of the substitute, we shall no doubt catch sight of something like a primordial differance. Yet we could no longer even call it primordial or final, inasmuch as the characteristics of origin, beginning, telos, eschaton, etc., have always denoted presence— ousia, parousia, etc. To question the secondary and provisional character of the sign, to oppose it to a "primordial" differance, would thus have the following consequences:

1. Differance can no longer be understood according to the concept of "sign", which has always been taken to mean the representation of a presence and has been constituted in a system (of thought or language) determined on the basis of and in view of presence.

2. In this way we question the authority of presence or its simple symmetrical contrary, absence or lack. We thus interrogate the limit that has always constrained us, that always constrains us—we who inhabit a language and a system of thought—to form the meaning of being in general as presence or absence, in the categories of being or beingness (ousia). It already appears that the kind

经典性的确定结构——意指延宕化的延异。这种结构预示了,延搁在场的符号,仅是以它所延搁的在场者为基础而被构想的,是以它向被延搁的在场者的移动为基础而被构想的,符号的目的就是为了占用这种被延搁的在场者。根据这种古典符号学,符号对物本身的替代是第二性的和临时性的:第二性是由于符号派生于某种原初和缺失的在场者;临时性的则涉及终级和隐匿的在场者,在这个意义上,符号是传达在场者的中介活动。

在质疑替代的这些第二性和临时性特性之时,人们将会理解类似于原初性的延异这类东西,但是,在本源、原初、目标、结尾等等的含义总是意味着在场——本质、说话等等的这一范围内,人们不再称延异为原初性的和终极性的。要质疑符号的第二性和临时性,要让它们和"原初性"的延异相对立,这样就会产生两种后果:

1.人们可能不会将延异纳入这样的符号概念中:符号总是意味着某种在场的再现,它总是在某个系统(思想或语言)中构成的,这个系统为在场所控制,或者向在场靠近。

2.人们就此可以质疑在场的权威性,或质疑它的简单的对称式对立面,即缺席或缺失的权威性。这样,人们就质疑总是束缚着我们的界线,这些界线仍在迫使我们——我们是语言和思想系统中的居民——在存在者或存在性(ousia)的范畴中,来阐述作为缺席或在场的存在意义。

of questioning we are thus led back to is, let us say, the Heideggerian kind, and that differance seems to lead us back to the onticontological difference. But permit me to postpone this reference. I shall only note that between differance as temporalizing—temporalization (which we can no longer conceive within the horizon of the present) and what Heidegger says about temporalization in *Sein und Zeit* (namely, that as the transcendental horizon of the question of being it must be freed from the traditional and metaphysical domination by the present or the now).

But first of all, let us remain with the semiological aspects of the problem to see how differance as temporalizing is conjoined with differance as spacing. Most of the semiological or linguistic research currently dominating the field of thought (whether due to the results of its own investigations or due to its role as a generally recognized regulative model) traces its genealogy, rightly or wrongly, to Saussure as its common founder. It was Saussure who first of all set forth the arbitrariness of signs and the differential character of signs as principles of general semiology and particularly of linguistics. And, as we know, these two themes—the arbitrary and the differential—are in his view inseparable. Arbitrariness can occur only because the system of signs is constituted by the differences between the terms, and not by their fullness. The elements of signification function not by virtue of the compact force of their cores but by the network of oppositions that distinguish them and relate them to one another. "Arbitrary and differential" says Saussure "are two correlative qualities."

As the condition for signification, this principle of difference affects the whole sign, that is, both the signified and the signifying aspects.

这已经表明，我们面对的新问题类型，我要说，是海德格尔式的；延异似乎返归至实体——本体论的差异。请允许我在这点上不要深入，我只是注意到，延异，同海德格尔在《存在与时间》中所说的时间化之间存在着某种严格的相通性，即使不是完全的和绝对必要的相通性的话。延异是作为延宕化——时间化的差异，它不再是在场者的视域内被构想；海德格尔的时间化则作为超验的存在问题视域，应通过现在或现时——从传统的、形而上学的控制中解放出来。

但是，我们首先还是待在符号学的问题框架内来看看作为延宕化的延异是如何与作为间隔的延异连接在一起的。主宰着今天思想领域的大多数符号学和语言学研究，不管是因为他们在各地都得到承认的结论还是他们都得到惊人的规范的模式，在谱系上（正确地或错误地）都将索绪尔指为他们共同的创始者。索绪尔首先提出了符号的任意性和差别性作为普通符号学，尤其是语言学的原则。正如我们所知，这两种主张——任意性和差别性——在索绪尔这里是不可分的。仅仅因为符号系统是由词语差异性而非统一性构成，才可能有任意性。表意元素起作用不是因为它们紧密的语核力量，而是因为对它们进行区分进而使它们彼此相关的对立之网。“任意性和差别性”，索绪尔说，“是两个有关联性的特性”。

作为表意条件的差异原则，影响着符号的整体性，即既是能指又是所

The signified aspect is the concept, the ideal sense. The signifying aspect is what Saussure calls the material or physical (e. g. acoustical) "image". We do not here have to enter into all the problems these definitions pose. Let us only cite Saussure where it interests us:

The conceptual side of value is made up solely of relations and differences with respect to the other terms of language, and the same can be said of its material side...Everything that has been said up to this point boils down to this: in language there are only differences. Even more important: a difference generally implies positive terms between which the difference is set up; but in language there are only differences without positive terms. Whether we take the signified or the signifier, language has neither ideas nor sounds that existed before the linguistic system, but only conceptual and phonic differences that have issued from the system. The idea or phonic substance that a sign contains is of less importance than the other signs that surround it.

The first consequence to be drawn from this is that the signified concept is never present in itself, in an adequate presence that would refer only to itself. Every concept is necessarily and essentially inscribed in a chain or a system, within which it refers to another and to other concepts, by the systematic play of differences. Such a play, then—differance—is no longer simply a concept, but the possibility of conceptuality, of the conceptual system and process in general. For the same reason, differance, which is not a concept, is not a mere word; that is, it is not what we represent to ourselves as the calm and present self-referential unity of a concept and sound (phonie). We shall later discuss the consequences of this for the notion of a word.

The difference that Saussure speaks about, therefore, is neither itself a concept nor one word

指的符号。所指是概念、是理念意义;能指是索绪尔所称之的"形象",是物质的,物理的(如声学的)。我们无需讨论此时的这些定义施加于我们的全部问题。我们只是在令我们感兴趣的一点上援引索绪尔:

意义的概念一方只是由关系和差别形成的,这种关系和差别是同语言的他项的关系和差别。意义的物质一方也是如此……综上所述:在语言中只有差异。更为要紧的是:一种差异一般都暗含两种确定词项,差异就在这两种词项之间确立:但在语言中,只存在无确定词项的差异。不论是所指还是能指,语言既没有先于语言系统的理念,也没有先于语言系统的声音,而只有来自于该系统的概念和语音上的差异。符号所包含的理念或语音物质较之环绕在它周围的其他符号而言无关紧要。

从这里得出来的第一个结论是,所指概念决不会自我出场,决不会在一个充分的自我指涉的在场中出场。从本质和规律上来说,每个概念都刻写在链条和系统内。其中,概念通过系统的差异嬉戏,指涉他者,指涉其他概念。这样一种嬉戏,延异,因此就不再简单地是一种概念,而是概念化的可能性,是一般的概念过程和系统的可能性。由于同样的原因,延异,不是一个概念,不简单地是一个词,也即是,它一般不表现为安静的、在场的和自我指涉的概念和语音物质统一体,后面我们将概要地考察一下这个词。

因此,索绪尔所说的差异,其本

among others. We can say this a fortiori for differance. Thus we are brought to make the relation between the one and the other explicit.

Within a language, within the system of language, there are only differences. A taxonomic operation can accordingly undertake its systematic, statistical, and classificatory inventory. But, on the one hand, these differences play a role in language, in speech as well, and in the exchange between language and speech. On the other hand, these differences are themselves effects. They have not fallen from the sky ready made; they are no more inscribed in a topos noetos than they are prescribed in the wax of the brain. If the word "history" did not carry with it the theme of a final repression of differance, we could say that differences alone could be "historical" through and through and from the start.

What we note as differance will thus be the movement of play that "produces" (and not by something that is simply an activity) these differences, these effects of difference. This does not mean that the differance which produces differences is before them in a simple and in itself unmodified and indifferent present. Differance is the nonfull, nonsimple origin; it is the structured and differing origin of differences.

Since language (which Saussure says is a classification) has not fallen from the sky, it is clear that the differences have been produced; they are the effects produced, but effects that do not have as their cause a subject or substance, a thing in general, or a being that is somewhere present and itself escapes the play of difference. If such a presence were implied (quite classically) in the general concept of cause, we would therefore have to talk about an effect without a cause, something that would very quickly lead to no longer talking about effects. I have tried to indicate a way out of

身既非一个概念,也非存在于其他词中的一个词。延异也可以同样如此地说。因此,我们就得去解释它们彼此的相关性。

在语言里,在语言的系统内,只有差异。因此,某种分类学操作可以对语言进行系统的、统计学的和类别的清理。但是,一方面,这些差异在语言中,也在言语中,在语言和言语的互换中起作用。另一方面,这些差异本身就是效应,它们并不是从完全成形的天上掉下来的,它们也不是铭刻于认知领域中,也不是刻写于大脑的灰色物质里。如果"历史"一词并不自身地表达出对延异的最终压迫动机的话,人们就可以说,只有差异,从一开始,在它的方方面面,才是"历史"的。

作为延异的文字,就是嬉戏活动,这些活动利用不单单是某种活动的东西来生产这些差异、这些差异效果。这并不意味着生产差异的延异在差异面前只是一种简单的、不加修饰的、无差异的现在。延异是不完全的、不单一的"本原",它是造成差异的,有结构和有差异的本原。

既然语言(索绪尔说它是一种分类)不是从天而降,它的差异就是被生产的,是被生产出来的效应,但这些效应没有在主体或物质中、在普遍性的物中、在某处出场因而就排除了在差异的嬉戏的存在中找到起因。如果这样一种在场以一种最古典的样式被包含在普遍性的起因概念中,我们就不得不提出一种无起因的效应,这就会十分迅速地导致我们提及

the closure imposed by this system, namely, by means of the "trace". No more an effect than a cause, the "trace" cannot of itself, taken outside its context, suffice to bring about the required transgression.

As there is no presence before the semiological difference or outside it, we can extend what Saussure writes about language to signs in general: "Language is necessary in order for speech to be intelligible and to produce all of its effects; but the latter is necessary in order for language to be established; historically, the fact of speech always comes first."

Retaining at least the schema, if not the content, of the demand formulated by Saussure, we shall designate by the term differance the movement by which language, or any code, any system of reference in general, becomes "historically" constituted as a fabric of differences. Here, the terms "constituted", "produced", "created", "movement", "historically", etc., with all they imply, are not to be understood only in terms of the language of metaphysics, from which they are taken. It would have to be shown why the concepts of production, like those of constitution and history, remain accessories in this respect to what is here being questioned; this, however, would draw us too far away today, toward the theory of the representation of the "circle" in which we seem to be enclosed. I only use these terms here, like many other concepts, out of strategic convenience and in order to prepare the deconstruction of the system they form at the point which is now most decisive. In any event, we will have understood, by virtue of the very circle we appear to be caught up in, that differance, as it is written here, is no more static than genetic, no more structural than historical. Nor is it any less so. And it is completely to miss the point of this orthographical impropriety to want

一种完全的无效应。我已试图通过"踪迹"表明走出这种封闭框架的方式,踪迹不再是效应,它也没有起因,但是在其文本之外,它不能靠自身自发地、充分地进行必要的逾界活动。

既然在符号的差异之前、之外,没有在场,索绪尔有关语言的论述就能扩充到一般性的符号:"为了言语能被理解,为了产生它的全部效果,语言是必要的;但言语的必要是为了让语言被确立起来;从历史的角度来看,言语的事实总是最先的。"

要至少保留索绪尔所提出的这种要求的框架而非内容的话,我们就将这样一种活动表示为延异:根据这种活动,语言、或任何符码、任何一般性指涉系统,都被"历史性"地构成为差异的编织物。"被构造","被生产"、"被创造"、"活动"、"历史性地"等等,都有必要超出形而上学语言来被理解,在形而上学语言中,它们连同它们的含义一道被保留着。我们本应该表明诸如生产、构造、历史等概念仍旧同此处有争议的东西是同谋。但是,这会使我今天离题太远,走向我们似乎封闭于其间的"循环"的再现论。我像运用许多其他概念一样来运用这些概念,仅仅是由于它们在策略上的便利,也是为了在目前最紧要的关头对它们进行解构。在任何情况下,根据我们似乎卷入其中的循环,这点都会被理解:延异,如同它被书写在此一样,既不是静态的,也不是生成性的;既不是结构的,也不是历史的;或者就是如此。要依据最古老的形而上学对立来对此进行反驳(比如,通过建立生成性观点

to object to it on the basis of the oldest of metaphysical oppositions—for example, by opposing some generative point of view to a structuralist—taxonomic point of view, or conversely. These oppositions do not pertain in the least to differance; and this, no doubt, is what makes thinking about it difficult and uncomfortable.

来反对结构—分类观点),最重要的是不要去读解拼写伦理中的失误处。这样的对立至少与延异无关,毫无疑问这也使得对延异的思考变得不安、不适。

If we now consider the chain to which "differance" gets subjected, according to the context, to a certain number of nonsynonymic substitutions, one will ask why we resorted to such concepts as "reserve", "protowriting", "prototrace", "spacing", indeed to "supplement" or "pharmakon" and, before long, to "hymen", etc.

如果我们根据上下文,根据某些非同义替换词来考虑“延异”所从属的链,人们会问,为什么我们还要借助于这样的一些概念,如“保留”、“原书写”、“原踪迹”、“间距化”,还有“增补”,或者“药”,而且不久又用了“婚姻”等等。

Let us begin again. Differance is what makes the movement of signification possible only if each element that is said to be "present", appearing on the stage of presence, is related to something other than itself but retains the mark of a past element and already let itself be hollowed out by the mark of its relation to a future element. This trace relates no less to what is called the future than to what is called the past, and it constitutes what is called the present by this very relation to what it is not, to what it absolutely is not; that is, not even to a past or future considered as a modified present. In order for it to be, an interval must separate it from what it is not; but the interval that constitutes it in the present must also, and by the same token, divide the present in itself, thus dividing, along with the present, everything that can be conceived on its basis, that is, every being—in particular, for our metaphysical language, the substance or subject. Constituting itself, dynamically dividing itself, this interval is what could be called spacing, time's becoming-spatial or space's becoming-temporal (temporalizing). And it is this constitution of the present as a "primordial" and irreducibly

我们继续。正是因为延异,也只是每一个所谓的“在场”因素,每个出现在在场场景中的因素同非他自身之物相关的情况下,表意活动才是可能的。现时在场因素因此也使自身保留过去因素的标志,它已经通过表明与未来因素的关系让自身变质,这就构成了踪迹,此踪迹同未来、同过去有同等的相关性,且通过和他者的相关性构成了所谓的现时在场者,此他者乃现时在场者绝对的他者,甚至不是过去和未来的修改过的在场者。某个间歇应将现时和非现时分开以使现时成为自身。但是,将它构成为现时的这种间歇,依据同样的标记,它本身也分割现时,根据它所能想象的一切事物,即一切存在——尤其是用我们的形而上学的语言来说,本体或主体。在自我构成中,在动态的自我分割中,这种间歇可称为间距化、时间的空间化或空间的时间化(延宕化)。正是在场者的这种构成——

nonsimple, and, therefore, in the strict sense nonprimordial, synthesis of traces, retentions, and protentions (to reproduce here, analogically and provisionally, a phenomenological and transcendental language that will presently be revealed as inadequate) that I propose to call protowriting, prototrace, or differance. The latter (is) (both) spacing (and) temporalizing.

它作为"原初"的,不能减约的非初级的(因而也是严格意义上的非原初的)符号综合,或者是作为保留和延续的踪迹(与此类推和临时性地再生产某种很快表明自己并不胜任的现象学和超验语言),我才主张命名原书写、原踪迹,或延异。后者(同时)(是)间距化(和)延宕化。

3. Questions for Discussion

(1) What is Derrida's purpose of coining the word "differance"?

(2) Summarize the deconstructive strategy used by Derrida in "Differance"?

(3) Analyze the overlooked marginal details of a classical work with deconstructive strategy.

3. 讨论题

(1)德里达为什么要创造"延异"一词?

(2)请总结德里达在《延异》一文中所用的解构策略。

(3)用解构策略分析一经典作品中被忽略的边缘细节。

Chapter 14

第 14 章

1. Introduction to Edward W. Said

Edward Said (1935-2003) was a prominent Palestinian-American literary theorist, critic, and activist of the late 20th and early 21st century. He is regarded as a founding figure in post-colonial theory.

Said was born in Jerusalem. His father was a Palestinian man who soldiered in the U.S. Army (1917-1919) in the First World War (1914-1918) and his military service earned himself and his family American citizenship. His mother was born in Nazareth of Christian Lebanese and Palestinian descent. In his formative years, he lived in both Cairo and Jerusalem. He attended the British St. George's Academy in Jerusalem in 1947. During the 1948 Arab-Israeli war, his entire family became refugees in Egypt. His family moved to the U.S.A. in 1950. In early September 1951, his parents deposited him in the Northfield Mount Hermon School, a private preparatory high school, in Massachusetts, and immediately returned to the Middle East.

Said earned a B.A. from Princeton University

1. 爱德华·萨义德简介

爱德华·萨义德(1935—2003)是20世纪末、21世纪初著名的巴勒斯坦—美国文学理论家、批评家和活动家。他被认为是后殖民理论的奠基人。

萨义德出生在耶路撒冷。其父是巴勒斯坦人，第一次世界大战(1914—1918)期间他在美国军队服役(1917—1919)，此经历为其本人和家人获得了美国公民身份。其母亲出生于拿撒勒，是信仰基督教的黎巴嫩和巴勒斯坦人的后裔。少年时代，萨义德在开罗和耶路撒冷生活过。1947年，他就读于耶路撒冷的英国圣乔治学院。在1948年阿拉伯—以色列战争中，萨义德一家在埃及成为难民。1950年，一家人移居美国。1951年9月初，其父母将其送至马萨诸塞州著名的私立学校北野山高中后，立刻返回了中东。

萨义德在普林斯顿大学获得学士学位，在哈佛大学获得硕士学位和

and an M.A. and a Ph.D. from Harvard. He joined the faculty of Columbia University in 1963, serving as a professor of English and Comparative Literature for several decades. Said also taught at Harvard, Johns Hopkins, and Yale universities and lectured at more than 150 universities and colleges in the United States, Canada, and Europe. He was fluent in English, French, and Arabic.

博士学位。1963年,他成为哥伦比亚大学的教师,任英语和比较文学教授数十年。萨义德还任教于哈佛大学、霍普金斯大学、耶鲁大学,并且在美国、加拿大和欧洲的150多所大学做过讲座。他的英语、法语和阿拉伯语都极为流利。

Said published many articles and books and the well-known ones are *Joseph Conrad and the Fiction of Autobiography* (1966), *Orientalism* (1978), *The World, the Text, and the Critic* (1983), *Blaming the Victims* (1988), *Culture and Imperialism* (1993), *The Politics of Dispossession* (1994), *Peace and Its Discontents* (1995), *Out of Place: A Memoir* (1999), and *Reflections on Exile and Other Essays* (2000).

萨义德发表了很多文章和著作,广为人知的有《约瑟夫·康拉德与自传体小说》(1966)、《东方主义》(1978)、《世界、文本、批评家》(1983)、《谴责受害者》(1988)、《文化与帝国主义》(1993)、《流离失所的政治学》(1994)、《和平及其不满》(1995)、《格格不入:回忆录》(1999)、《流亡反思及其他散文》(2000)。

Said is best known for describing and critiquing "Orientalism", which he perceived as a constellation of false assumptions underlying Western attitudes toward the East. In *Orientalism*, Said described the "subtle and persistent Eurocentric prejudice against Arabo-Islamic peoples and their culture." He argued that a long tradition of false and romanticized images of Asia and the Middle East in Western culture had served as an implicit justification for Europe's and America's colonial and imperial ambitions. He denounced just as fiercely the practice of Arab elites who internalized the American and British orientalists' ideas of Arabic culture.

萨义德以描述和批评"东方主义"而最为著称,他认为"东方主义"是西方对东方的态度中潜藏的错误假想的集合。在《东方主义》中,萨义德描述了"西方世界对阿拉伯—伊斯兰世界的人民和文化持有的微妙却非常持久的偏见"。他指出西方文化对亚洲和中东的错误和浪漫化的长久传统使欧洲和美国的殖民和帝国野心得到公开的合理化。他以同样激烈的方式谴责了阿拉伯精英将美国和英国对阿拉伯文化的东方主义思想内化为己的做法。

Said's "Invention, Memory, and Place" can be regarded as one of the examples of putting post-colonial theory into practice. It combines "memory", the topic of the humanities and social sciences with geography and discloses the complicated narratives of international politics and historical politics by close investigation into and thinking about landscape, land and place.

萨义德的《虚构、记忆与地方》(2000)堪称其将后殖民主义理论付诸实践的范例之一。它将人文和社科领域的议题"记忆"与地理学相联系,通过对风景、土地、地方等的细察和思考揭露复杂的国际政治和历史政治的叙事。

2. Selections from "Invention, Memory, and Place"

Invention, Memory, and Place①

Edward W. Said

Over the past decade, there has been a burgeoning interest in two over lapping areas of the humanities and social sciences: memory and geography or, more specifically, the study of human space. Both of them have spawned an extraordinary amount of interesting work, work that has in effect created new fields of study and inquiry. The concern with memory, for example, has branched out to include such increasingly prevalent forms of writing as personal memoirs and autobiography, which nearly every fiction writer of note has attempted, to say nothing of the outpourings of academics, scientists, public figures, and so forth. The national fixation on recollection, confession, and witness has run the whole gamut from public confession—as in the Clinton-Lewinsky scandal—to various studies of the meaning of collective memory, extended reflection and analyses of instances of it, plus numerous chronicles embodying it. I shall have more to say about that later. In addition, and somewhat on the margins, has been a serious, sometimes bitter inquiry into the authenticity of certain memories, as well as, at the other, calmer end of the spectrum, a remarkable academic analysis of the role of invention in such matters as tradition and collective historical experience.

2.《虚构、记忆与地方》选文

虚构、记忆与地方

爱德华·萨义德

过去十年,人们对于人文和社会科学的两个交叉领域:记忆和地理,或更具体地说,对于人类空间的研究,越来越感兴趣。两个学科都催生了大量有趣的作品,且这些作品事实上开创了新的研究和探索领域。譬如,对记忆领域的关注衍生出诸如个人回忆录与自传之类越来越流行的写作形式。几乎所有著名的小说家都曾尝试此类书写,更无需提及专业学者、科学家、公众人物及其他人群的大量相关著述。国家对记忆、忏悔以及目击证明的重视表现为各种形式,从公开忏悔——如在克林顿-莱温斯基丑闻中——到关于集体记忆意义的各种研究、集体记忆实例的扩展性反思以及为数众多的体现集体记忆的编年史。我在后面的内容中会对此进行追述。另外,在稍微边缘化的地带中,人们对某些回忆录的真实性进行了严肃、有时甚至尖刻的审视,在此范围更为理性的另一端,人们也对传统与集体历史经验中的虚构作用做出了非同凡响的学术分析。

① Selected from "Invention, Memory, and Place", *Critical Inquiry*, 2000, Vol. 26, No. 2.

Some examples of intense and even anguished controversy are the following: Was Anne Frank's diary really hers, or was it so altered by publishers, members of her family, or others in its published form so as to conceal the disturbances in her domestic life? In Europe there has been a great and often acerbic debate over the meaning of the Holocaust, with a whole range of opinions as to what happened, why it happened, and what it tells us about the nature of Germany, France, and several other involved countries. The celebrated French classicist Pierre Vidal-Naquet wrote a powerful book some years back called *Assassins of Memory* about French deniers of the Holocaust, and more recently the Papon trial in Bordeaux raised uncomfortable questions related not just to memories of the Occupation but the centrality of French collaborators with the Nazis and what it said about French selective memories of the Vichy regime. In Germany of course debate on the testimonials of the death camps and their philosophical as well as political meaning periodically receives new infusions of controversy, fuelled most recently by the publication of the German translation of Daniel Goldhagen's book *Hitler's Willing Executioners*. In the United States consider the anger provoked by representatives of the official culture and members of the government by the Smithsonian Institution—seen correctly as a sort of embodier of official memory in the country—in its unsuccessful attempts to mount exhibitions, one about the Enola Gay① and another on the African American experience. Earlier there was a furor over an impressive exhibition at the National Gallery of American Art, America as West, which set out to contrast representations of the land, the

一些激烈，甚至极为痛苦的争议事例如下：安妮·弗兰克的日记果真出自她的手笔？或者付梓的日记被出版商、她的家人或其他人篡改过以掩盖其家庭生活的不和谐之音？在欧洲，关于犹太人大屠杀的意图一直存在剧烈并且经常是尖锐的争论，争论观点涉及：发生了什么事？为什么会发生这样的事？关于德国、法国及其他牵连其中的国家本性，我们能获知什么？法国知名古典学者皮埃尔·维达尔-纳凯数年前写过一本颇有影响力的书，名为《记忆的暗杀》，讲述法国那些否认大屠杀的人。最近，帕蓬在波尔多接受审讯，审讯引发令人不安的问题，不仅关系到德国占领法国的记忆，还关系到与纳粹合作的法国人所起的关键作用和法国对维希政权的选择性记忆。当然在德国，关于死亡集中营的证词及其哲学与政治意义周期性地被注入新的争论意见，最近丹尼尔·戈德哈根所著的《希特勒的自愿刽子手》一书的德文译本的出版为这些争议再添一把火。在美国，只需了解由官方文化代表、政府成员和史密森学会引发的怒火便可。史密森学会被恰如其分地认为体现了这个国家的官方记忆，它试图推出几个展览，均未成功——一个有关艾诺拉·盖伊号轰炸机，另一个有关非裔美国人的经历。此前美国国家美术馆举办的令人印象深刻的"西部美国"展览，也引发愤怒的情绪。该展览再现了 19 世纪 60 年代美国西部大地、印第安土著人及其生活状况，并将此与白人以

① 艾诺拉·盖伊(Enola Gay)是第二次世界大战期间把原子弹带到日本广岛上空的美国 B-29 轰炸机。

Indian natives, and the conditions of life in the Western U.S. during the 1860s with the way the land was being forcibly settled and the Indians destroyed, and the transformation of a once peaceful rural environment into a predatory urban one. Senator Ted Stevens of Alaska decried the whole thing as an attack on America even though he avowed that he himself had not seen the exhibit. In any event these controversies raise the question not only of what is remembered but how and in what form. It is an issue about the very fraught nature of representation, not just about content.

Memory and its representations touch very significantly upon questions of identity, of nationalism, of power and authority. Far from being a neutral exercise in facts and basic truths, the study of history, which of course is the underpinning of memory, both in school and university, is to some considerable extent a nationalist effort premised on the need to construct a desirable loyalty to and insider's understanding of one's country, tradition, and faith. As is well known, there's been a robust debate in the U.S. on the matter of national standards in history, in which issues such as whether George Washington or Abraham Lincoln should be allowed more time than they have at present in history curricula have generated very angry arguments. Similarly, as Howard Zinn has suggested in his work, there has been skepticism expressed as to why the study of American history should glorify only the big deeds of big people and neglect to mention what happened to the small ones, the people who built railroads, worked the farms, sweated as laborers in the enormous industrial companies that lie at the heart of this country's immense wealth and power. (He redresses this imbalance in his impressive *People's History of the United States*, which has already sold

武力手段强行在此定居,印第安人遭杀戮,曾经和平的乡村环境转变成弱肉强食的城镇进行了对比。阿拉斯加的参议员泰德·史蒂文斯谴责整个事件是对美国的一次攻击,尽管他声称本人并未观看此次展览。不管怎样,这些争议引发的问题不仅关乎记忆的内容,还关乎记忆的方式与形式。这是一个关系到再现行为本身令人棘手的本质问题,而绝不仅仅是其内容。

记忆及其再现触及身份、民族主义和权力权威问题,意义重大。历史研究,当然是记忆的基础,但又不仅是在事实和基本真理中所做的中立训练,学院和大学的历史研究在很大程度上是一种民族主义性质的工作,其前提是研究者需要对国家、传统及信仰抱有适当的忠诚以及真切的了解。众所周知,在美国,关于历史中的国家标准问题一直引发热烈讨论。其中有关乔治·华盛顿或亚伯拉罕·林肯的内容是否应在历史课程中占有比当前更多的篇幅,诸如此类的问题产生了相当愤怒的争论。与此类似,霍华德·辛在其著作中提出,美国历史研究为什么只应美化伟大人物的伟大事迹而忽略不提小人物事件,是小人物修筑了铁路,在农场劳作,在位于国家巨大财富与权力中心的大型工业企业里挥汗如雨。人们对此类问题一直表示怀疑。(他在其引人注目的著作《美国人民的历史》中重新论述了这种不平衡,该书已售出愈 50 万册。)他在最近的一篇

well over half a million copies.)① In a recent article he goes even further. Having been asked to participate in a symposium on the Boston Massacre, Zinn reflected to himself that he wanted to discuss other massacres "because it seemed to me that concentrating attention on the Boston Massacre would be a painless exercise in patriotic fervor. There is no surer way to obscure the deep divisions of race and class in American history than by uniting us in support of the American Revolution and all its symbols (like Paul Revere's stark etching of the soldiers shooting into the crowd). I suggested to the people assembled at Faneuil Hall (the wall around us crowded with portraits of the Founding Fathers and the nation's military heroes) that there were other massacres, forgotten or dimly remembered, that deserved to be recalled. These ignored episodes could tell us much about racial hysteria and class struggle, about shameful moments in our continental and overseas expansion, so that we can see ourselves more clearly, more honestly.②"

文章中的论述甚至走得更远。在受邀参加一个关于波士顿惨案的研讨会后,辛对自己说他想要讨论其他惨案,"因为对我来说,似乎专注于波士顿惨案是毫不费力的爱国热情练习。美国历史中没有什么比团结我们支持美国革命及其所有象征(如保罗·瑞威尔记录士兵向群众扫射的令人触目的蚀刻画)更能掩盖种族与阶级的深刻分歧。法尼尔大厅的墙上挂满了开国元勋和国家军功英雄的肖像。我向聚集在大厅的人们提示过,还有其他被人遗忘或淡出记忆的惨案,同样值得回忆。这些被忽略的事件可以告诉我们关于种族歇斯底里症、阶级斗争,以及我们在美洲大陆与海外扩张的许多情况,如此我们便能更清晰更诚实地看清自己。"

These remarks immediately transport us to the vexed issue of nationalism and national identity, of how memories of the past are shaped in accordance with a certain notion of what "we" or, for that matter, "they" really are. National identity always involves narratives—of the nation's past, its founding fathers and documents, seminal events, and so on. But these narratives are never undisputed or merely a matter of the neutral recital of facts. In the United States, for example, 1492 was celebrated very differently by people who saw themselves as victims of Columbus's advent—people of color, minorities, members of the

这些话立即将我们带到那个棘手问题上,即种族主义和国家身份问题,过去的记忆如何依照"我们"或,就此而言,"他们"确实是以什么这一特定概念而形成。国家身份总是包含着关于国家过去,开国元勋及文件与重要事件等等的叙述。但这些叙述从来不是无争论的,也不仅仅是不偏不倚事实的详述。比如,在美国,有人以不同的方式纪念 1492 年,他们认为自己是哥伦布到来事件的受害者,他们是有色人种、少数民族、工

① 参见霍华德·辛,《美国人民的历史》,纽约:哈珀,1980。

② 霍华德·辛,《对历史的屠杀》(*The Massacres of History*),《进步思想》(*The Progressive*),1998 年第 62 期,第 17 页。

working class, people, in a word, who claimed they had a different collective memory of what in most schools was celebrated as a triumph of advancement and the collective march forward of humanity. Because the world has shrunk—for example, communications have been speeded up fantastically—and people find themselves undergoing the most rapid social transformations in history, ours has become an era of a search for roots, of people trying to discover in the collective memory of their race, religion, community, and family a past that is entirely their own, secure from the ravages of history and a turbulent time. But this too has provoked very sharp debate and even bloodshed. In the Islamic world, how one reads the orthodox tradition (sunnah) is being debated, as are the questions of how one interprets stories about the Prophet, which are, basically, memories reconstructed by disciples and friends, and how one can derive an image of contemporary Islamic codes of behavior and law that is consonant and in accordance with those precious, early, in fact aboriginal, memories. Similar questions arise in interpretations of the Christian Gospels, as well as the Judaic prophetic books; these questions have a direct impact on matters of community and politics in the present. Some of this lies behind the much-touted controversy over family values that have been vaunted by political candidates, moral philosophers, and public scolds.

人阶级成员,简言之,对于大多数学派视为进步的胜利和人类共同前进的事件,他们是声称有着不同集体记忆的人。因为世界变得越来越小,例如,通讯速度的提高令人吃惊,人们正在经历史上最快速的社会转变,我们的时代已经变成一个寻根的时代,人们试图在其种族、宗教、社群和家庭的集体记忆中寻找完全属于自己的,免于历史与动荡年代破坏的过去。但这也挑起了相当尖锐的争论,甚至流血冲突。在伊斯兰世界中,一个人如何阅读正统传统(即圣行);如何解读先知穆罕默德的故事,这些故事基本上是由他的门徒与朋友们重新建构的记忆;如何形成与那些珍贵的、早期的、实际上原始的记忆相符合一致的当代伊斯兰法律与行为准则的图像。这些问题正在遭受热议。对基督教福音书、犹太人先知书的阐释也出现同样的问题;这些问题对当下的社群与政治问题有直接影响。部分影响隐藏于大肆吹捧的关于家庭价值观的争议背后;这些家庭价值观被政治候选人和道德哲学家大加颂扬,但饱受公众指责。

To this whole matter of memory as a social, political, and historical enterprise has been added a complication, to which I referred above, namely, the role of invention. In 1983 two distinguished British historians Eric Hobsbawm and Terence Ranger edited a book of essays by various other

整个问题使得作为一种社会、政治和历史事业的记忆变得更为复杂。如上文所述,这个问题是虚构的作用。1983 年,两位著名的历史学家埃里克·霍布斯鲍姆和特伦斯·兰杰

well-known historians entitled *The Invention of Tradition*①. I won't try to summarize the ideas in this subtle and rich collection except to say that what was being studied was the way rulers—social and political authorities in the period since about 1850—set about creating such supposedly age-old rituals and objects as the Scottish kilt or, in India, the durbar, thereby providing a false, that is, invented memory of the past as a way of creating a new sense of identity for ruler and ruled. In India, for example, the durbar—whose status as "tradition" was a total fiction—was said to be a great ceremonial pageant designed to be implanted in the Indian memory though it served the British colonial authorities to compel Indians to believe in the age-old history of British imperial rule. "In Africa, too," writes Ranger, "whites drew on invented tradition in order to derive the authority and confidence that allowed them to act as agents of change. Moreover, insofar as they were consciously applied to Africans, the invented traditions (such as compelling Africans to work as laborers on European gentlemen's farms) of nineteenth century Europe were seen precisely as agents of 'modernization'."② In modern France, according to Hobsbawm, the demise of Napoleon III's empire and the emergence of a politicized working class as evidenced in the Paris Commune convinced the "moderate Republican bourgeoisie" that only it could head off the dangers of revolution by producing a new kind of citizen, "turning peas ants into Frenchmen ... (and) all Frenchmen into good Republicans." Thus the French revolution was institutionalized in education by developing "a secular equivalent of the church ... imbued with revolutionary and republican principles and

编撰了《传统之虚构》,收录了其他几位著名历史学家的著作。我不想在这里总结这本书中精巧且内容丰富的文集观点,我只想说,它研究的是,约1850年以来的社会领袖和政治统治者如何着手创作一些被认为年代久远的仪式和物件,比如苏格兰的短裙和印度藩王的接见仪式,以此制造出一种虚假的,也即虚构的过去记忆,作为统治者和被统治者新的认知的一种手段。比如在印度,藩王的接见仪式——其所谓的"传统"地位完全是子虚乌有——被说成是一次盛大的庆祝盛会,其目的就是要使其根植于印度人的脑海中,辅助英国殖民政府强迫印度人民相信那由来已久的英帝国统治。兰杰在书中写道,"非洲的情况也一样。白人利用虚构的传统来获取权威和信心,使自己变成革故鼎新的代理人。而且,由于这些虚构的传统(如强迫非洲人在欧洲绅士的农场里劳作)是被有意识的加在非洲人的身上,因此这些19世纪的欧洲虚构传统完全可以看作'现代化'的代理"。据霍布斯鲍姆所言,在现代法国,拿破仑三世帝国的消亡以及政治化新阶级的出现,正如巴黎公社所证明的,"温和的共和派资产阶级"相信,只有通过产生新公民,"把农民变成法国人……把所有法国人变成良好的共和党人"才能摆脱革命的危险。因而通过发展"一种教堂的俗世对应物……充满了革命与共和的信念和内容",法国革命在教育中被制度化了。除此之外,还有"公共

① 参见霍布斯鲍姆和兰杰主编的《传统之虚构》,剑桥:剑桥大学出版社,1983。
② 同上,第220页。

content." In addition, there was "the invention of public ceremonies. The most important of these, Bastille Day, can be exactly dated in 1880." Thirdly, there "was the mass production of public monuments," of two main kinds—images of the Republic itself such as Marianne—and images of the "bearded civilian figures of whoever local patriotism chose to regard as its notables."①

In other words, the invention of tradition was a practice very much used by authorities as an instrument of rule in mass societies when the bonds of small social units like village and family were dissolving and authorities needed to find other ways of connecting a large number of people to each other. The invention of tradition is a method for using collective memory selectively by manipulating certain bits of the national past, suppressing others, elevating still others in an entirely functional way. Thus memory is not necessarily authentic, but rather useful. The Israeli journalist Tom Segev shows in his book *The Seventh Million* that the Holocaust was consciously used by the Israeli government as a way of consolidating Israeli national identity after years of not paying much attention to it.② Similarly, historian Peter Novick, in a recently published study of the image of the Holocaust amongst American Jews, shows that before the 1967 war and the Israeli victory against the Arab states, American Jews paid very little attention to that appallingly horrible episode (and in fact tried consciously to deemphasize it as a way of avoiding anti-Semitism).③ It is a long way from

典礼的发明。最重要的是巴士底日，能够被准确追溯到 1880 年"。最后，还有"大量公共纪念碑的产生"，主要有两种类型，一种是共和国本身的形象，像玛丽安；另一种是"胡子拉碴的爱国平民，他们被认为是当地最优秀的人"。

换句话说，虚构传统是统治者通常使用的一种实践，其作为一种对大众社会的统治工具，尤其是当像村庄和家庭这样的小团体的凝聚力在解体，当权者需要找到其他方式将大量民众联合起来时。虚构传统通过篡改部分国家过去，压制他者，通过完全功能性的方式提高他人地位，是选择性地使用集体记忆的一种方法。因而，记忆不一定是真实的，但是很有用。以色列记者汤姆·塞格夫在他的《第七个一百万》一书中提到，在多年未重视国家身份之后，以色列政府有意将大屠杀作为一种巩固政权的手段。无独有偶，历史学家皮特·诺维克最近发表了关于大屠杀在美国犹太人心中的印象的研究，其表明，在 1967 年以色列战胜阿拉伯国家之前，美国犹太人对那段极其恐怖的经历关注甚少(实际上刻意尽量降低其重要性，以此作为避免反犹太主义的方式)。从早期的这种态度，到华盛顿大屠杀博物馆的建成，中间经历了漫漫长路。同样的，关于亚美尼

① 霍布斯鲍姆，《批量生产传统：1870—1914》(*Mass-Producing Tradition*：1870—1914)，剑桥：剑桥大学出版社，1983，第 271，272 页。

② 参见汤姆·塞格夫，《第七个一百万》，海姆·沃兹曼(Haim Watzman)译，纽约：希尔和王出版社，1993。

③ 参见皮特·诺维克，《美国生活中的大屠杀》(*The Holocaust in American Life*)，波士顿：休顿·米夫林公司，1999，第 146-203 页。

those early attitudes to the construction of the Holocaust Museum in Washington. Similarly the controversy surrounding the memories of the Armenian genocide is fuelled by the Turkish government's denial of its role.

My point in citing all these cases is to underline the extent to which the art of memory for the modern world is both for historians as well as ordinary citizens and institutions very much something to be used, misused, and exploited, rather than something that sits inertly there for each person to possess and contain. Thus the study and concern with memory or a specifically desirable and recoverable past is a specially freighted late twentieth-century phenomenon that has arisen at a time of bewildering change, of unimaginably large and diffuse mass societies, competing nationalisms, and, most important perhaps, the decreasing efficacy of religious, familial, and dynastic bonds. People now look to this refashioned memory, especially in its collective forms, to give themselves a coherent identity, a national narrative, a place in the world, though, as I have indicated, the processes of memory are frequently, if not always, manipulated and intervened in for sometimes urgent purposes in the present. It's interesting to contrast this more modern and somehow loosely malleable form of memory with the codified, rigorous art of memory in classical antiquity described by Frances Yates.① Memory for Cicero was something organized and structured. If you wanted to remember something for a speech you were about to give, you imagined a building with all sorts of rooms and corners, and in your mind's eye you subdivided the parts of the memory you wished to recall and placed them in various sections of the

亚大屠杀记忆的争议因土耳其政府否认在其中扮演的角色而升级。

我引用这些例子是想强调,记忆的艺术并不是一成不变的待在那儿供每个人占用或拥有。在当今社会,不管是历史学家还是普通大众抑或是组织机构,大抵都会利用、误用和滥用记忆的艺术。因此,对记忆,或者某种理想的、可恢复的过去的研究和关注是20世纪末期特有的一种现象。出现这种现象的时代背景是,时代急剧变化让人手足无措,国家大到令人难以想象却又很分散,种族间竞相争逐;最重要的可能当属宗教、家庭和政府纽带效力的式微。如今,人们试图通过这种重塑的记忆,尤其是集体记忆,来获取一种身份认同、一种民族叙事、一个立足于世界的位置。尽管,如我前述,有时为了当下迫切所需,记忆过程经常(如果不是一直的话)会被操控和干预。这种记忆形式更为现代,某种程度上可塑性也更高。而弗朗西斯·耶茨所描述的古典时代的记忆艺术则是典籍化和严密的。对这二者加以比较,非常有趣。对西塞罗而言,记忆是有组织、有结构的。如果你想记住即将要做演讲的某些内容,你会想象出一所房子,里面有各式各样的房间和角落。在脑海中你将想要记住的内容进行细分,再把它们放置到房子的不同地方。你演讲时,就像在脑海里穿过这所房子,边走边留意每个角落、

① 参见弗朗西斯·耶茨,《记忆的艺术》(*The Art of Memory*),伦敦:劳特里奇出版社,1966。

building; as you spoke you walked through the building in your head, so to speak, noting the places and the objects and phrases as you went along. That way order was maintained in the memory. The modern art of memory is much more subject to inventive reordering and redeploying than that.

物件以及对应的字词句。这样,秩序便留在了记忆中。相比而言,记忆的艺术在现代则更受制于虚构性的再组织和再分配。

As for geography, or geography as I want to use the word, as a socially constructed and maintained sense of place, a great deal of attention has been paid by modern scholars and critics to the extraordinary constitutive role of space in human affairs. Consider, as an easy instance, the word globalization, which is an indispensable concept for modern economics. It is a spatial, geographical designation signifying the global reach of a powerful economic system. Think of geographical designations like Auschwitz, think of what power and resonance they have, over and above a particularly specifiable moment in history or a geographical locale like Poland or France. The same applies to Jerusalem, a city, an idea, an entire history, and of course a specifiable geographical locale often typified by a photograph of the Dome of the Rock, the city walls, and the surrounding houses seen from the Mount of Olives; it too is overdetermined when it comes to memory, as well as all sorts of invented histories and traditions, all of them emanating from it, but most of them in conflict with each other. This conflict is intensified by Jerusalem's mythological—as opposed to actual geographical—location, in which landscape, buildings, streets, and the like are overlain and, I would say, even covered entirely with symbolic associations totally obscuring the existential reality of what as a city and real place Jerusalem is. The same can be said for Palestine, whose landscape functions in the memories of Jews, Muslims, and Christians entirely differently. One of

说到地理学,或说地貌,我用这个词是想说明,这是被社会所建构和使用的地方概念。现代学者和评论家大量关注空间在人类事物中所起的超乎寻常的构建作用。想一想,全球化这个词就是一个很好的例子,全球化是现代经济学一个不可或缺的概念。这是一个空间和地理学名称,标志着全球强大的经济体系。想一想诸如奥斯维辛这样的地理名称,想想它们对于波兰和法国这样的地方,或者对于某一特定历史时期来讲所具有的作用和反响。耶路撒冷也是一样,它是一座城,一个概念,一部完整的历史,当然,也是一个特别的地理位置。耶路撒冷给人的典型印象就是圆顶清真寺、城墙,以及环绕着橄榄山的房子。说到记忆以及各种各样虚构的历史传统,这也是由多种因素所决定的。尽管所有历史传统都是来自记忆,但它们之间大多是相矛盾的。神话中的耶路撒冷的地理位置——而非真实的地理位置——加剧了这种矛盾。神话中,耶路撒冷的风景、建筑、街道等诸如此类都被赋予,甚至可以说全部被覆盖上,象征意义,以致模糊了耶路撒冷作为一个现实之地和城市的真实模样。巴勒斯坦也一样,其风景在犹太人、穆斯林和基督徒的记忆中所起的作用千差万别。有一件我认为匪夷所思

the strangest things for me to grasp is the powerful hold the locale must have had on European crusaders despite their enormous distance from the country. Scenes of the crucifixion and nativity, for instance, appear in European Renaissance paintings as taking place in a sort of denatured Palestine, since none of the artists had ever seen the place. An idealized landscape gradually took shape that sustained the European imagination for hundreds of years. That Bernard of Clairvaux standing in a church in Vezelay, in the heart of Burgundy, could announce a crusade to reclaim Palestine and the holy places from the Muslims never fails to astound me, and that after hundreds of years of living in Europe Zionist Jews could still feel that Palestine had stood still in time and was theirs, again despite millennia of history and the presence of actual inhabitants. This too is also an indication of how geography can be manipulated, invented, characterized quite apart from a site's merely physical reality.

Simon Schama's book *Landscape and Memory* chronicles the to-ing and fro-ing between specific geographical locales and the human imagination. Surely the most compelling aspect of Schama's book is that he shows in dozens of different ways that forests, villages, mountains, and rivers are never coterminous with some stable reality out there that identifies and gives them permanence. On the contrary, as in the example he gives of his family's original village in Lithuania, most of its traces disappeared; he finds instead through the poetry of Adam Mickiewicz how Jews and Poles "were snarled up... in each other's fate" despite his contemporaries' belief that they were "necessarily alien to each other." Geography stimulates not only memory but dreams and fantasies, poetry and painting, philosophy (as in Heidegger's *Holzwege*), fiction (think of *Walter Scott's*

的事情是,这个地方曾经多么强烈地吸引过欧洲的十字军,尽管他们与此地相隔千万里。例如耶稣降生和受难的场景,出现在欧洲文艺复兴时期的绘画中,这些绘画中的场景似乎是发生在一个并不真实的巴勒斯坦,因为这些艺术家没有一个亲眼见过这个地方。继而,一个理想化的风景画面逐渐形成并被欧洲人想象了好几百年。明谷修道院的伯纳德站在法国勃艮第中心的维泽来的一个教堂中,宣布发动十字军东征,要从穆斯林手中夺回巴勒斯坦和其他圣地。这让我一直都觉得很震惊。并且,在欧洲生活了数个世纪以后,犹太复国主义者仍然觉得巴勒斯坦自始至终没有变化,还是他们的巴勒斯坦。他们再一次无视了历史的变迁和真实居民的存在。同样,这也表明了地理可以被如何操控、虚构和刻画,成为或具有完全远离一个地方的真实情况。

西门·沙玛所著的《风景与记忆》讲述一些特定的地理位置与人类的想象来回穿梭的情形。这本书最吸引人之处莫过于他以不同的方式展现出森林、村庄、山河与其命名赋予永恒性的稳固外在现实从来都是密不可分的。但是,在他给出的家乡立陶宛山村的例子中,情况却不是这样的,大多数的遗迹都消失了。然而,沙玛在亚当·密茨凯微奇的诗歌中看到了犹太人和波兰人"是怎样纠缠在自己的命运中的",尽管同时代的人认为"他们彼此肯定是陌生的、疏离的"。地理场景激发人们的记忆,还有梦想、幻想、诗歌、绘画、哲学(譬如海德格尔的《林中路》)、小说(沃尔特·司各特的苏格兰高地小说),

Highland novels), and music (as in Sibelius's *Finlandia or Copland's Appalachian Spring*).①

But what specially interests me is the hold of both memory and geography on the desire for conquest and domination. Two of my books, *Orientalism* and *Culture and Imperialism*, are based not only on the notion of what I call imaginative geography—the invention and construction of a geographical space called the Orient, for instance, with scant attention paid to the actuality of the geography and its inhabitants—but also on the mapping, conquest, and annexation of territory both in what Conrad called the dark places of the earth and in its most densely inhabited and lived—in places, like India or Palestine. The great voyages of geographical discovery from da Gama to Captain Cook were motivated by curiosity and scientific fervor, but also by a spirit of domination, which becomes immediately evident when white men land in some distant and unknown place and the natives rebel against them. In the modern era Defoe's *Robinson Crusoe* is the essential parable of how geography and conquest go together, providing an almost eerie prefiguration of historical figures like Clive and Hastings in India, or scientific adventurers and explorers like Murchison in Africa decades and decades later. These experiences enable complicated memories for natives and (in the Indian case) Britishers alike; a similar dialectic of memory over territory animates the relationship of French and Algerian accounts of the 130 years of French rule in North Africa. We should never have left or given up India or Algeria, say some, using strange atavistic sentiments like the Raj revival—a spate of TV shows and films like

以及音乐(像西贝柳斯的《芬兰颂》和科普兰的《阿巴拉契科亚山脉之春》)。

但是最使我感兴趣的还是记忆与地理对征服和统治之欲望的控制。我的《东方主义》和《文化帝国主义》这两本书不仅是基于我所说的想象性地理——例如我们可以虚构和构建一个称之为东方的空间,这样的空间并不关注地理的真实性及其居民——而且也基于领土的制图、征服,还有吞并,这些不仅出现在康拉德所言的地球上的黑暗之地,而且还在人口稠密的地区,像印度和巴勒斯坦这些国家。从达·伽马到库克船长的这些具有地理发现的重大航行,在好奇心和科学热忱的驱使背后,还活跃一种统治的精神和欲望。在白人登上遥远和不知名的地方,并且被当地人反抗时,这种精神欲望就会表现得非常明显。在现代,笛福的《鲁滨孙漂流记》就是地理与征服的相互融合的重要寓言。它诡谲地预示了几十年之后像印度历史人物克莱武和哈斯丁斯,以及非洲科学探险家默奇森的出现。不管是对当地人(以印度为例)还是对英国殖民者来说,这些经历都会带来复杂的记忆。这种类似的领土记忆激化了法阿两国的关系,法国占领阿尔及利亚,至此开始了法国对北非长达 130 年的统治。尽管有些人会说我们永远都不应该离开或放弃印度或是阿尔及利亚,并使用诸如王侯复活一类怪异的吊古情感——这催生了一大批的电视节目和电影,比如《皇冠上的宝石》、

① 西门·沙玛,《风景与记忆》,伦敦:哈珀柯林斯出版社,1995,第 30 页。

The Jewel in the Crown, *A Passage to India*, *Gandhi*, and the fashion of wearing safari suits, helmets, desert boots—as a way of periodically provoking nostalgia for the good old days of British supremacy in Asia and Africa, whereas most Indians and Algerians would likely say that their liberation came as a result of being able after years of nationalist struggle to take hold of their own affairs, reestablish their identity, culture, and language, and, above all, reappropriate their territory from the colonial masters. Hence, to some extent, we witness the remarkable emergence of an Anglo-Indian literature by Anita Desai, Salman Rushdie, Arundhati Roy, and many others, reexcavating and recharting the past from a postcolonial point of view, thereby erecting a new postimperial space.

It is easy to see the fact of displacement in the colonial experience, which at bottom is the replacement of one geographical sovereignty, an imperialist one, by another, native force. More subtle and complex is the unending cultural struggle over territory, which necessarily involves over lapping memories, narratives, and physical structures. No one has studied this more powerfully than the late Raymond Williams in his classic book, *The Country and the City*. What he shows is that literary and cultural forms such as the ode, the political pamphlet, and different kinds of novels derive some of their aesthetic rationale from changes taking place in the geography or landscape as the result of a social contest. Let me explain this more concretely. The mid-seventeenth-to eighteenth-century genre of the country-house poem, with its emphasis on the house's calm stateliness and classical proportions—"Heaven's Centre, Nature's Lap" is not the same thing in Marvell, Ben Jonson, and, later, in Pope. Jonson draws attention to the way the house was won from

《印度之行》、《甘地传》,还使身着狩猎装,脚穿沙漠靴,头戴头盔的着装成为时尚——这些都能时不时地勾起大英帝国对亚洲和非洲殖民的回忆,然而大多数的印度人和阿尔及利亚人认为他们的民族解放是因为他们源于多年来的民族主义斗争。他们现在总算可以掌握自己的事务,重新建立自己的身份、文化和语言,并且最为重要的是,从殖民者的手中重新夺回自己的土地。因此,在某种程度上,我们见证了英籍印度文学经由安妮塔·德萨伊、萨尔曼·拉什迪、阿兰达蒂·罗伊以及其他很多人的伟大崛起,他们从后殖民的视角对过去进行重新挖掘、重新绘制,以此建立一个新的后帝国主义空间。

很容易看到殖民经历中的置换事实,其本质是以一种地理主权,一种帝国主义的地理主权,代替另外一种权力,当地的权力。对于领土的无休止的文化抗争,越来越微妙,越来越复杂,它不可避免地包含着重叠的记忆、叙述以及实体结构。不过还没有谁能超过刚刚过世的雷蒙·威廉斯,他的《乡村与城市》是这方面研究的经典著作。书中阐释了文学以及文化形式,像颂诗、政治宣传册,还有各种类型的小说的美学原理都衍生于地理或风景的变化,而这些变化是社会斗争造成的,下面对这一点我会更具体地解释。17 世纪中叶到 18 世纪的乡村别墅诗歌强调别墅的宁静庄重和古典的对称——"天堂的中心,大自然的怀抱"。不过这与马尔维尔,本·琼森,以及后来的蒲伯他们笔下所描写的是不同的。琼森所关注的是房子是如何摆脱那些令人

disturbing, encroaching peasant populations; Marvell in a more complicated way understands the country house as the result of a union between money, property, and politics; in Pope the house has become a sort of moral center; and later in Jane Austen's *Mansfield Park* it is the very embodiment of all that is benign and actively good in England. Property in all four writers is being consolidated; what we watch is the gradual triumph of a social dialectic celebrating the virtues and necessities of a propertied class, which itself seems to stand for the nation at its best. In each case the writer remembers the past in his or her own way, seeing images that typify that past, preserving one past, sweeping away others. Later writers, say, urban novelists like Dickens and Thackeray, will look back to this period as a sort of rural paradise from which England has fallen; the beauties of the field are replaced by the grimy, dark, sooty, industrial city. Both the retrospective image and the contemporary one, says Williams, are historical constructs, myths of the social geography fashioned in different periods by different classes, different interests, different ideas about the national identity, the polity, the country as a whole, none of it without actual struggle and rhetorical dispute.①

All of what I have been discussing here—the interplay between geography, memory, and invention, in the sense that invention must occur if there is recollection—is particularly relevant to a twentieth-century example, that of Palestine, which instances an extraordinarily rich tense conflict of at least two memories, two sorts of historical invention, two sorts of geographical imagination. I want to argue that we can go behind

烦恼的、不断入侵的农民;马尔维尔以一种更复杂的方法解读:乡村是集金钱、财产、政治为一体的结合体;在蒲伯看来,房子就是一个道德的中心;之后在简·奥斯汀的《曼斯菲尔德庄园》中,房子代表的是在英国所有善良、积极、美好的东西。财产在四位作家的作品中都得以巩固。我们看到的是一种社会逻辑逐步获得胜利,即对有地产的阶层的美德和需要大加赞扬,而该阶层似乎代表了全盛时期的英国。在每一部作品中,作家都以自己的方式回忆过去,他/她将自己看到的东西视为过去的典型代表。他们都保留了某一过去,而将其他过去全部扫除。后来的作家,例如狄更斯和萨克雷这样的城市作家,在回顾这个时期时都会把它当作乡间天堂,英国就是从那里堕落的;田野之美被工业城市的肮脏、黑暗、阴沉所取代。威廉斯认为,古今的意象都是历史的建构,是不同时期的社会地理神话,由不同的阶级、不同的利益以及关于民族身份、政体和国家整体的不同的思想所塑造,这些意象没有一个不是没有实际的斗争和修辞争议的。

我在这里所谈论的一切——地理、记忆和虚构的相互作用是基于有回忆就会有虚构这样的理解——与一个 20 世纪的例子,特别是巴勒斯坦的例子相关。它引证了至少两种记忆、两种历史虚构和两种地理想象之间极其频繁和紧张的冲突。我想表明,我们可以钻到关于中东冲突的

① 参见雷蒙·威廉斯,《乡村与城市》,纽约:牛津大学出版社,1973。

the headlines and the repetitively reductive media accounts of the Middle East conflict and discern there a much more interesting and subtle conflict than what is customarily talked about. Only by understanding that special mix of geography generally and landscape in particular with historical memory and, as I said, an arresting form of invention can we begin to grasp the persistence of conflict and the difficulty of resolving it, a difficulty that is far too complex and grand than the current peace process could possibly envisage, let alone resolve.

报纸头条新闻和反复还原的媒体报道背后,在那里发现一种比我们经常谈论的那些更为有趣、更加微妙的冲突。概括地说,只有理解这种地理,尤其是风景,与历史记忆和一种引人注目的虚构形式的特殊结合,我们才能够开始理解冲突的持续性和解决它的困难性,这种困难比目前的和平进程中所能想象的困难要更复杂、更艰巨,更不用说解决了。

Let us juxtapose some relevant dates and events with each other. For Palestinians 1948 is remembered as the year of the nakba, or catastrophe, when 750,000 of us who were living there—two-thirds of the population—were driven out, our property taken, hundreds of villages destroyed, an entire society obliterated. For Israelis and many Jews throughout the world 1998 was the fiftieth anniversary of Israel's independence and establishment, a miraculous story of recovery after the Holocaust, of democracy, of making the desert bloom, and so on. Thus, two totally different characterizations of a recollected event have been constructed. What has long struck me about this radical irreconcilability at the origin of the Palestinian-Israeli conflict is that it is routinely excluded from considerations of related subjects concerning ethnic or collective memory, geographical analysis, and political reflection. This is most evident in studies of the German catastrophe as well as of ethnic conflicts in former Yugoslavia, Rwanda, Ireland, Sri Lanka, South Africa, and elsewhere.

让我们把一些相关的日期和时间并置在一起。对于巴勒斯坦人来说,1948 是他们记忆中的灾难年。这一年,我们中有 75 万人,占人口总数的三分之二,被驱逐,财产被掠夺,数百个村庄被毁坏,整个社会被消灭。1998 对于以色列人和世界各地的犹太人来说是以色列独立并建国的 50 周年大庆。以色列的独立是一个传奇的故事,包含了关于大屠杀后的复苏、关于民主、关于让沙漠绽放花朵等等的内容。因此,对于同一回忆事件两种截然不同的描述就这样被建构。巴以冲突的根源存在着巨大的不可调和性,而一直让我震惊不已的是,人们在思考与民族或者集体记忆、地理分析和政治反思有关的问题时,会习惯性地忽略掉这一点。在研究德国制造的大灾难,还有前南斯拉夫、卢旺达、爱尔兰、斯里兰卡、南非以及其他地方的民族冲突时,这一点尤为重要。

Take Germany first. There is little doubt that it is important to prevent assassins of memory from denying or minimizing the Holocaust; but it is also

先说德国。很少有人会怀疑防止记忆抹杀者否定或轻视大屠杀是

important not to forget to show the link, well-established in contemporary Jewish consciousness, between the Holocaust and the founding of Israel as a haven for Jews. That this link also meant the disestablishing of the Palestinians from their homes and farms is practically never stated, although for Palestinians it increases the agony of their plight: why, they ask, are we made to pay for what happened to the Jews in Europe by what was in effect a Western Christian genocide? The question never emerges out of the debate in or about Germany, even though it is directly entailed by such facts as the enormous amount of money paid by Germany to Israel in Holocaust reparations and has surfaced again in the claims against Swiss banks. I have no hesitation in saying, yes, Germany and Switzerland ought to pay, but that also means that Palestinians over the past fifty years whose own losses are staggering deserve a hearing, too, especially since to us these payments to Israel go to consolidate Israel's hold not only on what we lost in 1948 but on the territories occupied in 1967. The Palestinians have never received even the slightest official acknowledgement of the massive injustice that was done to them, much less the possibility of staking material claims against Israel for the property taken, the people killed, the houses demolished, the water taken, the prisoners held, and so forth. There is also the complex, almost equally dense and far-reaching matter of Britain's responsibility. What strikes me as more significant is the refusal in the Israeli official narrative to take account of the state's complicity in and responsibility for the Palestinian dispossession. For years and years an assiduous campaign to maintain a frozen version of Israel's heroic narrative of repatriation and justice obliterated any possibility of a Palestinian narrative, in large part because certain key components of the Israeli story stressed

一件很重要的事;而同样重要的是,不要忘记揭露在当今的犹太人意识中存在的一种根深蒂固的联系,即大屠杀与以色列的建立、犹太人的避难所之间的联系。但这种联系也意味着巴勒斯坦人被驱逐出自己的家园和农场,这点却从来没有被公开地提出过。对于巴勒斯坦人来说,这种无处言说的无奈给他们的困境雪上加霜。他们问道,犹太人在欧洲的遭遇实际上是西方基督徒的一次种族灭绝行为的后果,为什么要我们为此付出代价?尽管这个问题是由诸如德国向大屠杀中的以色列支付巨额赔款这样的事实引起,并在对瑞士银行的索赔案中再次浮出了水面,但是它从来没有在德国或关于德国的争论中出现过。是的,我会毫不犹豫地说德国和瑞士应该赔偿,同时,我们也应该聆听在过去的 50 年中巴勒斯坦人民遭受了巨大损失的声音,尤其是对于我们来说,这些赔偿给以色列的钱增加了以色列对 1948 年我们失去的一切以及 1967 年被占领的土地的控制力。巴勒斯坦人遭受了巨大的不公正待遇,但没有得到官方的一丝承认与回应。更不要说对那些被掠夺的土地、被屠杀的百姓、被烧毁的房屋、被夺走的水源、被关押的战俘等等问题提出索赔。还有英国的责任问题,它同样复杂,令人费解,但意义深远。在我看来更为重要的是,以色列在官方讲话中,拒绝谈及自己在巴勒斯坦所驱逐的事情中存在的共谋关系和责任。这么多年来,以色列的人民努力地维持着一种英雄主义式的自我叙述,回到故土,正义凛然,以抹杀任何巴勒斯坦叙述的可能性,因

certain geographical characteristics of Palestine itself. Take the key notion of liberation: so strong was the story of Jewish independence and reemergence after the Holocaust that it became virtually impossible to ask the question, Liberation and independence from whom? If the question was asked it was always answered as liberation from British imperialism. Or, as the story got elaborated, it was defense against invading Arab armies that wanted to crush the young state. The Palestinians thus faded into the encircling and menacing obscurity of "the Arabs", the fact that they were actual residents occluded and simultaneously denied.

为在以色列的故事中,依然强调巴勒斯坦本身的地理特征。比如谈及解放这个概念:犹太人民的独立以及遭受大屠杀后的重新崛起的故事如此强大,我们根本不可能提出这个问题:解放和独立从谁手上得到?即使被问到,答案总是说从英国帝国主义的手中得以解放。或者说,随着故事细致化,答案就变成了要抵御那些入侵的阿拉伯军队,他们想要扼杀这个年轻的国家。巴勒斯坦人就这样被隐没在"阿拉伯人"这个包含一切、具有险恶模糊的词汇中,而事实是他们是被堵隔又同时被否认的公民。

...

……

Thus the dominant pattern in thought about the geography of Palestine, for a millennium and a half inhabited by an overwhelming majority of non-Jews, has been the idea of return: to return to Israel for Jews who have never been there was to return to Zion and an earlier state from which Jews had been exiled. Carol Bardenstein notes in a sensitive study the way the same images of prickly pears, oranges, trees, and return thread their way into discourses of memory for both Jews and Palestinians. But the Jewish discourse eliminates from the landscape the former Palestinian presence:

在过去的一个半世纪里,在这块绝大多数非犹太人所居住的地方,最主要的思维模式就是"回归"。对于那些从未到过以色列的犹太人来说,回到以色列就是回到锡安山,而犹太人民也是在此处被驱逐流放。卡罗尔·巴登斯坦在一篇敏感的研究中发现相同的意象,如刺梨、橙子、树木在犹太人和巴勒斯坦人的记忆话语中交替出现。但是犹太人的话语消除了巴勒斯坦人在该地区风景中的存在:

I had the opportunity to visit a number of sites of former Palestinian villages that have been variously reshaped through tree-planting and related JNF projects, in ways that would appear to promote "collective", if selective, forgetting. If one visits the site of the destroyed village of Ghabsiyah in the Galilee, for example, upon closer scrutiny the trees and landscape themselves yield two very different and contesting narratives converging on the same site. One has to rely on landscape readings,

我曾有机会参观一些前巴勒斯坦村庄的遗址。这些地方被植树计划和相关的犹太国家基金项目进行了各种程度上的改造。这样一来,明显促进了"集体主义"的遗忘,这种遗忘可以说是选择性的。例如,如果你去参观加利地区被摧毁的村庄加布斯亚村,经过仔细的观察,你就会发现相同的地点,同样的树木和风景会

because little else remains. What is most readily visible to the first-time visitor are the JNF trees planted on the site the recognizable combination of pine and other trees that have grown over the past four decades in a manner that makes it seem as if perhaps that is all that was ever there.①

存在两种截然不同的叙述。人们只能依靠景观阅读,因为这已经没有什么遗留下来了。对于第一次参观这儿的人来说,最容易看到的就是犹太国家基金项目的树木,这些树木都是一些比较容易辨别的松树和其他树木,已经在那里生长了四十多年,就好像这个地区一直以来都是这个样子。

Let me note in a very brief conclusion what the interplay among memory, place, and invention can do if it is not to be used for the purposes of exclusion, that is, if it is to be used for liberation and coexistence between societies whose adjacency requires a tolerable form of sustained reconciliation. Again I want to use the Palestinian issue as my concrete example. Israelis and Palestinians are now so intertwined through history, geography, and political actuality that it seems to me absolute folly to try and plan the future of one without that of the other. The problem with the American-sponsored Oslo process was that it was premised on a notion of partition and separation, whereas everywhere one looks territory of historical Palestine, Jews and Palestinians live together. This notion of separation has also closed these two unequal communities of suffering to each other. Most Palestinians are indifferent to and often angered by stories of Jewish suffering since it seems to them that as subjects of Israeli military power anti-Semitism seems remote and irrelevant while their land is taken and homes are being bulldozed. Conversely most Israelis refuse to concede that Israel is built on the ruins of Palestinian society, and that for them the catastrophe of 1948 continues until the present. Yet

在这个简短的结论中,我将指出:如果不是被用在驱逐的目的上,即如果是被用在解放以及不同社会的共同存在上(它们的相互毗邻需要有某种尚可接受的持续性和解),那么记忆、地方和虚构的互相作用还能够做些什么。我还是以巴勒斯坦问题为具体例子,在历史、地理、政治现实方面,以色列人和巴勒斯坦人纠缠在一起。因此在我看来,只考虑其中一个的未来而忽略另一个的做法,是十分荒唐的。美国发动奥斯陆和平进程所存在的问题是,它以分割和隔离作为前提,而忽略了在历史上的巴勒斯坦,犹太人和巴勒斯坦人生活在一起。分离把这两个遭受了不平等和苦难的社会团体拉在了一起。大多数巴勒斯坦人对犹太人受苦受难的故事漠不关心,也常感到愤怒,因为他们的土地被侵占,房屋被铲平,反犹太主义对他们这些屈服于以色列的人来说似乎很遥远,跟他们毫无瓜葛。相应的,大多数以色列人拒绝承认他们的社会是建立在巴勒斯坦这个社会的废墟之上,也不承认在他

① 巴登斯坦,《记忆与有根性话语之线:以色列/巴勒斯坦的树木、橙子以及刺梨仙人掌》(*Threads of Memory and Discourses of Rootedness: Of Trees, Oranges, and the Prickly Pear Cactus in Israel/Palestine*),《艾德比亚特》(*Edebiyat*)第 8 卷,1998,第 9 页。

there can be no possible reconciliation, no possible solution unless these two communities confront each's experience in the light of the other. It seems to me essential that there can be no hope of peace unless the stronger community, the Israeli Jews, acknowledges the most powerful memory for Palestinians, namely, the dispossession of an entire people. As the weaker party Palestinians must also face the fact that Israeli Jews see themselves as survivors of the Holocaust, even though that tragedy cannot be allowed to justify Palestinian dispossession. Perhaps in today's inflamed atmosphere of military occupation and injustice it is perhaps too much to expect these acknowledgements and recognitions to take place. But, as I have argued elsewhere, at some point they must.

们看来 1948 年的灾难至今依旧存在。然而不和解,那么冲突就无法化解,除非双方在面对各自的经历时能够顾及另一方。我认为问题的本质在于,如果作为强势的一方,以色列犹太人不承认他们驱逐了整个巴勒斯坦民族这个事实,那么和平的希望是不存在的。作为弱者的巴勒斯坦人要直面这个事实:以色列犹太人把自己看作大屠杀的幸存者,即使是这种悲剧也不能使巴勒斯坦人遭到驱逐合理化。也许在现在军事占领和不讲正义的环境下,想得到承认和认识是有点过分了。但是,正如我在其他地方讨论的那样,到了某个时候,他们必须这样做。

3. Questions for Discussion

(1) Why are memory and its representations significant?

(2) What does Edward Said mean by "the invention of tradition"?

(3) How does landscape function in the memories of people?

3. 讨论题

(1)为什么记忆及其再现意义重大?

(2)爱德华·萨义德所说的"虚构传统"意指什么?

(3)风景如何在人们的记忆中发生作用?

Bibliography
参考文献

Aristotle and S. H. Butcher. *Aristotle's Theory of Poetry and Fine Art, with a Critical Text and Translation of the Poetics*. New York: The Macmillan Company, 1902.

Arnold, Matthew. "The Function of Criticism at the Present Time," *Essays in Criticism*. London: Macmillan & Co., 1865.

Barthes, Roland. *The Eiffel Tower, and Other Mythologies*. Translated by Richard Howard. Berkeley: University of California Press, 1997.

Derrida, Jacques. *Speech and Phenomena and Other Essays on Husserl's Theory of Signs*. Translated by David B. Allison. Evanston: Northwestern University Press, 1973.

Eliot, T. S. "Tradition and the Individual Talent," *The Sacred Wood: Essays on Poetry and Criticism*. London: Methuen & Co. Ltd., 1920.

Freud, Sigmund. "Creative Writers and Daydreaming," *The Standard Edition of the Psychological Works of Sigmund Freud*, Vol. 9. Edited and Translated by James Strachey, in collaboration with Anna Freud. Assisted by Alix Strachey and Alan Tyson. London: the Hogarth Press, 1956-1974.

Jung, Carl Gustav. *The Archetypes and the Collective Unconscious*, 2nd Edition. London: Routledge, 1991.

Hegel, G. W. F. *Aesthetics: Lectures on Fine Art*, *Vol.* 1. Translated by. T. M. Knox. Oxford: Clarendon Press, 1975.

Kant. *Critique of Aesthetic Judgement*. Translated by James Creed Meredit. Oxford: The Clarendon Press, 1911.

Leopold, Aldo. *A Sand County Almanac*. New York: Oxford University Press, 1949.

Nietzsche, Friedrich Wilhelm. *The Birth of Tragedy*. Translated by Ian Johnston. Arlington: Richer Resources Publications, 2009.

Plato. *The Dialogues of Plato*. Translated by Benjamin Jowett. Oxford: The Clarendon Press, 1892.

Rivkin J, Ryan M. *Literary Theory: An Anthology*, *2nd Edition.* Oxford: Blackwell, 2004.

Said, Edward. "Invention, Memory, and Place," *Critical Inquiry*, Vol. 26, No. 2, 2000.

Wehr, Gerhard. *Jung: A Biography*. Boston/Shaftesbury. Dorset: Shambhala, 1987.

Woolf, Virginia. *A Room of One's Own*. New York: Harcourt Brace Jovanovich, Inc., 1929.

艾略特. 传统与个人才能，卞之琳，译，载《二十世纪文学评论》，戴维·洛奇编，上海：上海译文出版社，1987.

艾略特. 传统与个人才能，曹庸，译，载《外国文艺》，1980年第3期.
巴特. 埃菲尔铁塔，怀宇，译，载《罗兰·巴特随笔选》，天津：百花文艺出版社，2005.
巴尔特. 埃菲尔铁塔. 李幼蒸，译. 北京：中国人民大学出版社，2008.
柏拉图. 理想国. 郭斌和，张竹明，译. 北京：商务印书馆，1986.
柏拉图. 理想国. 顾寿观，译注，吴天岳，校. 长沙：岳麓书社，2010.
德里达. 言语与现象. 刘北成等，译. 台北市：桂冠图书公司，1998.
德里达. 延异，汪民安，译，载《外国文学》，2000年第1期.
弗吉尼亚·伍尔夫. 自己的一间屋 伍尔夫随笔全集Ⅱ. 王义国，译. 北京：中国社会科学出版社，2001.
弗洛伊德. 作家与白日梦，孙庆民等，译，载《弗洛伊德文集7》，车文博主编，长春：长春出版社，2004.
黑格尔. 美学. 朱光潜，译. 北京：商务印书馆，1996.
康德. 判断力批判. 宗白华，译. 北京：商务印书馆，1964.
康德. 判断力批判. 邓晓芒，译，杨祖陶，校. 北京：人民出版社，2002.
利奥波德. 沙乡年鉴. 侯文蕙，译. 长春：吉林人民出版社，1997.
利奥波德. 沙郡年记. 王铁铭，译. 桂林：广西师范大学出版社，2014.
米切尔编. 风景与权力. 杨丽，万信琼，译. 南京：译林出版社，2014.
尼采. 悲剧的诞生. 李长俊，译. 长沙：湖南人民出版社，1986.
尼采. 悲剧的诞生. 周国平，译. 上海：上海人民出版社，2009.
荣格. 原型与集体无意识. 徐德林，译. 北京：国际文化出版公司，2011.
伍蠡甫. 西方古今文论选. 上海：复旦大学出版社，1984.
伍蠡甫. 西方文艺理论名著选编. 北京：北京大学出版社，1985.
亚里士多德. 诗学. 陈中梅，译注. 北京：商务印书馆，1996.
亚里士多德. 诗学. 罗念生，译. 上海：上海人民出版社，2006.
章安祺选编. 西方文论经典名著选读，北京：中国人民大学出版社，2005.